THE WHOLE WORLD

THE WHOLE WORLD

Polly and Liv are American students at Cambridge University. Both strangers to their new home, both survivors of past mistakes, they quickly become friends and find a common interest in Nick, a handsome, charming and seemingly guileless graduate student. But a betrayal, followed by Nick's inexplicable disappearance, brings long-buried histories to the surface. A police investigation raises countless questions, with the newspapers reporting all the most salacious details. Soon the three young lovers will discover how little they truly know about each other, and how devastating the ripples of long-ago actions can be...

THE WHOLE WORLD

by

Emily Winslow

Magna Large Print Books
Long Preston, North Yorkshire,
BD23 4ND, England.

British Library Cataloguing in Publication Data.

Winslow, Emily
    The whole world.

        A catalogue record of this book is
        available from the British Library

        ISBN   978-0-7505-3985-2

First published in Great Britain by Allison & Busby Ltd. in 2013

Copyright © 2010 by Emily Winslow

Cover illustration © Nic Skerton by arrangement with
Arcangel Images

Published in Large Print 2014 by arrangement with
Allison & Busby Limited

Magna Large Print is an imprint of Library Magna Books Ltd.

Printed and bound in Great Britain by
T.J. (International) Ltd., Cornwall, PL28 8RW

For Derek Black,
who loves books

Part One

POLLY

PROLOGUE

'Come on,' Nick said, tugging my arm. He pulled me past the plesiosaur and iguanodon skeletons and unlocked a stairwell. He prodded the button to call the elevator. When the thing came it had one of those old iron grilles, which he shoved aside for entry. He pressed me against the back wall of the box and kissed me.

He has lovely hands. Later, when the people making 'missing' posters asked for a detailed description of him, I uselessly went on about his perfect hands.

When the elevator went *ping* at the top floor, he stalked out down a long, dingy hallway. I trotted after him. I'd forgotten that he had an office up in Earth Sciences – but of course he would. It was a tiny space, nothing more than books and a coffee maker and a desk and a lock on the door, which was enough. We perched on the desk and he pulled my face to his.

I don't think he meant for much more than petting – he didn't seem like someone who would rush anything. But when he started to unbutton my shirt, I said no. I'm certain I did, but it got muffled in his cheek. So he undid the next button. I said no again. I pushed his shoulder, hard. Nick was surprised. I was too. I mean, it's fine to say no to anything, but this was abrupt. He leant in to kiss me again. I don't think he deliberately ignored me; I think he was just on a roll. So was I, frankly. I kissed him back, which was disorienting – he had a right to be even more confused. It was all so…

There was this line. I wanted to be on one side of it. I tried to stay there, and haul him back. But he couldn't see the line. All he knew was that I was still leaning into him. He kissed me all down my neck, and then lower, down into where my shirt was open from the first two buttons. It made me crazy, in a good way, and it made me angry, which was strange. I shoved him so hard that he was suddenly standing upright; I had pushed him off the desk onto his feet. I leant over the other side of the desk and vomited into his trash can. It had papers in it, not crumpled, just all smooth and rounded, clinging to the side of the basket. I vomited in it, and then over it onto the floor.

The sounds were horrible. I tried to stop. I covered up my mouth but just ended up with stuff on my sleeve.

Nick put his hand on my back. I elbowed him off. More stuff came out of me. I didn't think I'd eaten enough for it to go on this long.

When it finally stopped I held still. A minute flipped on his clock, one of those old 'digital' clocks that has the numbers on little cards attached to an axle.

Nick said something. I made a noise to cover it up and bolted. I didn't wait for the elevator; instead I lurched onto the stairs, which I hadn't realised go on forever. Every corner I turned there was another flight down. I passed the museum level by mistake. Then the ground floor stopped everything.

Through the window in the stairwell door I saw a dozen students gathered, for a club or a meeting. My shirt was still open at the top. I turned to the wall. It took me a few tries to mash the buttons back through their slits.

I wanted to brush my teeth. I wanted to change my clothes. I rushed back up one flight to get my jacket from the window seat in the gem room. On Trumpington Street I started running.

CHAPTER ONE

That whole thing in Nick's office happened just around what would have been Thanksgiving. Home was, no doubt, drenched in crackling, flashy leaves. England does the season differently. Students at Cambridge are discouraged from having cars, so autumn comes with a flurry of bicycles. Leaves barely bother to brown before falling listlessly – the bikes make up for that in their number, variety, and motion. They swirl everywhere, as if blown into little cyclones by the wind.

I used to live in New Hampshire, which is all spectacular falls and knee-high winters, and summers thick with humidity and mosquitoes. It's a parade of nature there; that's what makes it special. But here in Cambridge, instead of trees and mountains and extremes of weather, there are buildings, all these towers, like something cartoonishly Atlantean that you'd put in a fish tank for guppies to swim through. Everything is made of stone, not clapboard. This city is like people, instead of God, made the world, and turned out to be good at this creation business.

The University has thirty-one colleges, which house, feed, and tutor students. The University departments provide lectures and exams. The older colleges downtown, founded by Plantagenets and Tudors, dominate the shops and houses like tall ships in a busy harbour. They're huge and solid and walled, each with an arched entryway giving a peep of courtyards beyond. There's usually a sign telling whether or not they're open for tourists, and always a sign remonstrating that the courtyard grass is not to be walked on.

Peterhouse is on Trumpington Street. The college itself is on one side of the big art museum, and my room, in the dorm extension St Peter's Terrace, is on the other.

I love these old buildings because they're still in use. They haven't been made into museums. There's something so sad about people filing through a famous rich person's bedroom to ogle a made, never-again-slept-in bed. These college rooms are all lively with activity, just as they were built to be. They're as different from museums as a wild animal is different from taxidermy.

I chose Peterhouse because it's the oldest of the colleges, more than seven hundred years old. That seemed the right thing to do. If I was going to go to Cambridge, and live in actual architecture, and wear a monkish academic robe called a 'gown' just to eat dinner, it seemed best to go all the way. Peterhouse had been the first of the colleges to get electricity, but it still lit meals only by candlelight. Its stained glass windows were by William Morris. There was a fireplace in my dorm room. When I saw that I laughed out loud.

Liv is American too, which is why we became friends. She was my first friend here. She's Californian, and could have gone to Stanford.

I met her my first week. It wasn't the way she talked that gave away her nationality. She hadn't even spoken yet. It was that she sat cross-legged on the floor in a public place. British people don't do that. She was sketching an empty windowsill inside the Fitzwilliam Museum.

I was above, surrounded by paintings of elaborate flower arrangements. She was below, on the middle landing of a fancy staircase, with two sets of steps going up on either side and another set heading down between them. She caught me looking at her drawing, and quickly hugged her sketchbook to her chest. Then she lowered it back to her lap, and smiled hello. She explained that there used to be three Chinese vases on this windowsill. 'Close your eyes,' she said. 'Go ahead and close your eyes. Just try to see it, okay?'

I'd descended the steps and was right in front of her. I closed my eyes.

'Three big vases, right? Right here. And this guy,' she said, 'this guy – I swear this is true and you can look up the newspaper stories – he tripped, I swear, he tripped on his own stupid shoelaces right into those vases, and he totally took them down. I was in the gallery above those stairs, the floral room, right, and I heard it. It was, like, *pow!* – at first a hollow kind of sound and then a clatter. They shattered into six hundred pieces.'

I flinched.

'No kidding,' she went on. 'I ran to the stairs. It was terrible to see them like that, all splattered, chaos where there should have been this – grace, you know?'

I couldn't keep my eyes closed any longer. Right here, right where I was standing, they'd broken up into shards. I backed up onto a step, to get off of where they'd fallen.

She nodded. 'I know, right? I know. I was horrified too. But then I was, like, kind of elated. And I was, like, springier and more alive, somehow. It made me think:

'This is all really here. It's not like a picture in a book or on a screen. It's not even under glass or behind ropes. It's all just amazingly here. Until I saw some of it broken, I hadn't really understood. I'm here, you know? And this is all real, real enough that if you bump into it something could break. I'm really here.'

She was beatific with the memory.

Then she grinned and snapped out of it. 'It's amazing, you know?' she said.

I smiled back. I just stretched my face and held it tight. I was remembering something broken too. I never should have closed my eyes.

'Where are you from?' she asked. 'Is this your first year?'

I didn't answer right away. I nodded, to buy time. I made my mind imagine vases. Over and over again my mind went *clatter-pow*. I forced it to be vases in my mind.

Liv's college is Magdalene, which is pronounced like it means 'sentimental'.

She lives in a riverside building with brick windowsills and fancy wooden banisters. The architect who designed it made every banister different so that drunk students could feel if they were on the correct stair. Hers had a kind of obelisk, and posts carved like chequerboards.

She'd covered the wall over her bed with pages from her sketchbook. I recognised details from paintings in the Fitzwilliam – lots of Monet poplars – and sights from around town. She didn't choose obvious targets. There was no King's College Chapel, its towers jutting from either side of its roof like the tufts on a great horned owl. Instead she drew two-storey buses, shop-window mannequins, and the snack aisle of the supermarket. There are literally dozens of flavours of potato chip here, and the many bright colours all lined up on the shelves give the appearance of a busy, upright garden.

'Here, give me a hand,' she said, plonking down a stack of printed pages on her bed. 'Reusing is even better than recycling, right?' She had two pairs of scissors, one for each of us.

The pages were old essay drafts. She'd been cutting them up into intricate little snowflakes that now nearly filled a plastic grocery bag.

At first I watched her: She'd cut a small piece off, no worry about its shape, and then fold it twice. *Snip, snip, snip,* then unfold. The folding gave the cuts a symmetry within the random edges. I took a page. Cut, fold, snip. Each sheet made a dozen or more sharp flakes, each one different. When we were done, she undid the fancy iron fasteners on the casement windows over her bed. She grabbed a handful of paper snowflakes and heaved them out. She pressed another handful into my open palm.

We threw fistfuls of paper snow down onto the busy path below, while Liv shouted, 'Ho ho ho!' Some people stopped to look up at us in annoyance, shaking the papers out of their hair or brushing them off their shoulders. One didn't. He bent to sweep up the scraps. At first I thought he was a neat freak, some kind of anti-litter crusader. But then he stood and pulled his arm back, and pitched the debris at us like a snowball. It couldn't make it up to Liv's window; it didn't have the weight or cohesion for that. Instead it showered back onto him, drifting down past his great, huge smile.

That's how we met Nick.

Liv was out in the hall before I even turned around. Her footsteps clattered down the stairs while mine padded. Out on the path, we tried to have a snowball fight, but even a ream of paper isn't enough for that. We half-heartedly threw bits around, but the wind had carried a lot of it away. The river would be dotted with it.

A dozen paper flakes were caught in Nick's hair. They were, by chance, arranged in a ring like a halo. Liv reached to tousle them out, but he ducked away from her hand. He reached up and rubbed them out of his hair himself. So Liv sprinkled another handful on, and he gave in and left them there. We all smiled. Teeth were everywhere.

Nick had to leave. He was a graduate student, a paleobiologist, at Magdalene too. He had a meeting. Liv got his phone number.

'Oh my God!' she said, laughing. 'Oh my God!'

'What?'

'He's so cute! Do you think he likes me?'

'Yeah! Of course he does. I think he really does.'

She hugged herself and spun around. She almost slipped on the mess of scraps, but caught my arm and righted herself. Someone else didn't quite manage that.

'Oh!' A surprised woman fell backward. Her skirt rode up, and the side of one soft leather boot scraped against the walk. A thin white cane pointed straight up into the air. *Oh crap, she's blind...*

'Shi–!' Liv said, rushing to help her. 'It's me, Liv. Here, let me...' She pulled on the woman's hands to haul her up. Resistance; confusion. Liv ended up whacked in the face by the cane. She stepped back with her hand on her cheek while the woman got herself back up to standing unassisted. She wiped her damp knees and smoothed out her skirt. She demanded to know what was on the ground.

'Some idiot dropped paper all over the walk,' Liv explained. I sucked in a breath.

The woman's thick beaded necklace was caught on her top button. Despite brushing her hands together and wiggling her fingers, a few paper flakes still stuck. 'They should be reported to the porters,' she declared.

Liv agreed, gravely. It took both my hands to keep the laughing in my mouth.

There was a smear of dirt and scraps on the back of the woman's peacock blue coat. 'You look great,' Liv assured her.

Her heels and cane tapped on the path: *click click click* away from us.

'See you tomorrow, Gretchen!' Liv called out after her.

'Was that Gretchen Paul?' I asked, grabbing Liv's arm. I'd heard of her from two girls in my building who studied English. 'What class do you have with her?' Liv majored in Art History, so I didn't know what she would be doing with a Lit professor.

'I don't. I work for her. Shit, shit, shit. I hope she's not mad.'

'She probably just needed to get somewhere,' I said, but actually she had looked pretty mad.

'Really?' Liv said. 'Do you really think so?' She squeezed my hand.

I opened and closed my mouth. A porter saved me.

He boomed out, 'Do you know who did this?' The broom in his hand contrasted with his neat, formal suit.

'Some first years,' Liv said easily, pulling me along like we had somewhere we needed to go. We didn't slow down until we were out on Magdalene Street, heading for the bridge.

'What does it take to get someone to lighten up around here?' she shouted, with her hands cupped around her mouth. Quayside was full of people: waiting in line for coffee, hanging out, eating at

22

outdoor tables. All of them looked at us.

It turned out we were both turning twenty that week. So we went out to a pub to celebrate. Liv was in her second year, and twenty because she had taken time off to paint before coming here. I was twenty as a first year because our school district had had a draconian cut-off for starting kindergarten. And I took time off after high school too.

'They call that a "gap year" here. What did you do?' Liv slowed down with her own beer, even though she really didn't want to, to keep pace with me, which was nice.

'Nothing. Just a break, you know?'

'Sure,' she said. 'But really, doing what?'

The whole group at the next table cheered about something.

'Look, nothing, leave it alone.' I didn't recognise any of the beers advertised on the cardboard coasters. I hadn't smelt cigarettes in a restaurant since I was a little kid.

She waved her hand in front of my face. 'Hello? You were drifting away there for a minute.'

The pub was really noisy. I could barely hear her.

'I think I need to go back to my room. I might be coming down with something.' I got out into cooler air.

It was happening again. I felt strange and kind of out of it. I thought back to those vases she'd told me about before. *Clatter-pow.*

Newnham is the part of town where a lot of faculty

live. It has big houses and pleasant, uncrowded doctors' and dentists' offices. Stephen Hawking lives there; I saw him once, whirring by.

Liv took me there to Gretchen Paul's house to help with the project she was working on.

She rang the bell, and then got out a key without waiting. 'Gretchen doesn't mind,' she explained. 'She just wants me to get it done.' The furniture inside, all dark and solid, was interspersed with exotic objects. I figured they must travel.

Liv hadn't yet been able to figure if their money was hers or his. Gretchen's husband, Harry, didn't work. Well, he worked hard, but he didn't work for money. He bred canaries in a special room upstairs, and was almost always home. He was gentle and seemed like the kind of person who would repair something thoroughly. His last name was Reed; Gretchen used her mother's last name.

Harry offered us tea and brought it to us in the library: a pot, cups and saucers, milk and sugar. British cookies are brittle, meant for dunking. These had been made from scratch. Harry had a towel tucked into his belt, and wiped his hands on it as he left us to the work. We giggled. I felt like I was in kindergarten, playing tea party. We clinked our cups together in a happy toast. This is what saucers are for: I almost splashed onto Liv's work, but the little dish caught it and saved me.

There were photos spread all over the table: sepia grandparents and black-and-white babies, vacation shots from the fifties, and orangey snaps of seventies teens. They were in piles, some large and definite, others small and spread out, in the

24

beginnings of a system, like Liv wasn't sure yet exactly of their classification. 'Those are the same person,' I pointed out, indicating two black-and-white photos near each other but not stacked. The woman was beautiful; her eyes and mouth were striking, even at the two different ages represented.

'Maybe,' Liv said. 'Or they could be sisters. Or, if they are the same, which of the two sisters is it? See?' There were two 'definite' piles, one each for two similar-looking but not really identical women. In those, you could clearly see the widow's peak on one, and the pointier chin and side part on the other, that differentiated them. The unsorted photos I'd pointed out could each be either.

'No idea,' I finally laughed. It wasn't a simple project.

One of those sisters was Gretchen's mother, Linda Paul. The other sister was Gretchen's aunt, Ginny. Gretchen needed Liv to figure out which was which.

'Gretchen's mother died recently,' Liv explained. 'Linda Paul was this novelist, well, was a long time ago. She was kind of a big deal back in her day. Anyway, Linda always forbade Gretchen from writing a biography of her. She wouldn't even let Gretchen have these. They were all boxed up in her attic. But now...'

Gretchen was in the garden; we could see her through the window, kneeling, pulling up weeds. She had to identify them by feel. Liv said she worked out there to think. She said that you could tell how stuck Gretchen was on something

25

by how she tossed or punished the weeds as she piled them up.

Harry came into view behind her. He gathered up a small tree that had been leaning up against the shed. Its roots were still in a ball. He took it away and we heard the car doors open and shut.

'What's he doing?' I wondered. The tree was pretty. It was a lilac.

'Oh, they had a fight about that a couple of days ago. He bought it for her, but she didn't want it.'

'Mmm,' I replied, still staring out the window. Liv tapped my arm.

'Do you notice anything about the garden?' It was lush and vivid, but so were so many gardens here. The rainfall makes it easy for things to grow. 'All the colours...?' Liv hinted. 'Don't you find that funny?'

I wasn't sure. 'I guess it's strange for a blind person to focus on colour.'

'Do you get it now?'

'Get what?'

Liv looked up at the ceiling, annoyed with my incomprehension.

'Just pretend I'm stupid, okay?' I told her.

'He wanted her to have a lilac because she'd smell it. But she thinks that's condescending. She hates any kind of special consideration. Newnham or New Hall or Lucy Cavendish,' she said, naming Cambridge's three women-only colleges, 'would have loved to have her. Instead, she came to Magdalene, not too long after they'd finally gone mixed. Some students wore black armbands over women getting in. Does that sound to

26

you like she wants it easy?'

I looked out the window. Gretchen hunched over the earth, digging at something resistant. It was weird to think about how even if she looked up she couldn't see me back. She probably didn't even know I was there.

Liv said, 'She hates that she needs my help to sort these pictures. I think she picked me because I'm not in her department. It would be, you know, awkward, to let one of her own students see her vulnerable.'

A tune started up in my bag. It grew in volume as I rooted around for the phone. It was Nick calling. 'Oh, hi!' I said. Liv didn't have a cell phone; that's why he had to call me. 'We're in Newnham.'

The three of us had gotten together before, at the Fitzwilliam. Liv had shown us around, art being her thing. 'No,' I said. 'This time it's my turn. We'll go to the Whipple.' The Whipple is the museum of the history of science. That was my thing.

Later Nick would take me to the Sedgwick, which has geology and dinosaurs. And privacy, in his office upstairs. But there were weeks before we'd get there.

I mouthed to Liv, 'Nick?' and she gave a thumbs-up.

'He says he'll come meet us here in an hour or so,' I said after I hung up.

'Who?' Gretchen asked. I jumped. The house has plush rugs all over; I hadn't heard her approach.

'Gretchen!' Liv chirped. 'This is my friend Polly. She's helping me with the photographs. I hope

27

that's all right. I know you want the work done quickly and, well, two heads and all that...'

'I certainly hope there's been progress.'

'Oh, yes!'

'If you require assistance–'

'I don't require it, it's just helpful to bounce thoughts–'

'So long as she isn't a distraction.'

'She won't be.'

'I won't be,' I echoed.

Gretchen turned to me. She knew where I was because of my voice. 'Are you a student?'

I squeaked out, 'Peterhouse. NatSci.' It's an abbreviation for Natural Sciences, pronounced like it has a K instead of a C.

'You're American,' she said, getting that from my few words. 'My mother attended a boarding school in Virginia.'

I couldn't take my eyes off the box in her hands. It was a dirty, decrepit shoebox nestled in a plastic grocery bag.

'Can you tell me what this is?' she asked.

We stepped close and looked in. Small bones and plastic jewellery. Altogether it was shaped like a little dog. The plastic necklaces had been wound around the rib cage. The beads were bright, like tiny beach balls.

Liv jumped back. 'Uh, that was a dog, I think.' Her hand went over her mouth, like she might throw up.

'I found it in the garden,' Gretchen said. 'Someone must have buried it a long time ago. What are those plastic nodules...?'

'They look like a kid's toy jewellery,' I said.

28

'Ah!' She smiled. 'How Egyptian.'

She turned toward Liv, still holding the thing. Liv backed up a little. 'I want to emphasise to you the importance of the photographs set in foreign countries. Linda's travels are an essential aspect of her character. As foreigners yourselves, I'm sure you can appreciate that. I expect results won't be compromised by socialising. You have responsibilities. You have *obligations*.' She was really serious. The box quivered in her hands. The bones and beads in it rattled lightly.

She turned and headed back outside.

'Oh my God!' said Liv. 'What was that?'

We held hands like little girls.

Later, at the Whipple, Liv revelled in the children's activity corner, full of compasses and telescopes and other fun things for kids to try. She put on a felt vest and offered Nick the box of Velcro organs, teasing that he couldn't put them all in the right place.

He wasn't listening to her. He was looking at a telescope. He looked up and asked me if I knew the constellations. I don't, really, besides Orion the obvious.

But I think about stars a lot. How, up close, they'd be fire and death; and just far enough away, like the sun, they're life and warmth and daylight; and farther still, even so far away you'd think they wouldn't be anything, they're navigation and myth and poetry. Gretchen was like that about her family: Past the age when she needed a mother, and even past Linda's death, Gretchen was still getting something out of her.

Gretchen's mother, Linda Paul, had written a series of five books about a young woman, Susan Maud Madison, trying to make it as a writer in the fifties. Presumably this was all semi-autobiographical. I saw the books in Gretchen's library, on their own shelf, with dust covers still well intact though aged. Her mother had inscribed each one to her – 'To my darling daughter' – with what I calculated to be the year Gretchen would have finished the equivalent of high school. Next to them were braille versions, which Gretchen had commissioned. The covers showed a woman with short blonde hair and an exaggerated expression apparently romping through comic adventures with her social set, who, the plot summaries informed us, didn't approve of the heroine's ambition.

Nick and Liv and I saw a pyramid of paperback versions in the window of Heffers bookstore downtown. Heffers used to be Cambridge's indie bookstore, and even after being bought out by a chain it's still got a local feel. Prompted by Linda Paul's death, the store had made a special display.

We stopped in and I picked one up, reading aloud: "'Susan Maud did her duty: She spread her towel out on the sand next to Margo. She slid off her wrap to create the illusion that she intended to sunbathe. Margo nodded in approval, and then jogged to catch up with Dick. Susan Maud pulled a notebook and pen from her bag, leant on her elbows, and began chapter four. She hadn't written twenty words before a pail of water was tossed onto her back. 'Come on, Susie!' Dick called. 'Get your feet wet!' Susan's back arched in shock and, for a moment, anger. She pressed the soaked notebook face down onto the towel, blotting the words to stop them sliding down the page. Then she sat up, smiled brilliantly, and retorted, 'You bully! I'll bet you can't run fast enough!' She grabbed the bucket and filled it in the surf, tempted to add a stone or a crab. She chased him down the beach, finally soaking him on the top of his head. He shook his hair out like a dog and grinned, finally cool on the hot day. She hadn't hurt him at all."'

'Wow,' Nick said. 'Edith Wharton it's not, but still there's something *House of Mirth* about it, what with the heroine wanting to be two kinds of mutually exclusive person at once.'

Apparently, these books had made a minor splash back in their day. Gretchen had found several instances of real women with the main character's name, and she'd sent letters asking if their mothers had called them that on purpose. One was even a writer. Maybe it was a pen name, in homage? Maybe Linda Paul's influence had resonated. Maybe Gretchen wasn't the only one to adore her.

'My turn!' Liv announced, picking up a different volume. But when she read aloud the woman at the checkout glared at us. Liv speaks a little loudly. I nudged her to read a little more quietly, that was all. I didn't mean for her stop. But she closed the book and put it back.

This is how Nick got involved. It piqued his interest. We all started working on the photos together. Liv got paid to produce the actual index;

31

Nick and I just helped because we all liked being together.

Nick rented a room from a family in a town house on the east side of town, near the big shopping mall. The father was a lecturer in mathematics, the mom was a journalist, and the two girls, eight and ten years old, went to Perse Girls, an elite day school. They were an Indian family, and he got to share their spicy cooking, which he told me they're pretty generous about. The house was tall and narrow, with his room and bathroom on the top floor.

One time I waited for him in their small kitchen. Mrs Chander had covered the dining table with papers, which made the place feel productive and cosy. She too was sorting into piles. Aahana and Aashika played in the small garden out back, building something that looked complicated. Mrs Chander smiled and told me that they were building a replica of the Chateau d'If, the prison from *The Count of Monte Cristo*, to impress Nick, who'd challenged them to try it. They plainly adored him.

I'd seen Nick with the girls on the playground nearby. He took turns holding them up to reach the monkey bars. He was fair. They each got equal chance.

That's what it was like with me and Liv, and him hanging out with both of us. Liv joined the Magdalene choir, so they saw each other a lot at practises. He sometimes worked out at Kelsey Kerridge when I was there for yoga.

He was being fair, I think. We were given equal chance.

We made some progress with Gretchen's project, but it was slow going. Most of the photos weren't labelled at all, and those that were labelled were not necessarily done so correctly. Because Gretchen had gone blind gradually, she could describe people and places to us, veto certain hypotheses, and describe scenes that she remembered from childhood. She'd seen the oldest photos when she was small, and remembered when most of the rest had been taken. This was usually helpful, but often not; sometimes she would insist that something was some specific way when we could plainly see it wasn't. She got prickly having her memories challenged.

Gretchen tensed around me and Liv. She took offence. I think she was one of those women who interacts more easily with men.

Or at least, more easily with Nick. She was tense with her husband too.

In one of the baby pictures, Gretchen's little-girl dress reminded me of something I'd worn when I was little. That's all. I said to her, 'I had a baby dress like this. The plaid one.' I said it in a nice voice, and in a complimentary way. Gretchen asked, 'What dress?' which was a reasonable question, except that the way she asked it was like a wild animal sniffing the air. She was looking for a fight immediately. 'I didn't have a plaid dress.'

'It looks like a Christmas picture,' I described, trying to be helpful. 'You're sitting on a couch, holding an ornament, I think. You're maybe ... two?'

Gretchen pressed her lips together, then

33

squeezed out the words: 'I remember that. I wore a plain purple dress. No pattern. It was my favourite.'

Liv kicked my ankle. She's the kind of person to always defend the right to speak one's mind, except around Gretchen. She wanted to please her.

'There must be an unpatterned dress photo as well. We'll let you know when we find it,' Nick said. I didn't think there was one, really, but there could have been, I guess.

Gretchen's breathing got hard and fast.

'I know the photograph,' she insisted. I shrank down and Gretchen stood over me, taller in that way that angry people appear to grow.

The silence stretched on until it was taut. At breaking point, Gretchen abruptly left the room.

Liv went after her. I busied myself neatening a stack of photos that was only slightly askew.

'She didn't mean anything by it, Polly,' Nick said.

'I know,' I said curtly.

'It must be frustrating to have one's only visual memories be so old,' he explained, as if I didn't understand that.

'Everyone's memories are vulnerable that way,' I said. 'You don't have to be blind to remember things wrong and get really freaked out about it.'

'I don't think you're being charitable, Polly,' he said.

My head snapped up, indignant. I hadn't heard a tone like that since my fifth-grade teacher.

I opened my mouth to tell him off, but his ridiculous sternness cracked me up instead. I

34

laughed at him. I opened my mouth and laughed out loud.

Now his head snapped up. He leant back, surprised.

For a moment, I wasn't sure what would happen. Would he stand up and leave?

'I'm sorry,' he said at last. 'Sorry.' And he laughed too.

Gretchen's house was full of souvenirs. Not postcards or plates or thimbles, but carved wooden sculptures and thick-daubed paintings. Maybe they were Harry's, or maybe Gretchen got something out of touching them, feeling the brushstrokes. My first time among all those touchstones of adventure and achievement I'd felt intimidated, but they became familiar. There was an Asian ceramic dog by the front door. By my third visit I was ready to scratch his ears and bring him a biscuit.

Gretchen sat down with us the next time we went over.

'I want to apologise for my ... *possessiveness* sometimes about the photographs. You're being my eyes for me and it's just ... *difficult* sometimes to give up what I remember seeing. I want to thank you for all the work you're putting into it. I knew the photos were in a state, but I didn't realise how bad of one. I only thought: All I need is a pair of eyes.' She pushed her eyebrows together. I could tell how hard that was for her to say. 'I'm sorry it's turned out to be so difficult.'

Liv said, 'They must be very special memories for you...'

Gretchen teared up. 'It was magical, those youngest years. Not just seeing – though seeing was good, of course – but it was *what* I saw! Mother had such a way of creating moments. She lived a life then that was ... exotic and exhilarating ... hotels and aeroplanes ... I tagged along. Did you see the picture? At the Prater? On the horse?'

There had been several photos on horses, but Nick knew the one she meant. 'The white one?' he suggested.

'Yes! It was a carousel made of living horses. I've always remembered that, though I didn't learn it was the Prater in Vienna until much later. I just remember the child's view of things. I remember sitting on the back of a white horse, and it wasn't carved or painted, it was real.' She sighed ecstatically.

A bird flew suddenly past her face, coming to cling to the edge of her cup. It was steel blue, and she swatted at it. Her husband, Harry, came softly behind it, coaxing it with clicks and twitters. It hopped onto his finger and he took it back upstairs.

I found one of the Whipple's pretty compasses in Liv's room. Not a historic one, one of the kid ones from the activity corner. It wasn't expensive, but it wasn't hers either.

She had it out on her desk like she wasn't ashamed.

I didn't say anything.

We had on our black academic 'gowns' for dinner at one of Magdalene's daily 'formal halls': a fancy meal, candles and everything, for cheap.

You wait for the Fellows at the High Table to sit, and then the gong goes, and then the grace in Latin. I had to shush Liv sometimes to make her stop giggling. Then we would get to eat. There's a set menu of multiple courses served by waiters. There's wine.

We usually got tipsy at these things. This was one of those conversations. We hung out afterward, on the steps by the water in front of her building. Magdalene is one of the few colleges on the river. 'Why does she care so much?' I said.

'Mmmm?' Liv asked.

'Gretchen,' I said. 'Why does it matter so much to her that she had this posh childhood?'

'Do you really not get it?' Liv said this like I was stupid to have to ask. 'Money's important. What, are you so rich you don't need to care?'

'I'm not rich.'

'Well, I was, once. My dad made four million dollars at a dot-com startup. That's the truth. Then we lost it all when the stock tanked. Believe me, it matters.'

I gaped. 'Where does four million dollars go?' I asked, trying to imagine a number that big, and how something that big could just disappear. You'd need something on the scale of a meteor and total climate change. That kind of money is at least as big as a dinosaur.

'It was the whole Silicon Valley bubble. My dad's an engineer, and his company got bought by Racer. It was this huge deal. We moved up to Livermore, which is this mini wine country – no way near Napa or even Sonoma, but cute, and lots of new housing. We had a view of grapes through huge windows. There were Internet plugs in, like, every room. And we got it on a mortgage, not because we needed one, but because the rate on the mortgage cost us less than what we were making by keeping the money in stock. That was the thing to do. Everybody did it.

'Then, when NASDAQ crashed, we needed to sell but no one was in a position to buy. Our neighbours were trying to sell too. Half the houses hadn't gotten curtains and blinds yet, and now no one could afford it. We could all see each other. You had to find a corner to get dressed in. And we could all see down into each other's backyards, and half of them were still churned-up dirt. People couldn't afford to do the landscaping.

'So we eventually sold, for less than we'd bought. Dad got another job. We moved into an apartment, an okay apartment. I mean, it wasn't a house, but it was one of those nice places with cookies and newspapers in the pool house. So it was okay. But it wasn't special. You remember the special. It felt good to live in a house like that. It felt like ... it felt like you deserved it. I know that's not true, but that's how it felt. Just having it felt like you were the kind of person who was supposed to have it. That feeling is the kind of thing you hold on to.'

'Wow,' I said.

'Then my parents got divorced, and that sucked. I mean, that really sucked. So I remember not just the big house, and the Internet plugs, and that there had been this fountain, an actual fountain, in our yard. I remember that we were together there.'

I made a mental note to get friends tipsy more often.

She kept talking. 'Holy crap, Nick is so hot. He never comes to these dinners. I saw him earlier today and asked if he was coming. He was busy or something.' I felt embarrassed, like I always did when she talked about Nick. She went on, 'He was with his thesis supervisor. They were having this deep conversation. It just made me crack up, how serious they were. Richard – that's his supervisor; he's a Fellow here – is nice, but so weird. I heard that he's been *celibate*,' she whispered that part, 'between wives. Can you believe that? It's been, like, ten years or something. He's getting married again at the end of term.'

'Why would you even know that?' I asked, meaning the celibacy.

She laughed. 'It's a religious thing. It's okay to know if someone's religious. Can I help it if his religion is obsessed with sex?'

Just then – this freaked me out a little – he walked by. Being a Fellow, he'd eaten at the High Table at dinner. We'd stood up, as required, when he'd walked in. We ignored him now. I hoped he didn't notice us. He didn't stop to look or anything, but he might have heard us. I was mortified.

When he had passed, Liv leant over and moaned, 'Oh, *Richard!*'

'Why is it any of your business who has sex and who doesn't?' I was peeved.

She retorted, 'What do you care?'

Then she pretended to be from France to a couple of guys. It was weird but pretty funny too.

39

Her accent was terrible. At first I kind of distanced myself, but at last she cracked me up. She did a little victory dance. I clapped and, just like that, everything was right between us again.

I thought about Liv's lost money the next time I looked at Gretchen's photos.

The best of them were those from the Brussels Expo in 1958. This is something I didn't know about, but apparently it was a big deal at the time.

Gretchen told us about it. Liv used Gretchen's computer upstairs to Google for specifics about various scenes, so she could label them properly in the spreadsheet. There was the Atomium, a massive building in the shape of an iron molecule. There were pavilions representing different countries.

We laid all the Brussels pictures out on the table at once. The nanny was blonde and so always obvious. Until we could for sure call one sister Linda and one Ginny, we called them 'side part' and 'widow's peak'.

The two sisters had laughed together in front of an African hut in the Belgian Congo sector.

Side part, the nanny, and Gretchen posed in front of a pagoda in the Thai pavilion.

Three of them stood in front of a lawn dotted with white flowers, part of the German pavilion. 'Ginny took that,' Gretchen told us. 'She tripped backing up to get a second shot, and twisted her ankle. I stayed with her at the hotel the second day.' But that itself didn't solve the problem of telling the sisters apart, because the Linda in that photo had turned her head. She was facing away, and blurry from motion.

I noticed that there were four photos of 'widow's peak' and six photos of the nanny, each alone. Maybe that meant that those two went to the Exhibition the next day, and just took photos of each other. Gretchen agreed that that sounded plausible. That made Ginny the one with the side part.

This was confirmed by Gretchen's recollection of dinner atop the Atomium. In one picture, all four of them sat with a man at a table with an incredible view. They'd convinced the man to buy them dinner. 'They all flirted with him,' she said. 'The food was too fancy for me,' she added.

Then, 'Ginny accidentally dropped a glass! I gave her mine. A waiter took the photo for us.'

Sure enough, there in the photo, the sister with the side part had a shot glass in front of her while the other adults all had wine glasses. Gretchen didn't seem to have any idea what it was; I think she thought it was just some kind of kiddie cup. It must have been the only child-sized glass the restaurant had on hand.

So that was Linda (widow's peak) and Ginny (side part) solved! Liv whooped. She said we should celebrate.

She wanted us to go out for shots ourselves. She tugged on Nick's sleeve, past the point where it would have been charming, but he said he couldn't go. He had something else to do. So then it was just the two of us, but I didn't feel like drinking. I had a book to read for class.

'Aw, come on!' she said.

I resisted. It went back and forth like that as we walked toward town.

'This is why I don't always tell you stuff,' she finally exploded. 'You can be so prissy.'

'What?'

'Like about Gretchen's computer. That really hurt my feelings.'

Gretchen didn't want the photos leaving her house, so Liv used her computer upstairs to do research about the Expo. When Liv later tried to tell me stuff she'd read in Gretchen's email, I'd told her I didn't want to hear it.

I rubbed my forehead. 'I never meant to hurt your feelings.'

'The whole reason I tried to tell you about the emails is because what was in them is relevant. If Gretchen isn't going to tell us everything, then we have to look for it. Right?'

'I don't get it.'

She sighed. 'Well, can I tell you now?'

She stopped to face me dead in the middle of a little bridge across a mud patch on Sheep's Green. I couldn't get around her. 'Fine,' I said.

'Someone else is writing about Linda Paul.'

'Really?' I guess Linda Paul's general importance wasn't all in Gretchen's head.

'She's a real writer too. She said she already had the okay from her publisher. I think she thought Gretchen would be flattered. Oh, and she asked if Gretchen has any photographs she's willing to share. Ha!'

'Wow,' I said.

'She's emailed, like, three times. Gretchen has never answered. But it was about when the first one came that she hired me. That explains some of her moodiness, don't you think? The pressure?'

'Maybe.'

'Knowing stuff like that helps me help Gretchen, so it's all good. Right?'

'Sure.'

We'd hit The Mill pub. 'So you want to have a shot or what?'

Before Cambridge I hadn't even heard of Linda Paul, and here people were vying to write about her. It was crazy. But having looked through the photos, and getting a sense of Linda and Ginny's spirit and fun, it sort of made sense why Gretchen idealised those early years so much...

I shook my head to clear it. Liv asked, 'Are you okay?'

I was. 'I was just remembering my dad,' I said. When I was little, we used to walk to the bakery together on Saturday mornings. People used to wave at us and he'd wave back. That was as amazing to me as Gretchen's carousel of living horses, and Atomium, and purple Christmas dress.

'Is he, like, dead?' Liv asked. I was shocked that she said that, because he wasn't dead. Why would she think he was dead?

But I said, 'Yes.' It was easier.

Liv never did get to celebrate with shots the way she wanted, but Gretchen marked our finding the distinction between Linda and Ginny by having us three over for dinner. She had been disappointed at first to learn that many of the best photos were of Ginny, not Linda. Ginny had really liked the camera. But anyway, Gretchen could get on with things now, and that was worth throwing a little party.

I brought wine. I had no ulterior motive here except hospitality, but I did wonder what effect it might have on Gretchen, already inclined to reminisce.

Then, with dessert, Harry poured us port. I was going to get loopy, no doubt about it.

Gretchen rambled about her childhood again. She asked Nick to read aloud a poem her mother had treasured. He blushed like a girl.

The poem had been found with the photos. It had obviously been important to someone. There was a clipping of it, from a newspaper, and several handwritten transcriptions. First Gretchen had thought that her mother had written it, but it was credited in the newspaper to 'A. Simms'. Then she'd decided that it must have been her mother who cut it out and copied it. Either way, she was excited about sharing something that had been important to the woman.

Nick demurred. He really didn't want to read it. Liv put her hand on his shoulder and shrilled, 'Aw, Nick, you've got to!'

'Nick, it's okay...' I said, meaning he didn't have to if he didn't want to. I think he really was embarrassed. But Liv is louder than I am. I don't know if she wanted him to do it because she liked him a little off-kilter and embarrassed, or if she just wanted to make him do what Gretchen wanted. Either way, I said, 'Liv, Nick can decide for himself what he wants to do.' Liv glared at me.

To keep the peace, Nick stood and read aloud:

'I hunger for a perfect fruit, a pear.
Its cello curves pressed heavy in my hand,
its robust, rounded flesh all swollen full
of juices pressed against the straining dam
of yellow-reddish skin. I'll not be moved
by any lesser offering of food.

My empty belly whines to be indulged,
indignant at my forcefulness of will.
My salivating mouth anticipates
its base desires soon will be fulfilled.
But cheese is now too thick and bread too dry.
No arid compromise will satisfy.

Let weaker others abdicate their selves,
disclaim their true desires for a play
at momentary comfort. They'll contort
to fit the shifting context of each day.
But I will stand within my inborn shape,
expose to all the scaffolding within.
I'll wait for what my true self most desires
and from all else I'll to the death abstain.'

Liv clapped, which embarrassed him even more.

'It reminded her of her commitment to me,' Gretchen rhapsodised. 'It wasn't a popular choice for her to even have me, never mind give up everything for me. But she did. And she never regretted it.

'When I was three and a half, she made a decision,' Gretchen explained. 'She made a sacrifice of her glamorous life to devote herself to my care. It was – sometimes I think it was too much. She left behind so much!' But Gretchen didn't sound unhappy about it; she sounded proud to have been worth it. 'The trips stopped. The handsome visitors, the cocktail parties. It all just ... the tap ran dry.' She blinked and smiled. 'From then on she mothered me. The nanny was dismissed.' She described this with a clipped voice, like the existence of the nanny was something on a par with rats in the house, something to be cleared up and ashamed of, something invited by bad habits. 'She resolved to fully be my mother and she did it.' She drained her glass. 'Sometimes I feel like my life has a dividing line – the life before, where I lived in her wake, sailing through a glorious world, and the life after, where I lived in her arms, thoroughly ordinary.' She seemed equally enamoured of both.

I tried to change the subject; Gretchen ignored me. She said loudly, nearly crowed, 'She gave up writing completely. She told me that I would be her story and she would write *me*. Isn't that a much nicer way of saying "mothering is a full-time job"?'

Trying to recover from embarrassment, Nick had bent himself over the transcription. He ran his fingertip over the words. Then he got up and went to the library. He returned with a few key photos, and turned them upside down on the dinner table.

The loopy, flourishy writing that had hand-copied the poem was also on the backs of several of the older photos. They were labelled 'Mother' and 'Father', so that writer would be Ginny or Linda.

But the newer photos, the colour ones of a

teenaged Gretchen, had a smaller, more careful style of writing on their backs. This was strong, though not certain, evidence that this writer was her mother. It would make sense for her to label the photos she took of her daughter's friends. That would make the first writer Ginny. I was beginning to like Ginny. She had her mouth open in several of the pictures, laughing out loud. And it was she who had copied the poem. I knew Gretchen would be disappointed again. Liv put out her hand to stop Nick, but he told Gretchen anyway.

She took it better than I expected. 'All right, then, the poem wasn't Linda's. So I had an aunt who liked pears. Who doesn't?' The words were flippant, but her voice was tight.

Pears. Picasso's violins. The female figure.

As if reading my mind, Gretchen defended her aunt's heterosexuality. 'You don't know Gin. Love affairs with inappropriate men were her speciality. She died in a boating accident on the Mediterranean when I was seven. Mother told me that she'd been with a married man.' She whispered those last two words in an exaggeration of scandal.

Nick ducked his head. Liv would say that he was a prude. Gretchen's memories of her mother were full of sexual conversations.

Still reminiscing, she told us about Brussels' Motel Expo, a temporary building designed only to last through the fair. They'd stayed in a cheap-looking room that was identical to all the others. The layout of the building was also repeated without variation throughout. Gretchen said that, one evening, they walked into the wrong room, interrupting a couple having sex. I winced, embarrassed for the three-year-old walking in on sex, and embarrassed for the fifty-year-old telling us about it. The man threw a shoe at them. Linda and Ginny and the nanny all laughed, and Gretchen says she laughed too, because they did. She laughed telling it.

Nick interrupted. 'Do you really remember that, or did your mother tell it to you?' He shouldn't have used the word 'really'.

She bristled and insisted that she knows she remembers it, because she sees it in her mind. She says the man had a hairy chest, and that the shoe he threw was pointy in the heel and actually could have hurt one of them. But it hadn't, and they'd laughed.

Harry tried to break the tension then by talking about his birds. Gretchen overrode him. He looked pretty beaten down, so I said, 'May I see them?'

His face widened, I swear. It had to, to fit a smile that big.

The bird room was at the top of the house, a converted attic. The fluffy Norwiches chirped and flitted in their cages when we entered. Maybe they were anxious about strangers, or happy to see Harry. It was hard to tell the difference.

Harry greeted them as individuals, recounting their pedigrees and awards. They were all linked. He narrated every connecting thread: That one sired that one; that one mated with that one. The relationships made a web of the room. It was like being inside a mathematician's brain.

The three of us walked home. We were tipsy and happy. Nick was between me and Liv, and we had our arms linked with his.

Liv teased him about the poem he'd been made to read at dinner, and she joked about his perfect life. 'My life's not really perfect,' he said. 'But I know I've been lucky.'

And she said 'Lucky!' to emphasise the understatement.

He said she should talk to his sister about luck. She hated British weather and wearing a school uniform. She read teenage novels set in America.

Normally you'd hit Peterhouse first, but Nick took us up Queen's Road to drop Liv off at Magdalene.

Then he and I walked through town, past St John's and Trinity. At Trinity Lane, Nick grabbed my hand and pulled me into a shadowy corner next to a cobbled wall. His mouth had the tang of port still in it. We kissed like mad.

That's not the time I had to push him away. That time I was as into it as he was. It's not like we were in private or anything. It's not like anything else could happen there.

Someone came around the corner and Nick jumped back about two feet. 'Sorry,' he said.

I wasn't sure if he was apologising to them or to me.

'I'd forgotten where I was for a moment,' he explained, looking down. 'They took me by surprise.'

'Okay,' I said.

'Is something wrong?'

'No.'

He didn't kiss me again, but he held my hand. 'I really like you,' he said earnestly. Everything flip-flopped: It wasn't an insult that he'd jumped; it was a compliment that he'd been so carried away that he'd kissed me in public in the first place.

'Do you know,' he said as we moved on down King's Parade, 'I saw you once before. Before we met at Magdalene. It was at the Penrose lecture. I sat behind you.'

I remember that lecture. It was soon after I'd arrived in Cambridge. Even though I'm not up on theoretical mathematics, I'd attended because Penrose is famous. I'd expected his presentation to be polished and intimidating. But he used an overhead projector, like one of my old grade school teachers, instead of a laptop and Power-Point. He'd made the illustrations himself, in a dozen different colours of magic marker, with underlines and squiggles, and dashes radiating out around the most important words. Each sheet was like the cover of a thirteen-year-old girl's note-book. A thirteen-year-old who's really, really good at math.

'You had a stack of library books in front of you. Some Muriel Sparks and Hilary Mantels, and then, on top and out of place, one of the *Famous Five* books. I thought you were charming.'

I felt ridiculous and foreign. I'd stuffed myself with British authors when I first arrived, mostly authors my mom used to read, right down to a children's book on top. I didn't think anyone would have noticed my silly burst of Anglophilia. 'I just went kind of crazy with Englishness when I got here.'

'It was sweet,' he assured me. Our arms swung together as we walked. 'Do you like it here?'

I stopped and looked around. I didn't know. 'I'm having a good time,' I said. The thumping in my chest sped up.

'I'm glad you're here,' he said. He squeezed my hand.

I unhooked from him and pointed with the hand he'd held. I could have used my other hand, but I didn't. 'Oh! Look!' Fitzbillies had put new cakes on display. We crossed the street and stood in front of the window, arms touching. There was one with a pirate ship on top of a delicate icing sea. There were little white tips on the blue waves, to show how wild the water was.

'That's why I'm here,' I said, still pointing. 'That's why I like science. It's bigger than me. Like the ocean is bigger than a ship. A ship isn't trying to control the ocean, or make the ocean. A ship is just trying to get along with the ocean, and figure it out. If you get to know the way the ocean works well enough, you can ride it. You can, like, go for this amazing ride...' I put my hand over my mouth. Sometimes I blather.

'That's why I like science too,' he said. He didn't think what I'd said was weird. He didn't think it was profound or impressive or intimidating either. It was just ordinary conversation. It could happen every day.

'I love it here,' I said, meaning it.

He put his arm around my shoulders. I let myself lean a little.

'So do I,' he said.

That's not the time I had to push him away

51

either. He walked me the rest of the way home and we pecked goodnight in front of St Peter's Terrace.

Telling Linda from Ginny wasn't quite the job done. There were still the rest of the pictures to sort out, which was now much easier work but even so required thoroughness and effort.

'Is there anything after she turned four?' I asked Liv. She grabbed a small pile and handed it to me. These were mostly photos from puberty onward. Gretchen had the typical adolescent awkwardness and animation, and I could tell her sight had dimmed considerably. The fashions were laughable. The house behind her looked homey and plain. She looked happy. The photos usually had friends in them, boys and girls matching her age.

'I guess her mom was less interested in being the centre of attention once their lifestyle changed,' I said. Previously, Linda had put herself into most of the photos. In these she was always behind the camera.

'That's just age plus vanity,' said Nick. 'The last time I have a photo of my mum and me together I'm in a chorister's robe.'

'Are there any of her dad?' Liv asked.

'He's the one in the white dinner jacket with a martini glass in his hand.' Gretchen was suddenly there. She didn't need to tap a cane in her own home. Liv stammered, embarrassed to have been caught prying.

Gretchen overrode her. 'Do you have the photo to hand?' She leant against the door frame while Nick fished it out. 'Jim' was written on the back.

'He was my mother's accountant. They remained good friends. They were never really lovers. Well, of course they were, but I mean in the social sense. They were never a couple. He was kind to me. He always had a toy or something in his briefcase for me, I remember that.' She smiled. This seemed a genuinely pleasant memory to her; there was nothing of the deprived or abandoned about it. 'Their friendship ran its course. The only thing she'd ever really been devoted to utterly was me.'

'Do you want us to keep this one out, to frame it?' Liv asked.

'He's not a "daddy" to me, dear. He was just a friend of Mother's. I don't need to have him on display.' She moved to face the window. I think she could see strong contrasts – light and shadow. 'Nick, do you have the one on the island to hand? There are palm fronds and such. It's Mother, Aunt Ginny, and me. We were all laughing. I remember when that was taken. Mother's Pekingese had run off with a cutlet from the kitchen and was wrestling it on the carpet. We all laughed instead of stopping him. We spoilt that thing rotten.'

Nick found it. 'I could scan this and have it blown up for you. It would be really nice in eight-by-ten.' He was gallant at heart, and earnest and courteous.

'Thank you, Nick, I'd like that,' she said, patting him on the shoulder. *Good boy*, I added in my head, as if she were scratching him behind the ears too. She was so cold to me and Liv, but with Nick... Sometimes what he inspired in others made me laugh.

If he hadn't been so good with people, I wouldn't have ended up in this position. I would have sidestepped the whole thing. But everything he did was so spotless in its motivation that going along with him always seemed the right thing to do.

Since the night we'd kissed on the way home, Nick hadn't changed his demeanour toward me. He was, as ever, courteous and attentive, but there was no new possessiveness or pushiness. I would have bolted at the first sign of it.

The only outward show of his interest was the way he looked at me. But he'd looked at me that way for as long as I had known him.

When my old boyfriend Jeremy and I had started having sex, when I was sixteen, the most awkward part had been finding where to do it. I was too tall to manage in his car. Our parents were all home in the evenings. We had siblings with varying schedules in and out of our houses after school. My cousin Rain had solved the problem by letting us use her house when her dad was away on business. Rain didn't have a mom, and her dad travelled a lot. She was in college and spent a lot of time at her boyfriend's anyway. So that gave us the place to ourselves on some afternoons or weekends – whatever we could arrange around my cello lessons and Jeremy's soccer.

I refused to do it in Uncle Joe's bed or Rain's bed; that would just have been gross. So we'd put a sheet on the couch in the TV room. We had to bring our own sheet. This is what I mean about it being complicated.

The TV room was on the back side of the house, with the lumpy couch. The good couch was in the front room, but being there would have necessitated closing all the blinds, which would have looked suspicious. There was no air conditioning, so when it was hot we had to be quiet because of open windows; all the windows had to be open for a cross breeze if you didn't want to choke on the heat. We'd turn on the TV to further mask the sound; we'd have sex to cartoons or talk shows and sometimes we'd just crack up. It was all very cloak-and-dagger. And of course we used condoms. Preparing to do it was this huge effort of planning each time, which means sex, to me, had this incredible lead-up with logistics and scheduling and packing. I don't think of it as improvisational.

So, unless he sent me an explicit invitation, Nick was going to take me by surprise.

It was daytime when we visited the Sedgwick. It wasn't like a dinner date, or anything else self-conscious. The Sedgwick has dinosaurs and fossils and rocks. I like geology.

I flitted around the gem room, admiring the bright colours and natural sharp facets. I took off my jacket. He watched me. He leant back on the red cushion of a window seat.

'You are gorgeous,' he said, and it wasn't casual.

I was really pleased. I wasn't thinking ahead. I did that duck-the-head-shyly thing, to show I was both modest and delighted.

'Come on,' Nick said, tugging my arm. He pulled me past the plesiosaur and iguanodon skeletons and unlocked a stairwell. He prodded the button to call the elevator. When the thing came it had one of those old iron grilles, which he shoved aside for entry. He pressed me against the back wall of the box and kissed me.

I didn't see him again, even though he wasn't yet gone. We avoided each other. Of course we did. I'd made an idiot of myself. He'd offered me something, and I'd acted like I wanted it, and then I'd gotten angry, and sick, and who does that? Who acts like that? Who's going to kiss a girl he's watched throw up, who's going to want a girl who throws up over a kiss? I'd messed up everything. I'd messed up something good.

I think I did it to protect myself. Which is roundabout and stupid, but I think it's what I was trying to do. I remember long ago thinking about Jeremy, 'He means the whole world to me.' I meant that at the time, really meant it, and that was how big my world was: It was as big as the ten blocks between my house and his. You could have told me there was more, you could have drawn me maps and told me myths of a bigger world, or other worlds, or however you wanted to define whatever there was outside of that space, but the whole world as far as I could perceive it and touch it and cared about was the size it was. It had him and me in it, and my parents, who made a mess of things. And that – not him, or my parents or the mess, but really the size of my world – is why I've done everything I've done since, and why I came here, and why I pushed Nick away.

Cambridge is, in its way, another small town.

56

But looking back to the start of the universe, and looking ahead to new ways to figure it out, is a wide world to me. Studying expands me, whereas sex had squeezed me to within a little pinpoint.

Jeremy had meant the whole world to me. I never want my world to be that small again.

Nick disappeared two days after I'd been sick in his office. So I continued to not see him, but this not seeing was worse. He really wasn't there any more.

CHAPTER TWO

I could still taste my vomit and smell Nick's shampoo. My body was electric with everything he'd stirred up in me. I'd run the whole way from the Sedgwick. I only wanted to get into my room and close the door. And brush my teeth. I desperately wanted to brush my teeth.

She stood in front of my building, framed between two columns. She fit there, in front of the blue door. I've always known she grew up here, but that was a long time ago. I hadn't noticed before that she actually looked English.

'Darling!' she called.

I didn't move.

'Polly!' She advanced. 'Which window is yours? That one?' She pointed to one with a little stained glass suncatcher. 'That one?' She pointed to one with a teddy bear looking out. The rest were anonymous from here.

I willed myself not to look at mine, behind its iron juliet balcony. I didn't want her to know.

'Polly,' she said, the way all mothers say their kids' names. Exasperated. Proprietary.

The quivering started in my stomach and radiated outward. I didn't figure it for anger until she tried to hug me and I shoved her away, hard.

She wobbled, and backed up into sitting on the low wall along the drive. She looked up at me, some kind of puppy look, and I said, 'I can't, Mom. I can't deal with you right now.'

'I'm sorry. I needed to see if you're all right.'

'I'm all right,' I lied.

'Polly – darling – please...'

What did she mean by that? That I wasn't all right? That I'd just pushed away a good thing, and didn't have any control over my feelings or my body? That I was a freak and a coward and broken, and stupid for not realising it until I had a good guy practically on top of me? Is that what she meant?

'I'm all right,' I repeated. 'You could have called–'

'It's about your father–'

'No!' I shouted. 'No, absolutely not.' I started breathing way too hard.

She got smart right then. I think that even a year ago all this would have been a cue to hold me and rock me, or try to anyway. But there's a difference between a hysterical little kid and a hysterical adult. I stood up straighter, hugging myself across my chest. I said one more 'No.'

'All right,' she said, rising, smoothing her skirt.

'Not now.'

She held a business card from a Cambridge hotel up to my face. I saw the name, which is what she wanted. She left.

My hands shook. It took me a while to get my key out of my pocket.

I got upstairs to the bathroom and scrubbed minty toothpaste all over the inside of my mouth. I spit.

I wanted to rinse my hands under warm water but the old sinks come with two taps, one very hot and one frigid. I let them both run and rubbed my hands quickly between them, attempting the effect of tepid, but all I got were two simultaneous extremes.

The recognition hit me hard. I numbly sat down on the closed toilet. I bent over in that position they show you on airplanes, the one where you get your head between your knees.

I wanted him so much. He was warm and gentle and the nicest person I'd met in Cambridge. He was a little older than me, which made me feel older. There was this wriggly feeling inside me of things unfinished.

But the cold water rushed just as hard. I had to stop him. I had to. I couldn't do it again.

The two extremes didn't cancel each other out. They didn't add up to indifference. They just kept rushing, burning and frigid, right next to each other.

I got up from the closed toilet seat and turned off the taps.

In my room I meant to undress, but pushing my top shirt button through its little slit reminded me

59

of him, of his hands, pushing that same button. And the next.

I wanted to try again. I wanted to tell him I was sorry and I'd do better next time. I'd mentally prepare myself. It was the surprise of it all that had done me in.

I took off just my shoes and got under the covers fully dressed. I undid my fly and slipped my hand in, rubbing around. It was a good feeling, right? It was good. I kept going, thinking of his hand on my buttons, and his mouth on my neck. The feelings kept rolling over me. His blond hair tickled my cheek.

Then his face lifted, and it was Jeremy. I screamed a little scream, I screamed and then I strangled it. I sat upright and retracted my hand. The rolling feelings had stopped.

This is why I have sleeping pills.

The winter dark here comes as early as four o'clock. I didn't realise Cambridge was so much farther north than I was used to, but it is.

The next day, Wednesday, I made myself take a shower and attend a lecture. I used to feel silly that Liv and Nick, and even Gretchen, were all at Magdalene, and me at Peterhouse, odd one out. Now I was relieved. I made it through the whole day without running into anyone with expectations. I only had to breathe and smile and listen. I only had to be polite. The girls in my building who were my friends just believed me when I said I had stuff to do. Erika wanted my cello to join her clarinet and Claudia's piano to make a trio, but she stopped asking when I told her that I really, really couldn't.

My mother stayed away from me. I felt calmed by this because I wasn't thinking.

Since I wouldn't talk to her, she, I discovered, went after my lecturers and friends. On Thursday, Dr Birch said something nice to me about meeting her. I smiled politely and made excuses to get away. I was so distracted imagining that Mom was stalking everyone around me that I didn't think about what time it was. Liv had a class getting out, right by St Peter's Terrace. I almost walked right into her. The spokes of our open umbrellas jabbed at each other.

'Oh my gosh – what's up with your mother? She cornered me coming out of the library yesterday,' Liv said. Tuesday was when I'd been sick; it was now Thursday. Nick was gone, but we didn't know it yet. 'She totally must have followed me. It was so weird...'

I must have looked appalled, because she reined herself in.

'I only mean – it was strange that she found me there, not someplace obvious like after a class or even at the museum. It's not like she would have known when I would be at the library.'

Had she trailed Liv through town, waiting for the perfect, private moment? Mom would consider that courtesy. God.

'Anyway, she just asked me how you were doing, and she said she was glad you had me for a friend. I told her that you're fine – you like England, you know lots of people. Nothing in particular.'

I'd saved up to buy all new clothes to bring. I hadn't wanted anything from home to come with

61

me. Not one thing. God. Couldn't she stay back where she belonged? I felt faint. This was ridiculous.

'I'm supposed to meet my supervisor; do you want to walk with me?' she offered.

'Okay,' I said, though I didn't want to. I felt floaty, and didn't have it in me to resist.

Liv did all the talking, about random stuff. She had lots of Anglophilic facts to share. I didn't have to say anything. 'Did you know that Cambridge was founded by Oxford scholars fleeing the aftermath of a murder?' She said this like she was talking about people we knew.

I stopped walking. This was news.

'Really?' I asked.

'One of the students killed a townsperson in an archery accident. But the locals called it murder. There were riots, and the University shut down. Some of the students didn't want to wait it out, so they came here. Not really that interesting. Nothing salacious or gory.' She laughed to be unserious about it.

'Of course they had to leave,' I said.

'Well, I guess.'

'Of course they had to leave,' I repeated. I felt like I was walking backward.

'Hey!' she said, and the sound of it stretched out in the middle, like it was thinned and elongated by a rolling pin. I think I was swaying. It was hard to tell. It might have been the world. The world did spin, didn't it? Perhaps I was just perceiving it for the first time. Perhaps everyone else was in denial.

The doctor shone a flashlight in one of my eyes, then the other. He took my blood pressure. My body did everything right. He pronounced me physically well and advised me to relax. Liv called a taxi to take us back to my room. She stayed with me and wouldn't go, even when I demanded it. She made me lie still and brought me water to help me down some paracetamol.

'Have you seen Nick?' she asked. This was the first time someone asked that. Later it would be asked over and over again.

'No,' I said, meaning not today or yesterday. I didn't want to talk about when I had seen him last.

'He'll want to help me pamper you. I'll send him over to sit with you while I'm at supervision.' College tutors meet their assigned undergrads every week to monitor progress. Liv grabbed my phone off the nightstand.

'No!' I protested in a sharp bark.

'Look, no one's accusing you of being a baby, we're just looking out for you like friends do. Stop being so stubborn.'

I knew I had to get it together. I couldn't keep making a big deal out of things. So a man kissed me. So I had a mother. So what? These things happen; the world turns. You can't dwell on it or you'll just get dizzy. Liv left Nick a silly message in a Cockney accent, just to make me smile. It finally got a laugh out of me and Liv looked satisfied.

'Okay,' I said to myself, having no idea what I would say to him when he came. I knew he would come, to be kind, but I didn't know what he would want from me any more. Liv left me with a bottle of water and an energy bar. I propped myself up and read.

Nick didn't come. Maybe his cell phone was off. Maybe he was in a lecture. I wasn't worried; actually I was relieved to be alone. I slept. By the time I woke up on Friday, he was officially considered gone.

A policeman came to Peterhouse.

I was with my supervisor, Allison. I'd already been told that Nick was missing. Allison said we could reschedule, but I didn't want to. I needed to hold on to whatever hadn't disappeared.

We were talking about evolution, which is just a charged word for change. Things change. I know some people back home who don't believe in it, but I hope every day that it's really true.

A man knocked and entered without waiting for the invitation. 'I'd like to ask you a few questions, Miss Bailey.'

This was different. See? Find what's changed. The accent was different. It helped to be in another country. This was not the same. It was not happening again.

He asked Allison to wait outside and took her place across the table from me. I gathered up the papers that were spread there, and reached to close an open book. He splayed his whole hand across both pages. He read the chapter title upside down. It was 'Mating Systems'. As soon as he backed off to get out a small notebook I slammed the textbook shut.

'Do you know Nicholas Frey?' he asked.

'Yes.' He wrote that down, just the one word.

'And what is the nature of your relationship?'

'We're friends.' The policeman nodded and wrote *Friends*. He put a dot after it, like it was a whole sentence, and looked back up at me.

'We've been alerted that he failed to appear for a meeting yesterday morning, then missed an appointment with his supervisor. He hasn't been to the house where he rents a room since Wednesday. When was the last time you saw him?'

'Uh – three days ago. Four? It was Tuesday. Today's Friday. I saw him Tuesday.'

He wrote that down. He wasn't hiding his notes from me. I was clearly meant to see my own words transcribed. 'I see,' he said. 'May I ask what you were doing, what was his mood, and so on?'

'I – we – went to the Sedgwick. That's the geology museum. He seemed normal.'

'Normal?'

'Just Nick.'

'Ah. Did he have any plans?'

My face heated up, but the policeman was still talking. 'Was he going out with friends, heading out of town?'

'It's nearly the end of term. He wouldn't go out of town now.'

'No,' the policeman agreed. He wrote down: *End of term.* Then asked, 'Is there any reason you can suggest why he might have chosen to leave so suddenly?'

'You think he left on purpose?' Surely Nick was too stable to run away over a mere embarrassment. For all he knew I'd had stomach flu and it was nothing personal. This wasn't my fault.

He leant in, fascinated. 'You don't? What do you think happened?'

'I don't know.'

'But you don't think he left willingly.'

'He wouldn't do that.' He wouldn't. He wouldn't let anyone down; he wouldn't make anyone worry.

The policeman folded his notepad and put it back into his pocket. 'You've been described to us as his girlfriend...'

'By whom?' I was indignant. I was on the offensive now.

'Various sources. It isn't true?'

'No,' I said.

'Maybe he wanted it to be true?'

'No.' It was a lie, but it didn't feel like a lie.

'Anything on his mind lately? Troubles with his work...?'

'Nothing that I know of.'

'All right,' he said, punctuating his words by clicking his pen closed.

'Are you worried about him?' he asked, as if it were a personal question.

I swallowed. 'Yes.' If the police were involved, I was pretty sure we all needed to worry.

He waited, but I didn't say anything else.

'All right,' he finished at last. 'Thank you for your time, Miss Bailey. May I give you my card? I'd like you to ring me if you think of anything else. I'll come by again.'

I'd hidden my hands inside my sleeves. Two fingers peeped out to take the card.

'He's not really missing,' I called out to the policeman's back. He turned around and stared

66

hard at me. I realised what I'd said was ridiculous. 'I mean,' I added in a whisper, 'that this isn't happening. Okay?'

The policeman nodded slowly. Allison stepped in. I think she'd listened through the door. 'We have a lot of work to do,' she announced.

She watched out the window to see the policeman leave. She waited for him to pass the porters' lodge before turning back to me. 'Polly, you look awful,' she said, surprised. Then, to make everything better: 'I'll make you a cup of tea.'

I burst out laughing. Now I know where my mother got it from. It's not a personal tic, it's just English.

'The police came to talk to me,' I told Liv. We faced each other cross-legged on my bed, in my room at the top of St Peter's Terrace. The ceiling was all jagged from the slant of the roof and the protruding window. 'Well,' I amended. 'One policeman. Singular.'

'What? About Nick?'

'Yes. Did someone talk to you too?'

She picked at the clasp of her bracelet. 'No. Not yet. Why did they want to talk to you?'

'Somebody said I was Nick's girlfriend.'

'What?'

'I know.'

'You're not his girlfriend.'

'I said I know.'

'Why would somebody say that?'

'Because they're stupid? Why does anybody say anything?'

'What did you tell him?'

67

'He wanted to know if Nick had problems. I told him that Nick was the last person in the world to be in trouble.' Nick had started life as a coddled baby, become a much-flattered boy soprano, and finished his childhood at fancy boarding schools. He easily attained an undergraduate 'first', the highest grade, at Magdalene, and currently pursued his doctorate there, much doted on by the faculty. He did what he did because he loved it, and had absolutely nothing to prove. I'd never met anyone with such a lack of unfinished business. 'Nick is, like, the nicest person I've ever known. He's just ... he's a sweet, gentle person, and I just–'

'You sound like a girlfriend,' she accused me.

'I'm not anybody's girlfriend, okay? I'm not. And I know you like him. But I can't make him like you back. Okay? He's not even here any more. What is it that you want me to do?'

She sprang across the duvet and hugged me. She did this crying thing that made her head bounce on my shoulder.

Then she showed me a card she'd made for Nick's family. She'd folded a piece of parchment paper and sketched one of the arches of Pepys Library on the front. 'They put those flower baskets up in the spring,' she explained. I felt like a little kid, needing to be told. I'd only been here two months, months too cold for flower baskets. Liv had seen them hanging from the arches last year.

I was surprised by the envelope. 'His family is in Cambridge?'

'Sure. They moved here when he was a kid, when he became a chorister at King's.'

68

'I didn't know that.'

Liv sat up straight and smiled. 'That's okay,' she comforted me. 'I mean, you're not his girl-friend, right?'

'He told me about his sister. I just didn't know she lived *here*.'

'It's okay, Polly. You don't need to get com-petitive.'

'I'm not!'

But she knew his family address. She knew his parents' first names. She knew that flowers are hung from the arches of Pepys Library in the spring. She knew everything that I didn't.

A group of undergraduates made the 'Have you seen...?' posters that went up all over town. One of them wanted me to tell them Nick's eye colour, which is when I blathered about his hands.

The poster had two photos on it, recent enough, but both before his last haircut: a formal picture in a tie, and a candid shot of him punting on the river, on one of those thin, flat boats. It wasn't the time he'd taken me and Liv.

Of course he'd taken many people punting in his life, of course he had... He had a whole other life, a history. Of course. I wondered who'd taken the photo, who'd been sitting in the boat, looking up at him standing at the end, driving the pole into the water. I was jealous, which was stupid. The posters were everywhere, wet through from that week's unusual, near-constant rain. Because it had become December, the posters shared space with holly and fir branches, tinsel and little twinkling lights.

The policeman came back to me like he said he would. His name was Morris. I don't know if that was his first or last name, but he said I should call him that. I'd lost his card.

Morris told me that the cleaner for Earth Sciences said Nick's office was a mess on Tuesday evening. Apparently he'd been sick. Did I know anything about this, since I'd been with him Tuesday?

This was the worst thing he could have asked me. I didn't lie immediately. I considered whether and how much to lie.

'That was me. I had a bug. When he saw I wasn't feeling well he brought me up to his office.'

'Oh. All right.' Morris fiddled through his notes. 'I understand his office is up several flights of stairs and near the end of a long corridor? How is it that he thought that would be a comfort to an ill friend?'

'I don't know, Morris, but that's how it was.' There was something about calling him by his name that felt satisfyingly insubordinate, even though he had asked me to call him that.

'Look, Miss Bailey, I don't think you've done anything wrong, but I do think you could shed some light on his state of mind. I really don't see the motivation behind your brevity. If you're not attached, and neither was he, there's no one to protect...'

Morris may have been a shrewd cop but he was a naïve person. There was myself to protect, of course. My sanity. Who else would be more important?

'It's all right to tell me,' he said. Then he waited. His not-going filled the room more and more until it pressed me near flat.

I sucked in a breath. He cleared his throat. It took that little to crack me.

He swore he didn't know how it ended up in the news. He wouldn't share his case notes with the press, he said. Nevertheless, there it was, all I'd told him, leaked by whatever usual gutters ran between the police and the paper. They described it more luridly than I had, but they did capture my vehemence that we were nothing to each other.

It was reported in Monday evening's edition. On Tuesday, everyone knew.

I was grateful for the rain; it allowed me an umbrella to hide under. I didn't want to look at anyone, even my friends. Liv would lord it over me. I was broken and she wasn't.

She was coming out of the big brick library as I headed in. I'd just pulled my umbrella down for the revolving door. We saw each other through the glass, spinning around the same axis. She went all the way around to end up back inside. 'You bitch,' she hissed at me.

I wished to be outside, anonymous in the rain. I wished to be upstairs among the books, where she wouldn't be allowed to talk to me. I wished she would let go of my arm. My closed umbrella pressed against my leg and soaked my jeans through.

People stared. The person behind the desk asked if there was a problem. Liv said in a raised voice that the problem was that I was ungrateful, which was baffling. Did she mean I'd been ungrateful to her for something? But it was Nick. She meant toward Nick. She called me an ungrateful bitch. We were asked to leave.

I pushed through the revolving door as fast as I could. Liv squeezed herself into the next compartment and spilt out onto the front steps right after me. She chased me down them, out into the parking lot. A car pulled out right in front of me. I had to stop. Liv put her hand on my shoulder. 'I'm sorry, okay?' she said. We were both breathing hard. We were both wet.

Nick had been gone six days by this time. Speculation was drifting more toward death, either by murder or by accident. No one had suggested that he might have killed himself; no one could make his personality fit that. But, however it had happened, it didn't look like he was coming back. I guess that's a good reason to get hysterical. All of us were kind of hysterical, just set off by different things.

Liv asked me to go with her to Kettle's Yard. She held my arm, but loosely, squeezing it gently. I said okay.

We went into a gallery full of life-sized photographs of empty walls where famous works of now-stolen art had once been displayed. It was more stunt than art, but effectively mournful. We sat on the floor with our knees tucked up and our backs against the wall. 'I'm really sorry,' she said.

'That's okay. This has been awful for everyone.'

'Do you think he's dead?'

I just shook my head because I no longer had it

72

in me to say a confident no.

'Why did you call me ungrateful?' I asked.

She sighed. 'Because you didn't want him. He offered you something good, and you didn't take it.'

I understood her jealousy, but I didn't have to explain myself to anyone. She could tell I was bristling.

'Okay, I know,' she soothed. 'I'm not saying that I have a right to feel that way, just that I do. Okay? I'm just explaining.'

'I know you liked him.'

'Yeah.' And she smiled, like I didn't really know, not everything.

'What?' I asked.

'I was out with Gina that afternoon. You know Gina?' I shook my head no. But it didn't matter. 'She'd given me a cute sweater she didn't want any more, and a pair of earrings. I felt really pretty. I ran into him later. He seemed kind of down. I tried to cheer him up, you know, I was being silly. I pulled him into this staircase party. It was just what he needed. And we ended up dancing a little, I mean it was too crowded to really dance, but there was music and we were standing near each other. I pretty much threw myself at him. Then the porter broke the party up and we went into my room and went at it.'

'Oh,' I said. My mouth was dry. This was agony. This recitation was a form of revenge.

'We didn't do it all, okay? It was a kind of President Clinton thing.' She smirked, but her hands were shaking. 'I'm a virgin, okay? And I'd never done that before either. And I knew he was yours, but I wanted to try.'

'He wasn't mine,' I said. She said 'yours' like this was borrowing a shirt and getting a stain on it. She said 'yours' like when she had taken ten pounds from my bag without asking.

'Whatever,' she said. 'When everyone else said that you were the girlfriend, what was I supposed to say? That I was, really? Because I didn't know that. I was waiting to find that out. I knew that what we'd done wasn't a sure thing, it wasn't a "progression" in our "relationship". It was a thing that maybe would make him see me that way, or maybe it wouldn't. I was waiting to see what it was to him.'

She wiped her face on her sleeve and went on. 'I knew I was second choice, okay?' she blurted. 'But it wasn't until yesterday that I found out *from the freaking newspaper* what had really happened that day. I thought he'd gone upstairs with me because I'm maybe more exciting than you are, or prettier, or more enthusiastic, or more obviously into him.' She took a deep breath, glanced at me to see how I was reacting. 'He only let me do it because that was the day you got him all high like a kite but then wouldn't get him off. I was just ... finishing the job. But he wasn't hard for me, you know?'

She was a mess by this time. For a few minutes she couldn't talk. I stared at a photo of an empty wall. Finally she said, 'You're my best friend and I hate you.'

I got up. I had to get out. Liv followed me. We almost knocked into a sculpture of a woman made out of hard wire knots.

74

'I have to go. I'm meeting somebody.'

'Who?' she demanded.

I hesitated. This would make her angry too.

'Nick's sister,' I confessed. 'She asked to meet with me.'

She gaped. She shook her head. Liv had sent the card to his family. Liv had sung with Nick in the choir. Liv had put out. But his sister wanted to meet me.

'Sometimes the whole world is just crazy,' I agreed.

We'd wandered into the way of the gallery's spot lighting. Liv squinted and looked down. I put my hand, flat, above my eyes, like I was looking at something far away.

'You'd better go,' Liv said. 'It must be pretty awful, missing a brother.'

That's all it takes to realise you have no right to be so precious about your feelings, your loss, your trauma. There's always someone with more rights to it than you.

Liv's story made sense of the mention in the paper that Nick had been seen at a party at Magdalene in the days before he disappeared. Some person there had noticed that he'd been friendly with a girl, and it had been reported, I guess by someone making assumptions, that that girl had been me.

Alexandra went to Perse Girls, like the Chander daughters. It's not far from St Peter's Terrace, where she offered to meet me after school. She looked nothing like Nick, and much, much younger. She was about fourteen and dressed, as required by her school, entirely in navy and light blues.

We couldn't fit on the sidewalk with two umbrellas, so she ducked under mine. She was headed for town and we walked together. 'I know this is going to sound stupid,' I said. 'But, until last week, I didn't know Nick's family was in Cambridge.' I immediately regretted it. What a rude thing to say. 'I mean, he talked about you. You especially. I know you play cello. I play cello. I just... I didn't know you were here.'

We stepped over the great gutter called Hobson's Conduit and slipped through a break in traffic to cross the road. When we got to the other side, we continued up the street and she said, 'When Nick started boarding at King's, my family relocated. I was born a year later. Before that, Mum and Dad and Nick lived in London.'

'Do you like it here?' I asked, stupidly, as if she'd been dragged here instead of born here. 'I mean, do you ever wish your family had stayed in London?'

She shrugged. 'I'll go to uni in London if I want,' she said simply. 'I didn't know about you either.'

Okay, touché. Nick hadn't mentioned me to his family.

'I read about you in the newspaper...' she said.

Of course she had, and in light of the latest it made me cringe. 'Yes, well... Nick is my good friend. One of my best friends. I don't think he was my boyfriend. It's all gotten a little out of hand.' I didn't want to talk about this. 'Did your parents name you after the Romanovs?'

She rolled her eyes. 'You have no idea how many people ask me that.'

How Cambridge. I doubt many people back home would have noticed.

'Mum's brother who died was Nicholas,' she explained. 'Dad's dad was Alexander. It just worked out that way.'

Wait, what? 'Your mother's brother died?'

She looked right at me. 'He drowned when Mum was my age. He was ten. Now her second Nicholas is gone.'

She looked so sad.

'I know he'll come back,' I said.

'What do you mean? Do you know something?' She stopped walking and got right up in my face all of a sudden, my height, eye to eye.

'No! No, I just...' I didn't know. I didn't know anything. 'He's got to,' I said. 'He's got to come back.'

She backed down, started fiddling in her bag, digging around. 'The last time I saw him I was really angry,' she confessed.

At Nick? I didn't think he could make anyone mad.

Alexandra looked both ways. She turned off the main avenue onto a side street; I followed.

'He'd hate that I'm doing this,' she said, putting a cigarette in her mouth. 'Do you want one?'

'No, thanks,' I said.

Her lighter was made of purple plastic. She lit and sucked in. 'He's such an older brother,' she said, looking just straight ahead, leading the way.

We turned again, onto Tennis Court Road,

parallel to Trumpington but much more private.

'What do you mean, "older brother"?'

'You know what I mean. He just thinks he knows everything. If he were still here I'd still be angry. But because he's gone, I don't get to be angry any more.' She raised her voice. 'I'd be really, really angry. I probably wouldn't even talk to him.' Tears squirted out of her eyes.

We stopped again. Because we were under one umbrella, her little curls of smoke got caught around my face.

'Why does he live at the Chanders' house?' I asked, as if this little girl weren't baring her grief to me. I didn't want it. I didn't have room for hers too.

'He's a grown-up,' she said, incredulous at my ignorance. 'Grown-ups move out.'

Of course. He was twenty-four. He was a 'grown-up'. That description was unbearably sweet.

Alexandra threw her cigarette stub onto the ground and stomped hard on it.

Nick is a grown-up. I'd treated him like a junior high boyfriend. Hold hands, kiss kiss. It made sense he'd gone to Liv. I'd taken him for granted. It wasn't fair that I was being treated like a grieving widow. I hadn't earned it.

Finally I realised that we'd stopped because we'd arrived at the juice bar where she was meeting her friends. Two girls in school uniforms that matched each other, but not Alexandra's, waved at her from inside.

Alexandra got to the point. 'Did you phone on Wednesday? To our house?'

She sounded so accusatory that I tilted my head in response. 'What? No.'

'Oh.' She rubbed the sidewalk with the bottom of her shoe. 'I was kind of rude. I just wanted to apologise.'

She was in the shop in an instant. One of her friends hugged her. The other one stretched her neck to get a look at me.

Back at Peterhouse I put my academic robe on over my clothes.

I found its anonymity a comfort. I ate more and more at formal hall in the evenings, for an excuse to wear it.

Nick had been gone only a week when I found out that the police were planning to dredge the Cam. I almost phoned Morris to tell him not to do it. They should keep looking for Nick alive, not scrape the bottom of the river for a body. But telling him that wouldn't change anything. I've dealt with police before. They listen to everything, in case your words might be useful to them, but they never do what you say.

I went to Magdalene to tell Liv, but she wasn't in. I was just outside the porters' lodge writing a note for her when Richard Keene, Nick's thesis supervisor, came out of the chapel. I'd met him once, with Nick. I'd heard he only walked, never drove or cycled or took the bus. He said it kept the pace of life human.

'Good morning, Polly,' he said.

'Hi, Dr Keene.' He offered that I could call him Richard, which was nice. But he wasn't even one of my teachers, or someone whose house I go to, like Gretchen. I wanted to call him Dr Keene. It felt safer to live in an organised world.

'Congratulations,' I said. 'Nick told me that you're getting married.' He was marrying a medical doctor and going off on a honeymoon at the end of term. Was that really the coming Sunday, four days away? 'I mean, he told me that before ... before he was gone.'

My hands had been shaking since I got there. My handwriting on the note to Liv was all over the place. Now that I spoke, my voice was shaky too. Dr Keene looked worried about me. 'Are you all right?' he asked.

'They're going to dredge the Cam,' I blurted. I showed him the note I'd written Liv. It said the same thing, in a diagonal line across the paper: 'They're going to dredge the Cam.'

Dr Keene paled.

'Not today,' I clarified. 'They'll wait for the rain to stop.' To illustrate my point, water suddenly sheeted down, obscuring the view through the arch of Magdalene's gatehouse.

We waited under the shelter of the entryway.

'You go to church there?' I asked, meaning the college chapel from which he'd just come. I couldn't discuss Nick any more. And I was curious. From the creationists I knew back home, I'd just assumed people who worked with evolution stayed away from church.

'My Sunday church is near Lion Yard,' he said, waving his hand toward town. 'But I sometimes go to Magdalene's chapel for a more formal service midweek.' He looked back into the courtyard, at all the windows lined up just so and the

80

neatly trimmed grass and the designated paved paths. 'I find that formality is a comfort in the midst of chaos.'

So he felt the world spinning too. That was good to know.

'Dr Keene,' I said, 'do you really think–'

And then I saw her. My mother. She was on the other side of the road, looking for me.

I grabbed Dr Keene's arm, then let it go. I hardly knew him. I shouldn't be touching people I don't know. Mom crossed, ignoring the bicycles and the enormous red double-decker buses going both ways. For a moment I couldn't see her, as one of those buses drove between us. Then she was closer. Then she was there.

Dr Keene is the same size as my dad. I stepped back to put his shoulder between me and Mom. The wind changed direction; rain from the open courtyard behind us soaked my back.

Mom joined us in the shelter of the gatehouse. She dripped. She looked like a melting candle. She shook herself off and gave a little conspiratorial smile to us, like a stranger commiserating about the weather.

Dr Keene spread his arms protectively. He didn't realise who she was. It was refreshing to find someone I knew in Cambridge whom she hadn't already hunted down.

'You shouldn't be here,' I said from behind him. I meant in England.

'I know. It's such an expensive city. But I've been looking at apartments. The rents are higher here than I'm used to, but–'

'No.'

She looked at me with coolness instead of her usual beggar's eyes. 'I still have British citizenship and I can live where I wish. It's not up to you.'

I stepped out from behind Dr Keene. 'You can't leave Will,' I said. My brother.

'Polly,' she said gently. 'Will is in college now. You know that.'

Of course he is. But I still pictured him at fifteen. Everything at home is frozen there in my memory.

'I'm divorcing your father,' she said formally, embarrassed to be saying it in public. My refusal to meet with her more conventionally had reduced her.

I'd expected it, but, good God, I didn't need this now. *Later, later,* my eyes pleaded. *Not now.*

'Okay,' I said. Really, what else was she supposed to do?

It's not like I hadn't known this was coming. She'd started taking birth control pills again just before I left. We only had one bathroom, and she took one right in front of me, while I was brushing my teeth.

'And there's something else. Your father...'

'No!' I said. 'Not now, I have an appointment.' Lie, lie. 'With Dr Keene. We were just...'

'I'm Richard Keene,' he introduced himself, shaking her hand. 'Mrs...? You must be Polly's mother?'

'Yes, I am,' she said possessively. 'It's good to meet you, Richard.' She called him Richard! That really made me mad. Who does she think she is, that she can call these people she's only just met by their first names?

I sucked in a deep breath. 'Mom, I know you want a fresh start too. I get it. But Cambridge is mine. It's mine, okay?' I tried to reason with her.

'You're not all right, Polly,' she whispered. 'You're still...'

'What? What?' I deliberately raised my voice against her purposely delicate tones.

'You're still very fragile,' she said. 'And it's nothing to be ashamed of.'

I hate psychology. 'I like it here and I'm good at it,' I defended myself.

'Nick–' she started to say, and I exploded.

'First, you didn't want me to have sex. Now you think I'm "fragile" because I don't want to have sex. Pick one or the other, Mom – they can't both be evidence of pathology.'

This was wearing on her. I'd said 'sex' in front of a teacher.

'Polly, you're a good girl.' This didn't mean she approved of my behaviour. It was just mother-speak for general affection.

'I spoke to Nick,' she went on. 'He wasn't angry at you. He just didn't understand why you'd reacted the way you–'

'You told him?' I was incredulous. This was outrageous. 'You told him?'

'It's all right, darling, he understood.' She smiled instead of steeling herself against a blow. How little she herself understood.

It's like she'd brought it with her in her suitcase and set it free. It was sniffing me now, nipping at me. It was dripping its spit on my feet. It was curling around me with a loyalty I would never be able to escape. I'd left it behind on purpose, to starve without care, and she'd dragged it across the ocean.

'You had no right to tell anyone!' I screeched. 'You had no right!' I pounded at her chest while she tried to pull me into an embrace. We were locked a few inches apart, too close to punch as hard as I wanted to, too far to stop me from trying. 'You had no right!' Keene's arm slipped between us.

A porter emerged and commanded us to stop. Richard inserted his other arm and firmly parted us. I took one step back.

Mom spun out against the wall as if he'd tossed her. She covered her face and cowered there. Passers-by stood in the rain to stare. I panicked for a moment that, in the midst of everything else, someone with a cell phone would call the police.

So it seemed perfectly reasonable that, suddenly, a policeman was there. 'Hi, Morris,' I said, still catching my breath.

'Hello, Polly.' He nodded at me with formality. Then he turned toward my mother.

'My mom and I were just having an argument. It's not a big deal,' I explained.

'Polly, step aside, please,' he said. Then he repeated that I should step aside, so I did.

'Miranda Bailey, I'd like you to come with us,' he began.

Mom brushed her hair with her hands. She wiped under her eyes.

'You don't need to do that,' I said to him, as if he were taking Mom away for harassing me.

'Polly, get back,' he said sharply.

Dr Keene tried to intervene. 'Is this really necessary?' he hissed at the policeman.

For a moment everyone held still. I pressed back against the message board on the wall.

Morris squared his shoulders to Dr Keene.

'It's all right, Polly,' Mom said firmly. 'The Inspector knows I'm happy to answer any additional questions he may have.'

Morris kept looking at Dr Keene, waiting for him to back down, but he didn't. 'Mrs Bailey,' Dr Keene said to my mom, but looking directly back at Morris, 'would you like me to come with you?'

'No!' I said. 'No, she doesn't have to go...'

'Polly,' Mom said firmly. 'I'm happy to help.' She took Morris's arm like they were going to the theatre. He passed her off to a uniformed officer. She said to Dr Keene, 'Thank you, but I'll be all right.'

'Sorry, Polly,' Morris said quietly.

Dr Keene grabbed Morris's arm. I couldn't believe it. I think it's really important not to touch a policeman. I pulled on Keene to make him stop. I wanted to protect him. I hadn't jumped up for my mother, but here I was jumping for him.

'I can take it from here, Dr Keene,' Morris said, shaking him off. 'Take a step back, Richard.' I thought, How did he know his name?

'Did you really need to do it this way, Morris? In front of her daughter?'

Morris wagged his head back and forth, then laughed, which was horrid.

'You do your job, Richard, and I'll do mine. Come along,' he said to the officer. They had a car parked nearby.

'How could you?' I shouted, and I meant, *How could you laugh?* How could he have a personal squabble about it?

'I'll be fine,' Mom mouthed at me. I'd forgotten about her for a moment. I'd made myself forget.

I turned and ran the other direction, into the courtyard. First court, second court, around Pepys Library and into the Fellows' Garden. Some of the colleges are fussy about their Fellows' Gardens, but Magdalene's is open. I followed the path that leads away from the river; there are always too many people near the river. I hid in a private little wood that turned out to be a pet cemetery. I sat on the tombstone of a dog that had died a hundred and fifty years ago and put my face between my knees. Breathe.

I thought my mom had been arrested, tactfully. And I thought to myself, *My God, she did it. It happened again.*

I ran to Millington Road, panting. I knew Liv was at Gretchen's.

Harry let me in. 'Polly! What can I do for you?' He wore an apron and smelt of vanilla.

'Please. I need Liv. Can she come out, please?' I had meant to ask to come in, but I couldn't face it.

'Liv!' he called over his shoulder, keeping me in sight. I had never heard him speak above a polite volume. I must have looked a wreck.

Liv came around the corner. 'Polly?' she asked. We hadn't spoken since the revelations at the gallery.

'Liv...' I said, and then my eyes cracked open to

release a torrent of tears.

'Nick?' she asked, of course assuming that the worst had been discovered.

I shook my head, tossing tears to both sides. 'No, no. At least, I don't think so. I – please come with me.'

She told Harry that she had to go and pulled her jacket out of the closet next to the door. Her arm was in one green sleeve when Gretchen came up from behind. 'What's going on? Is there an emergency?' She sounded concerned but also annoyed.

'Please,' I said. Meaning, *I just need to speak to my friend*. But she took it differently. She insisted I come in and pulled on Liv's arm.

She dragged us both into the lounge. Harry prepared hot drinks in the kitchen. Gretchen tried to be stern and parental with me, which was exactly the worst thing under the circumstances. I sobbed till I was almost choking. It was minutes before I could speak.

'My mother,' I croaked out. 'My mother,' I said again, with a bit more control. I was getting it together.

'Is she hurt?' Liv asked. It was like Twenty Questions. All I could manage were short answers.

'No. No, she's all right.' They waited for me to elaborate. I could only hiccup.

'Is she still in Cambridge?' Liv is so sensible. I really admire her.

'Yes, she's here. She wouldn't leave.'

'Polly.' Gretchen took me by the shoulders. 'You've got to talk. You must.'

'Okay,' I said. Harry pressed a cup into my

hand. It burnt my fingers. That kind of got me together. 'Okay. My mother's been arrested. They took her away.'

'Harry,' Gretchen interjected. 'Call Jim. He'll have a recommendation for a solicitor.' Harry jogged upstairs. Gretchen continued: 'Drink up. You're in shock.'

'Thank you,' I said. I sipped. Time passed.

'I'm lost here,' Liv admitted. 'What's she been arrested for?'

Gretchen knew. She'd connected the dots.

'It's Nicholas, Liv,' said Gretchen. I nodded to thank her, which was thoughtless.

Harry had come back. He put a pink Post-it on the table in front of me. 'Grant Tisch. Would you like me to phone him for you?'

'No,' I said, honestly surprised. 'No, I think she did it.'

Gretchen sat up straighter. 'Harry, phone the man.'

Things happened around me. Liv gaped. I tried to protest the lawyer, but Gretchen was a force.

The room seemed to be growing larger. The cushions on the couch swelled up and pressed on all sides, lifting me up toward the ceiling. Liv and Gretchen lengthened before me. Liv asked, 'Are you all right?' and I said, 'Yes,' because I had no force of my own. I didn't have it in me to explain anything to anyone.

The inside of my head had become bigger than the world around me. It was a terrible place.

Gretchen spoke to the solicitor in front of me, to reassure me that my mother was in good hands.

She used a tone with him that suggested he should have pre-emptively prevented my mother from being arrested in the first place.

'Grant Tisch is going to meet your mother at the police station, Polly,' Gretchen said. Harry put food in front of me, which I ate, I think. Liv was doing whatever she was asked, and generally wringing her hands. I missed a lecture on 'Order and Disorder in Material Science'.

No one asked me again what I think it was my mother did.

Gretchen put me into the guest room even though it was daytime. Gretchen has this way. It wasn't physical how she did it, but with force nonetheless. I said, 'I think I should go home now,' and she acted like she didn't hear it.

There was a telephone in there, which I unplugged. I locked the door and considered climbing out the window. If only the world outside the window didn't have my mother in it.

I opened drawers. There was stationery and pens and stamps. Also an address book. This must be Harry's writing room when it wasn't accommodating guests.

I considered writing Nick, but where could I send it and what would I say? I couldn't apologise, because I'd tried to save him. That I'd failed was not my fault.

I eventually collected myself and wandered back down to the lounge. Liv wasn't there any more. Harry wasn't around either, not even in the sounds of distant puttering. The curtains were pulled. Gretchen sat at the table, running her fingers over a book.

She was startled by my steps. 'Polly!' she said. 'I urged Liv to attend her lecture. The most important thing was for you to rest.'

'Okay,' I said, still not fully under my own power.

I sat down across from her and she closed the book.

'Polly,' she said, 'I think you should tell me what happened.'

I've played in chamber groups and I've played in orchestras. In a quartet, we follow each other, we follow the music, we follow what we'd agreed together in practise. Orchestras are a whole other thing. In performance, the orchestra itself becomes an instrument, played by the conductor. His hands point and waft, dictating pace and emphases. We absorb the emotions from his face and posture, to return them through our instruments. We're open receivers. It's an unequal situation. An orchestra does what it's told.

'Polly,' she repeated, just that one word, just my name. It was like that moment when the conductor raises his hands. Everybody sits up straight. Elbows out, bows hovering over strings.

'Okay,' I said. And I opened my mouth to tell her.

CHAPTER THREE

I'm surprised Gretchen let me leave the house. She was pretty upset by what I'd said.

I walked up Grange Road, turned left onto Adams and then straight to the Coton Footpath. It took me over the rush hour M11, still full at eight p.m., then past fields to a cheap little playground: a slide, a spinning thing, and two swings. I pumped with my legs, back and forth, higher and higher. The air was misty but it wasn't actively showering. It was dark.

Before Jeremy and I had gone all the way, we used to make out in a park like this one.

Usually we came to the park together, but sometimes we met there. Once, I got there first and sat on a swing. He came just a little later, but for a few minutes watched me from a distance. He told me later that he liked to just look at me. And that my skirt blew up above my knees when I went up, and that my legs were the longest and prettiest he'd ever seen. I was, he said, the prettiest girl in school, which at the time had staggered me as an impossibly enormous compliment. It had made me the prettiest girl in the world.

I waited for him now. He might step out from behind a tree any moment.

He sat on the seat next to me. I said, 'Hi.' He started to swing too, but we weren't quite in sync. So it was hard for me to be sure it was him. He was behind me, then blurring past, then it was the back of his head. Over and over again. I kept trying to change my pace, to widen or shrink my arc so as to catch him. He stayed out of range. I couldn't look him in the face. Perhaps this was a purposeful kindness. Perhaps this wasn't five years ago, and was instead three or two or less. Perhaps his face wasn't whole any more, and he was sparing me from seeing it. He was a gentleman that way.

I stopped trying to catch up with his swing and just enjoyed his company. 'Jeremy,' I said. 'Do you like England?'

I didn't expect him to answer. I knew he wasn't really there.

Jeremy had blond hair. It'd been lighter than mine, except when I caught up in the summer. He was nice, a good swimmer, funny.

My father stormed in on us once while we were in the living room playing cards. 'Polly,' he said seriously, clearly holding something back, 'I need to talk to you.' Jeremy offered to excuse himself; Dad had been obviously ready to blow up about something. 'No, son...' Dad said, seemingly conversational. 'You need to stay.'

We'd looked at each other, Jeremy and I, feeling the hook pierce our gaping mouths. It was obvious what this was going to be about.

He'd found a cache of condoms in my room. He held up a sample.

I tried the offensive. 'What were you doing in my room?' But he just shook his head. He wasn't going to be derailed.

I tried again. 'Okay. So what? You can see we're

being responsible.' At 'we', Dad's head swung to Jeremy, who shrank a little.

'I care very much about your daughter, sir,' he said, as steadily as one can. It felt like a script, even though it was true.

'Do you?' Dad said, nodding to himself. 'Okay, okay. You care. That's nice.' He paced.

'Where's Mom?' I asked, because he was kind of freaking me out.

'She's out. She doesn't know yet.'

My face gave it away. He put the condom into his pocket. 'I see,' he said. I had told Mom months before.

He made Jeremy leave, then yelled at me. He told me I lived under his roof. It was all standard, as I understand these things. Dad seemed pretty okay afterward, like he'd got out what he needed to.

Jeremy and I became careful. We didn't do anything for weeks. I stayed in most evenings too, to show Dad. The condoms were gone and I didn't buy new ones; I didn't want the pharmacist or one of the supermarket cashiers to maybe tell him something and set him off. But it wasn't just me being good. Dad and I had this truce going on. Dad didn't say anything when I spoke to Jeremy on the phone sometimes. Once, Dad even handed me the handset and told me who it was.

About a month later, my brother, Will, broke his arm. He and a friend had been horsing around on skateboards, his favourite summer activity, which Dad didn't like. Mom took the minivan to the hospital, where Will's friend's mom had taken him. I was out with the yellow car and didn't know what was going on. That left Dad stranded at the bus stop when he came home from work. It was later revealed at trial that he'd had an ugly confrontation at the mill with his supervisor, about a forklift accident that had been covered up and some structural damage Dad was certain was worse than was being admitted. Dad had been the good guy in that conflict, and risked his job over it. Coming home that day, he'd been indignant and afraid of being fired. He'd been worried about the people who might get hurt if the company didn't take action. He was worried that my brother was skateboarding at the parking lot of the vacant strip mall, which he'd told him not to do. He was worried about me and Jeremy. And then there was no one to meet him, which was either fundamentally disrespectful on a day he totally didn't need that, or evidence of bad news. He was in a panic, or a rage, to get home.

I need to linger here, because if my brother hadn't broken his arm, Dad probably would have been a hero. He would have followed through with things at work. Maybe he would have gotten fired for it and sued them and gotten the press after them. Or he would have forced them to shape up himself, and maybe no one would have known what he'd done, but he wouldn't have minded that. My dad was a good person and, if Will hadn't broken his arm, would still be one.

Because Will broke his arm, Dad had to walk home. The walk from the bus wasn't too long, but it was a drizzly day. If Mom had picked him up, she would have driven the long way around,

94

down Campbell Street, because she didn't like the left turn onto Warwick. In a car it doesn't really matter if you go the little-bit-longer way. But Dad was walking, and turned onto Warwick no problem, and then right onto Minerva, and then left onto Cowper. This was the more direct way. As he was walking he imagined all the things that could have made Mom miss picking him up. They involved hospitals, police, or fire trucks. He was really worried, and, just underneath all that, suspicious that there hadn't been an emergency after all, and that no one really cared how hard he worked or what he'd done that day.

When he turned the corner from Cowper onto Lang, he saw our yellow car parked in the driveway. This is where his brother, Joe, lived. He wondered if we were all in there; if perhaps Joe had had a heart attack, or Rain had been arrested for shoplifting (he didn't like Rain). He bounded straight across the lawn rather than detouring the long way up the walk. He could vaguely hear the TV running, but it could have been a lot of people talking. He pushed in the front door, and heard worrying, potentially medical sounds under the TV noise. Was someone having a terrible asthma attack?

I know all of this because 'state of mind' figured heavily in his defence.

Just a few steps farther in, he recognised the sounds. He knew what they were and, worse, recognised me. He said later, on the stand, that he knew it was me because I used to breathe just like that when he tickled me when I was a kid: a distinctive kind of breathy whooping.

95

He didn't walk through to the TV room, but he called out to make us stop.

We did so immediately. We dressed. When Jeremy turned off the TV, I squeezed my eyes shut. I needed something to dull the full effect of what was about to happen.

'Are you dressed?' Dad boomed from the front room.

'Yes,' I called back. Jeremy shoved the sheet into his backpack and took my hand to go meet him.

Tears slid down my face, but I didn't cower.

Dad told me to walk myself home. He wanted to drive Jeremy to his house to talk to his parents. Jeremy shrugged. What else could we have done?

Jeremy kissed me on the cheek and said he would call me. I smiled bravely in return, and walked out past Dad without acknowledging him. From the next street I heard the yellow car start up in Uncle Joe's driveway.

Dad said that when he and Jeremy got into the car, he saw Burger King bags on the floor of the passenger side, and a couple of big bags from a camping store in the back. We had used the car that day to buy a tent from a store out of town; a bunch of us were going to go up into the White Mountains later in August. Jeremy and I might have otherwise met at Uncle Joe's on foot, and Dad would never have known we were there. But we'd had the car and, after getting a tent and a small grill, had stopped at Burger King on the way to Uncle Joe's. When the lawyer prompted him, Dad described everything from this point onward – Burger King bags, camping stuff – in emotionless detail. He gave everything equal weight, to dull it, I guess. To flatten it all out.

When I got home no one was there, and I'd given Dad my key ring for the car. I sat outside on the step. I heard it happen, three streets over.

Dad admits that Jeremy didn't say anything during the ride, which made it difficult for Dad's lawyer to prove provocation in the moment. Dad says he doesn't know why he did it, he just felt, compellingly, that it needed to be done. He makes it clear that this feeling wasn't rational, and it isn't one he retains. In fact, he says, as soon as it was over he recognised it for the horror it was. But as he did it, he said, it was as unthinking as a routine. You don't put on your tie in the morning because you want to, he said. You do it because that's what you do.

The prosecution had a slow ramp-up to their full description of the act. They had street diagrams and skid marks and experts on that particular engine to indicate where and how quickly Dad had accelerated. Apparently, Jeremy would have briefly seen it coming. Dad drove straight for the oak tree in the Palmers' yard, no swerving. He had nothing against the Palmers; it was just a big tree near the road.

The defence tried to make it look like an act of suicidal depression, but Dad had aimed the car so the passenger side would impact the tree and the driver side wouldn't. One could argue that that was luck more than good aim, but Dad admits it was intentional.

Jeremy had been thrown into the windshield. His face got shredded and sprayed blood like a cloudburst. His head was cracked open by the impact, and Dad said he could see Jeremy's brain. He said it like it was just a detail, the same way he had seen the Burger King bags. Dad said Jeremy had seemed unconscious, but breathed in a rattly way for a while beside him. The coroner says that death was instantaneous, but I believe Dad because he was there.

Dad had had an airbag. He cracked three ribs.

In the trial, there was some haggling over whether Dad knew that the passenger side didn't have an airbag, whether he knew that his side did, and whether he'd noticed that Jeremy hadn't put on his seatbelt. He was given seven and a half years, and will likely serve only five.

And all of this happened because Will broke his arm.

I finished high school at home with tutors. I didn't have too many credits outstanding, so there wasn't that much to do. The school was nice. They didn't make me come in for classes, but let me continue to be in the orchestra. I like being surrounded by the swell and flow of all those musical machine bits; I like being one of those bits. I like being part of something that works.

I spent the year after that at home with Mom and Will, planning. I was going to get away, there was no doubt about that. I had to get away, but I wanted to get somewhere good.

I haven't seen Dad except at the trial. He sent me a present for my last birthday, a beautiful copy of a sixteenth century planetary model, a pre-Copernican Earth-centered universe, to go with my intended studies. It spins beautifully, representing the best effort of an early scientist, all of whose hard work hinged on an error. I think Dad was admitting that he'd been wrong about a lot of things, fundamentally wrong.

The card was in Dad's writing, and the model was the kind of detailed, physical, well-engineered item he liked to share. But I think my brother helped him get it – I assume it was he who bought it and wrapped it. He probably helped Dad figure out to choose it in the first place. Why would Will do that? Why would he want to help Dad?

I didn't try to see Jeremy's family or attend the funeral. I think they would have flipped. I know that if you pressed them they wouldn't say they held me responsible, but of course they did. I actually didn't know his family that well. Jeremy and I had mostly seen each other at school.

The media was kind to me. I was never mentioned except sympathetically. They didn't draw Dad right, though. They just assumed conservatism was involved. Dad's actually agnostic and liberal. Who the hell knows what happened in his head?

I was made to go see a counsellor; that was part of getting such a sweet deal with school attendance. I actually got a great one. Her name was Laurel Bell. Two nouns, just like that.

She said I didn't have to say anything, but I did have to stay for the full hour each week, to give myself the chance to say something.

For most of the sessions I just played my cello.

For the last month before I left, I swear to God, we played poker. No kidding. She was awesome.

99

We actually laughed.

When I told all this to Gretchen, she'd said, 'What about your mother? How did she deal with all of it?'

And the answer was, I didn't know. I didn't think about her.

This is what I think happened here in Cambridge: I think Mom talked with Nick and found out what had passed between us. I think she saw another Jeremy. And I think she was another Dad.

It's probably not rational to think that. Mom hadn't been in the car with Dad and Jeremy. She hadn't freaked about the condoms. But I'm sure there is this orbit around me, this moon-path, that Mom follows as much as Dad ever did. She takes too much of an interest in me. She's too attached. I keep trying to cut her loose, but my gravity hauls her even across oceans. Some people think that Dad must have been anti-feminist or Saint Paul obsessed, but they don't understand that it wasn't philosophy steering that car. It was an attachment to me. It's me.

I walked back to St Peter's Terrace in the dark. The dark was nice. I feel safe when no one can see me.

My mother had been recorded on closed-circuit TV talking with Nick at New Square, at ten o'clock on the Wednesday night. That was the night before he was gone. The camera recorded her catching up with him and having a conversation that looked serious and, at the end, confrontational. When they parted, he went on toward the Grafton, chased by her a few minutes later. Mr Tisch told me that the police actually don't care about Jeremy. Isn't that bizarre? They would have arrested her even without the taint of his death.

It also came out that Nick's room at the Chanders' had been burgled that night. It's unclear exactly what's missing, but the room was a mess and his laptop was nowhere to be found. Mrs Chander has admitted that they sometimes leave the front windows partly open, because of the uneven winter heating of the town house.

To make it all worse, Nick's friend Peter, who'd been with Nick that evening, says that Mom had been looking for Nick. Like how she did with Liv.

I'd never even met Peter. Apparently, he's Nick's best friend. Which is why it's incredibly stupid that anyone thinks I was Nick's girlfriend. I didn't even know his best friend. Peter's a grad student too. Liv says he always has a different girlfriend. Even Liv knew him. I know she's been here a year longer than me, but that's not the point. Liv knew him.

Nick's wallet was found in a skip on Trumpington Street. A student says he saw it just lying on the top of the trash. Mom wasn't anywhere near that part of town yesterday morning, but I guess she could have dropped it anywhere and someone else picked it up. I mean, that's what the police think.

I'm not sure what I think.

I haven't asked Mom what happened because I don't visit jails. I made that decision three years ago and I've stuck to it.

Gretchen got pretty mad at me, actually, when I told her I didn't want to help my mother. She didn't seem to understand that this isn't my problem. She took it far too personally. I know she worships her mother and all, but not all of us do.

While she lectured me about my 'duty', she accidentally knocked over a small unlit candle. It split from its brass dish and rolled off the coffee table. Before that moment, I'd never seen her scramble for anything. She thrust herself after it, missing again and again. For the first time she really seemed blind to me.

I tried to avoid the river on the day they dredged it, but little brooklets all over the city lowered with the Cam. The assumption of Nick's death was everywhere.

An urge to memorialise him blew through the University. The choristers at King's dedicated a service to him, tactfully aimed toward praying for God's care for him, whatever his current condition. The voices of those little boys flew up to the ceiling, that elaborate ceiling eighty feet up. I'd not heard boy sopranos before. Their voices lack the weight and ringing of the grown female versions; they have a hollow, airy sound that floats and fills instead of aiming for a target. The effect is truly corporate, rendering the individual voices anonymous. It was difficult to imagine Nick once so small, a skinny little thing inside a cloud of white surplice.

It was difficult to imagine Nick at all, actually. And he'd been gone barely a week.

Part Two

NICK

CHAPTER FOUR

The envelopes were snatched out of my pigeon-hole just as I reached for them.

'What the hell?' I demanded.

'Ooh, love letters?' Liv held them behind her back with both hands. Stretching her arms behind her like that stuck out her chest. Her shirt was tight. Then she turned her back to me, bringing the mail around to her front, and rifled through the stack: a journal, a bank statement, a mobile phone bill.

'No,' I said, not laughing, not cracking a smile. Not bloody love letters. Polly had run out of my office at Earth Sciences like I was a monster. I still smarted from it.

'Bor-ing,' Liv sing-songed. She put the mail back into its slot and tugged on my shirt.

'What are you doing?' I asked, brushing her hand off. She rolled her eyes towards the porters and waved that I should follow her outside.

Out on the cobbles of First Court she whispered: 'There's a party. Come on.' She pulled my hand. I resisted at first. I leant back to counter her weight. 'Come *on!*' she said again, giggling, adding her other hand and pulling harder.

Polly. She'd pushed me away, with her hands and then with her elbow.

It was nice to be pulled.

'All right, let's go,' I said. My sudden compliance

with Liv's drag almost toppled her backwards.

'Okay!' she said, slipping, righting herself, holding on. 'Wow, okay.'

I followed her lead across the road and up her staircase. We stood close. We had to; there were too many people in the corridor and the music was loud. We were close enough that the bottles in our hands clinked together as we pulsed to the rhythm unconsciously.

The porter broke it up half an hour later. Students dispersed to their rooms.

'Well, goodnight, I guess,' Liv said, shrugging. 'Thanks for coming anyway.' She was right in front of her door.

I pushed it open. She pulled me in.

Liv stood up. I kissed her on the forehead, like a niece would be kissed.

Ridiculous. She was half-naked.

Her sweater was on the bed. Somehow, I was standing on her bra. I'd tossed it to the floor. First I'd struggled to unhook its clasp, scraping my knuckles on the wall behind her. Then I'd thrown it on the floor, not caring about anything except getting my hands on her skin. In the ensuing tangle it had got under my foot.

The blue cotton was now marked with dirt from my shoe. I picked it up. 'Sorry,' I said. She took it, and lifted her shoulders, like she didn't mind. She covered her mouth and laughed or sneezed, some small sound. Her breasts bounced and she crossed one arm over them. But she didn't dress. She smiled.

'I have to go,' I said. I did up my trousers. I

looked around for my coat and realised, in amazement, that I was still wearing it.

She shivered. I got her sweater from the bed. The coverlet was dented where the sweater had landed, but the rest was all smooth. Everything we'd done had been against the wall. She'd untucked my shirt and rubbed her hands over my stomach. She'd turned us to switch places, to steady my back against the wall, right next to the window well, where the side edge of a short red curtain had tickled my ear.

I offered her the sweater now. I righted the inside-out sleeves and held it out, limp.

'I don't want to get dressed,' she pouted, again with that smile. She reached out to me, again with that hand; she has soft, avid hands, with short fingernails, and one smooth, cool ring.

'I have to go,' I repeated, backing up and knocking into her fan heater. The corridor must have been empty by then; at least I hoped it would be.

Her hair was wild. The light from the long-armed desk lamp made strange shadows that elongated one of her nipples. Everything that had urged me on had finished. *I shouldn't have done this.*

'I have a meeting, Liv,' I lied. 'Richard's expecting me.'

'Isn't it a little late?' She laughed nervously.

'I meant to see Richard earlier, but you, uh, you distracted me.' Actually, I'd come only to collect my mail and Richard was the last person I'd wanted to see. He wouldn't approve of what I'd got myself into with Polly. How could I possibly explain *this?*

'Did I do it right?' she asked.

I stopped breathing. She looked at me so hope-fully. She was still bare. She was lovely and waiting.

'I've never done that before. Was it okay?' she persisted.

My fingers grazed the door handle.

I exhaled the answer: 'Yes,' I finally said. 'It was very good. Thank you.'

I got out the door.

Stairs, then the whoosh of the outer doors sliding apart like in a grocery store. I sucked in the cool air outside.

Knock, knock, knock. I looked up. She waved from her window. She had the sweater on now. I wonder how much of us had been visible, or audible, from outside.

I waved back and ducked around to the front of 'O' building. It was far too late to call on Richard, but I had to make a show of an appointment, for Liv's sake. So she wouldn't think I was escaping her.

The walkway leading out to the street was in full view of her window, so I waited. She'd think Richard had let me in. I stood in the dark against a brick wall. My hands were cold. Somewhere along the way I'd lost my gloves. I'd had them on when I got to Magdalene, but later I'd put bare hands all over her.

I sat on a bench, between the river and an alley with a locked iron gate.

I hid there until I was sure she'd given up on me for the night.

I showered for half an hour. I didn't usually waste the Chanders' hot water that way. Nothing about me was as usual, nothing. Polly had been right to run away from me. I evidently wasn't to be trusted.

I pressed my wet hair with a towel, then rubbed my face, hard. I had to be honest with Liv tomorrow, and early. I couldn't let her think that this was the start of something.

If she had a phone I would have called her then. Liv was the sort to tell all of her girlfriends, wasn't she? I had an obligation to spare her the embarrassment of bragging and then being broken up with.

Laughs pumped out of me: 'ha -ha-ha!' I hadn't even got her off. I'd got mine and got out. What would she brag about?

But her face. She'd looked ... grateful.

A knock rattled my bedroom door. I wrapped myself in a dressing gown and opened it. There was Aashika. She's eight.

'You should be asleep,' I said.

'I know,' she said. 'But I made you something at school. I heard you in the shower and I waited.'

She offered a carefully painted ceramic tortoise. She's been studying Darwin and the Galapagos. The paint had glitter mixed in. She held it out with both hands, and I took it.

That look on her face, so pleased and proud that I'd accepted her gift? Liv had looked just like that.

I didn't recognise her at first. She had on a skirt instead of jeans. The expression on her face was sweet. 'Hi,' Liv said softly. I'd never heard her speak softly before.

'You look nice,' I said, only to acknowledge the effort. She clasped her hands under her chin.

Gretchen drummed her fingertips impatiently. I'd finally found Liv there, after missing her at Magdalene, and outside a lecture that had been rescheduled, in between appointments of my own.

'I'm so happy to see you!' Liv said. 'But I need to finish up here, and then I have an appointment with my supervisor...'

'Back at Magdalene? I'll walk you.' Perfect. There would be an end point to cut short her inevitable acrimony when I told her that last night had been a mistake.

She was satisfied too with her own expectations. She bounced as she followed Gretchen. I trailed them into the library. Gretchen opened a first edition of one of the Susan Maud books to the title page. 'I received this in the mail yesterday. It had been flagged by the bookseller as having an inscription. Please read it to me.' Her finger stabbed right down onto it, having found the indentations by feel.

Liv said, 'To Mickey with gratitude. Linda Paul, 1959.'

Gretchen strained to remember a Mickey she'd never met. Liv packed up notebooks and pens into her bag, out of which she pulled a sheet of paper. 'Gretchen, this is a list of my hours. I know the index isn't quite done yet, but I figured you could pay me for these now...'

'Yes,' said Gretchen absently. 'Put it with the

mail.' There was a stack of it on a table near the door. 'I'll have a cheque for you when you come next.'

'Oh! Thanks. Yes. But I was wondering if maybe you could deal with these hours now...'

I stared at the handwriting. 'Linda didn't write this,' I said.

'What do you mean she didn't write it?' Gretchen wanted to know.

'This is Ginny's handwriting.' The loopy one, same as copied the poem.

'I guess Linda got Ginny to do some of the autographs,' Liv said lightly.

Gretchen turned on her. 'Is your time so precious that you weren't going to tell me?'

I knew that tone. Once, one of her students had plagiarised and she'd dressed him down right in the centre of Magdalene's First Court, on a warm day when everyone's windows were open.

'I didn't know,' Liv said. 'You asked me to read it and I read it.'

'You have eyes!' Gretchen railed. 'I pay you to *look* at things for me. If you think you're here to do the minimum, only to read or only to sort, then I don't know how I can trust *any* of what you've done.'

The look on Liv's face was awful. I'd seen other undergraduate girls hit this wall. They admire Gretchen so much. But Gretchen's not really the mentor type.

'Gretchen, it's my fault,' I said. 'If I hadn't interrupted just now, I'm sure Liv would have noticed and called it to your–'

'What neither of you seem to appreciate is that

111

this is all that's left of a woman's *life*, a significant woman's life!'

'Does it really matter,' Liv said, 'that Ginny signed a book for her sister?'

I flinched in advance. Gretchen wasn't going to take that well.

'Now that you've revealed your fundamental laziness, I think we can all agree that your work is worthless to me.' Liv's eyes sprouted tears.

'Gretchen, that's not so. The photo index is sound,' I insisted.

'I'll skip my supervision,' Liv said. 'I'll double-check everything.'

She shouldn't do that, not at end of term. 'I'll do it,' I offered. 'I'll stay. Gretchen, I'll show you that everything is as it should be.'

'Thanks, hero,' is what I think Liv mouthed at me. She looked genuine but I could only hear it sarcastically. I walked her to the door.

'I'm happy to help a friend,' I said, not sure if I emphasised the final word too much or not enough. 'Can we talk later?'

Liv suggested we meet in the evening. 'I'm meeting Polly at the library at four, but I can lose her after that.'

Polly. They'd tell each other everything. 'Oh, I have to...' Something. Anything. Once she and Polly spoke to each other there would be nothing for me to add. 'I'll see you tomorrow,' I said, certain that neither of them would want to see me.

'Oh!' she said, rooting in her pockets. 'You left these in my room last night.' She held out my gloves. I reached for them and she held on, giggling.

'Nick!' Gretchen called.

I got the gloves and stuffed them into my own pockets. 'Don't worry,' I said. 'I'll get this hand-writing issue sorted with Gretchen.'

Liv stretched up and kissed me on the fore-head, the same kiss I'd given her afterwards, last night.

'I'll fix this,' I promised.

I opened the box of photos and pulled out the folder with the poem and its copies in. I took one of Ginny's copies to compare, and the original, clipped from a newspaper, fluttered to the floor. I picked it up carefully, wary of its fragility. 'Sorry. We tried not to handle the original much.' That's why I hadn't noticed that the back of it had part of the date on it: 'mber 1963'.

That was strange. I thought Gretchen had said Ginny had died when Gretchen was seven, which would have been 1962. But what does it matter – seven versus eight, or even nine, is nothing. Gretchen must have meant merely that she'd been young when it had happened.

'I don't know why she would have done it,' Gretchen persisted, about the autograph. 'Mother and Ginny didn't socialise much after Brussels. Ginny travelled so much and Mother and I didn't any more. I don't see how it could have been Ginny who assisted her. Unless my mother didn't know? Perhaps Ginny was pretending to be Linda?' But the books weren't famous enough to make a masquerade worth her while, even as a social prank. Gretchen twisted her hands around each other, around and around.

'Let's be sensible about this,' I said. I laid out the two signed books, one of the poem transcriptions, and three photos back-side up: one of the older photos of what might have been Linda and Ginny's parents, the photo of 'Jim' (purportedly Gretchen's father), and a photo of Gretchen and her friends as teenagers. I compared them again.

'Do you have anything else written by your mother?' I asked. I could have asked before, but frankly I hadn't wanted to add to the chaos. The puzzle had seemed straightforward. Now more information was warranted.

'She didn't write me letters. We talked on the phone. Her will was handled by solicitors. We can call our solicitor and look at the signature on the will.' She was talking too fast. I needed to bring her down.

'It's all right, Gretchen. It doesn't matter.' By that I meant that not having an extra handwriting sample didn't matter, as we would figure things out another way. She thought I meant something else – that it didn't cosmically matter, I would guess. She stomped out. I thought it best not to follow.

She came back from her study with a folder. 'These are my school reports. Mother had to sign them. And here, these are her cookbooks. She wrote notes in the margins.'

I compared the writing. Unsurprisingly, it matched the writing in the books signed to Gretchen at graduation, and on the teenager photos, and 'Jim'.

'Does it really matter why Ginny signed a book for your mother? Perhaps she promised to get a signed copy for a friend, and found it easier to make a fake than to go through the mail.'

Gretchen flexed and unflexed her fingers, kneading a memory out of the air. 'I had kept asking to see Aunt Ginny. You know how children can be – I just wouldn't take no. I wanted her to come for my seventh birthday. It was going to be just a usual child's party: cake and balloons. I wanted her to come, but Mother told me she was travelling. And then, the day after the party, she told me the truth – that Ginny had died. She hadn't wanted to spoil my day, so she'd waited. It had been a good little party, with my best school-friends. But after that I couldn't bear that I'd been happy while my aunt was dead. I threw the presents away in a desperate ceremony. I buried them beside the house. A snow globe and a cuddly toy cat and new jacks. I was good at jacks, which surprised people. I always won.'

She didn't stop. 'It was our first year in the new house. Later I buried my pets there. By the side of the house. What was the date on the poem? Was there a date?' She asked this suddenly, and I felt for a flash that she wasn't blind and had read it there on the back of the clipping. I hadn't mentioned the discrepancy because I didn't want to add more to argue about. Now, knowing that the seventh birthday was a fixed marker for Ginny's death, the poem date was vital.

I told her the truth: September or November or December. 1963.

'No,' she said, and then waited for me to give a better answer.

'That's what it says,' I insisted.

She took my arm, hard, which was not in character. 'It wasn't Ginny, was it? The person who copied the poem and impersonated my mother signing the book.'

'Maybe there was another sibling. Whoever she – or he – was, they were the child of the couple in the older photos. That's all I know.' What if Ginny hadn't died? Could Linda have just been saying that to shut seven-year-old Gretchen up about her? Or perhaps the couple weren't Gretchen's grandparents. 'Where did these pictures all come from anyway?' I asked. The old address on the box had a CB postcode for greater Cambridge. Perhaps Gretchen had lived there once. Or perhaps they'd used borrowed boxes in a move. 'Did you used to live in Haslingfield?' I asked. 'On Cantelupe Road?'

'What are you talking about? Cantaloupes?' Gretchen was angry again. 'Wait here,' she commanded.

A few minutes later she returned from upstairs with a heavy frame. It held an eight-by-ten photo of the dark-haired sisters in younger days, days before Brussels and before Gretchen. Gretchen turned it over and felt the fastenings, working at them. 'I want to know if there's writing here.'

She lifted the backing out, and there it was: 'Me and Ginny, 1950.' So, Linda must have written it.

The writing style matched the poem transcriptions, and the grandparents' photos, and the autograph. But it didn't match the teenaged photos, or the inscriptions for Gretchen's graduation.

So the one who'd labelled the framed photo couldn't be Linda.

116

I could have lied to Gretchen. But I didn't really think about the options or implications. I pounced on the paradox with a detached fascination.

'Maybe your mother didn't really write those books. Maybe she was someone with just the same name as the author–'

She smacked my face. I hadn't been hit since I was six years old. Our cleaner had hit me and been fired.

Gretchen's face was rigid in a passive mould but tears gushed out as if through cracks in a dam. They slid into the paths of the thousand wrinkles that suddenly scored her skin. She was old now. She was wretched.

'Gretchen,' I said, trying to be kind.

'You don't understand,' she whispered. And I didn't understand. I didn't.

She put her hands into the box and pulled up dozens of photos. They spilt from her fists. She pushed them into my chest, grinding them in. 'Tell me again what she looked like. Tell me again.'

This was awful. She wanted me to be a conduit for something that was more electric than I could bear.

'Tell me again,' she demanded. She pushed me and lurched, suddenly disoriented. 'Tell me again.'

'Gretchen, please.'

She stopped and got her bearings. 'Take them,' she said, kicking at the photos, which were now a mess on the floor around us. 'Take them away.'

I knelt on the floor to pick them up, like when Alexandra as a child used to throw cards on the floor and call it a game.

'Thank you,' she said, while I crawled under the

table where some had fluttered or slid. When I passed her by she put her hand on my head, like a matron with a hunting dog in an old portrait.

I refilled the box in a jumble, and hefted it into my arms. I considered ripping the framed photo out of its place to take that as well. But there was a momentum leading towards my escape that I didn't want to disturb. I headed towards the door without it.

Gretchen remembered. She pursued me into the lounge. The corner of the frame scraped my ear. She piled it, frame and all, on top of the box in my arms.

I promised her that I would take them all away.

She said, 'Utterly, please. Utterly.'

If I'd been less rattled I would have stored the box somewhere, assuming that she would eventually change her mind. At this time, however, it seemed very important to take things literally. It seemed important to back away from making my own judgements about things. I hadn't made good decisions lately.

So I did what Gretchen asked.

Harry's car was just turning the corner, and I crossed the road quickly to avoid him. I didn't want to chat, but was relieved to see him. His presence would keep Gretchen from doing something drastic.

I took the box back home. Home-home, not the Chanders'. Mum would be out. Dad was away on business. We have a pond behind the house. Not a garden pond; this was a real jungle, a wildlife zone, hopping and buzzing and splashing with life. It was deep.

My arms tingled from carrying the heavy box so far. I dropped it at the water's edge and shook out my limbs to revive their circulation.

I considered sprinkling the photographs, like confetti, but that was too delicate a gesture. I hefted the box up and dumped it out.

I'd forgotten that they'd float. Photo faces dotted the water surface. Ginny and her side parting stood out to me. I hadn't noticed before that Liv's hair is parted in the same way, but after last night, looking down at the top of her head, I wouldn't forget. It's a side parting, to my left, and it had moved back and forth in front of me, my back up against the wall of her room.

The box itself bobbed, and I wondered if it had ever held something simple. I wondered if it had ever delivered a toy, or a lamp, or a book by someone who wasn't Linda Paul.

I looked back at our house. I still had a key. My old room was still there, with my bed in it, even if Mum had her computer set up in there now too.

Gretchen didn't like the idea of a nanny getting between her and her mother. I'd noticed that in one of the photos the nanny wore a pin from some society on her jumper. I tried to decipher it but Gretchen scoffed. She hadn't cared. 'She's just the nanny.' Still, the photos told a different story. In the photos, she and the nanny seemed close. I'd had nannies. They were nice. Anna from Germany, and Marie from France. Anna taught me how to crack an egg, and how to cook on an Aga. Marie was retired from competitive

119

tennis, and I spent most Marie days outside. Mum brought us lemonade and made me wear a hat. My mum was still my mum.

Briefly, I considered unlocking home and going back in time.

A car pulled up. I heard Alexandra and a friend pop out of it, spilling bright conversation. They didn't see me, around the back of the house.

It was enough to shake me out of my sentimental mood. Going into the house wouldn't undo being an adult.

Gretchen's photos still floated. The framed picture glowed gold in the early winter sunset, and looked for all the world like a raft. It had drifted too far to reach with a stick, even with this long branch that had come down in the last storm. So I threw a stone at it, which smashed the glass. That bull's-eye gave me confidence and I threw a larger one, which missed, and another, which pushed the frame perpendicular for a moment. Then it righted itself.

Something rustled in the bushes next door. Our neighbour, Mrs Cowley, wouldn't like me stirring things up down here. She didn't like people around. Usually I tiptoed around her sensitivities, but now I picked up the branch. No, it couldn't reach. But I hefted it up onto my shoulder and ran forward, releasing it like a javelin. It plunged into the water at least a metre from its target, the framed portrait. Scuttling noises retreated away towards the next house.

The lights in the ground floor of our house came on in a flash. The windows made a bright stripe across the whole building. I hadn't noticed before that the lights hadn't gone on as soon as Alexandra had entered.

My noise must have disturbed her. The back door banged open. 'You!' she called bravely.

I waved and emerged from the trees. 'Alex, it's me.'

I expected her to be relieved. But she tensed up.

'Alex, it's all right. It's Nick.' My voice sounded forced. I didn't sound like myself. She went back in without answering; the door slapped shut behind her.

As I got closer to the house, the angle of my view changed and I could see the whole of the lounge. Her companion wasn't one of her usual girlfriends. It was a boy. He was taller than she was, so he had to be older. Most of the boys her age have yet to catch up with her. They argued. She buttoned up her blouse.

That's what had looked so odd at the back door. Her shirt had been untucked and overlapped tightly around her, underneath her crossed arms.

I strode in. 'Alexandra, won't you introduce me to your friend?' I folded my arms across my chest.

She popped the last button in through its slit. 'Gordon gave me a ride,' she said. Meaning a car. I know she meant his car.

His shirt was untucked too. He held his blazer in front of himself, draped awkwardly over his arm.

'You can go now,' I said to him.

He tried to get a cue from Alexandra. She shook her head and lifted her shoulders. I stepped between them. 'Now!' I said.

121

When Alexandra turned to watch him drive away, I saw that her shirt had two lumps at the back where the ends of her bra were undone and poked up.

I took her blazer from the couch and handed it to her.

'Is there a problem?' she demanded, putting her arms into the sleeves.

'How old is he?'

'None of your business!'

'You're fourteen!'

She feigned shock. 'Oh my God, you're right! Better change my nappy and put me down for an afternoon sleep!'

She ran upstairs. The stair railing rattled.

I sat down on the bottom step. After a few minutes I was calm. I went up and tapped lightly on her door. She didn't answer. I opened it anyway.

She sat cross-legged on her bed. Her teddies were lined up behind her against the headboard. The duvet was neat underneath her. Mum must make her bed up; I know Alex wouldn't be bothered.

'I'm sorry that I embarrassed you,' I said.

She looked at me with red eyes. 'I don't forgive you.'

I nodded. I didn't expect her to.

'It's only that–'

'No! Don't tell me! I'm too young, right? And boys only want one thing? It's not like we came up to my room. We were just messing about.'

She still slept with bears and plush ponies. A boy didn't belong on this bed.

'Don't tell Mum,' she begged.

I promised.

'And get out of my room.'

I did. I shut the door so that it clicked.

The house phone rang. She snatched up her extension.

'Hello ... Oh, I'm sorry,' she said loudly enough to be clear to me. 'He's not allowed to talk to *girls!*' She hung up with an angry beep and threw the handset at the door.

'Who was it?' I demanded through the door.

'Some slag for you. Don't you know they want only one thing?'

Had the caller been Liv? Why would she call this number? Maybe it was Polly?

Polly wouldn't know this number either. Or think that I was here. Or want to speak to me.

She'd literally recoiled from me. Not just from me going too far, but then from me trying to help, trying to apologise, trying to figure out what had gone wrong. She'd run away from me.

And soon Liv would tell her where I'd ended up from there.

I leant against Alexandra's door.

The phone rang again. Alexandra let it ring. I dashed downstairs to the extension in the lounge. 'Polly?'

It was Mum. 'Oh, Nick! Are you staying for dinner?'

I said no. Mum was disappointed. But if I stayed Alexandra would refuse to join us, or she'd sit with us but not eat. She'd find a way to protest my presence, silently daring me to tell on her, and promising hate forever if I did. It wasn't worth it. Not tonight.

Mum said she'd be home soon, so I left Alexandra by herself. On the way out, I picked up a thick fallen branch and sent it sailing towards the neighbours' fence. The wooden slats rattled when it hit. I was tired of looking after people. I was tired of working 'round everyone's delicate feelings. Our neighbour, Mrs Cowley, was frightened by sudden noises, by any token of our existence, really; but what if I *wanted* to throw something? What about *my* feelings?

I didn't relax until I pushed in the heavy oak door of a pub.

By the time Richard Keene walked in I was past thinking clearly. He was with Alice. They would be married soon. I acted like it was my first drink. It wasn't anywhere near that.

'Working hard?' Richard asked. Because he was my supervisor. I didn't look like I'd been working.

I shook my head.

'Good,' he said, drinking. 'It's good to take a break.'

I should have talked to him. Alice said she'd be right back; we had the privacy. I could have told him everything that troubled me.

'I have to go,' I said, but I didn't move.

'I have to go,' I repeated, to prod myself. I turned.

He said, 'Wait,' I think, but then Alice came back. He stood up, and I got away.

I felt breathless outside, like I'd escaped something. Ludicrous. Richard's a good friend. I started to walk in small circles in front of the pub, convinced it would sober me up. I actually made myself go back in. They didn't see me. They were looking at each other. I thought, *Right, some friend he turned out to be.*

I pushed between several chairs and put my fist on their table. 'You want to talk? All right, I'll talk.' They looked shocked. I was shocked myself. What could I say? About Liv? About Gretchen? What could I say about anyone that wouldn't make it worse for them, not being wholly mine to share?

'Sorry,' I mumbled. Richard got up. He had to push Alice's chair forward to get to me. He pushed his fiancée to get to me.

'Go home,' he said, putting a hand on each of my shoulders. 'Get some sleep.'

That's the thing with Richard. His good advice is always so uninteresting. There's nothing arresting about it. No epiphany. It's easy to ignore.

I tripped walking out the door, and caught the jamb to keep from pitching forward. The door bounced off my back. A group of students on the pavement stopped talking and waited for me to get out of their way. One of them had dark hair. I thought it was Liv for a minute, and stared, frozen. She looked at one of her friends and laughed, which snapped me out of it.

A bicycle bell jingled behind me. I wasn't fast enough. The cyclist skidded sideways to avoid me and hit a parked car. Its alarm siren rose and fell, too close to my ears.

'What the fuck is wrong with you?' he demanded.

I didn't answer. He pedalled away, not leaving

a phone number tucked under the windscreen wiper. I groped in my pockets for an old receipt on which to scribble my number – it was partly my fault – but I didn't have one. I leant over a rubbish bin, and almost reached in to retrieve a paper bag. It had a wet stain and a bulge at the bottom, and I finally recoiled.

I leant against a concrete pillar. My mobile rang, again, and I assumed that it was Liv calling from a borrowed phone. I'd already ignored two of those, in the pub. But this call was from Peter. I answered.

Peter and I have known each other since we were teenagers. We boarded at different schools, but attended some of the same camps and summer courses. We were both at Cambridge now. We both had theses to finish.

'What?' I said.

'Careful, mate. You're being followed.'

I'd drunk too much to have a sense of humour. I flattened against the wall and demanded to know what the bloody hell he meant.

Peter laughed. 'That girl you know? Polly? Her mother's in town, and she's been asking for you.'

'What are you on about?'

'I told her you might be at Magdalene. That's why I'm phoning. If you don't want to see her, don't be at Magdalene.'

'I'm not.' I got myself together, and started walking along back streets towards Earth Sciences.

'You sound wrecked.'

'I thought you were Liv.' I shouldn't have said that. I didn't want to explain.

'Mmmm ... Liv,' he said, tasting her name.

126

'You're not responsible for her. She's not your fault. You didn't ask to be worshipped.'

'Some things are,' I said.

'Some things are what?'

'My fault. Some – a lot of things are my fault.'

He laughed again. 'You dog! I thought it was the other one you were after.'

'I don't want to talk about it.' I picked up my pace.

'So what happened with her?' he asked, referring, I think, to either of them. Whichever was a better story.

'Polly...' I said, then trailed off. I don't know what happened with her. I know what happened between us, but I don't know what happened inside her.

'Look, you did the right thing. Liv knows what she wants. You're better off.'

'I did the wrong thing. I did several wrong things. I'm doing a wrong thing right now.'

I skulked along the edge of Emmanuel College and crossed St Andrew's Street quickly.

I stopped short of my office. It wasn't a refuge. The stapler and pencil cup were probably still scattered on the floor, where they'd fallen when I pulled Polly onto the desk with me. The cleaners would have taken the rubbish bin, but the smell of sick would still be there, trapped in the poorly circulated air.

'Are you in your office?' I asked Peter.

He was. I crossed the road. The massive whale skeleton on Zoology's patio rattled in the breeze. Female voices in the car park froze me until car door slams shut them away.

127

That's the moment I thought of Lesley Harter. I hadn't thought about her, except in passing, for years. She was seven years my senior, which was an impossible distance when I was fifteen, at least to me it had been. Now she would be ... thirty-one. Which seemed equally impossible. She was probably married. She was probably a mother. She ran her family's businesses, and had done since she was twenty. But I thought of her as just herself.

I had met her at a dressage event, where one of her horses was competing. She knew Dad through work. Alexandra had wanted to see the 'horsies', which is why we were there. I'd only been out of choir for a year, having cracked my voice at fourteen. I'd never seen a woman so beautiful. While Mum chased after Alexandra, Lesley showed me the horses.

She asked me to carry a box of tack into the trailer attached to her car. I put it down in the corner and she followed me in. The trailer walls muffled the loudspeaker and applause. 'It's all right,' she said. She just stood there, waiting for something, and letting me know it was all right. I stepped close and kissed her, terrified I was doing it wrong. When I pulled away, she smiled again. 'You're a lovely boy,' she said. She waited a few moments more before turning to hang up a bridle. She left it to me, all on me. If I wanted to touch her I could. I could see the outline of her bra under her polo shirt. I couldn't move. It was overwhelming. She took pity on me. She kissed me again. I was mad with it in my response; I kissed her all over her face. She had earrings on, hard

128

little gems that scratched my lips.

That's all we did. Then we went to watch her horse compete. When he won, she raised her arms up in a cheer. Her breasts lifted with her arms. I could hardly breathe.

We became friends, and I never touched her again. I hardly saw her, just now and then. But when I did, she spoke to me like she valued my opinion. That wasn't new, exactly, but usually adults wanted to hear what I had to say about academic things. She wanted my opinions on life. Should she forgive someone, should she insist on some condition in a contract? It was somehow much the same as what had passed between us in the trailer. She treated me as an equal.

I would never tell Peter about her.

He opened the front door of the building for me, and we went up to his office.

An empty coffee cup from Fitzbillies bakery was on his desk. The last time we were in there together, he'd flirted with the woman at the till. I noticed that this paper cup had a phone number written on the side. Next to it was a stack of books with papers inserted between pages throughout. None of the books were open. There was an empire-building computer game on his screen. 'I thought you were working,' I said.

He grinned. 'Procrastination is part of my process.'

His whiteboard had notes scrawled on it in three different colours, and an idle sketch of a rowboat, surprisingly detailed. More of his 'process'. Polly rushed into my mind, her laughing that Penrose had illustrated his talk with colourful home-made transparencies. It's something to watch American standards and expectations get tickled like that.

Polly even looks American, though I can't quite explain what I mean by that. She looks like someone in an American chewing gum advert.

'So...?' Peter asked, leaning back in his chair, and I knew what he meant. I was in the stiff-backed guest chair, sitting straight up. I shook my head. 'You and Liv?' he persisted.

He was my friend. I had to trust somebody.

'I went too far...' I began.

'Holding hands is acceptable in this century,' he teased.

The opportunity shuttered. I couldn't make him understand without spelling it out. And once he did understand, he'd make a joke of that too, wouldn't he? He'd think it was hilarious.

'Tell me again about your brother,' I countered. His face froze.

'The hell?'

That was mean of me. His brother was the only thing he was sensitive about.

'Seriously, do you have a problem?' he wanted to know.

'Not me, mate.' I'd gone too far. It was out of character for me to bait him, but I had to get him off Polly and Liv. 'I want to talk about something else,' I said. 'The only things you're willing to be serious about are your brother and your work, so let's talk about them.' I pumped these words out in a rapid staccato.

'I don't want to be serious right now,' he pouted. Then, 'Fine, we'll talk about work.'

'How's your thesis?' I asked. This was a more normal conversation.

'It's all right,' he said. 'My thesis is all right. I'll be ready to submit soon.'

'It's about time!' I said, joking. I could finish this year too, but I'd probably drag it out. People don't think I've got laziness in me, but that's because thoroughness and laziness can look so much alike.

Thoroughness can be a cover for numerous less desirable things.

I shouldn't have gone on to analyse the handwriting on Gretchen's photos. But I'd gone on to 'see the job through', as my father had said to me a fair few times in my life, despite not being home terribly much. It was my personal sense of tidiness and completion that drove me to sort out the handwritings after Liv had left; compassion and responsibility, which is what I thought it was, would have involved observing Gretchen more carefully.

I take words at face value. Gretchen had said she wanted to know everything. I don't do well overriding what people say about themselves. I don't put body language and tone of voice over words themselves. I should, I know that now.

'You're a real shit, you know that?' Peter said, still hurt that I'd brought up his brother like that. But he wasn't going anywhere. He hadn't shifted his weight, or leant forward as if to stand.

I decided to respond to that, instead of the words.

'It's not just Polly or Liv. It's...'

He prompted, 'What?'

'Kepler.'

'Johannes Kepler?'

I nodded and he laughed at me.

'The cosmologist? From how many hundreds of years ago?'

Four hundred years ago. Kepler had defended the Copernican theory of a sun-centred universe. Circular orbits didn't work out; they couldn't explain the path Mars followed in the sky, seeming to backtrack on itself. Another kind of orbit might. He set out to prove that the orbits of the five known planets followed the shapes of Euclid's nested solids. This, to him, would have been a divine signature, proof that a sun-centred universe wasn't godless or random.

What he found instead were ellipses.

Elliptical orbits are one of the greatest, most perfect discoveries in scientific history. They explained Mars's apparent retrograde motion, the last scientific obstacle to a sun-centred system, and did so without any convoluted mechanics. Yet he despised them. They were too... I think 'natural' might be the word. He'd been looking for a perfect crystal and had found a beating heart instead.

'You know,' I rambled. 'Retrograde. Ellipses. The truth wasn't exactly as he'd pictured it. So he hated it.'

I'd found truth for Gretchen. She didn't want it.

'Are you drunk?'

'No.'

'You're not all here.'

'I had an uncle who drowned,' I said. This had little to do with the flow or point of the conversation. But I said it.

It was the intensity of Gretchen's faulty memories, I think, that triggered the thought. It was the way my mother always told me how much I used to look like my uncle; but, from the pictures I'd seen of him, I don't think I ever did.

'I never knew that,' said Peter.

'It was before I was born.'

He picked up the paper coffee cup and rolled it between his hands. 'Are you going to be all right? I'm supposed to meet someone. But if you want to talk about Polly or Liv, or your uncle, or Kepler...'

'No. No, thanks. Really.'

'Just a bit of advice, though, all right? Whatever you're not talking about – it's not as bad as you're making it.'

He would know, wouldn't he. He's always got a new girlfriend.

'Is it the woman from Fitzbillies?' I asked, flicking my fingers against the cup.

'I'll phone her this weekend. Tonight I'm meeting an old friend. We were a pair back in the old days.'

Old days? Undergrad, maybe? 'I'm really sorry that I mentioned your brother.'

'I know. It's done.'

'No, I'm really, truly sorry...' Regret and sentimentality inflated within me. 'That's not how to treat a friend.' I meant that in so many ways. I'd been poison to so many people in the space of two days.

'Nick. You're drunk. You should go home.'

'That's what Richard said.' Hours ago. Maybe by now the Chander girls would be in their room, doing homework or reading in bed. I wasn't up to facing their usual enthusiasm.

I got up.

Peter's phone rang. While he chatted and organised his laptop bag, I looked hard at that rowboat scribble on the whiteboard. The colours were vivid – red, green, and sun-bright yellow.

I remembered Wesley, a blind boy Peter and I had both known from a summer cricket camp. He'd been blind in the same way as Gretchen: able to see in his earliest years and then losing it. He couldn't play real games with us – it would have been too dangerous for him. But he could train. He was a decent bowler, actually. He couldn't tell what was going on in the field, but he could see people as 'blobs'. As for throwing the ball, he was excellent.

We'd been room-mates. He confided to me back then that his memory of colours was fading. The red he had that summer was less bright than the red he'd had five years before. I didn't see how he could know it was less bright, since he would have to mentally compare it with the bright colour to notice. He repeated that he didn't have the bright colour any more – he couldn't call it up in his mind – but he knew its absence. He knew that the red he used then wasn't fiery or sharp or any other kind of feeling word that one might use to capture the saturation of a colour. He knew it like someone knows they don't remember when they were one year old, or where they left their keys. So his memories were literally fading like an old photograph. Not a metaphor like most people mean – the details going away – but the colour actually draining. And these memories were his visual vocabulary, so his visual present and future and even his imagination were drained as well. I presume that Gretchen had had a similar experience. It put her attachment to her youth, and to the brightness of her early life, in perspective.

'Shall I go first, as a lookout?' Peter joked. I'd almost let myself forget that Polly's mother was looking for me.

I laughed. Maybe I should have said yes.

I'd forgotten what the Georgian buildings on St Andrews Street look like. They'd been covered for months, three cranes sticking out like antennae, while the new shopping centre was being constructed behind their facades.

I could have crossed at Emmanuel, but in my cowardice I craved the shelter of the scaffolding. I turned left down the pavement alongside the construction site and kept under it until I had to cross the street. More construction obscured me there, between Christ's College and the bus station. I'd been under cover since coming out of Downing Street. The open green of Christ's Pieces stretched in front of me. I hesitated to step out from the covered alley.

'Don't be an idiot,' I said out loud. I made myself step onto the path.

Approaching footsteps beat behind me, under the alley's temporary roof. I quickened my pace to keep ahead of them. Once into the park, I looked over my shoulder, but couldn't make out more than a silhouette.

It was a woman. I don't think she was a student;

at least, she didn't come across as studenty. Maybe it was the hair. The hair seemed like it belonged to someone's mother. Polly's mother.

I walked faster.

She was as quick as me, quicker. The distance between us shortened, despite my longer legs.

When she inevitably caught me up I whipped around to face her. 'What do you want?' I shouted. I shouted it into her face.

She stepped back.

'Why are you following me, Mrs Bailey?' I demanded.

She stepped back again. She wore a tracksuit, with a stripe down each leg. She had trainers on her feet. She flicked earphones off of her head.

'I'm sorry,' I stammered. Her glance flitted over all possible directions of escape. Back through the alley? Across the grass?

I pushed my hair off my forehead. 'No, I'm sorry. I'm sorry. I thought you were someone else...' I walked closer, so I wouldn't have to raise my voice.

She ran for the alley, probably because there was a homeless person in there. I suppose she thought I wouldn't hurt her in front of a witness.

She wasn't Mrs Bailey – I realised that from her reaction – but she reminded me of Polly just the same. It was the turning and running.

I leant over, hands on my knees, and tried to slow my breathing. The grass looked awfully close, closer...

'Nick?'

A soft, feminine voice. I sprang back upright.

'What? What do you want?' I spluttered. In that

136

instant the voice was Liv, it was Polly and Gretchen and my sister. It was my mother, disappointed that I wasn't staying home for dinner. I held my hands up in front of my face.

'I'm Miranda Bailey. Are you Nick Frey? Are you,' she asked, in light of the ridiculous outburst she'd just witnessed, 'looking for me?'

She hadn't followed me. Anyone with my address could guess I'd come this way. She'd simply waited.

'No, I, no...' I babbled.

'Are you all right?'

'Never better!' I flung my arms out wide. Then I started walking.

It was a public park. It's not like I could stop her from walking beside me. It's not like I could stop any of this.

We crossed the road together to New Square.

'Polly wrote me such nice things about you.'

'That's very kind of her,' I said, staring straight ahead.

'I need to talk to you because you're her friend.'

'You'll have to ask her about that.' Polly had made it clear how she felt about me now.

'If you and Polly have been ... intimate...'

'Good God, Mrs Bailey.' I stopped in front of a rubbish bin. 'I'm not going to talk about that with you.'

'There's something you need to know.'

What? A disease? This was horrible. 'Mrs Bailey.' We faced each other. I put my hands on her shoulders. 'You've got to stop. Please leave me alone.'

'You need to know that she's a fragile person.

You need to be gentle with her.'

Gentle. Had I been? I remembered pushing her up against the back of the lift.

She continued, 'I think you're good for Polly, you're a good person. So I'm going to tell you this, so that you'll understand what Polly's going through, and why.'

And then she told me. I was stunned, of course, and sickened. She was matter-of-fact about it, having, I assume, gone over it so many times. She didn't cry. She didn't claim any part of the trauma for herself. I genuinely think she was telling me for Polly's sake, misguided as that may have been.

'I'm so sorry,' I said automatically. Manners are a good fallback during times of stress. 'That's awful.'

In the lift, Polly had put her arms around my neck. I'm sure she did. But had she really wanted to? Or had she forced herself, trying to conquer her trauma by will? Were there signals I'd ignored? I'd stopped when she wanted me to.

Hadn't I?

In my office, I'd only touched her shirt a second time because…

Because I wanted to. Because everything else about her acted like she wanted me to. There was just the hand, brushing my hand away. One hand, versus everything else about her: the way she was breathing and her open mouth.

And what I wanted.

'Polly's a good girl.' Polly's mother brought me back. 'She's a good girl, and she cares for you, and she's been punished for caring for someone before.' I noticed that she'd not once said the

138

name of the boy. 'So you can understand,' she concluded, 'why it would be a hurdle for Polly to let herself go again.'

I did understand. But, 'Why didn't she tell me?'

'She doesn't want anyone here to know.'

Miranda looked very like Polly. Obviously older, but with much the same face. It gave the illusion of a future Polly time-travelling back to now to share this important information. But this wasn't future-Polly. This was Miranda and she had no right. 'If that's so, then you shouldn't have told me.'

'You need to know...'

'Polly will decide what I need to know. Polly will tell me when she's ready to tell me. She's brave, and she tried with me, and it's no one's place – not mine and not yours – to rush her into *anything* she's not ready for.' I wanted to tell Polly that. I wanted to promise her patience. I wanted her to know that the lead was hers to take.

Miranda looked away from my indignation, staring at her handbag held tight in both hands. 'She's lucky to have you,' she finally said.

Liv had said something like that last night, at the party. Just before the porter came, she'd said, 'I'm lucky to have run into you tonight.'

Lucky.

I pressed the heels of my hands against my eyes. 'No, she's not.'

Miranda took a deep breath. She wasn't done with me yet. 'If you'd just go to see her...'

I cringed. No. Polly would have talked to Liv already. She'd be done with me. 'I don't think so.'

Miranda was offended, actually offended. She

gasped. How dare I.

'Truly, Mrs Bailey, I'm sorry. I just...'

'You just what? You just care about her, except for the part of her that hurts? That part of her that's vulnerable? Is that "just" it?' She looked so much like Polly in that moment, yet so angry. I don't think I've seen Polly angry in that way. Then Miranda deflated. 'I'm sorry. It's only – she cares for you. I think you're good for her.'

I shook my head. 'I don't think I'm much good for anyone at the moment.' Not Polly, not Liv. Not even Gretchen, on whom I'd forced an unnecessary truth.

Miranda reached for me and I stepped back.

She reached again, and I stepped back again, almost tripping backwards over the low fence that lined the path.

'I'm sorry,' I said.

I turned and headed towards the Grafton. Miranda didn't follow me at first. I got almost as far as the compass rose embedded into the pavement where Fitzroy and Burleigh Streets meet. I heard her footsteps growing louder and I turned.

She ran for me, charged at me, really. When she reached me, she begged. 'Polly will think it's her fault. And it's not. You've got to let her...' It ran down into incoherence, and then, at last, apology. 'This is madness. I'm sorry. I know you'll do what you feel is right.'

That was a laugh. So I laughed, a ridiculous, strangled giggle. I'm sure Miranda could smell the drink in me. This was the nice man Polly wrote to her about?

I turned down Burleigh Street to end the conversation. I hunched up my shoulders to discourage her. 'Leave me alone, Mrs Bailey!' I said loudly.

But we'd already diverged. I saw over my shoulder that she was headed the other direction down East Road, towards her hotel. At the pedestrian light I finally felt far enough away from her to unclench my hands. I didn't pay attention to the stranger next to me.

This person also crossed the street. He stayed just a step behind and beside me. At the mini-roundabout just off the main road, he grabbed me by the collar of my coat and shoved me up against the wooden fence. He wrenched my backpack off my shoulder. I got twisted around, and for a moment the strap caught on my wrist. He pulled, hard, and the bag jerked free. He ran, pounding his steps into the pavement.

My arm quivered. Ridiculous. He was just a teenager. There wasn't any danger. He didn't want to hurt me; he just wanted my backpack.

And the laptop that was in it.

My thesis. *Shit.*

That was my excuse. I took off after him. He was faster than me, but it felt good to run.

In my mind, I caught up with him. I slammed him up against a fence, like he'd slammed me. I wrenched the backpack off his shoulder. It was only fair. But my imagination had momentum; it didn't stop there. I took out the laptop and raised it over my head. I slammed it down onto him. The plastic casing cracked, creating sharp edges. I beat him with it. I beat him bloody.

It never happened. He outran me through the park and I stopped and caught my breath.

I sank down onto the kerb, my shoes nestled in broken glass. Nothing desperate had been lost. A little money, a few cards in the front pocket, two books. My phone and computer could be replaced. I had backups of all but my latest work.

Thank God he'd got away. I couldn't even hear his steps any more. Thank God.

I waited for the adrenaline to subside. I didn't want to bring rage inside the Chanders' house.

I no longer had my keys. I didn't want to chat in answer to the doorbell. It was late for them anyway – they go to bed by nine, usually. The front window was partly open, as usual; the house thermostat against all reason goes by the temperature of the unheated entry hall and so never stops pumping heat into the lounge. I pushed it up the rest of the way and climbed in. I still had on the gloves that Liv had returned to me.

On the next floor up, the girls were in bed. I stepped carefully and slowly, to dull the inevitable creaking of the floor. Their parents were making love, quietly, tactfully, so that the girls wouldn't know. The door was closed and their sounds were discreet but definite as I went past.

Up another flight. In my room, on my desk, Mrs Chander had left me a note: Miranda Bailey had phoned this afternoon. It was probably she who had been hung up on by Alexandra as well. She'd probably been behind the unidentified calls I'd got on my mobile earlier. I'd thought they were Liv. I'd made a lot of assumptions today.

I threw a shirt and socks into a bag. I needed only one more thing.

I pulled open the Russian inlaid-wood box Alexandra had given me Christmases ago – but there were only some francs and lire inside, my pre-Euro collection. Where was it? I always kept it in there.

I rifled through my wardrobe drawers, the contents of which were never well folded to begin with because I do my own laundry. I checked the top shelf of the cupboard – knocking down two shoeboxes that then spilt out shoe-polishing tools and a mini-humidifier. It wasn't there.

Then I remembered the girls. They'd been through the boxes on my desk, in an innocent, curious way, and had admired it. Aahana said she'd always wanted a great key like it – like something out of *The Count of Monte Cristo*. I'd told her that great keys come with big old houses, and that this wasn't for her. I remember putting it back inside and closing the lid. Aahana was usually a good child, but apparently not always.

Past the closed bedroom doors, all quiet now, down the carpeted stairs and into the cramped kitchen. The stove-top espresso maker was still full of this morning's grounds and filled the room with an incense-like sharpness. Through the patio door at the back I could see the girls' replica Chateau d'If, made of crates and scrap lumber.

The cardboard box making one end of the structure was mouldy and sagging from repeated damp, but the main part of it was grand, if precarious. It also had only a tiny opening, possibly to keep out adults, but mostly, I suspected, to heighten the dramatic prison effect. They were dramatic girls.

I probed with my hand, banging on the outside first to frighten spiders. On a nail inside the entry hung my key.

CHAPTER FIVE

I cycled out of town on Barton Road.

I switched off my headlamp where there were streetlights, to conserve the battery for the dark stretches, which were utterly black. The route took me down curvy lanes, past the lit church towers of Haslingfield and Fowlmere, and over the moderately busy A505. The repetition of pedalling dulled my anxiety. I panted in exertion instead of panic. Suddenly the steeply banked single track I was on spilt out into an expensive cluster of new-build homes. There, in the last, weak glint from my weakening bicycle light, was a sign for Dovecote.

I tried to remember it, to calibrate my expectations. I knew the version in my mind, exaggerated over the years, would be less than accurate. Would the driveway stretch as long as it had appeared to me then, would the main, house loom as massive and solid? Up till then, my experience with buildings of that size had all been school-related, all shared space. That Dovecote was owned by a single person had thrilled me. I used to fantasise about being one of those boarders whose parents didn't bring them home for school holidays. I knew it didn't work this way, but I imagined they got to roam the school grounds, and camp out on their own in the empty classrooms. I wanted to run up and down the stairs, and yell to hear the echo. In my memory of that fantasy, I'm slamming doors. It doesn't feel angry, it just feels strong. Does everybody want to do that?

Lesley Harter had bought Dovecote to convert it into a hotel. To celebrate her purchase, she'd held a garden party on the grounds, avoiding the interior of the manor house, which had been in need of major renovations. I was nineteen then. I came with my family. I told a story that had happened to me just weeks before:

I'd been accused of stealing a woman's handbag in a crowd. A policeman had detained me but could find no evidence that I was the thief. I'd felt confident of my honesty, and never feared they would take me.

Everyone who heard it laughed. No one ranted on the unfairness of the accusation, because they had all felt it: I was unassailable. No authority would ever believe I had done it. It was a fine adventure – that was all.

But Lesley took me aside and said, seriously, 'Nick, you're a good boy. But if you're ever in actual trouble, you can always come here. All right? It's yours if you need it.' She gave me a key to Dovecote. 'It may be a mess of reconstruction for the next few years, but it's a place to go.' Her security code, she said, was the year Hatshepsut became Egypt's first female pharaoh. I looked up the numbers when I got back to our family house, in a history almanac that had been kept in the bedside table of my old room ever since I was a little boy. I wasn't surprised that it was still there.

It's amazing to me now what I'd taken for granted.

The sign ahead of me didn't indicate whether Dovecote had yet become a hotel. For all I knew, Lesley might have sold the place. There could be a conference going on, or a wedding. But I didn't really think so, just as I didn't really think Lesley was changed. Lesley, who wasn't fragile. Lesley, with whom no carefulness was required. I wanted to hold something durable, something that wouldn't shatter if I dropped it.

I was certain that nothing had altered while I'd been looking the other direction, except that the cars had gone, full of party guests, leaving just a few special people or none. I felt I was nineteen, fresh from the hands of the police. I felt free.

Gates put a stop to my fantasy. Two expanses of chain-link fencing abutted sharp holly hedge on both sides. Pulling on the obstruction did little more than rattle the chain and padlock holding them together. I pressed my face up against the fence: There was a tarp-covered hill to one side, probably earth from digging foundations or a pool; and an incongruous temporary building on the other side of the drive, presumably a site office for builders. But the manor house beyond appeared whole. I know Lesley had planned only interior renovations for it; the more drastic work must be aimed at the outbuildings. I saw no cars. But there – a light in a window!

Richard had once said to me, dead earnest: 'Don't rush.' Meaning, I think, everything. Don't rush with women, don't rush away, don't rush into.

I abandoned my bicycle, threw my bag over the fence, and scrambled to join it, squeezing my hands and feet into the many tight little squares until I was high enough to jump down the other side. I thudded onto the drive and skidded till I rolled backwards, gravel digging into my palms.

My new vantage point allowed me to see that the light had been a reflection of the moon off glass. The house was fully black inside.

I tilted my head back and closed my eyes.

Bloody idiot, I thought. Light rain dotted my jeans. This wasn't the first grand gesture of my life that had been completely ill-advised.

I remembered the flu I'd had as a child: the closed room, the pulled curtains, the piles of bed-clothes on top of me.

We were still in London then. I'd read *The Velveteen Rabbit*, set in the old days of scarlet fever, and had got it into my head that anything I touched while ill would be burnt. So I stayed away from all my things. I refused to have any toys or books in the bed with me, which Mum and Marie didn't understand. I had learnt the word 'stoic' in my Greek history phase, and applied it.

One night, while a vaporiser puffed damp white air towards the bed where I slept, one of them tucked my cuddly lion next to my head on the pillow. In the morning I woke up nose to nose with it; some of my saliva had dribbled onto its mane. I screamed out loud, over and over again, a 'horrible' scream Mum says when she tells this story. I thought I'd killed it, that it would have to be burnt up because it had touched me. I screamed and screamed and wouldn't touch my mother when she came for me. I'd become convinced in that moment that I could ruin anything. I yelled until she and Marie stayed at the edges of the room, pressed into the walls by my noisy threats. I was the captain of my own ghost ship, and all I could do to save them was to warn them off.

Marie and Mum had looked so shocked at me those years ago. I'd gone suddenly wild, suddenly vicious. Eventually they left the room; otherwise I wouldn't have calmed down. They didn't know why I was upset, so they couldn't explain the truth to me. They called for a doctor to come, which he did, and I let him examine me because, if I didn't, Mum would have tried to help him. I'd rather he died than she, so I submitted.

It came out to him what I'd been thinking, and he talked me down like a man. It all deflated out of me. I hadn't been brave, I'd been idiotic. I'd never felt so ashamed in all my life.

Mum sat on my bed but I wouldn't say anything. She didn't try to make me talk; she kept smoothing the covers. Eventually she told me about my uncle and how someone dying was the worst thing in the world. She told me that I'd been brave and good to try to protect her, and Marie, and Lion. She thanked me.

She told me I could have anything I wanted for lunch. I asked for a cherry lollipop and a butter sandwich. She offered to tuck my soft toys in with me, but I felt too grown up for that, suddenly. I felt heroic.

There was no one to bring me lollipops here. It was puerile to have come. I got up and readied to

148

re-scale the fence.

My leap back onto it knocked over my bike on the other side. I hung there off the ground, in a staring match with my bike's headlamp. It wouldn't have enough charge to get me home. It couldn't even get me back to the last pub I'd passed. I had to wait for daylight.

I got down off the fence and turned to face the building. It was bigger than I remembered. My memories hadn't exaggerated; if anything, they'd minimised the length of the drive. By the end of walking it, the door couldn't shock me. Its immensity was inevitable.

I poked my key at it, but the lock had been changed. It was smaller, for a modern key. This key she'd given me was large and old-fashioned.

The rain intensified into cold stabs against my shoulders and scalp. I shivered and followed the perimeter.

There were two more doors on that part of the house, both with new, small-holed locks. I kept on. The house was massive. I felt like the bricks were multiplying to keep ahead of me. I jogged, half believing I really did have to outrun them. I didn't slow down until I got round the corner.

Around the back at last were the remains of the original house, much older than the impressive, decorative front that had been stuck onto it. This solid block had been adapted into a grand kitchen wing, at least it had been planned to be used that way.

It had its own door, which predated the rest. The key fitted and turned.

The door opened outward. As soon as I swung

149

it towards me, beeping emitted from a box on the inside left wall, echoed by distant beeping elsewhere inside. Really, I didn't know if the house was occupied or not, and, if so, whether it was still owned by Lesley. I leant in, not technically entering, to press the glowing green number keys in the order she'd told me five years ago. The noise persisted until I pushed in the largest button, an 'enter' rectangle. The beeps cut off, leaving only the loud hum of the now pounding rain. The house must still be Lesley's. I leant into the blackness inside, giving a few seconds for a dog or person to come investigate.

When nothing happened, I put my foot onto an old stone block, the step down to the original floor. At first I felt it was a hollow under my foot, smooth from centuries of use, wobbling me. I sought to steady myself with my left leg, planting it down hard, alongside my right. But it too wobbled and then swung out forward. My first foot pushed sideways, sliding behind and under my other leg, stretching them past each other into a horrible right angle.

Cheap plates. Lesley had rigged the one unmodernised door by putting actual dinner plates on the slippery step below it, as a bit of extra homemade security for the old door. Whether this was a Victorian method of security or one of Lesley's own invention, it had served its purpose.

One plate spun and the other shattered. My right hand plunged down onto another plate, which sent my upper body falling. I ended up lying on the floor along the step, my legs blessedly together again, with a conk on my head from the corner of the stone and a sharp pain in my left ankle.

I lay there for a while, until the cold blowing in from outside and the cold coming up through the stone floor pushed through my daze. I hauled myself up to sitting. Pressure on my left foot caused a starry burst of agony around my ankle.

The weather had gathered itself into a temper. I managed to close the kitchen door by hopping up and out on my right foot. Bringing the door back with me was harder, necessitating a hop back onto the slippery concave stone, which, even empty of plates, was slick. I fell again and this time bashed my hip.

'Shit!' I said out loud. 'Bloody hell.'

The thermostat didn't respond to my nudging, but the heat was at least minimally on, I would guess to keep pipes from freezing. I was sceptical that the tap water was potable, but there were two long-dry glasses in the sink, so I took a chance that I wasn't the first to drink it. The pantry had a few long-life foods. It was obvious Lesley stayed here only occasionally, probably to monitor progress on the outbuildings or as a pied-a-terre. Telephone service was not yet connected.

My right foot started to swell. It too must have been hurt, but, in comparison to the horrid pain on the left, I hadn't felt it. I wrapped myself in a coarse blanket folded near the door; it was probably meant as a mat for wiping muddy feet when the place was occupied. I only needed, I was sure, to get through the night.

The utilitarian gates were convincing evidence

that Dovecote was not yet finished. The rain would stop and the builders would return. Surely.

The stone floor in the kitchen would only chill me worse, so I crawled out into the hall beyond. I reached up to press the button on the switch-plate by the door. A lamp hanging from a bulky chain glowed a sallow yellow in response. I pressed the second button. The room beyond suddenly dazzled – hundreds of pinpoint stars shone from the ceiling onto a wooden table near twenty feet long.

I shuffled into the dining room on my knees, staring up. Even with the enormous table, the room felt vast. There were no chairs yet, no sideboards. Just space. I leant back against a wood-panelled wall to marvel. Had she put in constellations? Or was the patterning random: space observed from another galaxy entirely?

The door to the hall fell shut, *crack!* My arms flung out in surprise, to steady myself. And my left hand recoiled from a sharp point.

More than a dozen sets of antlers were piled in this corner, some of them huge, and my disturbance sent them toppling towards me. One pair of spirals fell into my lap. They were monstrous up close.

Marks high on the walls showed where they all had once been displayed. Of course Lesley would have taken them down. She'd never tolerate anything along the lines of hunting or taxidermy.

I pushed them away, with a horrible clatter, and backed towards the now-closed door, sliding on my bum. Obviously, I'd nudged the door when I'd entered, that's all. For some reason I needed to open it again. It seemed important to confirm that the hall was still on the other side of it.

There it was: hall, stairs, yellow light from the hanging lamp.

A tiny marble rolled out from under the tangle of antlers, past me and out the door.

There must be a stuffed creature there too, now one-eyed. I didn't check.

There was no rug, but the floor here was wood, an improvement over cold stone. I crawled underneath the banquet table, as if it were a tent. Caught up in a figment of camping, and reduced even in my fantasies to mere expedience, I wished for a rock on which to lay my head.

I spread the blanket from the kitchen over me, and stacked my hands to form a pillow. The fibre-optic stars above twinkled mechanically, alternating between blue and white. In my mind, one-eyed owls hooted from antler-sprouting trees. I slept.

I woke the next day hungover. Rain streaked the tall, bare windows, adding a further filter to the daylight which was having enough trouble getting through the persistent layer of cloud. I could still make out the ceiling stars, but they had little effect without the contrast of full darkness. The aggregate of antlers was, of course, in exactly the messy pile in which I'd left it. My relief that they hadn't organised themselves overnight was absurd.

I tested my legs. Useless. I couldn't scale the fence now. I couldn't ride my bike.

I waited.

No one came. Even if the wet weather stopped, there was a good chance it would be too muddy for the builders to come the next day either, and then there was the weekend.

I crawled back to the kitchen and punched in the security code to set the alarm. Then I opened the door.

The siren sang at an unbearable volume. Its source was in the kitchen, twinned with another I could hear whining on the other side of the house. Sticking my head out the door, I could tell there was also an exterior siren. But in the wind it wasn't nearly as loud as I'd hoped.

I huddled on the step and covered my ears. After about twenty minutes, it all stopped.

Without phone service, there would be no connection to the police.

The driveway was a half-mile long, putting the road beyond the sound.

There were gardens and fields behind the house – perhaps she let someone graze their animals there?

I waited an hour. I ate Weetabix out of the box. No one came.

At first I resisted making any kind of settlement. That would be too much an admission of failure. I explored, using a lone golf club upside down as a cane. I'd found it in the pantry miscellany.

Most of the rooms were empty, punctuated only by occasional swatches and colour samples. One held rolled-up rugs stacked like a log pile.

Some doors were open and some I had to push. I did so with little expectation, just dogged thoroughness. I was mentally cataloguing the place: the rug room, the green room, the room with the ugly lamp. The wonder behind this panelled door rocked me back.

The fabric wallpaper, long tasselled curtains, and upholstery were all dizzyingly patterned, and accented with shiny gold thread. Framed prints of horses leant against the skirting boards, presumably testing where Lesley wanted to hang them. Several were already up, and the idea that she'd add the dozen more of them cracked a smile in my face. She was poking sly fun at her own house.

This must be where she spent her time here.

The down-filled cushions got flat underneath me in no time; I fell into a light sleep that must have filled hours. When I woke up, it was getting darkish outside. I thought I was hallucinating. The old-fashioned room, its colour faded in the dim light... I thought I'd woken up in Gretchen's eyes.

I shot up, startled.

I had to prepare for another night, or more. It was time to set up camp.

A red wagon was parked next to the fireplace. It held a box of matches and bits of wood chip, but no logs. I used it to drag in a cache of food from the pantry. A wheel caught on the threshold of the lounge as I re-entered, and I stumbled to the floor. I tried using the golf club to help me get up, but my hand was too stiff to hold on to it any more. I set it alongside the couch, for later when my hand had rested.

I shuffled on my knees back to the kitchen, to fill a couple of large empty Coke bottles with water. I briefly considered dragging back a large cooking pot too, but I swore to myself that it wouldn't come to that. There was a toilet near enough, just down the corridor.

Re-entering the lounge, my left ankle smacked into the door frame. I lay flat-out down on the floor, biting my sleeve, until the blast of pain subsided.

When I opened my eyes, the view from the floor revealed boxes lined up behind the couch. I retrieved the water bottles from where they'd rolled, and crawled over to look inside the cartons.

Books.

For a moment I revelled. Books and privacy and time are a heady mix. I rummaged through, pulling them out and scanning the titles, separating them into two stacks. I piled the Terry Pratchetts and Feynman lectures within reach from the couch.

Then my situation came back to me. I pulled the box with the rest of its contents over to the fireplace.

I picked up two paperbacks I didn't recognise. The pages resisted, but they were not in charge. I tore and crumpled, and tossed them in on top of the ashes that were already there. I opened the flue, and set the pages alight using the matches from the red wagon.

Maybe someone would see the smoke and worry about squatters. Even if Lesley's unpredictability would comfort any observers into assuming it was she herself randomly come home, at least I'd be warm. Briefly.

I grabbed more books and got into a tearing rhythm. I didn't burn the covers. I started a deck of them, face down, as a little book graveyard by the hearth. A batch of thick romances added lurid embraces to the pile. I stopped short at a blonde holding a champagne glass. I knew her: Linda Paul's Susan Maud Madison. I set that one aside, on top of the Pratchetts. I continued to tear and crumple and aimed paper snowballs between the andirons.

Polly and Liv's paper blizzard. I rubbed my hair as if little scraps still clung there.

The fire didn't last. I upended the box and pulled it apart. The cardboard burnt only a little longer. The cold coming in more than outdid any warmth from the brief flames. I put out the embers and closed the flue.

I stretched out on the couch, and put my feet up on the far armrest. If I rested, in a few days I'd be ready to climb the fence, or at least to troll the edge of the property, looking for a break in the hedge.

I tried to read. I chose the Linda Paul book because it was on top. It was described on the back as a 'romp': Susan Maud gets into 'hot water' pretending to be a famous reclusive novelist who has failed to show up for a party.

Most of the scenes take place in a borrowed manor house, so my imagination had little work to do. Despite the cover illustration, for the heroine I pictured Gretchen's nanny. She was blonde and from the correct era; why not? When, later in the book, contradictory features were specified, the nanny persisted in my mind.

I thought again of Wesley from cricket camp. Some of the other boys had played a stupid trick.

They told Wesley false descriptions of people: ginger hair, fat, even a limp, more and more exaggerated lies to see what they could get away with. Wesley finally caught on. It was horrible. He'd been betrayed in a way we couldn't comprehend. Despite learning the truth, he couldn't shake the false images out of his head.

I sat up. Perhaps neither could Gretchen.

The handwritings were intolerably contradictory. Something in our assumptions or her memory wasn't right. Ginny's death date? A misprinted year on the newspaper poem? Perhaps there was a third sibling who wrote 'Mother' and 'Father'; perhaps those older photographs weren't of relatives at all. What if the whole box had nothing to do with Gretchen? What if a former resident of her mother's house had left their own family mementoes behind?

No, that was too far. Too many of the photos matched her expectations for the whole to be entirely random. But an idea just as huge loomed up in my mind.

What if the 'nanny' was Gretchen's mother?

Her mother, and perhaps a hanger-on who'd joined Linda Paul for a few adventures, then been cut off? Who then pretended to actually be her idol?

It all made sense. She called herself Linda Paul. She gave Gretchen a set of books upon completing sixth form, and signed them herself. She took photos of Gretchen and her teenaged friends, and labelled them. Everything else, which perhaps she'd stolen, had been written by Linda – the real Linda – and her sister, Ginny. This fit. This justified the contradictions between the handwritings in the same way that ellipses had explained retrograde. Gretchen had been uniquely vulnerable to such a ruse: a small child, just losing her sight...

Words jumped around on the page in front of me; either my hands shook or I wasn't focusing. I looked at a print on the wall to test my eyes: It was still.

I looked back at the page. Susan Maud juggled two conversations, one as herself and one as the famous author. Double-meanings and misunderstandings were tossed and caught and balanced.

The words leapt again. I looked up at the wall; the print was steady. My hands were shaking, that's all, out of cold or exhaustion. I closed the book.

I checked the print regularly. If the horse in the picture stayed serene, I was well enough. It was only my body that shivered; my eyes, and by extension my head, were fine. I was fine. The horse never moved even one leg or flicked its tail. I know because I checked over and over to be sure.

The rain kept on. Not constantly, but enough to ensure that mud stayed mud. Builders failed to appear. I reread half a dozen Discworld books. The throbbing in my ankle dulled somewhat, though it still couldn't bear much pressure. Solitude and inaction squeezed me from all sides; after three days I popped out of Dovecote like a cork.

I thought the drive would be the safest and most direct route out. That's what comes from not paying attention.

Unlike in the house, where I held onto the golf club's flat metal head and used the rubber hand-grip against the smooth wood floor, outside it worked better right-way-around: with the head of the iron slicing into the thick mud. It hit hard-packed earth not far down. My progress achieved a nearly jaunty rhythm. How high was the fence, really? How long was the holly hedge? I was sure there would be someplace to burst through. There had to be.

When I'd come to Dovecote, it had been dark. But that was no excuse for not having noticed the brief change that had happened under my feet, a sudden switch from pounding dirt to thumping across planks, then pounding dirt again. The planks covered a ford across the drive, a ford which had been a ditch when I came and was now a rain-filled brook. The planks now just underwater kept cars from getting mired. Wheels would just splash through and ride them.

In my state, mud would have been preferable to wood. I plunged my golf club cane into the shallow, flowing water, expecting to work it deep into sludge until it was a secure hold to help me through.

Instead, it hit plank and slithered forward, splashing me face down into the wet. I hit the front of my head on the far side. It was all I could do to pull my face up out of the water. The brook wasn't running hard, but it was enough to nearly roll me. It prowled over me, an endless glide of cold. My forehead bled. I couldn't see where the golf club was.

I sputtered. It wasn't worth the energy to yell.

I propped myself up on my hands and knees. I didn't know if I could make it over the fence now. If I couldn't, but tried, I might not be able to get back to the house either. I backed out of the water on my hands and knees.

I looked back at the house. This time, the light in the window was true: my light, my little lounge, a real haven, not a trick of the moon.

I turned around and crawled back.

The fever lasted days.

The house, which had seemed so big, shrank down to the room around me. The patterned wallpaper hemmed me in. The fence and holly hedge around the grounds seemed hardly necessary.

I don't usually dream. People don't believe that. Or, I should clarify, women don't usually believe that. It's been insisted to me over and over that I must dream, and that my denial of it is some sort of a 'repression'.

An old girlfriend used to ask me first thing, before I was properly awake, what I had dreamt. Not if, what. I never had the answer she wanted.

But, in this fever, I dreamt.

I was back at school during a half-term, as I'd once fantasised. I had the buildings all to myself. I scrawled on blackboards; I ran in the corridors.

Then the holiday ended. I waited, but no one came back.

I rationed the food. When I was ready to try escape again, I went better prepared.

I had no cane any more. My right foot had improved, but the left still required some coddling.

I didn't want to crawl through the ford. It was too cold to get wet again. I tested the red wagon by the fireplace for my weight. It bowed a little but held. I could ride it over the planks.

I'd found secateurs in the kitchen. I could try cutting through the hedge, or even attempt cutting the wires of the fence. I tossed them in the little wagon and dragged it outside.

There was no rain, just a damp haze in the air. I shuffled forward on my knees, pulling the wagon behind. I looked like an actor playing at being a little boy.

I think it was that ridiculousness that made me first angry at rescue. That, and the single-mindedness that comes from desperation. I'd planned to go down the drive. This car blocked my plan.

Lesley had come back.

She didn't ask me anything, just helped me to get upright and back into the house. She had hot Indian takeout for herself in the car, which she brought to me. She put a blanket over my shoulders. I assume she eventually remembered giving me the key. It had been five years.

She took everything in without visible shock until she realised her part in what had happened. 'You stepped on the plates! Oh, God, Nick, I'm sorry...' She put her hands on mine. She tried to laugh at how pitiful I looked, but tightened her grip. 'God ... I hadn't thought ... I hadn't thought you'd ever really need to come. Nick, what happened?'

Lesley must have been over thirty. But she'd always looked 'grown-up' to me, so the changes were ... appropriate. She was still in the right proportion to me, always older and wiser, always beautiful. She was as beautiful as a person could ever be.

'I made some poor decisions,' I said. 'I didn't want to hurt anyone.' She looked alarmed so I quickly explained: 'I haven't done anything bad, not like that. I just... I had to leave.' It had seemed so urgent at the time.

I put more chicken tikka into my mouth. I didn't want to explain.

'Does anyone know you're here?'

I shook my head.

'God, Nick. Did you tell someone you were going?'

'I know,' I said, putting both fists against my head. 'I know.'

She looked at her phone. 'My mobile's out of charge.' She put it back in her bag. 'You should see a doctor.'

I think she meant for my ankles but, given my demeanour, she could have meant anything.

'I was worried about slipping in the shower, and getting in and out of a bath,' I explained, justifying my Robinson Crusoe look. Hitting my head crossing the ford had frightened me. 'I've been brushing my teeth and washing my hands; I've done that much,' I asserted, suddenly almost in tears.

She told me about her recent trip to Kosovo, from which she'd just returned. She was on the board of several charitable groups and had gone to inspect a children's home they'd funded.

I felt small, which was wonderful. I felt like

nothing in comparison to attempted genocide and potential independence. I felt like no one was looking in my direction, and I could finally relax.

'What have you been up to?' she asked, as if this were a normal conversation.

'I've almost completed my thesis. I'd like to get a Fellowship.'

'You want to be one of those eccentric old men who live in college rooms as lifelong bachelors?' she teased.

I shook my head, smiling. 'You know it's not like that,' I corrected her.

And it's not. It's just normal, a more peaceful version of normal. As a child I'd been treated as a prodigy. The truth is, I liked lecture halls because the seats were set out and the focal point was obvious. People had been impressed, thinking me clever. Really, I'd just been suited to the atmosphere.

'We'll go now,' she said, standing up when I'd eaten everything. 'Or would you like to shower first?' she added, reminding me what a mess I'd made of myself.

She would have to help me. It would be too embarrassing. It all would. Where would I let her drive me? Would I just walk into the Chanders' house as if nothing had happened? I'd have to go home. To my parents' house. It's what I'd been wanting, to put them out of their grief, but my shame swelled greater than my compassion.

'I can't,' I said.

But I whispered it, and she said, 'What?'

'I can't,' I said more loudly, pushing on the

second word. 'It's too embarrassing.'

This is not how I wanted to be in front of her.

'I'm not proud of myself right now,' I explained. 'I deeply distressed one friend, misled another, and stirred up things that would have been better left alone. Now here I am, a dirty hermit hiding out in the house of someone whose respect I would really like to have. I'm not respectable right now, at all, and I can't even wash myself.' I'd actually started a scraggly beard, which takes some doing with my fair hair. 'I've been brushing my teeth,' I repeated. It seemed important that she know that.

Lesley laughed again. It took great rib-spreading breaths to make a laugh like that. She put her hands on her face but even they couldn't make it stop. At last it petered out, and two little wet spots on her cheeks sparkled from reflected light. 'I've just been among people who, fifteen years ago, were murdering each other,' she said quietly. 'You can't shock me. All right? I'm not shocked.'

My supervisor, Richard, sometimes has to defend himself to creationists, because he combines his faith with his science. He told me about a time he got in an argument over Noah's Ark. He'd said to some devout person, or at least in her hearing, that his understanding of the idea of a 'whole world' flood had flexibility. That, depending on who was telling the story, 'whole world' could mean different things. The borders of one person's whole world may not match another's, or even overlap. This upset her a lot. But I know what he meant. And I realised in this moment, here with Lesley, that my whole world

165

was actually rather small. It matters, of course it matters, because it has people in it, but it's not the actual whole world, and I needed to get that straight.

'You're right,' I said.

If I'd been washed, I'd have reached out to her. I would have pulled her to me and made love to her somewhere in the house on some grand bed or uncomfortable Victorian sofa. I'd have again ignored Richard's admonition not to rush. I'd have rushed ahead and lost myself in it. I wanted to rush, even though rushing had, so far, been a terrible idea.

'I broke up with my fiancé,' she said, out of nowhere. 'He works in Kosovo right now, though he's being transferred to Congo. He's with an American charity. He's American. He's saving the world.'

'I'm sorry to hear that,' I said.

'His world, my world. You know. I don't want to live there. Either there. Maybe I should, but I don't.'

She stopped talking about it. I tried to picture her in Africa, but I don't know what Congo is like.

'Your father,' she said, 'will kill me if I don't promptly return you.'

'I would like to bathe,' I said, determined now to risk a fall coming out of the tub, knowing at least that I wouldn't be left shivering on a tiled floor for potentially weeks. 'I can do it myself.' God, I sounded five years old.

'Help yourself. There's a ground-floor suite with a tub in the east corner. Leave your clothes

166

on the bed and I'll put them in the wash. Soak. I'll put my toiletry bag in there. Some soap and a razor.'

She turned on a water heater in some far cupboard. The hot bath felt wonderful. I scrubbed myself, and shaved my face with her leg razor. I drained the tub and towelled off inside of it. Getting out was all right because she would be there if my one good foot slipped, though I was not going to let that happen. I hobbled into the adjoining bedroom, holding on to the tub edge, then the door frame. Of course my clothes weren't ready yet. She walked in just then with a robe in her arms. I shook my head.

'God, I want you,' I said, helpless to get her naked myself. I wanted to pull off her shirt but she was wearing a turtleneck. She pulled off her own clothes and guided me to the bed. It was an enormous, indulgent bed – maybe an American king, I've heard about those things. Right then it was big enough to be the whole world.

'I can't believe you don't drive,' she said.

'I've lived all my life in London and Cambridge; why would I drive?'

'I still don't believe you can't drive!' she mocked, and still hadn't started the car. We were in the curved drive in front of Dovecote's massive front door. The car was spattered with mud from her journey from the airport, but the weather was clear now. It was dark, but there was a bright moon. 'Are your legs really all right?' she asked seriously. I nodded. The left one still hurt, but it wasn't horrible. It wasn't broken. So she got out

167

and came around to my side.

'No, Lesley, I don't...' I don't know why I felt such an aversion to the idea, but I really didn't want to.

'I want to teach you,' she said. There was an absurd and irresistible sexual undertone to it. I shook my head and groaned, knowing I'd give in. 'It's dark. It's muddy. I don't know these roads.' Thank goodness the rains had stopped.

'I'll lead you,' she said, right up in my face, through the open window. I kissed her again, I had to. 'All right,' I said, getting out of the car. 'All right.'

I strapped myself into the driver's seat. I thought of the mechanics of the engine and the condition of the roads. I didn't think of how I would face my parents, what Gretchen would do, whether police would be involved. I was grateful that the battery of Lesley's mobile phone had expired en route from Pristina, preventing me from responsibly phoning home. There would be this privacy, this fantasy, for at least a while longer.

She pulled a map from a pocket behind the passenger seat, and showed me the route home. I objected to taking the M11 and insisted on village roads; they're skinnier and windier, but much less likely to have other cars on at that time of night. I didn't think I could face competition or confrontation. Bury Lane, Church Road, Crawley End ... The names of the streets washed over me. Across the A505, then through Newton, Harston, and Haslingfield. Polly and Liv popped into my thoughts, and the way those street and town names would sound so English to them. Then I put the girls out of my mind. I wanted to stay in Lesley's world as long as I could. Church Street, Brook Road, streets called after their towns, and then yet another Church Street. They all sounded familiar. Village streets tend to share the same names.

Lesley patiently explained the gears; I could manage the clutch if I squeezed my teeth together while my foot pressed down. I made the windscreen wipers whoosh and flashed the headlamps. I felt giddy like I had when visiting the war museum at Duxford with school, and had been allowed into the cockpit of a World War II T-6 Harvard Warbird.

'It's going to feel different when it moves,' I said aloud, when I had only meant to think it. Somehow this too was a kind of double entendre. Everything was.

'Take me to Cambridge,' she said, like it was an outing. She'd always made me feel like a grown man.

I used the bright headlamps, because no other cars were out.

I dismissed the thatched cottages and fields as we passed them to concentrate on the road itself, but, really, I've always ignored them. My blindness to the picturesque had driven Liv crazy.

I braked to cross the A505, and, when I tried to start again, the engine made horrible screechings. I pushed down the clutch, winced, and changed gears, though apparently to a worse gear, which I quickly corrected. 'You should take over,' I said.

'If you really want to switch with me you can

pull in at the pub in Fowlmere. It's not far.' She sounded tired, and her willingness to accept my surrender made me change my mind.

Driving was all right. I said it to myself over and over: *It was all right.* It all hummed along, between occasional dire gear changes. I even enjoyed it. We were almost to Newton, which sounded familiar, but most of them do. The road here was unusually long and straight. I looked over at Lesley, proud to be managing the car, to have accomplished something in this mess I'd made. She was fast asleep.

This is where things went wrong.

All along the way I'd been reassured by the signs pointing the direction towards nearby towns. I meant to be heading towards Harston. A sign in Newton assured me I was. Then a sign in Harston assured me I was heading for Haslingfield. This was all good. It was where I was supposed to be.

On the Haslingfield High Street, a sign for Harston pointed me up New Road. I couldn't remember if I'd been through Harston yet. All the place names had become a jumble. Was New Road somewhere I'd meant to go? It was too common a name for its familiarity to warrant confidence.

I took it anyway, and then a singular name stood out to me in the light of New Road's yellow streetlamps: Cantelupe Road. Like cantaloupes. Surely this street must be part of the route we'd sketched out. Why else would I remember it?

I turned. It was unlit, single track, and unpromising as a route to the distant ambient glow that was Cambridge. There wasn't room to turn around. I had no idea how to reverse without

170

stalling the car.

Still moving forward, I reached for the map in Lesley's lap.

I never saw it, not even in the headlamps. I must have been looking at the map at just that moment. There was just a horrible thud and then a *bump-bump*, a lump in the road under the left side of the car. Both left wheels went over it, and the car tilted to the right. It almost went over; I felt like it was going to; I pulled the wheel far to the left to compensate. We ended up sideways to the road, across the middle of it. The headlamps faced directly onto a house, Tudor-looking, very English, with a sign instead of a number: Rose Cottage. Our headlamps shone rudely into the front windows, but I dared not turn them off. We had to see. I wanted to move the car, but I'd become disoriented. I didn't want to run over whatever it was again.

'A dog?' Lesley asked. She was awake, already exiting the car, taking things in hand. She grabbed a torch from the glovebox and swept its beam over the road. I scrambled out myself, following the torch beam with my eyes.

It was a person. The mid-body had been crushed. The limbs were stretched apart at surprising angles like they were running away from each other. Lesley swept the beam over to the face.

I jumped backwards. I pointed. Lesley turned the beam onto me. I gibbered at her.

The face was Gretchen's. She'd been pushed almost in two by the weight of my driving over her abdomen.

I did something terrible: Instead of wishing for

it to not be real, I wished that I wasn't crazy. I wanted Lesley to see her too. I didn't want to be losing my mind.

Part Three

MORRIS

CHAPTER SIX

I had two opportunities to shove Richard into the river, and didn't act on even one.

Do you see the kind of restraint I put on around our family?

The first chance to push him was as everyone boarded their punts. It was darkish already, and the boats were lit by candles in glass lanterns. Thank goodness the driving rains of the past week had stopped.

This time of year, Scudamore's doesn't do daily business, so there isn't any crowding. We were our own crowd, though, around the weir of the Mill Pond. The women had high heels on, and narrow or short dresses, so boarding was a comedy. I got Gwen and Dora in, and then leapt up to Alice's other side. Gwen and Dora are my responsibility, and Alice is Richard's, but this was their day, so I helped. They'd just been married at a church in the city centre. Richard was in his only suit. How did my brother get to forty-two with only one suit? And a casual scarf that must have come from Alice, or from our mother. And a coat because it was bloody cold.

As Alice stepped in, dozens of cameras clicked like popcorn.

Richard leant over, to hand champagne bottles into the punts, to pass out hot water bottles for guests' laps, to tuck a blue plaid blanket up over

Alice's skirt. I could have turned around to hand him something and knocked him off the end of the dock into the water. He would have been fine. There would have been shrieks, then everyone would have laughed. He would have changed into something unsuitable, which would have ended up being funny. Ruining the groom's clothes is nothing like ruining the bride's.

Of course I didn't do it. I didn't do it in the middle of the river either, when we were trading places. That was my second missed opportunity. We had chauffeurs, but everyone goaded Richard to punt, and me too. I stood at the back, pushing us through the water, and then it was his turn. For half a minute we both stood at the end together, and the front of the boat sat up and begged like a dog. I had to get the pole into his hands and get myself back crouched into the body of the punt again. And it all went without a wobble because I don't take out petty frustrations by bullying my brother.

I take them out passive-aggressively on Gwen. She loves psychology! She'd say that admitting it is the first step!

In a normal family, I would have been the child who had grown up and done everything right. It's not normal to want your kids to be all in their heads forever, right? Because all I want is for Dora to not make any permanent mistakes in her teens, and then for her to get an education, and have a good job, and choose a man who has sense and kindness. This is pretty basic stuff. For some reason, in our family it's a good thing to still be living at university as a grown man, theorising. In a normal family, actually doing something would be expected and appreciated. But in this family, we applaud thinking. Thinking about thinking.

I went to university. I thought. I was good at it too. But when I hit statistics, I just couldn't fake it any more. I managed the calculations, I understood why the numbers worked. I just couldn't get past the meaninglessness. One thing being more likely than another is irrelevant to what actually is. Someone is dead or alive. Someone is here or gone. Statistically, the truth may be unlikely, but that doesn't make it any less true. Potential life has statistics; real life is binary. Things are or aren't. That something shouldn't have happened doesn't change that it did.

I finished my exams, but I did something practical with them. I have a real job and I do real things. Richard thinks about potentials. He theorises the origins of life, he lets his religion interfere, and he qualifies everything he proposes, citing 'scientific humility'. Atheists hate him, and so do fundamentalists. The people who like him mostly misunderstand. Students take his advice, which baffles me. Two women have married him.

My family should have seen it coming. Me, I mean. Even choosing Churchill instead of Magdalene – Dad had been at Magdalene – had been a rebellion. I chose a Cambridge college with no history or architectural significance. Ha! Take that, family!

They acted like it didn't matter.

Dad died within a year of my signing on with the force. And the point, the whole point, of joining the police had been to be able to actually do

177

something about what happens in this world. But he died on a research trip outside the country. Nothing nefarious, just a bad accident. There was nothing to solve. I'd been as useless as the rest of them.

When the punts arrived in Grantchester, Richard was the first to step out. He helped Alice out, then our mother. I think he would have stayed there, personally emptying the boats of every guest, but Alice nudged him away. She pulled him to the field path, where waiters stood in the tall grass with champagne. The men had jackets, while the female servers shivered in their blouses. The drama of this set-up was the doing of Alice's parents. Their daughter's first, they hoped only, wedding.

Gwen's shoe heels sank into the wet ground with every step. She clung to my arm. We've been married for sixteen years.

At last reaching The Orchard, a rustic tearoom tarted up with lanterns, there was one last hurdle. I'd forgotten about that stile. Two benches had been stacked and threaded through the fence to make a way over. Keeps the cows out. People can clamber over it. I didn't mind, but if Gwen ripped her tights I'd hear about it all night. Richard set the bar for the rest of us by lifting Alice over. Great.

Next came photos and the smell of dinner. The canvas sling folding chairs in the garden were nearly dried out from the past week's rain. The mud under the grass stuck to everyone's shoes.

'Dora!' Gwen hissed to our daughter, miming buttoning up. Dora has cleavage now. She pre-

178

tended to misunderstand and continued in conversation with some boy. He's older than her, I think. Most boys her age are shorter, but he had an eyeful from his height.

'It's all right,' I said automatically.

Richard waved us over to get into a picture, so we went. He put his arm around my shoulders. That's the kind of person he is: making sure people feel comfortable and included. Which makes me uncomfortable.

Of course coats were removed for the photographer. Alice had on a dress that wasn't big. It was almost a normal dress, not one of those bride dresses. It was normal, and it covered her up, but watching her take off her coat, watching Richard watch her ... it was far too personal. It was like watching her strip. They've made this huge deal of not living together before the wedding, not sleeping together, which is why this wedding is in the winter, right? They didn't want to wait. That's what I think. Which is fine, whatever you want to do with yourself is fine. They're getting married to sleep together; I got married because Gwen and I had been sleeping together and after six months she said the next step is a ring. Fine. It's all fine. We're all adults. We all know that marriage is a kind of containment system for sex, which ... in my line of work I've seen enough of the crap that can come from messing with that. Sex can use some containment. So, all right. But still, I could do without the looks Richard and Alice were shooting each other. It was embarrassing.

Gwen came up from behind and circled me with her arms. 'Do you remember when we got married?' she asked, her chin on my shoulder. Still tall, still well organised, still herself.

I wasn't quick enough to answer. 'At least pretend to be happy,' she whispered sharply, and walked away.

I patted at my suit pocket as if my phone had vibrated and waved to excuse myself out the gate. Across the road was that old church famous for its clock reading 'ten to three'. To rhyme with 'tea' in a poem.

I jogged up the street, and the wind pushed against my face. It felt great.

I turned in to follow the footpath. I'd walked it a dozen times. I used to come this way into Grant-chester with my flatmates from Churchill: through Newnham and then fields and then to the Green Man pub. Once, I got so drunk that I couldn't manage the cow gate between fields on the way back. You could walk over a kind of grate, or you could use the swinging gate, a 'kissing gate'; either are too challenging for cows. I swear I was no better than a cow. You could have locked me up in a pasture with one of those. My friends couldn't believe it. They *moooo*-ed at me from the other side of the gate. I wouldn't give in and use the grate side. I persisted with the kissing gate. All you have to do is push it forward, follow it in, step to the side, and then push it past back behind you. I kept thinking I was standing aside but I just kept pulling the gate into me. After a while I didn't even try, I just pulled it into me, over and over, to keep everyone laughing. Then I'd climbed over it and fallen on my face.

I missed dinner. They were pushing back tables for the barn dance when I got back. More people had arrived. Gwen was busy but she would deal with me later. 'Work,' I mouthed at her from across the room. She rolled her eyes.

'Dance with me,' said the bride, coming up behind me. Richard was paired up with his new mother-in-law. Our father is dead so... I would be the obvious counterpart. Where was Uncle Max, damn it? Or Albert – he counts, he's a cousin. Why weren't Richard and Alice dancing with each other anyway? No doubt Richard would say, 'We can be selfish on our honeymoon, Morris, but the wedding itself is about our families, not only ourselves...'

'No, no, no...' I demurred. 'I don't even dance with Gwen. Sorry ... Alice.' Damn. I hate that I still hesitate. It's been long enough that I shouldn't get caught any more by Richard's successive two wives having the same name.

She had noticed my pause. 'Am I still the "new Alice", the "second Alice"?' she asked.

'No, of course not,' I quickly assured her, embarrassed that she knew we had ever referred to her that way. 'You're just Alice.' Richard's first wife has been downgraded to 'first Alice' or 'other Alice' or 'Mrs Lapham', which is her last name now. She'd married again too.

Gwen swooped in from behind. 'You must dance with the bride,' she chided me. She took my coat. Apparently, I would dance.

The caller gathered us four forward. I put my hand on Alice's waist and followed his instructions. Finally the music started up with a waltz and we made a swirl in the centre of the room that pushed the rest of the guests back. I willed them to join in rather than stare at us. 'Sorry,' she said as we turned, obviously embarrassed by my reluctance.

'No, no,' I protested. 'I don't mind.'

Around and around. 'You're good at this,' Alice said over the music. I smiled in return. I'm not actually good at it.

Alice is kind. Richard knows what he's doing; both his Alices were good choices. There had been a divorce, yes, but it had been more of a widowing than a divorce. Alice, the first Alice, had become a different person. Of course people were gossiping about that. Members of our family were telling it to Alice's family (this Alice: Alice the doctor, Alice the bride). Dora is the worst about repeating it – she finds the story impossibly romantic and dramatic and tragic. She's fourteen.

I thanked Alice for the dance. She nodded and caught her breath back and partnered with someone else for the next set of instructions. I wondered when she and Richard would dance together. At what point does selflessness become ridiculous? At what point does confidence become showing off?

Gwen appeared at my side, pulling me in to learn the reel. I knew it would go like that. If I danced with Alice, there'd be no excuse. Which is why I hadn't wanted to dance with Alice. Do you see how these things go?

Eventually, the band took a break. Someone put on a CD to keep the music going. I was tempted to slip out again – Gwen would give me hell

182

anyway, why not earn it – but the song pulled me up short. I'd played it before.

When I'd swapped classical violin for fiddle music, in my Churchill days, Richard had been the only one in the family ever to come hear me play.

We played mostly for folk dance groups. Supporting dancers has a different feeling to it from playing concerts. There's more obligation to fit in, and less obligation to impress. It suited me fine.

Alice, the first one, had played flute with us. During the two months she'd been with us I'd been going out with the sister of one of my fellow constables, but it was nothing serious. I wanted Alice. She liked me too. She was casual but kind of deep, with long skirts and long hair. It was the eighties but she was still flower-child-like, and so pretty that I couldn't really think straight. We'd already messed about once, not a lot, just kissing this one time that had been cut short. She was finishing up her last year at the local polytechnic, which she chose over university because she said she wanted to play music, not study it. I never in all my life would have thought there was something in her for Richard, who'd just that past spring handed in his thesis and was already a Fellow. Never.

He'd come to hear us out of kindness. This was the tune I played as a solo. Alice and James and Mick stepped down off the stage to give me space. James and Mick took off outside to smoke, but Alice stayed to listen. Richard stood next to her. She made him dance – he's as bad as I am, but a more willing sport about it.

By the end of the number, she'd invited him to join us at the Folk Festival the next week. Later I asked him not to, so he didn't. It was supposed to be a date.

The festival was loud and good. Everyone sweated in the heat. At the end of the first day I leant up against her, with her back to a wall, but she said there were people around. So I asked her to come back to my flat. This is where everything went to a crazy place. This is where she told me, and I believe she thought she was being nice, that a week ago she would have gone with me in a minute. Apparently, I'm a really great person, and she would have been flattered for the chance to go home with me. That's what she said. And I wanted to know what was wrong.

She said that she'd gone to Richard's church, and she'd had this 'experience', and she was trying to figure out what it all meant. It had to have been just that past weekend. Just one Sunday. She was adamant that it wasn't a Richard thing; it was, she said, something bigger than that. And then she said the usual about Jesus and God and it's nothing I haven't overheard for most of my life, starting when Richard read his first C.S. Lewis at age twelve. She said she was going to put things on hold for a while, while she figured out what she thought about all that. Meaning, I'm reading between the lines, that she wasn't going to have sex with anyone for at least a while. Definitely not that night.

'All right,' I said. 'We can just–' Meaning, I don't know, just fool around. Something short of everything.

She cut me off. 'It's amazing,' she gushed. 'It's all – Jesus made us, and we're all special, right? We're *beautiful*...' And the way she said 'beautiful' cracked, and then she cried. 'I'm beautiful,' she said between gulpy sobs. She said it like it was news.

She asked me if I wanted to come with her to church next week. I said no.

Ten months later they were married. Two years after that a teenager in the Bible study she ran smashed a brick into her skull. He was, he'd said, in love with her.

Alice survived, but she was different. Part of the front of her brain was broken.

By then I was married to Gwen, who was waddling in that pregnancy posture women get.

Richard stayed married to Alice for four more years. He didn't complain. Her mind was changed and her manner was changed, but he remained steadfast to the new person inside her body. Then she wanted to marry someone she'd met at the rehabilitation clinic, who'd had a similar injury. So he granted her a divorce.

'Aw, you look sad.' Suddenly Carmen was next to me. Our sister. I didn't feel like responding to that.

'Come on,' she said. 'Have a little fun. Are you still jealous?'

I stopped myself from answering. Answering Carmen just leads to trouble, gives her stuff to analyse. 'Get off it, Carmen,' I said.

She's convinced that I haven't 'let go' of the first Alice, that I hold it against Richard for 'stealing' her. Which is ridiculous, because Alice was never mine. Sure, I'd liked her, but we'd never been anything. We might have become something, but we hadn't. So how could he steal? And this is Richard. That's a commandment, one of ten. He doesn't steal.

I suddenly noticed a difference in her. 'What did you do that for?' I gestured at Carmen's head. Her hair was back in some kind of lump on her head. It's usually more like a bush around her face. She and Mother argue about it at every family gathering.

She rolled her eyes. 'You only notice things that don't matter.'

'No, really,' I said. I wasn't going to let this go. 'What made you give in?' I grinned. This was getting to her. This was older brother stuff. I could handle this.

'Do you want to know what got to me?' She poked my chest. 'My respect for Richard's happiness got to me. Accepting that this event is about him, not me, got to me. My desire for a conflict-free celebration, with Mum having no excuse for an argument, got to me. I wish that kind of thing would get to you.' Then she walked away.

All right. If she wanted to talk about that, we would talk about it. Walking away was no fair. I followed her.

'I'm going to the loo,' she insisted. There was one up here, but she took the stairs towards the ones in the corridor. Just to get away from me.

'Wait,' I said, following her to the narrow corridor.

She stopped so I could say something, but I froze up. 'The thing is,' I stammered, 'I don't know what you think the problem is.'

She sighed with exaggerated patience. That sound was the background score of my entire childhood.

'You've always been jealous of Richard,' she said, stretching 'always' out long and thin. 'You don't like when he gets anything.'

This wasn't true. I shook my head. 'We don't want the same things, Carmen, so what exactly am I supposed to be jealous of?' Someone exited the ladies' and we had to flatten against the wall to give her room to pass.

Carmen said it loud enough that the woman turned to look at me: 'You both wanted Alice.'

'This is what I think about Alice,' I exploded, too loudly. So I lowered my voice. 'The first one, all right? The first one. He ruined her. He made her into something different, and that difference led her into harm's way. I know those kind of kids she was working with. She had no business trusting thugs like that. There's no way she should have let herself alone with them, let her guard down. She trusted Richard and his ideas about how the world works. She sacrificed herself – that's what I hold against him. He turned a vibrant person into a vulnerable person. Now she's gone. Her body's still alive, and someone lives there, but it isn't her any more. She's gone. He didn't take her away from me, Carmen. This isn't about me. He took her away from the world. He took her away, full stop. Now she's gone.'

Carmen smiled. She had a look of glory on her face. 'That's a breakthrough, Morris.' Then she hugged me.

187

'Christ, it's not a breakthrough, Carmen. It's just – the way things are.'

She released me and wagged a finger. She was still smiling when our mother emerged.

'Oh!' Mum said, flustered for a moment to be confronted right out of the toilet, as if she'd been caught coming out of a stranger's hotel room. Her hands travelled over her dress, patting it to ensure everything was secure. 'I despise public toilets,' she announced. Then, suddenly, 'I'm glad you see I was right, Carmen. You look like an adult. A lovely adult.'

'Cheers, Mum,' said Carmen, smiling fake-brightly, and I had to give her credit for not saying more.

'Really,' I asked, after Mother had walked past, 'why now? You've been defying her with your hair for a good thirty years. What makes this time different?'

'You don't even notice, do you? This is hard on Richard. His friend is missing. You're supposed to be finding him. He almost delayed the wedding, out of respect, but I persuaded him not to. You dredged the river, Morris... He was a wreck.'

She expounded further but I'd stopped listening at 'You're supposed to be finding him.' I'd released Miranda Bailey that morning. A regular had been hauled in the night before with Nick's credit card who swore he'd mugged Nick near East Road after Miranda was already back at her hotel. We were at a dead end.

'Would it be better if I hadn't come? Do you think the trail's going cold because I took a day off? Do you think finding someone is just a matter of persistence? Is that what you think? It's not. Some people don't get found. Some people...' I grappled for a metaphor my family would understand. '...Some people ... there isn't the data available. With incomplete data, the conclusions are necessarily conjecture...' I stopped because it was absurd. 'No one is blaming you,' she said in an awful, placating tone. But everyone was. I was.

The band was on again. Richard and Alice danced together, finally. Everyone else had joined in too. Gwen danced with Uncle Max. Her head swivelled. She was looking for me.

I pushed right through the swirling crowd. My shoulders and elbows made a way. I walked right through them up onto the stage.

The band stopped playing. The caller tried to usher me off, but I put up my hand. It wasn't a threatening hand, more of a 'calm down' hand. I don't know if it was because I was the groom's brother, or have that cop way about me, or because it was crazy and it's best not to argue with crazy. I pointed to the fiddle. 'Let me,' I said. The fiddle player didn't move at first. Then he handed the instrument over. It felt like home picking it up. Almost home, because it wasn't my fiddle, but it was good.

I hadn't played in a long time. My group had broken up shortly after Alice had converted. The bass player moved, and what were Mick and I supposed to do, just the two of us? I'd got promoted and there was Gwen. I didn't play any more.

I faced the crowd but didn't look at anybody. I

was just into myself. The bow touched down on the string and I rode away with it. I pushed the instrument and it pushed back. That relationship, that push and response, is the whole thing. Sound doesn't fly or leap; it can only bump, from something to something, from one air molecule to the next. That's how it travels, by contact. That's what I learnt at uni. There's no sound without relationship. There's no sound without touch. Something has to touch something, even just a molecule of air, or else there's no sound at all. That proves it: Sound doesn't have to be music to be profound. But when it is music, this is it. This is the stuff. I didn't even know who was looking or who cared. This was contact, this was action, this was making something happen. I might be alone and I might be stymied and I might be useless, but, by God, at the molecular level I was shaking the world.

Something else shook. The inside pocket of my suit jacket rumbled against my chest. God, not now. My mobile. Not, not, not now. I pushed again and again at the repetition leading towards the end. Not now, not now, I chanted in my head along with the persistent rhythm.

I brought it down to Earth when I was ready. I slowed it when it was time. Everything up till then had been wild and delicate and 'How did he do that?' fast. But the end was something else, just the melody, nothing tricky. Three notes, the same three that had persistently underwritten the wildness before. One, two, three. Done.

The room didn't have sound in it any longer. The phone in my pocket had stopped as well. All held still for a moment, all held blessedly still.

Then – *crack!*

Someone outside rammed the patio doors with his shoulder, and they flew back to smack against the wall. Everyone turned around to see. It was that boy, the tall boy, wet and shivering. He had Dora in his arms; she was wet too. She was soaked. It wasn't raining, but it was cold. 'She fell in the river,' he said. The whole crowd surged towards them and I pushed through them all.

I would have hauled her up in my arms, but the fiddle and bow were still in my hands. I stood useless for only a moment, but in that moment Gwen took charge: She sent someone for warm coats, someone for hot tea. Dora had to be breathing. She had to be. The river can be cold enough to give someone a heart attack. But the weather had been warm lately, warm and wet. It hadn't been frosty. I'd only been joking about pushing Richard in. I'd never have done it. Jesus Christ. I'd never have done it.

Someone laid two coats over her, two big wool coats. I wanted to do something, but Gwen was already there, cradling her. Dora snuggled, and tugged at the wet hair sticking to her neck. It had fallen from some fancy style, and I think she was trying to put it back up. Or tear it all the way down. She was trying to fix herself. She suddenly reminded me of Alice, the first Alice, back at the Folk Festival. How is it that women don't know how beautiful they are?

'Dora...' I said. Gwen looked at me, looked hard. This was a test of some kind. There was some right thing I could say that would make me a good husband, a good father. I didn't know what it was.

The fiddle was still in my hand.

I waited too long again. Gwen looked away, exasperated.

Mother pushed past me with the tea. Dora said, 'It's too hot.' Gwen told her it wasn't and to just drink it. The boy was in the midst of his own family swarm. Alice, a doctor, had quickly checked him, and then came to Dora. She knelt in front of her.

There would be no breaking through this wall of women. And I still had the fiddle in my hand.

I returned it to the stage. Then I checked my phone messages.

Bloody hell. Nick Frey and a dead professor.

Richard knew. Somehow he knew.

'Duty calls,' I said lightly, snapping the phone shut.

I found where Gwen had put my coat. Richard didn't say anything. But he knew. I could tell by the way he stuck to me.

'Please,' he said quietly.

I had no right to tell him, certainly not before telling the parents. Really, I shouldn't tell anyone until I was certain for myself. Mistakes get made. There was no room for that here.

But he followed me outside. I asked him to tell Gwen I had to work. 'And congratulations,' I said. He turned my intended handshake into a pleading grip.

'Please tell me,' he said.

I shook my head. 'Can't do that.' It took shaking my fingers to get the blood back. I repeated the message: 'You know I can't tell you.'

He didn't fight. He only hoped.

That's what really puts me over the edge with him. He doesn't push for anything. He just – stands, and people join him. He'd take a beating if anyone ever bothered to hate him. He'd take it. He took what had happened to the first Alice. I couldn't believe how he took it.

The boy who'd smashed her head had done a runner, and it took some doing to track him down. The sergeant who picked him up got cut. The boy had had a knife, a stupid small kitchen thing. A dull paring knife, probably from someone's rubbish. The sergeant got cut but wrestled it off the kid and brought him in.

When I brought this news to Richard, brought it like a present, he pushed it back. This was one for our side, we're the good guys, right? A sergeant had bled to bring the boy in, because justice matters. Because Alice mattered. A policeman had risked his life, a cop like me.

Still Richard didn't say anything, so I repeated it: 'Richard, we've got him. It's done.'

He just covered his face. I couldn't get anything out of him.

Finally, he wrote something on a piece of paper from the pad next to the phone. Alice's paper. Alice's pen. I'd never had special paper for the phone before I was married, and neither had he.

He wrote something on the paper and asked me to take it to the kid. It said, 'I forgive you.'

I wouldn't take it. I held my hands up out of reach. 'What the hell is that?' I said.

'Please.' He pushed it at me.

I shook my head. 'What the fuck is wrong with

you?' I said. 'What the fuck is wrong with you? You don't deserve her. If anyone tried to hurt Gwen I'd fucking kill him.'

He covered his face again. When I left, he was pressing the note against his closed eyes.

That's what I remember whenever he says 'please' to me, like he was saying now.

I grabbed the front of his shirt to bring his face close. 'Don't repeat this, all right? Not even to Alice.'

He nodded.

'Nick's all right. He's back. All right? That's all I can tell you. Don't breathe a word.'

I let him go and he stumbled backwards. 'Thank you,' he said.

'Thank you,' he said again. His face shone. He was happy.

Alice came to find me. 'Dora's fine,' she said. I knew she was; the last I looked one of the servers was lending her a change of clothes.

'Thanks,' I said. Richard was still radiant. I wanted to kick him.

Alice wound an arm around one of his. 'You look happy,' she said.

He stuttered. He looked at me with guilt. Christ, he was terrible at secrets.

'He's happy he has you,' I said, trying to lead him with the obvious.

He caught on. He kissed her hand. But she looked suspiciously at me.

'Morris...' she said. 'Is this about Nick Frey?'

'No,' I said, showing Richard how it's done. But he looked at his shoes. Alice would know by morning.

I rubbed my forehead. I needed to tell Gwen myself that I had to leave.

I opened the door back to the tearoom, but that entrance was filled with Mother, apparently on her way out to me. 'I was looking for you. Working again, Morris?' she said.

There wasn't any point to arguing.

'Dora was in a punt with that boy,' she continued. 'She said they were *talking*.' She twisted that last word sarcastically.

'Dora's all right, Mother,' I said.

'Dora's a teenager, Morris. She needs a father who pays attention to her.'

'Look how great we turned out without a father paying attention to us,' I said through a fake, bright grin. Richard was so shocked he backed up a step.

Mother pushed back. 'Your father–'

It's all the same conversation. It's all we ever really say to each other, over and over again.

She kept talking as I walked away.

CHAPTER SEVEN

Detective Sergeant Chloe Frohmann picked me up in front of Grantchester's old church. I would normally be paired with a Detective Inspector on a murder case, but she'd worked with me on the missing person, so I asked to keep her on. 'How was the wedding?' she wanted to know. I wasn't in the mood to answer. It would only encourage

195

her. She was planning her own wedding for next year.

She didn't need encouragement. 'I ask because my cousin got married last year and she wore a suit. She said that any woman over thirty can't get away with wearing a real dress, but I think that's crap. Alice is in her thirties, right? Did she wear a suit or a dress?'

There was no getting away from it. 'A dress,' I said. Then she asked me this crazy thing: Was it a tea dress or a cocktail dress? I said, 'It was a dress.'

'That's exactly my point,' she said, punctuating 'exactly' with a vigorous swerve onto the roundabout.

I leant my head back and tried to focus. Someone was found. Someone else was dead. There would be two family visits to make.

'Shall I take the parents? Or the husband?' Frohmann does read my mind sometimes.

'We'll do them together.'

I'd never been up Cantelupe Road. It was a strange road to be on if you didn't live there. What were both of them doing there?

The crime scene was easy to find: Just follow the bright lights set up for the forensic team and pathologist.

Rose Cottage was a homely scene inside: soft, threadbare furniture, lit yellow by standing lamps with fussy shades. Nick, or rather his friend, had called the police from here. It wasn't until the paramedics arrived that Nick admitted his name, to a flurry of piqued interest and scepticism. Now he sipped hot chocolate at the kitchen table,

196

his left leg propped up on the chair opposite. Two women stood apart from him next to an Aga, one of those huge country ovens.

'Nicholas Frey?' I asked, to be official. I recognised him.

He nodded and pushed his cup away. 'Yes, sir.'

I needed to caution him, in relation to the death outside, but something else bubbled up as more important first. 'Richard Keene's my brother. He's been very worried.'

He blanched. 'I'm sorry, sir. I didn't mean to hurt anyone.'

This was murky. The caution had to come out. 'Nick. You don't have to say anything, but it may harm your defence if you fail to mention when questioned something which you later rely on in court. Anything you do say will be given in evidence. All right?'

He nodded again.

'Do you understand, Nick? You have to say that you understand.'

He said exactly that: 'I do. I understand.'

'Where have you been?' I asked.

He told me about Dovecote. He gestured towards one of the women, who nodded to affirm that she was indeed a family friend who had long ago given him a key. He claimed that she hadn't been home until today. If so, it wasn't an affair of some kind.

He explained something complicated and very, very young about letting people down, and trying to fix things, and only making everything worse: for Polly Bailey and Liv Dahl, and for the dead woman outside.

I'd interviewed Gretchen Paul about him. She'd said only that Nick had assisted with a research project that was now ended, and was 'competent' and 'thorough'. Normally I'd take bland adjectives like that to be avoidance, but from her I think they were praise. Her formal neutrality didn't mesh with the hysteria he insisted he'd caused.

'Were you having an intimate relationship with Dr Paul?' I had to ask.

He looked offended. 'No, sir,' he said, wagging his head hard.

'What do you think her problem was?'

'I don't know.' He let out a pent-up breath. 'It had something to do with her family, I think. Her mother and her aunt. I'd been helping with some organisation for her. She's blind, did you know that?' I nodded. I knew. 'I'd helped to organise photos for her mother's biography. She was distressed by the result. I – honestly, sir, I don't know what was in her mind.'

'Can you guess?' I persisted. I've found that people who don't 'know' anything for certain often have interesting suppositions that come out when they're given permission to muse.

He sat up straighter, as if I had called his name in class and he was ready to deliver the right answer. 'Well. I've been thinking about it. I think maybe her mother isn't who she thought she was. She said her mother was Linda Paul, the writer. Linda Paul wrote something a long time ago. And then she gave it all up, to raise Gretchen. But I think … I think that's what she told Gretchen but that that's not who she really was.'

'Really.' That was strange. 'So … who was she?'

'The nanny. I think. Except there wouldn't have been a nanny at all if the nanny was the mother ... Look. There were three women, all right? Linda Paul, her sister Ginny, and this other woman. Gretchen calls her the nanny. They were in Brussels together, for a World's Fair. It was one of the last things Gretchen saw.

'I think the woman she calls the nanny was her real mother. A friend of Linda Paul, maybe a hanger-on. Maybe Linda said she couldn't stay around them any more, with the baby. She was cut off, and made up this story to herself about how she was Linda Paul, and gave up that life. Fantasised that she was the one making choices, not the one being pushed out. That would make sense of the photos.'

I made him repeat much of that, and drew a diagram in my notebook. He leant over it to check my work, ever the good little helper. I shut it so fast that the pages fluttered against his chin. 'That's not your place, Nick.'

He swallowed. 'No, sir.'

I rapped the closed notebook against the table. 'What were you doing on this road?' I demanded. 'It doesn't go anywhere.'

He shook his head again. He opened his hands. 'I don't know. I don't know. I was following the *A to Z*. We'd mapped out a route, and I followed signs... We were in Haslingfield. The High Street. Lesley had fallen asleep and I couldn't well look at the map and drive...'

'Why didn't you just stop?'

He didn't answer right away. 'I'm not very good with the clutch,' he admitted. 'I didn't want to stop and start.' He shifted position. 'I was following signs and all the names were running together in my mind. One said "Cantelupe Road". I knew that name. So I took it. I figured it for part of the directions. It's not a name you'd think to follow if you hadn't planned to, is it? I recognised it, so I took it.'

I leant back and thought about how we'd just come. 'It's not the way to Cambridge.' I let the accusation remain implicit. He's a clever boy. He knew what I meant.

'I've never been here in my life, sir. I didn't expect to be here, I didn't know Gretchen would be here. Honestly, sir...'

'But you knew the name.'

'I knew the name of the street. I don't know from where. I thought it was part of the route we'd looked at. I don't know where else...' He stopped himself. He slapped his hand on the table. 'It was the box. At Gretchen's house. The box of photographs. It was an old packing box. Something had come shipped in it. The address label on top had been for where Gretchen lived years ago. In Brighton. Underneath that was the address for the place the box had been first. That was Cantelupe. Here, in Haslingfield. I noticed it. I suppose it stuck in my head...'

'And this box is in Dr Paul's house?'

'No ... not any more. She asked me to destroy it. I threw it in the pond behind my house. My family's house.'

I nodded, but not as if I necessarily believed or approved. I didn't trust any of this.

'The constable tells me you were driving

without a licence,' I said.

'Yes, sir.'

'And you claim you didn't see her at all? You–'

'I felt her, sir,' he said. He shook his head again. 'I felt her under the car. I'd been looking down at the map. I didn't see anything until I got out of the car and looked at her face.'

He looked like he was going to be sick. It was time to get him home. I could talk to him again after the pathologist's report. Frohmann offered to help him walk to the car, but he insisted on hobbling. He said to his friend, 'I apologise for taking advantage of your hospitality in this way.'

She said, 'I won't intrude on your homecoming, but call if there's anything I can do.'

'I understand. Tomorrow...'

'Nick. I think your family would prefer I didn't.'

'I don't care what they–'

She laid her hand on his cheek. He held perfectly still.

'I'll be in touch,' she promised.

He glowered. His hands made tight fists for a moment, then he opened them up and slapped his thighs.

Interesting.

She went into the lounge to call a taxi, as we had to keep her car. He watched her. If eyeballs were hands it would have been indecent.

Nick spun back to me. 'May I please go home now?' he said.

I sent Frohmann to take him to her car, and wait for me. I wouldn't be long with the other woman. She looked impatient to get rid of us.

'And you are...?' I asked.

She spelt her name for me: 'Melisma Cantor. An M instead of a second S. It isn't Melissa. It's like when you slide around on a note of music, dress it up, right? Melisma.'

I wrote down her name, correctly spelt. I omitted the explanation.

All the time I'd been talking with Nick, she'd been putting away kitchen things from a cardboard box. Coffee. Tea towels. Washing-up liquid, but it wasn't new. It was half-full. She looked to be in her late twenties.

'I got here a couple hours ago. Susan wasn't home. I'm her stepdaughter.'

'Susan is the owner here?'

'Yes.'

'Was anything out of the ordinary when you arrived?'

'No. No.'

'Did you hear the accident?'

'I heard – something. It must have been the accident. They rang the bell not long after. They asked me to call the police.'

'Had you ever seen them before?'

She shook her head.

'Do you know what Dr Paul was doing here?'

She shook her head.

'Did you know she was here?'

She bowed her head, and shook it, staring at the tabletop. 'Is something wrong, Ms Cantor?' She repeated no. 'Where's your stepmother?' She shrugged.

'I don't know. She's an adult, you know. She doesn't always stay here every night.'

'Do you?'

She shook her head, again. 'I broke up with my boyfriend, and I'll be staying here for a little while. I just brought all my stuff from his place.' She held up the half-used Fairy liquid. 'I was the only one who washed the fucking dishes. Sorry,' she quickly added. Suddenly she looked as if she'd been left out in the rain. Her long hair appeared limp, her face stretched down. It was the streak of a headlamp through the front window changing the shadows. In a moment she was restored.

'Have you ever seen Dr Paul with your stepmother before?'

'I don't know the name.'

All right. 'Where's your father?'

'He's in Bangalore. He works there. They're divorced. Look, I'm really tired. I'd like to go to bed.'

I got the father's name and address in India, and made a move to the cottage door. I fiddled with the handle. It had a proper lock. 'Do you have a key, Ms Cantor?'

'Yes, of course. We used to live here. When they were married.'

'Did your stepmother – what's her full name, please? Susan...'

'Susan Madison.'

'Was she expecting you today?'

'I'd called earlier. She didn't pick up, but that doesn't mean she didn't know. She screens.'

'Ah.' I nodded. That seemed sufficient for now.

Dr Jensen stood up from his crouch beside the body. 'Two sets of injuries,' he said, plunging right in. 'She was hit once, in the vicinity of four hours ago. Likely thrown. There's damage to the back of her head that matches with a stone underneath it. Lividity suggests that she's lying where she died. The other injuries occurred post-mortem. She was run over and nearly cut in two by the weight of the vehicle. That's preliminary. I'll have more for you tomorrow.'

I stood back to take in the scene. Hit twice on a road so little-used as this? Her body was on the part of the road well past the drive. If it had been dark when Melisma arrived, she wouldn't have seen the body.

I turned around to head for the car and bumped nose to nose into Nick, who'd been standing right behind me. 'Why the hell aren't you in the car?' I said.

'I was just – if it was going to be much longer I wanted to ask permission to phone... Is it true? Did she really die four hours ago?'

I rubbed the back of my neck and held in several expletives. Frohmann appeared over his shoulder. 'Greene asked me to look at something...' she explained, sounding guilty. It was hard to know whether to treat Nick like a suspect or a found missing person.

'That finding is not yet official,' I told Nick, as to the time of death. But he sagged with relief.

In the car, Nick said, 'Look, I'm really sorry for the trouble I've caused you. I have no doubt there were long hours put in on my behalf, and I'm not surprised that you're angry with me. I can only apologise.'

Who talks like that? What a perfect little gentleman he is.

I turned around inside my seatbelt and faced him in the back. 'Susan Madison. Do you know that name? Has Gretchen ever talked about her?'

'Of course,' he said. 'Is that a trick question?'

I held back a nasty retort. 'No.' I glared. 'Why would it be?'

He smiled. He was lighter and lighter the closer we got to home. 'That's her mother's character. Susan Maud Madison. She wrote five books about her. Well, Linda Paul did. Gretchen was looking for anyone who'd named her child after the character. You know, been influenced by the books. Looks like she found one.'

Looks like she did.

Nick's family lived in a white modernist box from the 1930s: all stacked and protruding rectangles, with a long, thin window striping across the whole thing. Tall trees spiked in silhouette behind it, filling the sky over the flat roof.

It was now ten o'clock. There were lights illuminating the ground floor, so we wouldn't be waking them up. Frohmann pressed the bell. I suppose Nick might have had his key, but he hung back obediently.

Mrs Frey called out 'Alexandra?' as she came down the stairs, and, again, 'Alexandra?' while unlocking the door. She saw me and Frohmann first, and recoiled.

We parted to display Nick between us. She pitched forward to embrace him.

Frohmann backed the car out onto the road and we were tossed in our seats by the ruts beneath the wheels. 'Damn private roads,' she muttered.

The private segment emptied out onto a proper city-kept street, and shortly thereafter onto a main road that eventually linked with the M11. We took the direction away from the motorway.

'Is it just a husband?' she asked. I think she dreaded facing suddenly motherless children.

'Just a husband,' I assured her.

'Did you know her?'

'Not really.' Richard knew her, but they weren't close. I knew Gretchen Paul more from this case. She'd paid for Miranda Bailey's solicitor but, from what I understand, didn't actually know her. It was odd. I hoped the husband could tell me why. I looked in my notebook for his name. 'Harry Reed,' I said. Frohmann nodded.

She turned down Grange Road, driving past Robinson, Selwyn, and Newnham colleges. Grand Victorian houses filled in the gaps between them. Frohmann turned left off Grange Road onto Barton and then almost immediately right onto Millington. The change was immediate: Orbs of gaslight glowed white in the fog.

'What did they do to rate the special effects?' she asked.

'Another private road. So the city didn't include them in the electric upgrade.' Millington Road has about thirty houses on it. The gas lamps don't shine much beyond themselves; they're just dots tracing the right angle of the street.

The house we wanted was typical of the area: brick, gabled, big. I'd not been here during Nick's investigation; I'd interviewed Dr Paul in her office.

Our feet crunched down on the thick scattering

206

of pebbles acting as a pavement. It was like walking on the bottom of a dry fish tank.

The bell control was a thin iron rod with a small handle at the bottom. Frohmann twisted it, and we were rewarded with a sound like scraping a butter knife over a glockenspiel.

We waited. She twisted the bell pull again.

'No one's home. Perhaps he's out looking for her,' she suggested.

'He's the husband. He's a suspect.' I pulled out my mobile and punched in their number. Some people keep a phone by the bed. 'Or a sound sleeper,' I said.

The phones inside rang with different bells: one a trill, one a buzz. And then another sound. Some kind of ... coo? chirp? Whatever it is that birds do, coming from inside the house.

'Look at this,' Frohmann called. She'd walked around to the side of the house. I joined her.

She shone a torch on a parked car. It had a cracked headlamp and dented front.

'Call for forensics,' I told her.

A sudden light hit my face. Someone else's torch. 'Police,' I barked. 'Lower it.'

A smallish man came out from behind the shrubs. 'Pardon me,' he said, stepping closer, 'you looked suspicious.' He wore a heavy jacket over a dressing gown over pyjama bottoms. 'I'd like to see some ID, please.'

We accommodated his request. 'Harry Reed?' I asked.

He frowned. 'No, I'm not.' He looked back and forth between my ID and my face. 'I'm the neighbourhood watch coordinator,' he said proudly. I'm surprised he didn't proffer identification of his own. He added as an afterthought, 'I'm his next-door neighbour.'

'Really?' I asked. 'Seen anything interesting lately?'

He pointed up.

Several small, colourful birds perched on the roofline. Two more were on the sill of an open window.

He sighed in disappointment at our incomprehension. 'They're cage birds. Norwich canaries.'

I started to get it. 'They're not in a cage.'

The neighbour had noticed the open windows and free birds when he'd come home for lunch. A plump orange bird flew in as a fluffy black-speckled one flew out.

'What time was this?' I asked again.

'As I said, lunchtime. One-fifteen. I always get home at one-fifteen for half an hour.'

'Anything else happen in that time?'

He frowned in thought. 'My wife made a proper cooked meal for once,' he said nastily. 'That's notable.' He shrugged again. Then: 'You want to get in? I've got a key.'

He had many more than one; it looked like every household on the street fell under his protection. He flicked through them, recognising the right one by some obscure system. He held it up and nodded, but when I reached for it he walked past me to the door. I shared a look with Frohmann, who shrugged in response.

The interior of the house was full of art and colour, in contrast to Gretchen Paul's stark office, where I'd spoken with her about Nick. I'd taken her lack of decoration there as a natural consequence of her blindness. Maybe it was, and this was her husband's taste. Or maybe she drew a thick line between personal and work.

Some of the birds had stayed inside; one perched on the back of a dining chair. Mindful of forensics, who were on their way, we separated to make a casual check of the home. I jumped when Frohmann called out upstairs. I bounded up to what turned out to be the study. There was another voice, droning. It sounded bizarre. 'Police!' I called out.

'You've scared it to death.' Frohmann laughed, leaning over the computer.

I leant over her to see. 'It talks,' she said. 'This must be Dr Paul's computer.'

It was reading out the webpage that was up on the screen. 'I jiggled the mouse,' Frohmann confessed. 'The screen saver disappeared and it started talking.'

It read from a maps page, telling us how to get to Cantelupe Road from here.

Things were not looking good for Mr Reed.

The neighbour's voice came from down the corridor, an urgent bark. He must have followed us in. 'What is he doing in the house?' I muttered, ready to be stern with him.

My lecture stalled in me as I joined him at the bottom of the attic ladder. A streak of seeds, droppings, and feathers dribbled down the steps, culminating in a man's body at the neighbour's feet. 'Get back,' I ordered, kneeling by the head. 'Is this Harry Reed?'

The neighbour only made some noises. Frohmann called it in. I felt the neck for a pulse, finding none.

'Is this Harry Reed?' I pressed, looking at the neighbour for a nod. He finally gave it to me, and Frohmann led him out.

Frohmann tugged on latex gloves she'd retrieved from the cache in the car boot. I did the same, and paper shoe covers. I wanted to eyeball the scene in the bird room.

The robot voice from the computer pulled me back into the study. 'Quote I love him completely comma quote she said full stop she pulled on her socks and trainers comma girlishly tying the laces in double knots full stop she's my sister but completely unlike me full stop she dreams about men comma but why should a fish dream about water question mark she's—'

Frohmann shook her head. 'I wouldn't be able to take that for a whole book...'

'Is that what it is?'

'A book excerpt.'

'Note the URL for me, all right?' I said, escaping the monotone recitation. Behind me I heard it switch to reading out an email header.

The steps had no visible footprints on them. I kept to the far left edge of the steps, and crept up, careful not to use my hands. Someone else might have held on. I just wanted to get my eyes to floor level and get an overview of the scene. More seed, droppings, and feathers, small broccoli florets, and splashes from overturned plastic birdbath bowls.

Flapping and urgent twittering alerted me to a bird with a foot trapped in the door of an over-turned cage. A whole wall of wire cages had been pulled down. The central aviary had been bashed down on one side, perhaps by the chair lying on its side across the room. The aviary's corner was bent in, which would have taken repeated blows, if the wire frame was as strong as it looked. About half a dozen birds were still in it, not having taken advantage of the open door. One flew from one perch to another, back and forth. Two others pressed together in a corner.

The bird with its leg in a cage door was too far to reach from here. I didn't want to compromise the scene, but I couldn't leave the animal in distress. I entered the room completely, stepping over debris, and freed the fluffy orange creature. I let it go. It flew up to the top of a wall of cages still standing on the other side of the room, and perched next to a red prize ribbon.

'Sir,' Frohmann called.

'Here.'

'Jensen's pulled up. Forensics won't like you in their scene.'

'I know,' I said, descending. I filled her in as we headed downstairs to let Jensen in. '...It's been savaged up there, especially the aviary and one wall. Maybe means something, or maybe the other cages are just better secured...'

I stuck with forensics until they left at two. Then someone from the RSPCA came to rescue what were left of the birds. I left them to it with a constable to keep an eye out. I slept on a couch at the station and woke with a rotten headache.

She could have killed him, and then been the victim of a random hit-and-run. Except that it was his car that killed her.

He could have killed her, and then returned home to die in an accidental fall down those steep stairs. Except for the condition of the bird room. No accident there.

They were both murdered. Even if one of them did kill the other, there was a third party involved in at least one of the cases.

I spent the morning on a computer, recreating Gretchen's web history and branching off into some investigations of my own. She'd taken a taxi to Rose Cottage: A page with the car company's phone number had been in her browser history, and she'd used a map website to print out directions for the driver.

I drove there myself. Susan Madison was expecting me.

'You can make yourself tea if you want to,' she announced when I arrived. I declined and followed her into the lounge. She sat down in a well-worn club chair and put her feet up onto a footstool.

There was no other seat in that room. Who has a lounge with only one chair? 'May I?' I asked, and she nodded. I carried a chair from the kitchen table and squeezed it into the lounge, which was crowded with small tables and chests. She was older than I thought she would be. I had expected fifties. She was seventies.

'You have a beautiful home,' I said, choosing charming.

'Why don't you ask what you came here for so I can get back to work?'

Work. Ms Madison is a writer. She was already demonstrating to me a mastery of directness and brevity.

'Where were you last night?' I asked, sitting down in the hard chair.

'I was with a friend. He lives in Great Shelford.' She gave his contact information.

'What time did you arrive there?'

'Around four. My ex-husband's daughter had announced to me her intentions of leaving her partner and coming to stay with me. I preferred to be elsewhere.'

'And you were with him till morning?'

She smiled. 'Yes.'

I tilted my head to one side. 'If you didn't want your stepdaughter to come stay with you, why didn't you just say so?' Sideways questions sometimes lead interesting places.

'I didn't want to talk about it,' she said simply. 'I didn't see any reason to engage it at all.'

I uncrossed my legs and leant forward. 'Did you see Gretchen Paul here yesterday?'

'Yes,' she admitted.

I nodded to myself. 'I understand she was tracking down people who'd been named after a book character her mother had created...'

'...But I'm too old,' she finished for me. 'Yes, I am. As was evident to her immediately. I told her it was merely a coincidence.'

'Is Susan Madison a pen name?' I asked. 'That would have been of interest to her. A writer having named herself after this character.'

She mouthed 'no'. I think she was unhappy with my jovial persistence.

'Are you sure? Because the publication of your first book in 1963 was also the first year that you paid any tax. Ever. There doesn't seem to be a record of you before then. And "S.M. Madison" has had a steady, low-key career since then...'

She looked straight ahead, not at me.

I pushed. 'Ms Madison? Was that your name before 1963?'

From Nick I knew the theory about the woman Gretchen called the nanny, Gretchen's actual mother, admiring her friend Linda Paul too much. She could have made life hell for her idol, enough that Linda had made a drastic escape. And a pretty obvious one, to be honest.

'All right,' she said. 'Don't gloat.'

'You're Linda Paul.'

She lifted her shoulders and waved her hands in little circles. 'I was, and now I'm Susan Maud Madison. It doesn't matter.'

'Why did you change your name?'

'It's not illegal to use a new name.'

Maybe. 'But why bother? Was Gretchen's mother harassing you?'

She closed her eyes, retreating.

'Ms Madison. Please answer.'

'Fine, fine, all right. It was easier to walk away.'

'Your writing career?'

She waved a hand dramatically. 'I write. I write.'

'I'm sorry...?'

Her hands balled into fists. She shook them on either side of her head. She didn't like explaining herself. 'I like my own company. I like being in

214

charge of my own small world. I write. And then I let it go.'

I pressed again. 'By giving up your name, you gave up your professional status. You had to start over. Why would you do that?'

She began to shiver. I was halfway to calling for an ambulance when I realised this was a fit of laughter. 'She wouldn't leave me alone! She followed me, she imitated me. Oh, oh...' She leant forward, head over her knees.

So I'd been right about the nanny being a stalker.

'How did Gretchen feel about this?'

She grinned. 'Oh, you seem to know everything.'

'Were you aware that Gretchen's mother used your name?'

'I don't care what other people do.'

'Were you aware that she – excuse me, what was her original name?' That was a puzzle piece I didn't have.

She laughed again, a small, mean giggle. 'That's what she wanted to know.'

'Excuse me?'

'She wanted me to tell her that woman's real name. I've forgotten. What was she to me? I've forgotten.'

'Gretchen? That's what Gretchen was asking – her mother's real name?'

'She got so angry when I didn't tell her. Then when I explained I couldn't remember – well, that got rid of her. She left.'

'When was this?'

She flapped a hand at me. 'I don't know. Three? Four?'

'Do you know where she was going?'

She rolled her eyes. All right, I got it – she wasn't anyone's keeper. I closed my notebook.

'We both left,' she told me. 'She wasn't stranded. She had a mobile. I saw her talking on it as I drove away. I assume she was calling a taxi.'

She'd called home. We found her phone near the scene. It had been thirty feet from the body. She'd been hit hard, and thrown far.

'There's only one thing I don't understand,' I said. 'What about the box? The box of photographs. Gretchen had it. It had once belonged to this address, and had been reused to ship to Gretchen's mother, when she and Gretchen lived in Brighton. They were your photographs. How did they get there?'

'I didn't want them any more.'

'You mailed them? You addressed them to "Linda Paul"?'

She didn't say anything else. She closed her eyes.

Frohmann met me at Millington Road. I wanted to look around the house again with a fresh mind. Black clouds of fingerprint dust covered strategic stretches of wall, rails, doorknobs.

Frohmann reported the latest: 'It was his car, for sure. Paint match. Tyre match. No fingerprints in it except expected ones, and in all the expected places...' We had the appropriate elimination prints from the investigation of Nick's disappearance.

'Steering wheel wasn't wiped, then,' I clarified.

'That's right. Must have worn gloves. Premeditated?'

216

'Or cold. It's December.'

She continued: 'The vehicle wasn't cited for anything last night – no speeding tickets, no parking violations.'

I prowled the house, touching all the furniture. I'd had to hold back last night, for fingerprints' sake. Now I could indulge in getting a feel for the place. Expensive. This was a well-kept house.

'What did he do for a living?' I asked.

She riffled through her notebook. 'He bred Norwich canaries.'

'For a living, Frohmann. Birds are a labour of love.'

'They were his only labour, sir. Ex-solicitor.'

I turned in a circle and marvelled. 'Look at this place, Frohmann. She was a professor. Where did the money come from?'

'Family, sir. Isn't that usually the way, with homes like this?'

'Exactly. Find out if it was his family, or hers.' She made a note.

'Also, sir, the driver's seat was adjusted for Harry's height.'

'So, driven by Harry, or by someone Harry's height, or by someone who had the sense to set it back when they were done.'

She sighed at me. I was being negative again.

'Look,' I said. 'The question here, the big question, is why bring the car back?'

'To frame Harry,' she answered too quickly.

'Maybe. But he's dead. How framed could he be?'

'Try this, sir. She messed with his birds, he found out, he killed her, came back here...'

'And had an accident while cleaning up? I don't believe it. He wouldn't have left those windows open. He wouldn't have left those cages toppled over. Last night I saw some of those birds – crushed in their cages, some of them not quite dead yet. He wouldn't have left them. He'd save them before he'd avenge them.'

'What if he killed her for a different reason? Killed her for something else, and then came home and found the birds? What if the reason she was angry enough to go after his birds might be the same reason he was angry enough to go after her?'

'The neighbour saw the car here at lunchtime, when he also saw the windows open. So, whoever took the car later knew about the birds. Not Harry. It wasn't Harry.'

I jogged up the stairs, and up again, to the bird room. Frohmann trailed me.

'The killer had no assurance that Harry's death wouldn't have been discovered,' I mused. 'The birds coming and going might have alerted someone. Returning the car was a risk. Why bring it back? Why?'

The empty cages had been restacked haphazardly. Fallen rosettes had been tossed into a corner: first prize, champion, best in show. The birds had been taken, but nothing had been cleaned. The mess on the floor had been swept into a now stinking pile.

'Maybe, sir ... to get his own vehicle? What if the murderer had parked here, and just needed to get his own car away? That would be worth coming back for.'

That was good. That was very good.

'Any witnesses to unusual vehicles, in the driveway or on the street?'

She flipped back through her notebook pages. 'Mr Neighbourhood Watch gave us a list. We ran the plates; no one popped as connected or suspicious.'

The doorbell clamoured before she finished. That grating sound.

Frohmann descended to answer it. I followed more slowly. From the top of the main staircase I watched her open the door to Miranda Bailey, of all people.

'May I help you, Mrs Bailey?' Frohmann asked politely. I ought to send a thank-you note to her mother for raising her right.

'I– Where's Harry? I heard about Gretchen. Where's Harry?'

Frohmann looked up at me for guidance. Polly's mother followed her gaze. 'Oh!' she said. 'Inspector Keene.' She looked upset. I'd been the one to interrogate her over Nick.

'Mrs Bailey.' I descended the stairs like a host. I wanted to be kind.

'If you think Harry had anything to do with it, you're wrong. Where have you taken him? Have you dragged him away to jail?' She was strangling her wrists with the strap of her bag.

'No, no, no, Mrs Bailey,' I said. 'Please, sit down. Please,' I said.

Frohmann got to the point as soon as she was off her feet. 'He's dead, Mrs Bailey.'

She jumped up. 'What? No! No, it's Gretchen. I was told by someone from the University.

219

Gretchen's dead.'

'They're both dead,' Frohmann assured her.

Miranda looked at each of us, back and forth, a little tennis game. 'Really?' she finally squeaked.

There was a box of tissues on the mantel. I handed it to her. Frohmann pushed her gently back to sitting, and sat next to her, on the arm of the couch.

'Was he in the car too?' Miranda asked, obviously having heard 'car accident' through the grapevine. Her misunderstanding of the facts spoke well for innocence.

I took over. Not everything would be released to the public. 'He died here.'

Miranda cried. Frohmann pushed ahead. 'Did you know him well, Mrs Bailey? Why did you come here today?'

I...' She looked around, as if surprised to find herself here.

'I'd heard about Gretchen. I wanted to see if he was all right.'

'How well did you know Mr Reed?'

She only blinked.

'Harry Reed,' I expanded.

She put her hand to her mouth, and looked back and forth from me to Frohmann. 'I thought his last name was Paul,' she finally said.

'A reasonable mistake,' I assured her.

She rocked back and forth. 'No, it's not. It's really not.'

Frohmann intervened. 'How well did you know him, Mrs Bailey?'

'Apparently, not well at all!' Her laugh was high-pitched.

'Can you tell us why they took such an interest in your arrest?' I pressed. 'Did you know either of them before your arrival in Cambridge?'

'They were friends of my daughter. They took an interest in justice. Do I really need to rationalise that?'

'No, Mrs Bailey,' I agreed. 'No, it's only that your concerns about one another seem to have been deeper than one would expect of friends of family.'

'Then I feel sorry for you,' she said. 'You must lead a very insular life.'

'When exactly were you here last?' I asked, ignoring her editorial.

'Yesterday morning. Around ten-thirty? I think?' Her hands were full of crumpled tissue. As she swivelled her head looking for a rubbish bin, she suddenly perceived her vulnerability. 'When I left he was alive!' she asserted. 'I left him and he was about to take a shower. And I went into town. I took Polly shopping. We bought things. I used a credit card at Robert Sayles! You can trace that! I bought a sweater. I bought her a coat. She wanted a new coat...'

'Sergeant Frohmann will take you home,' I suggested. We would check on that alibi later.

'Oh. No, thank you. No, I have a rental car. A hire car. I'm visiting my old village today. I used to live fairly near, when I was a girl. I wanted Polly to come with me, but she didn't want to. That's all right. It's been a good visit. She let me buy her a coat yesterday. We haven't been shopping together in a long time, too long. But yesterday she let me. She let me buy her a coat.' She was awfully excited about that coat. She covered her face and eked out a sound like a deflating balloon.

'What do you make of her?' Frohmann asked me, after she'd left.

'She seemed honestly surprised.'

Shouting outside distracted us. Across the street, Miranda and another woman were arguing in the driveway of a house for sale. The other woman sounded belligerent and Miranda cowered.

Frohmann bounded across the street.

The woman arguing with Polly's mother wore a suit and high-heeled shoes, all in red.

They stopped. Lady-in-red turned her glare to Frohmann. 'This car needs to be ticketed. It has no right to park here.'

'Can we back it up a little?' I suggested, catching up. 'You are...?'

'Rebecca Phillips-Koster. I represent this home for sale, and I'm tired of people using it as a catch-all parking space.'

Miranda was crying again. 'Yesterday a horrible man put notes on all the windshields of cars parked in the street instead of in driveways. He was on a crusade against Christmas shoppers parking in the road. I didn't want to deal with him today. You had the police cars in the driveway, so I parked here. I didn't think it would hurt anyone.'

'What horrible man?' Frohmann asked.

'That man.' She pointed to the house next door to Gretchen and Harry's. The neighbourhood watch.

'This driveway is not a public car park. This is trespassing!' the red lady insisted.

'All right, all right,' I soothed her. 'I understand your frustration. Has this been going on a lot?' I shot Frohmann a significant look.

The red lady looked embarrassed. 'Once or twice. But even once is too much! This is private property.'

'Yesterday?' Frohmann prodded. 'Was anyone parked here yesterday?'

Red lady shook her head, then switched abruptly to a nod. 'Students.' She rolled her eyes, inviting us all to commiserate. 'One had left a bicycle here. Propped against the side of the house, around here...' We all walked around the side of the house, and looked where the offending bicycle had once been.

'Did you see this student? Do you remember what the cycle looked like?'

She shook her head. 'I didn't see him. But–' She pulled a remote control out of her handbag. The garage door slowly inched upward. 'I taught him a lesson. I put the bike in the garage. Ha.' She looked satisfied.

I must have looked pretty satisfied myself. 'Please don't touch it,' I said, as she walked towards the garage. Frohmann called forensics on her mobile. I felt a vibration in my front pocket.

'Why haven't you phoned?' Gwen demanded.

'I've been working,' I apologised.

'I assumed so.' Her voice was deliberate. 'But I didn't know it. I was wondering if something had happened.' This comes from every police spouse.

'I slept at the station. Things went late. We found that student...'

'I know. And the professor. It's on the news.'

'It's ugly. Look, we're in the middle of–'

She cut me off. 'It's Dora.'

'What? What's Dora?'

'We left the wedding after you did. She was exhausted. She was cold. A waitress lent her some dry clothes. She went right to sleep as soon as we got home–'

'Right, right, yes, I get that. What's happened?'

'I wanted to brush her hair. It was getting matted with all that gel and pins in it. I opened her vanity drawer, to get her brush, and there was a condom in there.'

Shit. I stepped farther away and lowered my voice. 'It's not hers. It must belong to a friend.'

'Exactly,' she said. Meaning a male friend.

'She's fourteen, Gwen. She's fourteen...' She didn't say anything, so I kept talking. 'I can't deal with this right now. We're in the middle...'

Gwen cried. I couldn't not deal with this.

I called to Frohmann, 'Take care of the bicycle. I'll catch up with you at the station.' I walked down the driveway, holding the phone tight enough to squeeze the blood out of my fingers. 'All right. What can I do?'

'I don't know.' She was still crying.

'Have you talked to her? Is she there?'

'No. No, she was asleep the moment she fell into bed. I didn't say anything last night, I just walked out of the room. I waited for you to come home. I kept waiting...'

Sorry, sorry, sorry... 'Then what?'

'I fell asleep rather late. She was already out when I got up. She'd left the cereal box open on the table. She'd made herself coffee.' Dora drinks coffee? Since when does a fourteen-year-old drink coffee? 'I just kept waiting. I didn't want to bother you but I was going crazy.'

'Do you know where she is?'

Gwen didn't answer. I guessed she was shaking her head. When she's upset she forgets a person on the phone isn't right in front of her.

'Look, Gwen, she's probably with Stephanie, right? Stephanie and ... what's the other one?'

'Margaux.'

'Margaux. Right. They hang out together. I'll bet they're ... shopping or something.' What do teenage girls do? 'Have you checked her email?'

'Of course I checked her email. She doesn't use the email we gave her. She probably uses one of those free ones you can check at a website.'

'All right, all right. Try a few. The computer might be set to remember her login. Try Hotmail. Try Yahoo.'

'She'll hate us...'

Probably. I reasoned to myself that there was no reason to panic. If the condom was hers, she was either already in deep and today wasn't any more important than tomorrow, or she was just playing at being a grown-up and there wasn't any real worry at all.

'She'll come home for dinner. Or she'll call. You know she always does,' I said.

Gulping sounds, which I interpreted as more tearful nodding. Then: 'You know, what I really want is a co-parent in this situation. What I really want is a partner, a real partner...'

I know, I know, I know...

'I know our daughter's going to grow up,

225

Morris. I know what's part of that. I know. But I don't want it so fast, and I don't want to parent it alone.'

Sorry, sorry. 'I know.'

'She was so beautiful last night, Morris. She's so beautiful...' She is. She looks like Gwen.

'I'll come home for lunch. Will you make me lunch?' I felt a bit lord-of-the-manor saying that, but it would distract her.

'It's late for lunch–' she said.

'I'll come home,' I said.

The first time I'd met Gwen's dad I'd been in a panic to impress him. I wore a tie. I bought new shoes. I brought flowers for her mother.

'Mum, Dad,' she'd said. 'This is Morris.' It was such an announcement. 'This' was Morris: newly a detective constable. New shoes. A tie that had been a despised Christmas gift.

Her dad had shaken my hand. 'Gwen likes you,' he said.

'Yes, sir.'

'You're supposed to say how much you respect her,' he prompted.

'I do, sir,' I said. Nothing else would come out. What could I say to a dad? That I was hard all day thinking about her? That's what everything came down to. Her prettiness, her love of animals, her kindness, her cleverness – everything I liked made me want her. That's the way things are at that age.

The first time we'd done it, which had been a week after that dinner with her parents, I'd been too fast. I'd thought she wouldn't see me again after that. I'd been drinking, and selfish, and stupid, and eager.

226

We got better matched over time. We were good together. We were.

Gwen stood at the door, waiting for me. 'Oh, Morris,' she said, and started crying again.

I said, 'She's all right, you know. She's all right.' And Gwen nodded. It really wasn't the end of the world, was it? It really wasn't.

'It's just so early,' she said. 'I thought we had years...'

'We have years,' I said, suddenly fierce. 'We have years to be parents to a fine girl who's becoming a fine woman, who'll drive us crazy sometimes, and scare us sometimes, and make us proud sometimes. We have years of that ahead, so don't spend all your energy on today. We have years, Gwen, we have years...' At that, she wrapped her arms around my neck and pulled herself tight to me. She almost lifted herself off the floor.

I didn't know what to do with my arms. We'd been making love like usual, but we hadn't embraced in a long time.

I put my hands on her back. 'Oh, Morris,' she said. 'I've missed you.'

I'd been away, that was sure. I just wasn't certain I was entirely back.

'I'm sorry, Gwen, it's been...' I didn't know what it had been. Richard's wedding?

She released herself and led me to the table. She'd set out sandwich fixings, and coffee. 'I know yesterday was difficult for you,' she said.

I shook my head. 'Dancing embarrasses me, but I wouldn't call it difficult.'

She sighed elaborately but wouldn't face me. 'It

was Alice,' she said. Why do people think I carry a torch for Alice? Has Carmen been pushing her ideas on Gwen?

'I don't give a shit about either Alice, except in the most human, generic manner of wishing them both well,' I said.

She shrugged. We were at a stalemate again. The connection from the doorway was gone.

'Gwen,' I said, reaching across the table. 'Gwen, I was never in love with Alice. I hardly knew Alice. I liked her, and I might have had something with her, but I didn't. I had something with you.'

She ignored my hand. 'I always knew I was second choice...' *Shit.* Where was this coming from? Sixteen years!

'All right, Gwen, all right. When I first met you, we weren't serious, right? It wasn't serious for you either. We were just having fun. And I thought about having fun with someone else too, with Alice. That's ordinary. There's nothing big there. So I tried to get off with her, and she said no. She said no. And you and me, we kept going on, and we became something, and here we are. This isn't a contest with places. This is just ... life. We went from not being together to being together. Here we are.'

'Yes, here we are,' she said. I wanted to eat to stop the talking but I couldn't face food. She pushed on, 'What can I do, Morris? Is there something I can wear or something I can do to make you look at me again?'

'What on earth would you wear?' I said, knowing it was incendiary as soon as it popped out. But what is it with women thinking how they dress is

228

going to change something? 'Stop crying,' I said. 'Gwen...'

'Do you remember our first time?' she said. *Great.* One of my most embarrassing moments. 'You made dinner at your flat, and we had strong red wine. I felt elegant, having wine instead of beer. I was nervous so I just kept sipping. I didn't want the food because I was worried about garlic on my breath. I thought kissing the taste of wine would be nice. So I just kept drinking...' I'd just assumed she'd noticed that I'm a terrible cook. 'I knew we were going to go all the way. I was – we knew, didn't we? Without talking about it. We knew. Morris, I'd never felt so wanted. You were ... *wild* about me. You were on me like...' She shook her head. She couldn't find the best words. 'You were so hungry for me. I'd never felt so perfect in my life.'

Dora interrupted. She'd pushed the door open with a hand full of shopping bags, and had heard the last sentences. 'That's disgusting, Mum. Keep it to yourself,' she said lightly. 'Are you trying to corrupt me?'

Gwen pinkened. I jumped right in. 'You don't seem to need much help. What do you have a condom for?'

She froze. 'Which one of you went into my things?'

'Not the point, Dora. Just tell us what's going on.'

She put down the bags and joined us at the table, looking suddenly much younger. She stood holding the back of a chair, looking from one of us to the other. 'Margaux and Spencer are doing it. They've been dating a year, right, and they think they're in love.' She rolled her eyes at that, which made me glad. 'So she gave one to me and one to Stephanie "just in case", right? She said it was great and we should be prepared. I put it in my drawer, 'cause what was I gonna do, carry it in my handbag like an emergency tampon?' She rolled her eyes again.

I nodded. 'All right. That's a fine answer. In fact, that's a great answer. I like that answer. But you can come to us when the answer is different too, all right?'

'Ew,' she said, and went upstairs.

I rubbed the back of my neck. Gwen tapped one finger on her cheek.

'Do you believe her?' she whispered.

'I do. I do,' I said. She nodded too.

'Oh, Morris,' she said, relieved and embarrassed, and still fragile.

'You were in a right tizzy,' I teased her.

'No more than you!' We laughed dodged-a-bullet laughs.

'Morris, I'm sorry. Maybe all this' – she said, waving a hand around – 'is my fault. I've always felt like I was competing with what might have been, and then when Richard got engaged...' She shrugged. 'I don't know why that would have bothered me, but it did. It made me jealous. The newness of what they have. Their love is so ... shiny. It's shiny.'

'What, so their love is a puppy, and our love is an old, hairy, smelly, half-blind dog?' That made her laugh.

'We're smelly old dogs,' she agreed.

'Aw, Gwen. You'll always be one of those dumb yapping puppies to me.' I smiled hugely. She came round to my side of the table to swat me in the chest. I caught her wrists. 'No, babe, no,' I said. 'I'm a cop, you can't get the better of me.' There we were, about to wrestle.

'You haven't called me "babe" in years,' she said, like she was going to cry again.

My phone vibrated. 'Sorry,' I said. She knew my work-voice. It was Frohmann. I had to get to the station. She'd done something magic to get the bike owner's name so fast.

'I'm proud of you,' Gwen said, seeing me out the door.

'I'll be home tonight,' I said.

We kissed a kiss like we hadn't since we were pissed on cheap wine and empty stomachs.

Part Four

GRETCHEN

CHAPTER EIGHT

'The river was low today,' Harry said. He slipped in beside me under the duvet, which puffed the scent of an aggressively floral detergent as it settled.

'I don't know what you're talking about.'

His hollow in the mattress blended with mine. A tiny bead of birdseed rolled up against my thigh.

'They dredged the Cam. They didn't find anything,' he explained.

Anything. A body. They hadn't found a body. 'I wouldn't expect them to.'

'Why? Where is he? A drowning would make as much sense as anything else–'

'It would make no sense whatever. Why are you telling me this?'

He didn't answer immediately. 'I thought you'd want to know.' He opened the book so hard that its spine cracked. I winced. 'I thought you'd want to know if he was dead.'

'But you don't know if he's dead. You only know he's not drowned.'

'Yes, he's not drowned! Good news, I thought.'

'I never thought he was drowned in the first place.'

Was that a sunflower seed? I kicked my legs and brushed at the sheet under my knees.

'What?' he asked.

I threw back the duvet and sat up, legs over the side. There was no explaining it to him. He was inured to the hard little specks all over the house.

He put his hand between my shoulder blades and rubbed. 'Would you please just read the book,' I finally said.

'No.' Both of his hands were on my shoulders now. The book slid off his lap and a corner of it poked me.

'No,' I said too.

He dropped his hands. He slapped the book onto his nightstand.

Oh, for Heaven's sake. 'Don't pout,' I said.

'I'm going to sleep.'

I brought my legs back up onto the bed. I leant across to his side. 'Please.'

I hadn't told him why the books mattered. He only knew that one of my avenues of research for the biography had been to track the effect of Linda Paul's series character, Susan Maud Madison. Homage to her, with her three names, was obvious to spot. I'd written to several women of that name, to find out whether they'd been given it on purpose, and what it was their mothers had wished for them by doing so.

One of those, S.M. Madison, was a writer. Not famous, but reliably mid-list. This was one of S.M. Madison's books. It wasn't available in audio.

'Please, Harry,' I said again. I tried to wheedle with my voice, but I've never been much good at that.

'Gretchen,' he said, 'it's late.'

'No.' *It's not too late.* That's what I was discovering: It wasn't too late.

The dust jacket crinkled as he opened it.

He read aloud with a fervour more suited to an undergraduate auditioning for a drama society. It was useless to direct him otherwise. I filtered out his tone and emphases to get at the words, the raw words:

'"Gloria was swarmed by children: hot, fat, sticky ones, that had been eating with their fingers and clawing into garden soil. They nuzzled at every bend of her body: one in the crook of her arm, another behind the knees, a small neck slipped into the narrow of her waist. She put her fingers through the hair of that one, the one at her hip. They all breathed on her. It was overwhelming. This happened every afternoon, at the end of their trek home from school–" Good God, that's unpleasant.'

I tensed. 'Please don't comment.' It wrenched me out of the story.

He sighed.

This is exactly why I'd had to hire a student to work with the photographs.

He read on. A later scene put the protagonist on her front steps, while her neighbour, Gloria, was out.

'"Lily, the smallest one, came to me when her mother didn't answer the door. She wanted a drink. I denied having water, which made her laugh. The sound was frail and breathy and high; her fragility terrified me. Where was Gloria? Lily ran off; she grabbed a branch and swung herself up onto it. Where was her mother? I didn't want to be responsible for this. These small creatures, so fast and so needy. So empty all the time. They consume the adults around them. That's how they become adults themselves. They eat their parents up.'"

He stopped. 'Are you all right?' he asked.

'I'm fine,' I assured him. 'For God's sake, get on with it!' But I had gripped the duvet tightly in my fists. I let it go and smoothed it out.

I'd already listened to others of her books that were more current. This one was her first. It was the only one of them that had a mother in it, any mother at all.

I suddenly remembered myself as a child, lying half-asleep on a kind of sofa bed, pressed against a warm female body: leftover perfume, a brushed cotton nightgown over free breasts. We were asleep together, and suddenly the light flashed on. It woke me; I can still see very bright light even today. Clicking heels against the wood floor, a vaporous smell of drink. I clambered out from under the smooth sheet and itchy blanket to fling myself at the woman who'd just walked in the door. I reached up as high as I could, so high I felt the beads in her necklace. I was between her and a man. The handbag hanging off her wrist was at just the height to bounce hard into my head.

Behind me, the cotton sleeves pulled me back. That's all I remember, being sucked into a suffocation of warm brushed cotton, under a cool sheet and itchy blanket. The woman in beads with the handbag walked through to the bedroom. I don't know what happened to the man.

That was Linda Paul, my mother. The woman in the nightgown was my nanny. She raised me.

She raised me when she was with Linda, and then she raised me without her.

Nick had discovered that my recently deceased mother wasn't Linda Paul, and assumed that Linda Paul had never been my mother at all. But I knew, from research, that she had two relatives blind in the same way that I am. I was certain that Linda Paul had given birth to me.

Then she had given me away.

Nick hadn't realised that's what he'd shown me. I'd had to make him stop before he got that far himself. There's a difference between a noise downstairs in the night and someone suddenly standing over your bed. They may amount to the same thing, they may both be the same intruder, but the moment it might be and the moment it undeniably is are different.

I didn't notice that Nick had gone, truly gone, until the police came to talk to me. I was angry. This wasn't my fault. What had he done to himself? I told the Inspector that he'd informally assisted with a research project; that was all. That he seemed to be a generally untroubled person. The Inspector asked me if I was worried about him. What kind of question is that? What would my answer matter in the investigation? I didn't know if I was. Polly and her mother disturbed me more.

Most distracting of all, I knew who S.M. Madison must be. After Linda Paul abandoned me, where did she go? She wouldn't stop writing, would she? She wouldn't. That fantasy of sacrifice came from the nanny, a woman who'd never written anything. S.M. Madison had written a book every two years since 1963.

So I've known since the day Nick was gone.

I didn't tell anyone, not even Harry. I didn't know what he'd do if I did. He might try to protect me. He might close the book permanently. I couldn't let him do that.

'Harry,' I said, truly begging, 'please read it to me.' Unthinkingly, I rested my hand on his forearm. A static charge jolted us both, reminding me how long it had been since I'd touched him. 'Please,' I said again. I meant it desperately.

So Harry read on.

In the end, Gloria died. The children moved. I'd made Harry read the entire book, every word, one by one. A review on the back of the jacket congratulated S.M. Madison's bravery and originality in depicting an alternative to the self-sacrificing mother figure that society has colluded to perpetuate. Suddenly I, one of the first female Fellows at Magdalene and the first blind graduate of my college, was put on defensive as a party to woman-stifling, anti-feminist society. My eagerness to accept the fantasy concocted by the one who raised me, to see myself and the mothering of me as more valuable than anything else she might have done, made me an accomplice. Some feminists think men are the enemy, but I knew myself for what I was. Children are the enemy here. It's not men who demand a woman's undivided attention, it's children. It's the children who wake her up, and the children who come to her for everything, every little thing. It's the children who can't dress themselves or feed themselves or go on without her attention and approval. My anger was tempered into pity for my mother, and guilt. What had I done to her? What had my existence done?

Harry's voice was parched. He asked me again, 'Are you all right?'

Why couldn't he stop that? What was wrong with the man?

'I'm going to sleep,' I said. I rolled onto my side. I didn't hear the click of a switch, so he must have stayed up. He had books of his own to read.

Harry would have thought I'd gone out.

The next morning, I woke before he did, dressed, and drank my coffee at the kitchen table.

There was the scrape and thud of a magazine being thrust through our mail slot. I wanted to catch Lawrence, our postman, to hand him a card I needed mailed. Today was Richard's wedding, and I had yet to post it.

We have a cluster of bells attached to our front door. I made those bells shake.

But it wasn't Lawrence at the door. Of course not. It being Richard's wedding, it was Sunday. The magazine-person was someone who smelt of cosmetics. That, and finding myself standing on a pile of yesterday's mail, disoriented me. 'I'm sorry,' I said, stepping back and bending to retrieve the mail from the floor. Both Harry and I must have used only the side door yesterday.

The magazine-person's voice confirmed her gender. 'So sorry to have disturbed you,' she said. 'I'm an estate agent. Rebecca Phillips-Koster. I'm selling the house across the road.' She crouched with me. 'I was just delivering these informational

241

brochures around the neighbourhood.'

I assumed she was proffering one, but my hands were full of yesterday's mail. She twigged soon enough that I don't see, and compensated with a flourish of attempted assistance. She pulled at the letters in my hands, to aggregate them with her magazine. I was shocked enough that I let go. She layered them all into a neat pyramid, smallest mail on top, and returned the stack to me. We stood. 'Shall I tell you who they're from?' she asked loudly.

The pipes in the wall rattled; Harry was showering. He would only have heard the shaken bells on the door, not the obtuse Ms Phillips-Koster exaggerating her pronunciation for my sake.

'Oh dear,' she said. 'This one's been opened.'

'Which one?' I'd felt a tear in one envelope, but had assumed it to have been an accidental mangle from some post-sorting machine.

'It was mailed from this house. It's being returned. "No such person at this address." Tsk. Laziness – ripping open an envelope before bothering to glance at the name. Oh, look–' She plucked another from me. 'There's another being returned. This one hasn't been opened.' She told me who they'd been written to, and handed them back to me.

'Thank you,' I said, meaning 'goodbye'. She chattered about how good I was to have sent my holiday letters out with so much time to spare, and that the same happened to her every year: returned letters due to changed addresses. 'Not everyone,' she commiserated, 'can be so organised as we–'

I closed the door.

I carried the stack of mail into my study, and overturned it on my desk. The two returns were now on the bottom, thoroughly covered and held down. It was important to keep them under control.

Now I knew where she was. The letters had told me.

I'd written to the few Susan Maud Madisons I'd discovered, including author S.M. Madison. I'd contacted her through her publisher; no personal information about her had been available. A Susan M. Madison lived in Cambridgeshire, at Rose Cottage on Cantelupe Road. Both had returned my letters unaccepted. But one had been opened. And the estate agent had noticed that 'return to sender' had been written on each in the same terse handwriting. I'd found her.

I'd wait. I didn't want to explain it to Harry. I didn't want to say the words out loud. Soon, he'd come downstairs, drink coffee, and go out. Eventually. By patience, I could earn the means to go upstairs to the computer, uninterrogated. I could print directions to Rose Cottage, and phone for a taxi. I'd see her today. If I could just keep still, I wouldn't have to speak to anyone else before I spoke to her.

So it was my fault that Harry thought I was out. He'd heard the door; I was quiet here. What else would he assume?

My study is a small room. It had been added on by the previous owners as a large cupboard, had no windows, and had never been rigged for electricity. I had a desk in there, with a chair tucked under it, and a chaise along the wall, too full of books to sit on. Our computer was of necessity upstairs, in a room full of power outlets. I worked up there. I used my study to read, and to be alone. With the door closed, there was no tell-tale line of light from under the door or sound of typing to indicate occupancy. Harry wouldn't have known I was in there.

So it's my fault that he did what he did. He's not a monster. He never would have made me listen.

The doorbell rang, followed by the bell cluster jingling. Harry's feet on the stairs. The knob, and a click.

'Is Dr Paul here?' a woman asked. She sounded too mature to be one of my students, thank goodness. I've had enough of students. They remind me of Gloria's children.

'Oh,' this woman said, to what I assume was a shake of his head. 'Well, I wanted to thank her. And you, of course. Mr Paul?' That happened to him often.

'Call me Harry,' he said, not bothering to correct her.

'I don't know what I would have done. I would have hired some solicitor, of course, but Mr Tisch was a wonder.' Aha. Miranda Bailey. 'I got out last night. He made them wake me up and let me out. He wouldn't let them keep me till morning. There was a teenager. He'd seen Nick later that night. He'd mugged him. I hope Nick isn't hurt.'

The voices shifted. Kitchen. Harry serves food

as a reflex.

She blathered on. 'You and your wife have been so kind. Mr Tisch stood up for me. That policeman...' A pause. To shudder, to cringe? 'I know he was just doing his job. But he wasn't nice.' How fastidious of her to put it that way. How British. Polly told me that her mother was originally British.

'How is Polly?' Harry asked.

'I think Polly's ... depleted, you understand? I don't think she has it in her to deal with me and my problems, which she shouldn't have to anyway. She's just a baby ... I just want to pick her up in the middle of the night and hand her what she's dropped over the side of the crib and make everything all right again...'

The kettle whistled. 'It must have been hard on you, Mrs Bailey,' Harry said. The tea drawer squeaked as it opened, spoons clinked.

'I didn't care for it!' She forced a laugh. 'But whatever Nick's going through must be far worse. They were right to detain anyone who might have hurt him. I can't blame them.' Pause. Sipping at the hot stuff, stirring it, blowing on it. Tea gives something to do with one's hands. 'You don't have children, do you?' she asked him. He would shake his head. He doesn't use words for that subject. 'Well, I love my children, but sometimes it's very hard. Will, my son, sometimes I think he's been lost in all the fuss. He's become peripheral. Isn't that awful? Good grief, I'm a terrible mother...'

Here is where Harry would be embarrassed. He's terrible with tears. When my mother died he cooked for me. He didn't know what else to do.

Miranda must be hemmed in by biscuits now. He would be thrusting them at her, making hills of them around her. 'You've done well with Polly,' he said. 'She's a good girl.'

Miranda laughed, a sudden, horse-like sound. 'When I was a girl, "good girl" meant something else entirely. It meant sexless. I like that "good girl" means something else now. Strong. Determined. She's a good girl. I try to tell her that, over and over I tell her, but it's hard for words to compete with what her father did. I'm grateful that people like you tell her too. Maybe if we all keep telling her... Anyway, I'm glad there are people here who care. She must be very dear to you both, for you to have rescued me as you did. So thank you.'

She thinks Polly was like a daughter to me. I don't even like Polly. I don't think she's strong. She let go when it was most important to hang on. She would have left her mother to humiliation and punishment. She's spoilt. She thinks a mother is some kind of entitlement, something everyone just has, something easily replaced, or dispensed with entirely. She thinks mothers are permanent; she thinks mothers don't die, don't leave. That you can walk away and come back and there the mother will be, still breathing, still welcoming, still ... making dinner? Patching clothes? That a mother is a statue in a park, who stands through graffiti and bird shit and rain and time, not eroding, not falling apart. Not walking away. She thinks mothers are made out of rock, and have no choices, and can't shift position, and won't leave when the persistence and drudgery drive down on them day

246

after day. Polly thinks having a mother is her choice: Today I don't want my mother, maybe tomorrow I will. She doesn't know how tenuous it all is. She doesn't know about mothers being people, sometimes terrible people. She doesn't know to cling, to bribe, above all to not look away for a moment. She doesn't understand that any moment they may sneak away, that they can if they want to. She doesn't understand how tempting it is. She doesn't know that they can, and she doesn't know how much they think about it. How much they plan in their ticking minds what they could do if they ran away, and how it would feel. That it would feel good.

Footsteps between the carpets. Miranda wore hard heels. Into the lounge. The hiss of the heating system coming on. The neighbours driving away.

'Did she ask you to help me?' I pictured her big, hopeful eyes. Harry would want to lie but wouldn't.

'She's understandably confused just now,' he said.

Crying sounds again. 'I'm sorry, Harry,' she said, the name coming easily. 'I'm sorry. Poor Polly. She shouldn't have been put through any of this... Do you know, when she was a little girl, she used to cry at just about anything. She cared about other people. She'd cry if someone else's toy broke, or if they weren't chosen for a team she was already on. She was never just herself. She felt for everyone. I never saw her cry after ... what her father did. She must have. Maybe with the counsellor, or one of her friends...' Snuffling, weeping. 'She cried for everyone else her whole life but couldn't manage it for herself. Oh dear, I seem to be managing it entirely too well...'

I cried when my mother died. When the woman who raised me died. Harry circled me but didn't get too close. I was a maelstrom. He made tea.

'Have some more tea,' he said to Miranda. I put a hand over my mouth to smother laughter as Miranda snuffled and honked her nose.

'Mrs Bailey,' he began.

She interrupted, 'Call me Miranda.'

'Miranda,' he said, 'your Polly has been pushed around by some hard things, but she's going to be all right. If she's keeping her distance, well, it's just because she needs to for a small while. But a girl needs her mother. I well know that from my wife. A woman needs her mother...'

'Oh, I hope so, Mr Paul. Harry. She wasn't happy that I came to England and ... you don't think she thinks I hurt Nick, do you? She can't think that–'

'You're free now, Miranda. No one thinks that. No one.' More snuffling sounds. Cup and saucer sounds. 'It made me wonder, does your wife...?'

What?

Miranda said more: 'She seemed to take it all very ... *personally*. I understand she lost her mother recently. Is there anything I can...?'

Harry laughed. It boomed out. I hadn't heard that in years. 'No. There's nothing any of us can do.' Then, 'Would you like to see my birds?'

Harry's birds. We bought the house because of the top floor, an attic eyrie for Harry's canaries. The walls are covered with cages and prize roset-

248

tes, and in the centre is a grand aviary, waist high, for them to fly about in. They chitter all day, and birdseed has been ground into our carpet from Harry's shoes. His hands smell like sawdust and soap.

'I keep Norwich canaries. They always cheer me up when I need it. I have a grand champion. Let me show you.'

Harry's bloody birds. He doesn't even name them. But he loves them; I have no doubt that he loves them. He got glasses made with plain lenses in. He has perfect vision; but he wears them up in the bird room, so if they're ever confronted by a bespectacled judge they won't be frightened.

When we'd just met, he'd been mad for South American birds with their colours and magnificent tails. I'd thought he might become a counter, one of those people who make lists and try to catch sight or sound of every species in the world. But somehow he got here, with these fat, round Norwiches. He tells me that some are orange, and some are white. I've held one, briefly. He let me hold one, because I couldn't look. But he was impatient and nervous about it. Apparently, they ought not to be handled too long. Even when he holds them, it's just for quick transfer from one environment to another. Never to fondle or pet. Except for me, just that one time.

He led me upstairs, and had me hold still while he clicked his tongue and rummaged in a cage. Then he brought it to me. I cupped my hands. The heart beat so quickly, it felt like a racing clock. The claws of its feet scratched my palm. Harry wanted me to understand something, to

249

feel ... something. I tried. But all I felt were feathers, and a fearful heart, and sharp feet. It was a bag of bird bits. I don't have it in me to perceive a bird as something more than its parts. He wanted me to share something with him, but I don't know what it was.

I tried to support the birds. A hobby is good for the mind. Then he'd brought in the fosters.

Apparently, Norwiches aren't good at raising their own young. He takes their eggs as soon as they're laid, and puts them in warm little drawers. He marks the date on a calendar. He has several different pens for writing on his big chart; they squeak when they write. He has 'lizards' (birds so called for their markings) and fifes in cages apart from the Norwiches. He gives them the eggs, and they parent the new birds. I think that's disgusting. Why fawn over a breed so unsuited to the fundamental functions of life?

I don't enter the bird room any more.

I was sure Miranda would feel the same about it. How could any mother not? How could any daughter not? He would go on about shape and feathers; how he'd successfully campaigned to make the standard rounder. He'd go on. Miranda would mark time, those fosters impossible to ignore. The 'singing' is overwhelming. It comes from all sides.

Perhaps I ought to rescue her, I thought. Woman to woman. Give her a break.

The noise was indistinct, and strange. Wood smacking a wall. Was Harry building something? I couldn't hear the bird room from my study. I was underneath a guest bedroom.

Its bed has a wide wooden headboard, up against a plaster wall. The joints must be loose. It exaggerated every movement on it, thumping like a timpani.

People feel sorry for me, not being able to see, but very little in the world is exclusively visual. This rhythm didn't need looking at to know what it was.

There's nothing profound that uses just one sense. There's nothing that can hide itself by just holding up a curtain. Everything real has scent and sound and makes the air move differently. Real things shake. Real things loom. Being blind is bloody useless. For all its inconvenience I ought to be able to miss this. I ought to be able to not know, to walk by, to not see him on her. Everything I 'see' is in my mind anyway. This is as vivid as if they were in front of me. This is in my mind, made of pieces of Harry I know from my own hands, and made up of envy of Miranda, who in my imagination is younger than she could be with Polly for a daughter.

The last time Harry reached for me was the day I sent Nick away. He came home just after Nick left. It was my birthday. Harry had bought flowers in the market. I smelt juice on his breath. Grocery bags crumpled at his feet. He leant close to me but I put my hand up between us. I was still reeling from Nick. I'd remembered something. I used to have a trinket, a key chain I think. It had a lion on it. Someone had given it to me as a toy when I was very, very young. Children like lions, but that wasn't why. They'd given it to me because I was a

251

Leo. I suddenly remembered that. Someone, some friend of the family, giving it to me and telling me why. Because I'd been born in August. But I wasn't born in August. My birthday is in December, my birthday was that day. My mother used to make an extra fuss to ensure I wouldn't feel dwarfed by Christmas. But I remembered that lion. Harry put his face to mine but all I could see was an enamel painted lion head dangling from a cheap chain. I pulled back from him, from both heads, his and the lion's. I'd said, 'Liv's upstairs,' to make him stop trying, even though she'd left before Nick.

Upstairs now, the *thunk-thunk-thunk* of the headboard hitting the wall continued. Miranda cried out. Then Harry too. 'Oh!' he said, like he does. Like it's taken him by surprise. The hum of pillow talk, he more than she. I couldn't make out the words themselves but their content was predictable. Excuses. Explanations. Harry got out of bed, the squeaking, loose-jointed bed. His robe wouldn't be there; his robe hangs on the post in our bedroom, not this one. He'd reach, then remember, and rise with his bottom bare.

Pull up trousers. Zip and belt. The bathroom is en suite. Miranda with a few minutes of privacy: Find clothes, straighten the bedspread. That's the bed his mother sleeps in when she visits. That's the bed his nephew used when he came last year to interview for the engineering department.

He came downstairs. I heard the door of the guest room open and close, then the whooshing sound through our pipes; she was in the bathroom, then. She came down the stairs too, her steps clicking on the wood. Neither had showered. They would still smell like what they'd just done.

I could hear the words once they were downstairs, she first: 'I, I'm sorry. I shouldn't have–'

'Shhh,' he comforted her.

'I didn't mean to. I've been lonely. This whole... Polly doesn't want me here. But I need to be away from home as much as she does. Her father, he – I'm divorcing him, of course. Not that I – I don't mean that I'm trying to... You're married. I know. I'm not trying to impinge on that. I'm not looking for something – commitment... I sound like a slut. A slag, you'd say, right? I remember that. My mother once called me a slag.' She laughed, high-pitched. They were ten feet from the door of my study.

'You're not a slag. I shouldn't have taken advantage.'

'It's just... Sometimes I feel like right now is just this thing all by itself. I know that life is a ... a chain ... that moments are all in some kind of line and they connect and they affect each other. But sometimes I can't feel that. I only feel now, just now, and that's all there is. And ... it was good, just now. I've done something terrible, but it felt good. There must be something very wrong with me.'

'It's all right,' he said, 'for two lonely people to comfort each other.'

'Thank you for that,' she said. 'Sometimes I think I'm the only lonely person. But I know that's not true.' Then 'No.' As if he'd leant in to kiss her. 'I have to go,' she said. The usual kerfuffle followed: footsteps, coat, where did she put down her bag when she came in?

At the door, he said, 'Miranda, today was good. It was good.'

'I don't think Gretchen would think so–'

'Gretchen doesn't care,' he said firmly. He said it loudly. 'She hasn't for some time.'

'Oh, I–'

'No, I don't mean... I don't make a habit of... This isn't something I've done before. I don't mean that she would know or approve. I mean she literally doesn't care. About anyone. Certainly not about me.'

I pictured her hand on the doorknob, ready to flee his change from gallant to vulnerable.

Indistinct murmurs at the door. The bells attached to the door jangled for the open, then for the shut. There was quiet, then his footsteps back across the rug, then up the stairs. Our shower rattles the whole plumbing system. He stayed under the spray for what seemed like a very long time.

I'd been so relieved to get married the first time. The day after university graduation, one of my lecturers asked me out. He said he'd been waiting a long time to be able to do that. I admired his self-control. We dated for a year, then got married. I'd been happy to get that done, as advised in one of my favourite poems, by Adrienne Simms:

What is it that I grieve for when I weep,
when I leave my hair untidy, lank and long,
when my clothes are unrefreshed by wash or brush,
when I thrust the curtains shut though day is young,

254

when my every former joy before me palls
and I stay inside of doors, inside of walls
where torrid tears escape my eyes in squalls?

What is it that I miss now that you've left
no half-remembered hope behind unpacked
now that you've taken with you much of me,
which of those things are they which I most lack?
Your company, your touch, your voice, your face?
Or, worse, my trust, my smug protected grace?
The peace that came upon the end of chase?

For when I had you I thought I was done
with girlish wishing-fors inside my mind.
No longer wanting 'someone', some grand 'he',
I had, in you, completed that sad grind
of hoping, longing, yearning from afar
for one to be my match, my prize, my star.
And being done I could, I'd hoped, do more...

I'd been happy to get that done, and then be free to do more. Sex was work: with whom, how far, what it means. Marriage would just be marriage. Marriage would just be.

When Nick discovered that my mother, or aunt, had saved a poem by the same author, I'd caught my breath. That is the synchronicity that drives me, that linkage with my mother, as if I'd been built out of real flesh torn off of her.

Everything had been fine with Dan, until four years in, when he found my birth control pills. He'd wanted children. I didn't. He'd been assuming we were just unlucky.

I started at Magdalene a year after they started

to let women in. I received a research fellowship. I'd not been to Cambridge before. The divorce was final.

Harry, a Cambridge native, had given up his law practise, and spent his savings on a trip to South America, where he'd fallen in love with birds. Then he'd returned and fallen in love with me. Then... Well, here we are.

He went straight out of the house after his shower, despite his wet hair and the cold. He'd duck inside the first chance he'd get. The pub on the corner. They don't serve food until evening. He hadn't even had breakfast. He'd be drunk before long.

I let my study door hang open behind me. I walked into a chair that Miranda must have moved to sit in. Harry hadn't moved it back. He used to be careful about keeping things predictably arranged for me.

I went upstairs. Past the guest room; I didn't open the door. Past the computer room. I carried on to the attic stairs. Up to the bird room. The noise was stifling: bird shrieks and whistles from all sides. Cold pushed in through the one screened, open window. Mountain songbirds don't need heat. The room smelt biological: dry, thick, doughy, dirty. I felt caught by it.

I felt for the back of his chair. It's a straight chair, no cushion. I hefted it up over my shoulder and brought it down against the top of the central aviary, by my hip. The chair bounced against the cage, and sprang back up over my head. Its next time down it bent bars. I pulled it up again, and

256

brought it down again. The metal made a piggish sound, squealing as the bars ruptured. The birds squealed too, suddenly fat, shrieking pigs instead of light, insubstantial twitterers. A sound came out of me too. I was a pig. I groaned from my stomach, groaned like I had a baby coming out of me. My mouth stretched open even as I squeezed the rest of myself together in a crouch on the floor. I was still for so long that two of the creatures alit on me. I'd broken the aviary door. They were free.

I opened the window. Why not? It was windy out. The birds would be swept away as if with a broom.

The still-caged birds on the right-hand wall chattered with increasing volume and their jumping rattled their cages, right next to my head. These weren't the canaries. These were the fosters.

I felt myself trembling. My fingers wriggled easily between wire bars, grabbing two cages at once. I pulled them down, tumbling the ones above them as well. I was all limbs: kicking in the cages below, waving the two in my fists. The shrieking inside them increased in fear and then died away, one by one.

There's a pattern in S.M. Madison's books. She starts with contentment: a heroine in an exotic location, in communion with the place itself. Conflict follows, shoving the heroine up against other people. There's friendship and sex, but always as action, never as the goal. The end brings equilibrium again; her triumph leads back to the pleasures of her original solitude, enhanced by comfort, or confidence, or money, or safety. But still, alone, and happy. Enchanted by place, not people.

The House of the Dead begins at the Mena House Hotel overlooking the Giza pyramids:

The walls huddled together. We were all tired, the walls and I. Only the shutters were awake, begging to be opened, energised by the hot daylight on the other side. I hadn't slept on the plane. It had been impossible, with knees and elbows on both sides, and actors racing across the soundless screen at the front of the cabin. So I slept here: cool sheets, hard mattress, small room. The edges of the fluffed pillow made a high, soft wall around my heavy head. This sleep was delicious, and decadent like an evening feast after Ramadan's daily fasting. I was fat with this sleep. Outside, camel hoof stomps pounded sand. Outside, the pyramids faded in the strong sun. Outside, flies landed on moist, open eyes. The shutters kept all of them out. The shutters kept me in. I'm grateful to shutters. The door should take lessons. It quivered from pounding fists. Someone was getting in. The shutters held out the whole waking world, but the door couldn't keep out one man.

It ends in the southern city of Aswan, on the famous terrace of the Old Cataract Hotel:

Yellow and blue make green; it's true everywhere. The blue Nile and yellow desert make green life between them, a fresh, narrow swathe along each side of the river. Servants make coffee. Tourists make crowds. Rolling blinds, thick and patterned like carpets from

*the marketplace, make the terrace cool in the hot day.
The natural shape of a huge stone elephant makes
visitors photograph the island across from the hotel.
Wind makes dozens of white sails pull feluccas across
the water. All of these are true every day.*

She follows this pattern over and over. In *Out of
the Sea*, her heroine begins in an aisle seat on an
aeroplane, desperate for the window view of the
Aegean below. Her fellow passengers, like the
one blocking her view, are impediments to her
experience. Over and over, this S.M. Madison
prizes place over people. Over and over, she finds
peace in hotels, not a home.

Her fictional beginnings and endings became a
comfort to me. Her abandonment of me hadn't
been personal. Her affair with solitude was the
most consuming in her life; that was clear.

There are moments for me too, where the
primacy of place, and relationship with the in-
animate, is suddenly overwhelmingly satisfying.

I may be like her. I may be meant to be alone.

Harry sometimes asked me for help with
crosswords. He'd read the clue and describe how
many spaces and any letters he already had. I
threw answers at him, but I hated it. I hate crosswords. They seem such a waste of time. I pelted
him with words of the correct length, and suggested anagrams and interpretations of the clue
fragments. I reasoned that if I could give him the
answer it would end. Maybe he couldn't tell I
hated it; he kept asking. He kept talking to me,
until I was sick from words, mentally batting
them away from my head. The words were like

birds flying at me, his birds, always birds. Their noise was constant.

The two in the cages in my hands were dead. I'd beaten the cages against the wall.

I put them down and descended the ladder-like steps. In the den I pulled up the website with taxi numbers and called one. I must always explain that I'm blind, or they won't bother to push the horn on arrival, no matter that I've asked.

I printed directions to Rose Cottage to give the driver.

I brushed my hair in the bathroom. I changed my clothes.

The taxi's horn was louder than I thought it would be. I jumped, I dropped my bag. It blasted again, twice, hard. My head throbbed. I opened the door.

I knew it was nothing personal. I could see that. She got rid of me because of who she is, because she doesn't share life with anyone. It wasn't me, it had nothing to do with me. I comforted myself with that truth, pulled it around me like a smooth sheet, a coarse blanket, and a soft cotton sleeve.

CHAPTER NINE

The driver offered to walk me to the door of Rose Cottage, but I wanted the transition to myself. I'd brought my cane. Its tip swished through the longish grass until it scraped on hard path for me to follow. I rapped on the front door.

I tried to age the young woman that I carried in my mind: the woman from the Brussels photographs, the woman who wrote about children with fear and disgust. I tried to age her, but I didn't know what had happened between now and then. So a young woman opened the door to me, wearing the green dress she'd worn to dinner in the Atomium restaurant in Brussels. She spoke with an old voice, but I saw the girl in the green dress. I suddenly remembered her perfume. I don't know if she still wore it, or if it was another of those sudden memories that had been jumping out in front of me since Nick changed everything.

'What do you want?' said the old-woman voice.

My voice answered, also old. Amazingly old. In my mind I was young too: in my twenties, out of college, not yet married. We looked alike to me. We both looked like the young woman at the Brussels Expo. Then we spoke, and the vision splintered apart. 'Why did you have me?' I asked.

This wasn't the plan. The plan had been to persuade, to defend; to prove who I was and accuse who she was. Then to ask at last: Why did you leave me? But the question asked itself, and it was more important than the one I'd intended.

She didn't answer, not quickly. She was examining me. Of course she would be; I'd skipped ahead. Then she retreated, leaving the door open. I followed her into a low-ceilinged room; I could feel the pressure of it, and the air smelt like the windows were closed. A fire made scratching noises in the corner. A jungle of furniture grew wild in the dry heat.

Her voice came from near the fire. She was faced

261

away from me, poking it, I think. There were rustling sounds there, like a family of mice had settled into the flames. 'Calling you Gretchen wasn't my idea. A nurse named you. I didn't have a name ready, so she called you after her dead sister. Her sister had died in a fire.' I'm sure the fire was consuming crumpled newspaper and hunks of wood. I'm sure of it, but I saw mice there. And a little girl. In a purple dress at Christmas.

'I despise waffling,' she said. 'I'd come to hate Susan Maud. I hated what in me was like her. Equivocating. I wrote a scene; it was vicious. I had her raped in it. Never mind that there wasn't even sex in any of the other books. I let it rip in this one. I held her down. I made her grow up. I was sick of her.

'It was unpublishable, of course. Unfinishable too. There wasn't anything I wanted left to do with her after that.

'When I found out what was inside me,' and here I thought she figuratively meant her viciousness towards Susan Maud, but it became clear that she literally meant me, 'I said, all right. I'm not going to pretend. I'm not going to apologise. So I stuck my belly out and everyone knew. I forced myself the way I'd forced Susan Maud: no more chance to go along and get along.'

I rocked.

'You can sit down,' she said abruptly. She waited, then spat: 'It's right behind you.' I stepped back gingerly, until my leg bumped the seat. I sat. She still stood. Her talking came from over me, still near the fire. Still far away.

'What did you come here for?' She sounded exasperated. I was suddenly a teenager, railing against a college rejection letter, or appealing punishment for breaking curfew. She was my mother. She was suddenly my mother. I cried.

Clink-clink, metal on brick. The fireplace poker. Impatience. I had to get myself together.

'She's dead. She died,' I said, almost saying 'my mother', but I'd been training myself out of that. I'd been straining them apart in my mind: one slipping through the sieve holes, the other caught. Two mothers.

'I don't know what you want me to do about it.' She still stood, cornered. My chair was between her and the door.

'I wanted to meet you,' I said. 'I remember you.' I wanted her to remember me. Something precious and wriggly; something that looked like her. 'You kept me,' I added. 'For three years...' Instead of feeling abandoned, I felt chosen. Three years! Almost a thousand days. She could have given me up from the hospital bed.

'I didn't write for three years,' she said. 'Not anything complete. Pieces. I wrote Gloria, if that means anything to you.' The only mother her books had ever had. The children who were sticky, who terrified the protagonist. I was the sticky one. I climbed. I clawed. I consumed. I was the monster: small, agile, full of tricks.

The fire sighed. Wind in the chimney. My face and hands were hot; the backs of my legs were cold. I looked at the fire, which was a jagged-edged blob to me.

Another memory shot up in me like a rocket.

263

The dog. The one she carried on the island trip. What had happened to the dog?

I must have asked out loud. She said, 'It ran away.'

It did. I remembered it now. I was only two, but I remembered. She put it down in the garden and opened the gate. It ran away.

'No one could take away the money,' she said. 'It was mine. It bypassed my parents. I threw it at you. I buried you in it. I hired that girl. She carried you around. She carried you. But you just kept reaching. Your arms were ... so horribly long.' She shivered. 'The girl wanted you. It was easy. Keeping you was hard.'

I shot up out of the chair. 'What about boarding school? You didn't need to ... to *sever*. Why didn't you just *stretch?*' Would weekends have been so horrible? Holidays?

'You!' she bellowed, from a deep, echoey space in her chest. 'You've never had a child, have you.' It was an accusation, not a question. She panted. She snorted.

Men have wanted to put one in me, but I've said no. I've never wanted one. I didn't know what she meant. What is there in having a child that makes boarding school not far enough? She must have really loved me, to have required such a vicious severance between us. You wouldn't use an axe to slice bread.

'Did she steal me away?' This was my last fantasy. That I'd been wanted by both of them, only one had been more clever and more determined.

'I left open the garden gate,' she said, with a

high, trickly laugh. That was the dog. Did she think the dog was here?

I shouted back, 'I'm not the dog! I'm the baby!'

Suddenly we were old. Brussels was suddenly fifty years ago, Brussels was suddenly another country. I was here, in a cramped, too-warm cottage, in England, sturdy England.

'It was a long time ago.' She exhaled.

'I was born in the summer, wasn't I?' I said. A Leo.

'It was hot,' she agreed.

'She changed my birthday. December. She celebrated my birthday in December. Was that when she took me?'

I laced my fingers, squeezing rings against knuckles.

'I'll tell you how it was,' she said at last.

'She was friends with Gin,' she explained. 'They double-dated. Gin thought she was all right, a nice girl. Bland, but Gin would like that. She liked being the one to sparkle.

'She was jealous of me. Of both of us, me and Gin, but of me especially, because of the baby.' She meant me. I was the baby. 'She fussed over me, and brought me cold drinks that horrible, hot August. She offered to be the nanny. That was fine with me. She liked going fun places; she didn't have the money herself. She liked being a better mother than I was. She liked that a lot. We were the pretty ones, Gin and I, and I was the brilliant one. And she was the ... good one. None of us minded that. We all got to be the best at something.

'There was only one time it got out of hand. In

265

Brussels. She chided me. The stairs multiplied, and you didn't want to walk. You wanted to be carried. You'd been eating chocolate, and expected to be picked up. I said no. She wanted to lift you, but then what? Go all the way back to the hotel for a change of dress? I said no. She wiped your hands on her slip. She pulled it out from under her skirt and wiped your dirty hands with it, streaking the white linen muddy. It was disgusting. I was embarrassed. I told her I'd said no. She kept going. She even spat on her hand to swab at the most stubborn marks. Then she lifted you and passed in front of me, preceding us up the stairs. You waved your damp palms around as they dried to tackiness.'

I didn't remember that, none of it. Not chocolate, not sticky hands, not those stairs, nor that time being carried, waving my arms.

'She was smug at the top of those stairs. The hem of her dress had a brown stain, and her slip had gone askew and was showing out the bottom. You put your hands into her hair and ran the fingers through. I looked away. It was...' Her breath shuddered. This was Gloria. This was where Gloria came from.

'I told her to take you back to the hotel and change. She left with you, but I saw her later. She looked the same. She hadn't changed. She hadn't even put you down. She was still carrying you, and you had ice cream, and it was falling onto the front of her dress. A white linen dress embroidered with pink and yellow flowers. The ice cream was vanilla, but its white was thick and yellowish and showed on the fabric. It showed as much as if it had been blood. She bore it like stigmata, the sacrifice of motherhood. She even tickled you to make you shake. Drops of melted ice cream festooned her frizzy hair like dew on a spider's web.

'She was claiming you, as if she'd swollen up around you and squeezed you out. I don't know why she didn't have a child if that's what she wanted so badly. It's not difficult to get a child. I know that. Anyone can have a child. Even my mother had children, and she despised my father. She fought him off. But there we were, Gin and I.'

I never saw her, the nanny, touch a man. Not my whole life. She never left me with a babysitter for a weekend away, or had a man over for dinner. She worked as a secretary at my school during the day. 'What was her name?' I asked suddenly. It had only just occurred to me that I didn't know.

'What do you mean?'

'She called herself Linda Paul. She pretended to be you. You let her be you. What was her real name?'

'I don't know,' she said. That answer just popped out of her: no caginess, no shame, no reaching deep into the bag to see if it might be in one of the corners. 'I don't remember. It was a long time ago.'

'She said my father...' I'd never said that phrase before: my father. Compared to my mother, it hadn't seemed important. '...was her – your – accountant. She had a picture of him, in white tie. At a party.'

'He certainly was not.' She snorted. 'Our family

267

accountant was a pig-bellied dirty old man.'

'Who was he, then?' I asked.

'A man in white tie at a party? Any one of thousands, I would imagine. It doesn't matter, you know. They don't matter.'

'I just want to know,' I explained carefully, wary of using up her willingness to speak, 'in case it turns out to matter.'

She told me. There were two men, both married academics, and she'd had affairs with both of them around that time. I asked their specialities, and was unsurprised that one was an expert in literature. The other was a botanist. Of course the kind of genetic assumption I so quickly leapt to is faulty; the botanist would be the first to chide me that humans are not so predictably determined by their parents as are plants.

'I'm a member of the English Faculty at Cambridge. Magdalene.' I remembered handing my mother picked violets once. But I couldn't remember which mother it had been.

'You don't take after me, then,' she said. She snorted. I think she was laughing at me. Had she been bad at school? Had she disliked teachers?

'You must know her name,' I pressed.

'She wanted to be Linda Paul. She wanted it, so I let her have it. Fine with me.'

'Why?' I asked. 'Why would anyone want to be you?'

She laughed and laughed. 'Thank God. I was getting sick of you. That pleading face. So avid.'

'Why was she so eager to replace her name?' I persisted.

'Why not? So was I. Being a child is such a horrible thing: powerless, stifled. She admired what I'd been able to do with money. Travel and such. She hadn't, she wanted to. You can't tell someone that what they want isn't what they think it must be. You can't tell them; you can only let them go ahead with it. They'll find out soon enough. She wanted the name and the baby and the money. I let her have them all. We each thought we got the better deal.'

'What did she give you?'

A satisfied sigh. 'Nothing. Nothing, nothing, nothing, nothing.'

Her book *Half Moon* contained a scene in which that word was repeated, just that way: an exultation. It was the comfort of the nothing that comes after something too loud, too close, too much. A good nothing, without a needy daughter and the uncomfortable role of socialite shaping her from the outside. She was water spilt at last out of an uncomfortable jar; that was in her book *Noisy Birds*. Water can't resist its container's shape; it's free only if it leaves the jar entirely. She got out by inviting infill from ... the nanny. 'You must know her name,' I begged. 'To give her the money ... there must have been papers...'

'The money was in your name.' Of course it was. It was a trust. It had always been mine. 'The trustee was Linda Paul. I gave her my National Insurance number. I didn't want it. The books... I'd written them. I was done with them. I was sick of them.'

'But you became Susan–'

'We fled together, Susan Maud and I. Having the whole world to choose from, I named myself

269

the character I'd created. I became my own, from start to finish. My own mother. My own child. I was completely my own at last.'

Is that what she'd wanted? Had that been her 'pear'? Something worth sacrificing everything else for…

'You sent the photos to our house in Brighton. I have them.' She'd reused a box of her own. Someone had mailed something to her, here on Cantelupe Road, and she'd put a sticker over that address to mail the photos to me.

'That was years ago.'

She could have thrown them away. 'Thank you for doing that.'

I hadn't thought I'd thank her. I thought I'd bellow at her. I thought I'd push and cry and never forgive. But I hadn't the energy. I was old. My mother wasn't a girl, and neither was I. We were old and tired.

Her telephone had an old-fashioned bell, a jarring one. It shrieked four times. Then a click, a whir. 'Leave a message.' Succinct.

'Hi, Susan, it's me, Melisma. I'm … having a rather bad day, actually. A shitty day. Roger and I are done. Really done this time – he's such a prick. I hate him. I'm sorry to be springing this on you, but, really, I need to get out of here. I'm taking all my stuff so he won't have any reason to come by bringing me this or that, "Oh, Mel, you forgot your soap," or whatever stupid excuse he'd make. There are some things I'd like to leave but I won't because he'll think I want a reason to come back, which I don't. I'll just take everything and chuck what's useless. Fucking men. I need to

270

pack everything up here and then I'll bring it over. I hope you don't mind. Bye.'

'My stepdaughter,' she said heavily, before the machine had even clicked off. She got up and keys jangled. 'You'll have to leave now.'

Her stepdaughter. Another daughter. She was running to her now, to comfort her, to commiserate about her awful ex-boyfriend, to protect her, perhaps to put ice on bruises if he was a beast, and encouragement on her ego if he was merely horrid. This was a real daughter. Not one from inside her, but one for whom she'd instantly leap to action. She put her coat on. Shoes. Closet door, rustles, heel clicks, the bang of a handbag hitting the wall as she bent over to ... tie laces? Slip a finger between the back of her foot and tight shoe leather?

'You'll have to go now,' she repeated. I remained in my chair. I was pinned there by the image. There must be photos of her in this room, lovingly framed. Hundreds of them, interspersed with lit candles. Scrapbooks too. Newspaper items, degree certificates. That's what so crowded the room. That's why there was only one seat in the lounge. It was filled with shelves and stacks and icons and altars dedicated to this one creature, this real daughter. This horribly-named creature. Melisma? Linda hadn't named her. But she'd taken to her. I know that because of how she was running now, running to rescue her.

Together they'd carry boxes from flat to car. Clothes, books, bathroom things, kitchen things, art, photographs. Whatever had intertwined to make Melisma a couple with that rat, now uncoupled. Linda would make her tea here later, or get drunk with her, if she was that sort of mother. That sort of best-friend mother. Or perhaps she was a stern mother, a pull-yourself-together mother: Get a better job and stop throwing yourself at men who aren't worthy of you.

I couldn't match this with the mother I thought I'd figured out: defensive of her solitude to the point of terror. But here she was. The door was open. Melisma had phoned and everything in her jumped to attention.

Whatever this Melisma had done – been sighted, been of an independent age, been good and beautiful – she'd won. She'd swooped in and won. Now Linda was swooping to her. Rescue, rescue, with a metaphorical siren on top of her car.

I realised that I'd used Aunt Ginny's image for Melisma in my mind. Pretty Aunt Ginny, so like Linda, but a little more forward, a little more willing to be crazy in public. I had to ask: 'Did Aunt Ginny die on a boat? She' – the nanny-mother–' told me Gin died on a boat...'

'Gin married one of those Italian princes. I suppose she's still there. In a villa.'

That's good for Aunt Ginny. I felt such relief. Gin alive, and married. Probably skiing and sunbathing, and having affairs. She'd be old now, but still Gin. Heavy with jewellery and tight in a girdle, to lift and squeeze her body into remembered youth. I was suddenly happy, so happy. I think I was hysterical. I think I was making some noise. Linda shouted at me to be quiet and get out.

I stood in the garden. Linda got into her car. The door slammed but the engine did not immediately start. Was she waiting for me to go? I held my mobile up to my ear, to show her that things were in hand. I wouldn't be here when she and the real daughter returned.

I kept the phone pressed to my ear for show, mouthing 'Everything's fine, everything's fine, everything's fine...' At last the car pulled away.

The garden seemed enormous to me, probably larger than it really was. Everything seemed stretched out, as if there were an impossible distance between me and the road. I could dial anyone, anyone in the world. Gin? Harry? God? I could dial anyone. What would I say to my first husband? What would I say to my old thesis supervisor? What would I say to Nick?

That name was sudden in my mind, and stabbing. Nick. He was just a child. I'd bellowed at him like he was some monstrous adult, a stand-in for those who'd let me down. I'd scared him off. I'd scared him, perhaps, to death.

For a moment it was as if I might find him in the bushes there, or the flowerbed, there. Hiding, relieved to see me, eager to emerge. I wanted to hold out my hands to him, and raise him to standing. I think that was the first maternal instinct of my life. I think that was the first moment of not being the child myself.

I dialled Harry. The ringing went on forever. Then, our machine. He would still be at the pub. 'Harry,' I said. 'Harry, I'm so sorry. I'm sorry. I've been horrible. Harry. I'm at this place. Rose Cottage. The directions are on the computer. I need a lift. I'll wait for you to come. I'll wait for you. Please come. I want to... I want to change everything. I want to be different. I want to ... throw things away, and move house, and start something new. With you. We should start new together. I know what happened today. I understand it. I don't care about it. I don't care. I'm going to get rid of the money, Harry.' This decision surprised me to hear coming out of myself, but it was right. It was necessary. 'I don't want it any more. I don't want anything from her. We can put it all to charity. Tomorrow. Quickly. I want it gone. Oh, God–' I remembered. 'Oh, God, your birds, Harry. I'm sorry. Oh, God–' But the machine had clicked off. A sixty-second limit.

He would never forgive me. It was impossible. When I heard the car an hour later, his car, I knew there was rage inside. That's all it could possibly be; I'd waited for it. I walked towards the road; I stood on the last of the lawn before the dirt track. The headlamps angled to face me. I could see them, like the bright lights of the Centre for Mathematics. I regretted never having seen his face.

The inevitable acceleration hummed rather than shrieked. I thought about all the times in my life that that had been true: things that ought to rate a fanfare, or applause, some volume, some notice, but happen quietly, too quietly, without the yelling and pointing they deserve.

The bumper hit me lower than I expected, around the knees. I'd illogically expected more of a punch in the stomach. My legs bent the wrong way, like deer legs, bent backwards. But instead

274

of crumbling, I sailed.

This too stretched. My arc blazed long. At the top of it, my head opened up like a net, catching in it old memories and random thoughts from the air. I knew. Suddenly I knew everything.

Her name was Eleanor. That was certain, and clear. Eleanor. I'd called her that sometimes. Sometimes, even in Brussels, I'd called her Mummy.

Eleanor borrowed Gin's perfume. Eleanor wore Linda's clothes. She was soft-skinned but hard-boned; she stood up to Linda about me. She made rabbit shadows with her hands. She let me sit on her lap on the train to see out the window. She gave me sips from her cup. She loved me. She worshipped Linda.

She'd been pretty to me, in her gift clothes and borrowed cosmetics. Eleanor had been pretty to me. But Linda had been astonishing to both of us.

One night, Linda had modelled dresses for us. She was dressing for an evening out. I sat on Eleanor's lap, and we clapped and cheered at each successive outfit. There was one that Eleanor had particularly admired: It was girlish, layers of skirt and tight on top. Linda stepped out of it and tossed it to Eleanor. 'Try it on,' she said. 'I don't like it any more.' Eleanor undressed, curling herself up modestly, holding the dress up so its skirt made an impromptu curtain. It fit in size but not in shape. The waist stretched too tight, the bust sagged. She looked terrified in it. Linda said, 'It looks good.' Eleanor puffed up; the pride in her risen chest almost made it fit.

275

The doorbell rang, and Linda, in just a slip, said, 'I'm too tired to go out with him. You go.' Eleanor cowered. She shook her head, hard.

Linda said, 'Tell him to go away, then.' She went into the bedroom and closed the door. The doorbell chimed on. It was a nice doorbell, not one of those harsh ones. It had a ring, a real ring. I sang along with the tune as it repeated, and swung my short legs back and forth under my chair.

Eleanor said, 'Gretchen, you tell him. Tell him I can't go.' Then she locked herself in the bathroom.

I stayed in my chair. The bell sang me songs. Then it stopped. Later, Eleanor came out. She still had the dress on.

She read to me from a storybook illustrated by Marc Chagall. I was still young enough to see. I put my face right up to those pictures. His happiest people always float in the air. Goats too. Happy people, floating goats.

Eleanor loved books. She made me love them too; it was inevitable that anyone who lived in our house would become an expert in literature, whether they wanted to be or not. She loved adventure in books. She loved men in books. She was in awe of people who created books the way religious people are in awe of God.

Chagall contained happiness like that: colour and captured motion, tethered by a frame or windowpane. His figures aren't limited to feeling happiness inside; they float and fly, arc through the sky. And their goats fly with them.

The downward half of my arc sped up, rushing me towards the rutted road. I passed a goat. I trailed colour. Suddenly I was in the Fitzwilliam Museum, and the paintings were all Chagalls, from that storybook. Eleanor was there. Wearing that dress.

Part Five

LIV

CHAPTER TEN

Nick became a calendar.

Wednesday December second became: The Day Before Nick Was Gone.

I carried around his gloves most of the day; I finally got a chance to hand them over to him at Gretchen's house. Then Gretchen and I had a fight, and he stayed to fix it. He was gallant. I had to go, and he was doing something else later. It was all, 'See you tomorrow!'

Then, tomorrow, Nick was gone. That was Thursday, which became Day One, but we didn't know that yet.

It was the choir dinner. I knew he'd be there. It was black tie, not academic gowns. I had second-hand dresses I'd gotten cheap from the charity shops on Burleigh Street. Old May Ball dresses from last year. That's where I shopped with Polly when we were friends. Then we'd eat at the café of the public library, outside on the high-up deck: cheap baked potatoes, cups of tap water, and the tower cranes building the Grand Arcade swinging not too far overhead. We'd read our borrowed books. It had been enough. Someone's old clothes, borrowed books, and cheap potatoes. It was very *La Bohème*, a starving-student sort of thing. It was fun. I didn't mind.

But there's a boutique on Magdalene Street, just by the entrance to college. They have shoes and purses, and dresses. Not Cinderella-type fuss, just real modern, feminine dresses, in my face, every day.

There were two other customers in the shop: a tiny elderly lady indulging in a really great pair of shoes, and another Magdalene student whom I'd seen around. I knew she had money. She was buying three dresses and a purse. I could tell from the conversation that she knew the sales clerk.

I waited for her to leave. Then I asked the clerk, who had beautiful straight blonde hair, if she had the dress in the window to fit me. She took a long time to consider, and all I could think was: She'd fit into the bitty one in the window. Finally she went in the back and there was one in a normal, human size for me. I tried it on behind a curtain. The dress was knee-length and white, with a splash of red poppies clustered at the hem. The top was ruched around my chest, with smaller flowers scattered there. A skinny red ribbon traced the waist. I'd never had on anything so pretty.

I had to get shoes as well.

I keep my cards in a little zipper thing that fits in my pocket: credit card, ATM, public library, student ID. The zipper thing is only just a little bigger than the cards themselves, and it kind of holds on to them when I try to pull one out. The bag and I had a little fight about the credit card. In the end I snapped the zipper pull and now it doesn't close any more.

I might have stopped myself. I could have stopped somewhere between the dressing room and punching in my PIN on the little machine. I needed to make it through to Christmas, when my dad would pay tuition and top up my living expenses again. But when my own purse tried to stop me I just got defensive. I'm not going to let a stupid bag tell me what to do.

The price came in just three pounds under my limit.

I wouldn't be able to return the shoes; they would show scuffs. But I'd return the dress. So long as I was careful with it, I could return the dress, saying I hadn't used it, and get the money back.

After all that, Nick didn't come to the dinner.

It was held at Magdalene, with the usual formality. All the men looked alike, and the women looked different: different hems, different colours, different hairstyles. Except for the girl I'd seen in the shop, who was wearing the same dress that I was. Poppies on white.

I was angry. Nick was supposed to be there. Instead – what? I didn't even think of him being with Polly. I assumed him to be at some sort of family event, something to do with his sister, or maybe something with the Chanders. Some performance or presentation at their school. Because he'd spent his whole life going to dinners like this. They weren't special to him, so he had no respect that they were special to some people.

I was so angry I couldn't eat. I didn't want to risk dropping anything on the dress anyway. Dinner was roast beef. Even one drip would force me to keep the dress. I was careful with the wine, careful with the water even. I was between someone named Mark and another guy. Mark asked me if

I'd ever sung Scarlatti's 'Stabat Mater,' which I hadn't. He said it had more than thirty-part harmony. I told him he was full of shit. The girl on his other side said it does have that many parts, and what was my problem? I was really mad from Nick being so cavalier about where he bothers to show up, so I told her to fuck off. And she said, 'How very American of you.' Five or six people laughed at that. The girl who said it wasn't even English; she was Canadian. I wanted to leave but everyone would have looked at me walk out.

I picked up my wine glass, which was still full because I'd been avoiding it. Mark reached for his water at the same time, and our arms knocked lightly. If my glass hadn't been full, it wouldn't have been any big deal. But the wine was close to the top and sloshed over the side. Just one plop of it, but it hit my plate with momentum enough to send a drop sliding up over the edge. It hit my lap, on the linen napkin there, which I grabbed up quickly, to keep the purple from soaking through onto the dress. That's when Mark's water spilt onto the dress instead. Clear water, but any wet at all would ruin the fabric. It could be dry-cleaned away maybe, but not enough to make it look like it had never been worn. Two hundred and eighty-nine pounds. I gasped. Mark apologised, but the girl on his other side covered a laugh.

I was too angry to move, and if I swore again that would just set off the Canadian girl. 'It doesn't matter,' I said. 'It doesn't matter.' I thought, *It's Nick who should be apologising.* And, *It's Polly who would be laughing, isn't it?*

There was nothing Mark could do; it's not like

he could dab at my crotch with his table napkin. He stopped saying sorry eventually. Now I really couldn't get up; it would have looked like I peed myself. The guy on my other side finally said something to me. He said, 'These things go on forever.' What did he mean? Did he kindly mean my skirt would dry into a wrinkled mess before I'd have to get up? Did he obnoxiously mean that he hated being stuck next to me and my problems?

None of it even mattered. The hard rains had come. When I stepped outside, the dress got soaked.

We found out that Nick was gone on Day Two, which suddenly made sense of him missing the dinner. I heard it from the porter. I was worried, but in a light way, thinking he'd gotten a flat tyre on his bicycle or had lost track of time in the library stacks. I went to tell Polly, who already knew.

Polly had been interviewed by the police.

I had to call them myself to tell them I was Nick's friend too. This was Saturday, Day Three. The man said he was glad I'd called and that I was on his list, which was bullshit. He just said that to cover up that he didn't think I was much of anything to Nick. I made an appointment to go down to the Parkside police station, to tell them everything that had happened and let them decide who the girlfriend was.

'Hi,' said the policewoman. Polly had talked to a man. 'Thanks for coming in. You're at Magdalene?' I nodded. 'The porters tell me there was a little party Tuesday evening.'

'Oh, totally,' I agreed. 'I saw Nick collecting his mail and invited him over. He needed a break.'

'Was there any alcohol at this party?'

'Just some beer. I think he only had one.' He wasn't drunk, if that's what she was implying. He didn't need to be drunk to do what we did.

'When did he leave?'

'He stayed in my room for a while.' I smiled.

'How long is a while?'

'I guess half an hour.' *Long enough*, is what I meant. 'He had to see his supervisor.' It was important to explain why he hadn't stayed over.

'Richard Keene? No, he didn't.'

'What?'

'We've spoken with Dr Keene. They had no interaction on Tuesday night.'

I know that Nick saw him. He went around to O building and didn't come out.

'Why would Dr Keene lie?' I asked.

She leant back. 'Why do *you* think Dr Keene would lie?'

I held on to the seat of my chair with both hands.

'I guess he wasn't in. But Nick went to see him.' And didn't come out from around the front of the building for at least forty minutes. After forty minutes I went to bed.

'We'll investigate the discrepancy,' she said. 'Did Nick go to a lot of parties?'

'I don't know.' Maybe he did. Maybe this was a normal thing for him. Maybe lots of girls put their faces there.

'What did you and he do for half an hour?'

286

She was asking everything backward. She was supposed to have asked that before she told me that Nick hadn't really gone to see Dr Keene.

'Like, we talked and stuff. About ... school.' I shook my head. That was stupid. Why would we talk about school? But she believed me. She didn't even try to get it out of me that we hadn't talked at all.

'Do you know Polly Bailey? Was she at this party?'

'No!' I said.

I let them take my fingerprints, like they were doing with everyone who knew him well. 'For elimination purposes,' this policewoman said. That's right; someone had trashed his room.

My prints wouldn't be there. I'd never been in his room. Whenever I went over to the Chanders' house, we'd sat in the kitchen. I'd never even been upstairs.

By the time I learnt about Polly being sick in Nick's office – and when – it wasn't really a surprise at all.

Since he'd lied about needing to see Dr Keene, and lied about liking me, and lied about whether I'd done it right and if it felt good and if I mattered, maybe he'd lied about everything. Maybe he hadn't tried to smooth anything over with Gretchen. Maybe, instead of calming down her freak-out over the handwriting thing, he'd urged her on, picking apart my index line by line...

Never mind. I had to try. I had to get it done. I had to get paid.

She wasn't even in. And Harry was away for a

bird competition, which was actually kind of perfect. I have my own key for just this kind of situation, and I thought, *Great, no distractions.* But Gretchen had moved the photos. The whole box had been put away somewhere. Maybe she'd taken them someplace to get scanned or preserved, but I thought it was really rude to not have told me.

I'd set aside two hours to be there. I turned on the computer. What else was I supposed to do? It's not like she'd left me the ability to do my stupid job. I looked at some sites that I like and just felt really frustrated. Then I flipped through her bookmarks a little. Why not?

Polly thinks it's wrong that I looked at what was on Gretchen's computer sometimes, but I didn't even do it on purpose. It *talked* to me and that's literal. The first time it happened I freaked out. But then I got used to it, and it was like having a conversation. I'd press buttons and it would say stuff. It was funny.

One time when Gretchen had been using the computer, and I waited my turn out in the hall, I'd heard her. I wasn't really paying attention, but I noticed it spell out 'brussels1958'. I thought that was funny. I realised it was her password. It recited a series of numbers too. It was the password to her bank account. It's just funny to pay attention to stuff like that. One time I watched a friend of mine dial her locker combination and freaked her out for weeks after by putting stuff in there. Nothing mean, just funny, like stupid toys from the dollar store. It just makes sense to pay attention in life.

So, when I was alone in Gretchen's house, with

absolutely nothing to do – which wasn't my fault – I logged in. I just wanted to see how much she had. The checking account was normal; the investment account was enormous. Big to me anyway. Not like what had been kicking around Silicon Valley when I was a teenager, but still, it was a lot.

The thing is, I needed money for things, stupid things. Shampoo and food, stuff that I would have charged if I hadn't hit my limit. It's not like I could make it to Christmas. I was supposed to get a cheque today, and even then it would take time to clear. Now I'd have to wait even longer.

Since they had so much, it didn't seem any big deal to take a little from the cash in the top drawer. Just three twenties. Queen Elizabeth looked at me all judgmental until I crinkled her into my pocket.

Polly's mother was arrested on Day Seven. I was back at Gretchen's house one last time, trying to not have a fight with her. 'What do you mean you told Nick to "dispose" of them? What does that even mean?' I'd come one last time to try to finish with the photos, and they were gone. Just gone. She'd gotten rid of them.

'I'm suspending the project. You may return the house key. I'll get you your cheque. Harry!'

He was in the kitchen. His hands were covered with flour.

'What did Nick do with them?' I demanded. 'You can't just–'

That's when the doorbell rang. Polly was hysterical, which isn't really surprising. We knew by then how she'd reacted to Nick touching her.

Who knew how she'd cope with anything else?

Everyone forgot about my cheque. Only Polly mattered.

They forgot about my key too.

'It's one thing to use a girl because you're just so in the moment overwhelmed by her. It's something else to make her finish someone else's job. After that, he was gone. And good, you know? Why would I want him to come back?' I told Dr Keene everything, not about money but about Nick, to shock him.

He winced, then looked over my shoulder, as if the 'Building Stones of Britain' were really, really interesting. We were in the basement gathering area under the Sedgwick Museum. My art stuff was spread out over utilitarian tables. The walls were covered with rock samples, every one a slightly different colour. They were apparently a lot more interesting than me.

I'd volunteered to make models for a special exhibit at the Sedgwick: 'Creatures of the Burgess Shale'. Apparently the Cambrian period, which was way before dinosaurs, had far weirder creatures than most people know. The students who'd studied these fossils in the seventies had given them hilarious names, like *hallucigenia*. I love the seventies. I would have looked awesome with Farrah Fawcett hair. I have this friend who's fat who spends all her weekends at Renaissance Faires because the dresses look good on her. I think if I could be an original Charlie's Angel on weekends, I'd do it.

It felt good to be making art again, not just talking about it. I was making these outsized abstractions of these creatures that were wacky in the first place. No one knows what colour any of these things were, so I was free to really go for it. They needed to be paper pop-outs so kids could make their own spiky *hallucigenia*, or *marrella*, which is like a shrimp wearing elaborate headgear, or *wiwaxia*, which looks like Mercury's winged helmet. With glue and pom-poms and feathers too. Anything to make the kids like science.

I've thought about majoring in science. Not stopping making art, but coming at it from knowing more about life. Because experience is the foundation for art, right? So I'm tempted, and then I think, *What's the point of this school thing at all? Why not be like Gauguin and have an adventure?*

That's the kind of thing I said to Dr Keene, just to see if I could set him off. It was Day Ten, the rains had stopped, and the police were dredging the Cam. He'd come to take a look at my models, probably just to have something else to think about, and we ended up talking. But he didn't rise up in defence of formal education and good grades. He just nodded absently. So I told him everything about Nick and me.

He did that thing of freezing his face to not show any reaction. A person only does that if their real reaction is something they'd be embarrassed by, right? He's known Nick for longer than I have, so maybe it's happened before. Maybe he knows Nick is a dog. Isn't that the point of his religion? Knowing we're messed up, and just accepting that as inevitable? So he acted weary about it, but not surprised. What he said, though,

291

was 'I don't think you should be telling me this.'

'Why?' I said. I said it sharply, because that kind of prissiness about life is just what I'm trying to get away from. 'Why not tell you about this? You mean it's okay for Nick to be this way, just not okay to talk about it? Or it would have been okay, except Nick is gone and his victimhood trumps mine?' We were all imagining Nick bloated and grey from drowning.

'Or do you mean...' I was attacking him at this point, hurling words. 'Do you mean that I shouldn't tell you this because you're a man and I'm a woman and we shouldn't talk about S-E-X? Even about other people? Because I didn't think a biologist would be all squeamish about that; isn't that what you study all day long?' Which is absolutely true: the drive for sex, and the likelihood of sex and the success of sex, is the whole process of natural selection.

'So, like, isn't this exactly the point? My traits won't be carried on to the next generation because it's not like someone's going to fuck me. So, like, my belligerence and insecurity are going to die out. And that's good, right? And good manners and restraint are going to be passed on by people like Polly, and people like you.' I knew he was getting married. To a doctor, a medical doctor.

You have to specify 'medical doctor' here because Cambridge is stuffed with the other kind. Yelling 'Is there a doctor in the house?' would get you Ph.D. computer scientists and engineers and geomorphologists and historians. It wouldn't get you anyone practical. It wouldn't get you anyone

292

who knows how to apply a fucking Band-Aid.

I cried but I didn't stop working, because I had said I would make the models. I do what I say I'll do.

'I think it's a wonder,' he said, sighing, 'that any of us get past age twenty at all.'

I stabbed little spiny bits all over *hallucigenia*. I'd painted them purple.

'Why?' I challenged him. 'What happened to you at twenty?' If he was going to be all I-know-what-you're-going-through, I wanted to make him spell it out.

'That's the year my brother decided he hates me.'

'Poor you.' Stab, stab, stab. 'Was it over some girl?'

'Oh, no. He came to hate me over a woman a few years later. But the first time he hated me was when he joined the University. I was already here. We were in different colleges, different departments. We were completely different – nothing to have rivalry over.'

'So, what?' I pushed.

He shook his head. 'That's just it. There was no event, nothing to blame. He just realised he hates me. I've never been able to fix that.'

His forlorn gravity was overwhelming. It wasn't fair. Everyone felt sorry for Polly, and for Nick, and now I was supposed to pity Dr Keene for a bad brother. No matter how bad I felt, it was never bad enough to rate. It's like everyone just says, 'No big deal. It could be worse. Wake me when it's worse.' I never measure up, even in failure.

'Well, I wish my brother hated me. He liked me

way too much. He raped me when I was thirteen.' I don't even have a brother, but I spewed an eruption of tears. 'He said I was beautiful. I was so pretty he couldn't not do it, he said. It went on for, like, a year. Then my father found out and threw Will out. He still writes me letters. If my dad found out, he'd kill Will.' Then I remembered that Will is Polly's brother. But I couldn't change it once I'd said it.

I wasn't really in the floral gallery when the vases broke, like I told Polly. I hadn't been in the museum at all when it happened. But it had been important to make her understand that moment. I told it to her in a way that would make her understand. I had to make Dr Keene understand, and if he needed a lie to get it, I'd give it to him.

The whole point of cubism is to capture more than one side or one moment. Cubists tried to get a deeper accuracy than photographic representation by including many moments and many sides at once. It doesn't look literally, physically real. But it is real. It's the real that includes more than one moment, more than one viewpoint, more than just the physical. It's a truer real.

What I say may seem a mess, like a cubist painting, but that's only because it's even truer. It's how I really feel. It's what what's happened has done to me. That's truer than just what literally happened.

I finally got the look. I got it. His mouth opened and his eyes didn't blink. 'I'm so sorry,' he said. He said it with full attention. I feel like there hasn't been full attention from anyone in Cambridge, even from Nick when I was on my knees.

I leant forward. I filled his field of vision. I had to keep myself bigger in perspective to him than the fucking rainbow of British building stones.

'I know I shouldn't let him write to me. I don't write back. But I do read the letters. He's my brother, y'know?'

'Perhaps you ought to tell the authorities in your home state–'

'Oh, no, no, it's not like that. He's not writing things like that. It's over. He wants me to know how sorry he is. He writes to say that he's sorry. He has a girlfriend too. He saw a therapist and he's got a girlfriend. Everything's cool.'

'Have you talked to anyone professional?' he asked.

'I talk it out with my friends. That's good enough for me. Like talking it out with you right now. It's good. Thanks.' I smiled. He was hooked. I leant back in my chair. I looked down shyly. Then he ruined it.

'Can I call someone?' he asked. 'You're friends with Polly, I could see if she can come around...'

I shook my head back and forth. 'No. No, Polly and I aren't really friends right now. You know,' I said, bringing it back to Nick.

He nodded, and looked away. Everything flowed back into place again, inexorable: This was the day they were dredging the Cam. Only Nick mattered today. And Polly, with both parents in jail. It had been years since my brother had raped me, right? It had been more than a week since Nick treated me like a whore. God, like ten whole days.

'Let me tidy this up,' Keene offered, about my

295

art supplies. Isn't that just his whole drive in life.

'And me do what? Go back to my room and feel sorry for myself? Or join a volleyball game on Parker's Piece and pretend it's all good? It's not.' I bounced my giant paper *hallucigenia* from hand to hand.

Dr Keene looked past me. Then Peter strode in, Nick's friend. 'Richard,' he boomed out. 'Richard, it's done. They didn't find him.'

Dr Keene closed his eyes and it was like his body melted a little. All the tension that had been holding him up slipped away. He and Peter clasped hands. The testosterone in the gesture made me laugh. Keene looked at me strangely.

Peter said to me, 'He's not drowned. He's not drowned.' He didn't say 'He's not dead,' because by that time we couldn't be sure he wasn't, some way or other. But, at least, there would be no body today.

Isn't that a kick when that's the best you can say about a day? That there isn't a corpse in it, at least as far as you know? There's no certain corpse. It's like... Schrödinger's corpse. Until we see it, it isn't really dead. I laughed again.

'Peter...' Keene started, and in his pause I could tell he wondered about the wisdom of fobbing me off on a man with Peter's reputation, what with me in such a vulnerable state. But he wanted to get rid of me. That was obvious. Teacher-student, etc. There was potential for a fabricated harassment accusation if things got too personal and he had to be stern.

'I'm all right,' I said, standing up. 'I'm all right.' I said it without making eye contact, so he knew to keep worrying. 'I'm going to go down to the river,' I said. 'Now we can enjoy it again, right?'

I can only assume Keene gave some kind of nod or signal to Peter to follow me. It's not like he would bother with me otherwise.

'How are you holding up?' he said, keeping pace beside me, awkwardly matching his longer stride to mine. The three tower cranes building the Grand Arcade at the end of the road dominated the view. Each was a huge, latticed capital T. One swung around at the command of a little man in the driver's seat underneath. It wound up a cord to pull a massive load up over the tops of all the aged college buildings. It was making shops.

'They're beautiful,' I said. It had been pouring since Nick left, but today the sun was out, shining on the cranes. 'I'll miss them when they're done.' I would, really. They're so tall, so aggressively enormous, and perfectly balanced. The completed Grand Arcade won't be able to live up to them when they go.

'What, the cranes?' He sounded like I was crazy.

'Whatever,' I said, turning the opposite direction, to walk toward Trumpington Street instead.

'No, wait,' he said, and that's how I was sure this was Keene's idea. Peter has better things to do than chase me.

'Look, you may not want to believe this,' I said, 'Nick being your best friend and all. But he raped me. Just before he disappeared. I didn't have anything to do with him going, but I do know that I wouldn't care if he were in the Cam, because he'd deserve it. You can ask around at Magdalene. We were at a staircase party together, after Polly left his office. I guess he wasn't finished, you know? He asked if he could crash in my room, you know, from drinking too much. He acted like he needed to crash. But when we got there, he wasn't tired at all, I guess. He was plenty able to do what he wanted to do. That's what I think of your best friend.'

I'm not sure why I went with that. It was completely different from what I'd told Keene, but it's not like Keene would compare notes with Peter. It's not like anyone even listens, right?

Peter put his hand through his hair. He scanned whatever was behind me, same as Keene. 'Nick?' He put his hands on his hips and puffed out the word, as if winded from a long jog. He was so ridiculous I almost lost it and started laughing. 'Jesus, Liv–'

'Yes: Nick. I haven't told anyone because it would just make the police think I had something to do with him being gone. Which I don't. It may have been karma that got him for it, but not me.'

'Jesus,' he said again. 'Nick?'

Everyone acts so surprised that Nick would do anything wrong. Is what I was saying that much different from what he really did do?

'I don't want to ruin things for his family,' I explained nobly. 'He has a sister. I don't want to ruin him for her, at least, not unless he comes home. But if they have to grieve I'm going to let them have it nicely. When my dad died, everyone said only nice things about him. I appreciated that.'

'I don't really know what to do with this...' he said, holding his palms up.

298

'There isn't anything to do.' I shrugged. 'These things happen.'

'Maybe you should talk to Polly.'

I pushed him in the chest. 'What the fuck does Polly have to do with this? Why does everyone think of Polly?'

'I'm just saying she's been through a lot herself, maybe she would understand–'

'What the fuck has she been through? As far as I see it, she's been treated like a princess ever since she revealed her traumatic, scandalous past. Jeez, I gotta get me some of that, right? Because everyone's tiptoeing around her, all solicitous, all whatever-you-say, whatever-you-need. And anything she wants to be is okay, all of a sudden okay. If she wants to work, she's being strong. If she wants to hide away, she's "taking care of herself". And if she wants to act like a jackass and joke around like nothing's wrong, then she needs her space, because we all have to breathe, right? And it's all okay. If she turned around and went with some guy we'd all be proud of her for "healing", right, instead of thinking, "That's awfully quick..." – which is what it would deserve. And if she never goes with a guy again, it's not because she's a coward, or stuck, or just stupid, but something profound. Something that has nothing to do with her choices, but all to do with life whipping her around. And that's bullshit. We make like her dad made her in that moment, made in her the right to anger, and the right to grief, and the right to fear and frigidity. But I'll tell you – all that stuff is already in everybody. Maybe her dad kicked it up a notch, okay, but it's not like what he did invented

299

anything inside her. But when she acts fucked-up it makes people want to protect her, and when I act fucked-up it scares people away.' He had stepped back. We were still on the street, just down from the pedestrian crossing. Periodic clusters of people waiting for the green light had heard parts of what I said, making Peter's eyes shift from side to side, embarrassed.

One of the people waiting to cross the street was Polly.

Tears cut streaks down her face. 'Liv?' she said, incredulous, before taking off back toward Trumpington Street.

'Shit, Liv,' said Peter. Acting out my entire point, he left me and ran after her.

I hadn't told Dr Keene or Peter – or anyone – about the letter from my dad.

After the divorce, Dad married someone else and had a baby. I'd told him not to do that. I don't care who he's married to but I told him not to have a baby. I remember this one time that I had a friend over, this was when Dad and Mom were still married, I had a friend over, and he said: 'Excuse me, sweetheart...' as he passed by her to get to the patio. My head had snapped up. Because he always called me 'sweetheart'. That was what he called me. But he used it for this stranger to him, just because she was a girl. I learnt a lot about my dad. I learnt that what I thought was a special name was just really the way he talks to girls. It's just that I was usually the only one around, so I'd thought it was mine. I learnt a lot about my dad. So I knew what would happen if he had another baby.

It was a girl too.

They named her Viola, to go with my name. From *Twelfth Night*. I got here for college before they could make me do any babysitting. The baby was all right, I guess. But then Dad wrote me this letter.

Viola wasn't talking when I left, which was normal. She was a baby. But I guess she never got very good. So now he says she needs a speech therapist, and also to attend a special preschool, for 'special' kids. Which is fine. She'll do fine. But then he said that for him to pay for it, I'd have to come back to California, into the state system. And live with Mom.

That letter had come yesterday, the day before they dredged the Cam, so excuse me if Nick wasn't the first thing on my mind.

There is nothing wrong with UC Berkeley or wherever but there is a lot wrong with living at home. And a lot wrong with having your college money go to a toddler's preschool. There's no way I was going to go with Mom to family therapy, and spend my life shopping at strip malls and stuck in endless traffic. There's nothing aesthetic or bearable about any of it.

You'll notice he hadn't asked me to live with him. I wouldn't, but he was supposed to ask.

I'd first started painting because I liked being in charge of something, some small thing: this square of canvas. I liked being able to make it whatever I think it ought to be. And beautiful – I could make something beautiful. It could hang in a world of chain restaurants and giant parking lots and roads as wide as the Mississippi and clogged to a standstill, but be, itself, beautiful. I did it out of desperation.

Now, across the ocean, I'm feeling for the first time like I'm not gasping for beauty any more. It's here. I've found my inspiration here, and, instead of rebelling against my surroundings, I'm being fed by them.

He wanted to take that away from me.

Do you know that the British students pay hardly any tuition? Same for the Europeans. But everyone else really has to cough it up.

And do you know how Polly manages being a foreigner here, with her dad in prison? Her whole town has taken up a collection for her tuition and living expenses.

Do you see the difference? I can't get money out of my dad, and she gets money out of everyone she's ever known. People like to take care of her. It's that weak thing she has going on. I'm too strong. I come off that way. People think I don't need, and when I reveal that I do, like with Nick, when I make myself vulnerable, it freaks people out. It doesn't fit with what they've thought about me.

People want consistency over depth, which is bullshit.

My first plan didn't have any stealing in it at all. I wasn't going to be able to continue at Cambridge, that was clear, but I didn't have to go home. I had already set up with Therese, another Art History major; to spend the Christmas holiday with her family in Switzerland. The colleges rent our rooms

302

to conferences outside of term, so I'd had to find somewhere to go. And I did. It was going to be amazing.

And I thought, *Okay, I'll look for some kind of under-the-table au pair job while I'm there. I'll set up a real life. I'll paint. It'll be even better than Cambridge.*

There was time in that plan to make a change, like turning a slow barge.

So that proves that I'm adaptable. I'd already come up with that plan and the letter had only arrived that morning.

Then, after Peter ran after Polly outside of the Sedgwick, and I'd jaywalked across Pembroke Street, I saw Therese turn the corner out of Free School Lane. She was with someone who had to be her older sister. They looked just alike except the sister was a little taller. They had bags from the harem-like custom perfume shop.

'Oh, Liv!' Therese called. We fell into step together toward Emmanuel College. She introduced her sister Annick, and I said something about looking forward to the holidays.

'Yes, I know, but there's a little problem,' Therese said in her precise, pretty accent. 'You see, our cousins have invited us to meet them in the Pyrenees. To ski. I've missed them so much since leaving home that I really can't say no. It wouldn't be home at Christmas without them.'

'That sounds wonderful!' I said. 'Wow!'

I'd never gone skiing before. But I knew it was this amazing rush. It would be like all the good part of falling – the whoosh, the freedom – without a crash at the bottom or the jarring restraint of a bungee. You could, if the mountain was high enough, and you made wide enough S curves, fall for a very, very long time. The only maybe-problem would be equipment rental fees. Were we staying at a lodge or at someone's house? Would everyone bring their own skis and could I borrow? I had to hammer all this out.

They stopped short of Emmanuel and veered into The Rat and Parrot. I followed them into the pub, because I had to. Details needed sorting. I didn't have any cash on me, but I figured it was okay to sit with them so long as they ordered something. They each got a glass of white wine; I asked for water. Therese and Annick talked family stories while we waited at the bar for our drinks. I tried to memorise the names they used – Henri, Luc, Paul. All their cousins were boys. Maybe if I flirted the right way they'd pay for my meals. 'One pound sixty,' the man behind the bar said, pushing my glass toward me. He'd poured my water from a bottle, not from out of the tap. He'd put a lemon slice in it.

Therese and Annick clinked money onto the bar and took their drinks toward a table. I had exactly one pound in my pocket, just that one thick coin.

Everything froze. Everything in the arrangement of figures in this scene drew the eye to my glass.

I laid my coin on top of theirs. They'd overpaid with a round number, either to tip or just because they didn't want to waste time getting change.

He gave me 10p change from the whole transaction. I wrapped my fist around the skinny silver disc and held it tight.

'Do your cousins bring their own skis? Will I need a special outfit?' I asked, joining them at the table. I had to get practical. I had to figure out what to borrow. My friend Gina skis...

'No, you don't understand,' Therese said. Expensive water sloshed over the side of my glass when I lifted it for a sip. 'It's my cousins' invitation. It's not my place to extend...'

'I know that,' I said, like they were slow.

They looked at each other.

'I don't even ski,' I clarified.

She and her sister smiled. 'Then you won't be sad!'

I stayed to finish my water. I had, after all, paid for it. I listened to their stories and brainstormed about Christmas presents.

They walked off with linked arms. That's a European girl thing. Sometimes you see French girls hold hands. Their small posh shopping bags bounced off their thighs as they walked.

I had to be out of my room in a week.

I wanted to be like Gauguin. I wanted to have an adventure and paint it, paint from some wonderful life. I didn't need to study for that; I just needed to live it. I couldn't be satisfied with painting in defiance of banality any more. I needed to be surrounded by beauty – not luxury, but beauty.

It would be possible to make one great gesture and get away with it. It would be possible to take enough to get somewhere good.

I had to try. What kind of a person would I be if I didn't try?

I think about Gauguin a lot. He wasn't nice to his family, but he was important to the world. I think about that for obvious reasons. And when he ran away, it wasn't cowardly. He was running to something, not just away. That's a beacon to me.

When we still had the money we really had had all that money once – we spent a weekend in San Francisco, me and Mom. Dad was working. We ate at crowded restaurants, and stayed in a boutique hotel. We went to an exhibition at the MOMA about the effect of photography on Impressionism. There were examples of how photography became part of how some painters worked, like if they used a live model or a picture of one, and how they came to see discrete moments within action, like the breakdown of the motion of a galloping horse. But the best part, to me, was how they photographed each other, and how they experimented with that. These painters playing with their new toy had a grand time. They created. And they horsed around.

The photo I most remember was of Gauguin, in someone's house or studio. The label called it 'Gauguin playing the harmonium'. And so he was. But the label neglected to note the hilarious: Gauguin wasn't wearing any pants. I mean that in the American way, not the British way. He had boxer shorts on, but no trousers, and yet he was fully, formally dressed on top. It was hilarious. It was a moment between friends, nothing sexual but simply casual. Maybe he didn't want his trousers to get wrinkled. Maybe they were itchy. The museum label was disorienting; was I the only one who noticed? Was everyone else, including the curator, thinking, *That's just Gauguin. He's so often unclothed while playing the harmonium that I don't even notice any more.* I swear I was the only one who laughed out loud the whole time we were in that gallery. I felt isolated, but superior too; was no one else actually looking?

That's what it was like, living where I did. I was too often the only one who noticed something, or wanted something, or thought something was special or beautiful or funny.

There was this house in our town that was burgled. The thieves left a Picasso. It was hanging on the wall, right there, and they carried out the television and the computer, walking past it, back and forth. It was an original, signed Picasso litho worth $40,000. But in suburban California, only sappy, ostentatious Kinkades get treated like art. Picasso can't even get himself stolen. That's what it's like back home. If you recognise a Picasso, if you notice Gauguin isn't wearing pants, you're the foreigner. It doesn't matter that I was born there. I'm a foreigner.

Now thinking of that Gauguin photo just puts Nick in my mind: Nick half-undressed. Nick only half-rumpled, Nick holding back. He's ruined that for me. It's not funny any more.

It's important for me to make it clear that Nick's not all that. He's not. He's just some guy with an accent and floppy hair; God knows there are enough of them in this town. God knows, half the men in this town wear knee-length wool coats and winter scarves striped with their school colours. Everyone talks like he does. But I was vulnerable to that. Americans are. We feel superior to the traditions that sort people into classes, but we envy them too. They're romantic. I let myself get all romantic about the whole English thing, and he was a piece of it. I wasn't in love with him. I was desperate for him. Those are two entirely different things.

Because Polly was so prissy about me reading Gretchen's emails, I didn't tell her the interesting part. The other biographer had offered money for the photos.

I immediately thought about selling some to her, of course I did. It was the same as someone looking down at the ground from a height. You think about what a jump would feel like, and the fall, and the splat. It doesn't mean you're considering it, it's just a mental journey. You see it and think what it would be like.

After I got the letter from Dad, I thought about it a different way.

It would have been so easy to scan a few. I could even just take pictures of them. The biographer wouldn't be picky about the source. She wanted them, right? So she wasn't going to get all righteous and say no.

Except for Gretchen having gone all nuts. Just like that, everything done. Not just for now, but done in a final way. Even the portrait photograph of the two sisters together, which used to hang in Gretchen's bedroom, was gone. She'd told Nick to actually get rid of everything. That's crazy!

Maybe he'd thought so too...

I stood up straighter. Maybe he'd recognised that it was ridiculous. Maybe he'd tried to save

Gretchen from herself. Maybe he'd saved those photos somewhere before he disappeared...

Maybe he'd saved me.

It was easy to get to Nick's house: Just go all the way up Madingley Road. For all the web of curvy, crossed lanes downtown, the roads out of town are long, straight spokes. Madingley Road heads for, well, Madingley village. People take this road to get to Churchill College, and the Observatory, and the four thousand white crosses of the World War II cemetery of American soldiers. I took it to Nick's house, which is right across from the vet school horses.

The house is modest in that it's not some huge edifice. It's an aesthetic stack of all-white boxes with windows in a swathe all the way across. It was really built in the thirties, not an homage to the thirties, and you can tell the difference. It's kind of cramped, a little shabby with age, but full of strong shapes and interesting light. The whole thing is topped by a tangle of branches reaching over from the wood behind it.

I rang the bell. A girl answered. This had to be Nick's sister, Alexandra.

'Hi,' I said. 'I'm a friend of Nick's. He'd borrowed something of mine. I'm really, really sorry to bother you. I didn't want to do this, but I really need to have it back.'

She squinted at me. 'What was it?' She didn't open the door any farther, only kept it open enough to stick her face through.

'Some photographs. They were in a big box.' I gestured with my hands to indicate the size. 'And some papers and stuff, but mostly photos. Do you know if he left them here?'

'Nick doesn't really keep anything here.'

'I know. I know, but it isn't at the Chanders' house or in his office and so I thought...' The contents of those two places had been discussed in the press.

'Were they some really old photos?'

Yes! 'Yes,' I said. 'Really old. They were mine, and I'd like them back.'

She lifted her shoulders, then dropped them in tandem with an enormous sigh. 'Somebody dumped some old photos in the pond. I thought it was our neighbour. Why would Nick do that?'

I told her something about Nick trying to protect me from some old memories that he thought weighed too heavily on my mind. She squinted at me. Good girl for being suspicious; that had sounded stilted even to me. So I tried it a little different and beseeching: 'Oh, please, can you tell me where the pond is?'

She squeezed her arm out without opening the door any farther and pointed.

I thanked her and ran around the house. I didn't see any photos; just nature. The ground near the water was unmaintained, a wild mess of roots, leaves, and weeds.

It was nearing dark already. Winter afternoons don't last long here. I swept at leaves with a stick, to see what was under them. Nothing but bugs and dirt until, halfway around, a white corner stuck out. I picked it up and turned it over. It was of Gretchen and her friends, at some high school event. It was useless to me itself, but it was like a

310

big fat X in the dirt: The Linda Paul pictures were here. And they'd been discarded; I could collect and sell them legitimately. I could sell them *all*, not just a discreet few. How could Gretchen complain, when she'd thrown them away?

I got down on my knees to push the leaves around with my hands. Then a stick plunged down in the dirt, right next to me. It nearly impaled my wrist. I fell back and shielded myself. The person with the stick shined a flashlight on me.

'You're trespassing,' she said. 'I demand you leave immediately.'

'I'm a friend of the Frey family...' I said, but my excuse counted for nothing.

'Then you would do well to return to them before I phone for the police.'

I backed up like a crab, and she followed me, poking the flashlight at my face so I never felt comfortable rocking forward to stand up.

'Look,' I said, 'I just made a mistake, okay? I didn't mean to cross into your yard...'

Then she saw the picture in my hand. She snatched it up and scampered backward, out of my reach in case I planned to wrestle her for it.

She turned her back to me and trained the light onto the picture. Now, with the light facing away from me, my eyes readjusted.

Every one of those big trees had photos nailed to it. At first they were all just rectangles to me, but as my eyes coped with the fading light I made out the shapes of familiar scenes. There didn't seem to be any order to it – black-and-whites and colour ones were grouped haphazardly; baby Gretchen and teen Gretchen and young Linda Paul. The neighbour lady put her flashlight on the ground and I couldn't see much any more. But I heard her – *thud, thud, thud.* She must have been nailing up the picture she'd taken out of my hand.

I stood up and rubbed my arms. There! Hanging primly from its wire, the way you'd hang it in a drawing room, was the framed photo of Linda and Ginny. I remembered it. It was formal and beautiful and surely the biographer would pay something for that. Wilting flowers had been intertwined through the elaborate frame. The glass front was cracked. She was distracted. I stepped toward it.

The crazy lady was quick. She called out, 'Yaaaaaaaah!' and ran at me. Maybe she had the hammer still in her hand; I couldn't see. I just turned and ran. There was a large wooden fence between her land and Nick's, so I had to head back toward the pond for an opening to his family's well-kept grass. She stopped pursuing as soon as I crossed over, but I kept running until I got to the driveway. I stood there, hands on my knees, breathing hard.

Alexandra opened the front door, just the same amount as before: about eight inches. 'I told you I thought they belonged to the neighbour.'

I got on my bike and across the road to the campus of science labs. I was shaking. I rode just to clear my head. The streets and buildings here are named after Cambridge greats: Thomson, Maxwell, Bragg. Thomson discovered electrons and his street always makes me think of Seurat and pointillism: Aren't we all just made of little dots?

The reason Seurat painted like that, by the way, was to give viewers the ingredients of a colour – say, yellow and blue, in tiny bits close together – to be mixed fresh in their eyes each time they look. Instead of some stale old green cooked up ages ago. Isn't that generous?

That's the exact conversation I had with Juergen once. He studies explosives in the Bragg Building. He's nice and kind of geeky. He tried to kiss me once and I avoided it. We haven't really hung out since then but we say hi. And I thought, *Why not see if he wants to do something?* Just hang out and maybe bullshit about art and science and all that undergraduate stay-up-all-night kind of talk. Because I really didn't feel like running into Therese or Polly or anyone else.

I found a bench that had less dried goose shit on it than the others and sat by the pond. I know he cycles by the pond to the bike path to get back to his place. He shares a flat on Fitzwilliam Street. Next to Darwin's old flat, no joke. He tells me stuff about Darwin and other scientists, and I tell him stuff about art.

That's what I love about Cambridge. The smartest people don't think someone is stupid just because they don't know some fact or really specific thing. Specialists understand from experience that you can be deeply brilliant at one kind of thing and completely ignorant of something else. Because you've focused. Really smart people focus. Nick didn't mind explaining things to me. Juergen didn't mind explaining things to me. Rocket science, actual rocket science. And he didn't think I was stupid for not knowing already

– he thought I was smart for being interested and able to follow his explanations. He thought we were equals.

Back home everyone always acted like I was so smart. They meant it nicely, but it was isolating, you know? They said I was special. But 'special' means 'by yourself'. That's what it means; 'better' than everyone else means 'not the same' as everyone else. I love Cambridge, because being smart means fitting in.

Those thoughts and others filled two hours. Juergen never came by on the path lit by knee-high bollards. It was Saturday; what was I thinking? Full term was just ended. There was no guarantee he'd be here. He might have been out with friends. He might be flying home. He might be here, but working all night.

The big, boxy, quickly constructed warehouse-type buildings populating the West Cambridge site had the benefit of dozens of window offices. In the dark, the ones that were lit looked suspended. I knew Juergen worked in the Bragg Building; I didn't know which window was his.

I walked around Bragg, rolling my bike along beside me. Unattended bikes disappear quickly. Four window offices were lit. I saw Juergen at his desk.

I threw a pebble at his window. I felt like such a geek. He looked down and I waved at him. He met me at the entrance. It has scripture quoted above it. That's the way it is when a country still has a monarch whose role is head of the Church.

'Hi,' I said. 'Look, I feel really stupid, but I've just had a run-in with a crazy person and I've had a fight with this girl in my college and I just don't feel like being there right now. Do you want to go out to a pub or something?' I must have expected Juergen to be eager for an invitation. I was surprised when he hesitated.

'Uh, look, I've got to finish this up. But, uh, you can hang out if you want...' I locked my bike up outside. He waited at the door and then led me upstairs. We passed a model of the double helix. Watson and Crick had been Cambridge boys. Their favourite pub had a plaque on it about them. The ceiling of it is covered by graffiti from World War II airmen.

The biggest tourist attraction near my home town is a massive house so poorly designed by the crazy rich lady who built it that it's marketed as a 'mystery'.

I had books in my backpack, so there was stuff to read. There was a beanbag chair, so I wasn't uncomfortable. Juergen was doing something at the computer, something involving models and scenarios. He was into it, so I didn't talk. We passed the whole evening like that. I think he stayed up all night. I eventually fell asleep.

Do you know how I think people become sluts? It's like, pay attention to me. He wasn't even looking at me. There was no conversation. No sharing something from a vending machine, or talking sticky problems through aloud. There was nothing.

The Centre for Mathematics, which is new, is very 'wow' on the outside. But I've heard from someone who works there that it's disconnected inside. No feeling of being part of the whole; your office is just this isolated little cave. I told that to someone else, and Nick, overhearing, had said, 'Isn't that what a researcher needs at work?' He said it like, *Of course we want to be unconnected.* Of course. And this with Juergen was like that. It was like I wasn't even there. I think that's what makes someone into a slut. Because I don't even like Juergen that way, but I fell asleep thinking, *Pay attention to me, asshole.* I thought, *All right, I'll do it, whatever. Just notice that I'm here.*

CHAPTER ELEVEN

It was Sunday, Day Eleven: The Day After the Dredging. The morning after I'd slept on a bean-bag chair in Juergen's office.

Term was just done. Dr Keene was getting married. Nick wasn't dead in the Cam, but was still gone. The bells in Great St Mary's played a quarter-peal at nine. Churches filled up, after which shops opened, which I hear is new. Everything, I'm told, used to be closed on Sundays not so long ago.

There is a pair of shows on the BBC called *Springwatch* and *Autumnwatch*, made of footage of the effects of changing seasons on the natural world: deer mating, swallows nesting, that sort of thing. I think Cambridge should have its own show, *Termwatch*, where you can see footage of the sudden deflation in the bicycle population whenever students go home for break; the bloom of tourists at Christmas and summer; the after-

Easter switch of season in school uniforms, from navy blazers to school-colour gingham dresses on girls all over the city. Juggling buskers materialise on the corner by Holy Trinity Church whenever children have days off school. It's all as cyclical and inevitable as any pattern of mating and migration.

Early December sees Christmas lights and banners advertising garish pantomimes dominate downtown. No snow, but deep, damp cold.

Harry's told me that this is the time of year for the best canary feathers. Because they finish their moult, I think. He goes to bird shows most weekends this month. I'd know him gone or not by the car.

The only obstacle would be Gretchen. She wouldn't have lights on to warn me that she's home, so I had to keep an eye out for other hints. I got there early enough to assume that she'd be in: robe, coffee, whatever she does instead of reading the newspaper. Maybe listening to something on the radio. I wasn't near the house, of course; I stayed by the end of the street, where it hits Barton Road. There's a bench there. It isn't a bus stop, just a gift to tired walkers and cyclists coming from Lammas Land or the Grantchester footpath. That sidewalk is so full of both pedestrians and bikes that it's been split into lanes.

I fit in, wearing jeans and a sweater from yesterday, and my jacket. I looked all right. I'd had a hairbrush in my bag. I'd cycled straight there from Bragg. I needed to be there early to see her go for sure. If I came too late, and she went out in the morning, I'd never know if she was gone or not.

There were lots of cars passing me, and parked cars blocking me. No one would notice or remember me. On residential and dead-end Millington, sure. But not here on Barton, busy with cars, cyclists, and pedestrians. I looked natural. I was doing a book of Sudoku puzzles. Everyone did those.

Polly's mother drove straight at me. She was coming up out of Millington as if from Gretchen's. What was she doing there? Wasn't she supposed to be in jail?

Suddenly anyone could be anywhere. A policeman could be in the car idling at the light; Nick might be hiding up a tree. Who knows who could be under this bench? I'd assumed Gretchen was home, but maybe she wasn't. Maybe I was waiting for nothing.

Mrs Bailey turned to join the cars at the light. It greened and everything rolled on.

I don't think she saw me.

I picked up my pencil.

About fifteen minutes later Harry surprised me by being on foot. He turned toward Newnham Road and downtown. Later a taxi turned down the L of Millington Road, then came back up with Gretchen in it. She went in the opposite direction of Harry, out of town.

I walked my bike down Millington. I parked it around the side of a house for sale; I didn't want anyone to see it parked at Gretchen's. I used the key they'd given me for working with the photos.

Inside the house, I walked a wide arc to avoid the Chinese dog statue. Stupid. It wasn't going to bite me, it wasn't going to bark. I made myself go back, right up to it, and nudge it with a little kick.

And that's how I felt about Gretchen.

This whole time I'd acted like she has some kind of power. But she doesn't. I don't need to walk a wide arc around her. I can kick her if I want. She's just a person, like the stupid Chinese dog is just a statue. She's not anything I need to be afraid of.

I went upstairs. I examined their bill history on-line. I created a new payee, directed to my bank account, but named it to look in its record like a regular billing account. I transferred ten thousand pounds. It was easy. It would come through by the second business day: Tuesday. I didn't think they would notice the discrepancy before then. Gretchen had been distracted lately.

Then I'd have to go away. I'd be like Gauguin. I'd find my own Tahiti. I'd – not go home. It was important to not go home.

That meant the world to me. Polly would think it was too small, but it's not like I chose to be squeezed this tight. It's not like I asked for it.

The phone rang. I just about jumped. I'd ignored the computer narrating my keystrokes, but the phone was unexpected. At the same time, the front door opened. I could tell by the foot stomps on the doormat that it was Harry. It sounded like he had plastic bags, like from Sainsbury's. Groceries.

The phone kept ringing. Instead of picking up in the kitchen, he went for the stairs. A machine picked up, a machine in this room. It didn't seem like he was going to answer, but there was every chance he'd listen to the message. I do that. I screen. It's normal. He was coming.

I'd already shut down the banking site and the monitor. I slipped out of the den and could only follow the hall away from the main stairs. And the only thing there was the ladder to the bird room. Jesus. There were feathers and sawdust on each step, and the air smelt like balsa with a tinge of refrigerator rot.

The voice came from the den: 'You've reached Gretchen Paul and Harry Reed. Please leave a message.' Gretchen, Paul, and Harry – they sounded like a folk group. Ha. Then a long, irritating whine for a beep.

Harry had paused outside the den door to listen. I was wearing ballet Rats, but even so I didn't think I would get up to the bird room without obvious creaks. He might even be on his way there anyway. And – Jesus, there was a dead bird on the top step. A dead orange bird...

'Hello, Gretchen. I'm calling again to make sure you know that Miranda Bailey has been released. I thought you'd want to know that her situation has been resolved by a witness. Phone if you have any questions; I'll be in the office.'

It was the lawyer. So it wasn't Polly's mother who did it, whatever had been done. Sometimes I wondered if Nick had pulled a Gauguin of his own.

Harry came closer. I hunched in the corner, behind the ladder stair. I should have just grabbed some papers and said I was working. He didn't care when I was there. Shit. I closed my eyes. He gasped.

It was the bird. It wasn't me.

He'd seen it. Poor thing. The feathers were fluffed out, making it almost spherical. The body itself was rubber-chicken limp. He stood on the bottom step and scooped the body gently in both his hands together. Then he gasped again, and thundered up the stairs. He froze with his upper half inside the bird room, standing on the middle step. I looked up at him. There was nowhere to go. I kept still. His head fell forward and he saw me.

'Liv?' He sounded strangled.

'I was just... I was finishing up with the pictures...'

I wasn't even thinking about the money any more. I thought for sure he'd blame me for the birds. Indignance blossomed in my chest, blossomed so big it hurt. I defended myself: 'I don't know what the hell happened up there. Jesus.'

He was calmer than I expected. He's a big man. I thought for sure he'd grab me up by my shirt and throw me into a wall. He had that kind of energy in him all of a sudden. But it wasn't directed at me. The sound that came out of him was weird and keening, and he pounded the top step with his fist.

I wasn't sure how he was reading the situation, but I felt like I had to prove it hadn't been me. I followed him up the ladder. He squatted in the middle of the mess, righting cages. Dead birds flopped inside; living ones flapped and chattered.

I took a broom propped in the corner and pushed sawdust and birdseed together in a pile. Little bits of broccoli too. I swept around the cages. It was really important that he know this wasn't my doing. Jesus. There are some things I would do but this was horrible.

While I swept, he got all the loose cages piled up. The big cage in the middle was bashed in, one corner completely concave, and the door couldn't close any more. Some birds were still in there. A few had escaped. They were perched or lying dead or out the window.

A white one was on a chair seat. It was alive, but it wasn't sitting right. Like it was hurt. I picked it up, in my two hands together, like he'd done with the dead one on the stairs. It quivered. I switched to cupping it; maybe it was cold. I brought it to him, like, *What do I do now?* I thought he would open a cage. Harry turned from righting a cage and looked straight at me, this awful look. His eyes slowly lowered to my hands.

He freaked. He wanted me to put his bird down. I didn't know where to put it down. He stood over me. He's really tall. He started waving his arms around and there was really nowhere to go.

The bird twitched, making awful noises. He was trying to get me to let it go, but it was crazy. He was crazy, and all the grief and wonder in him about what had happened up here made this wall of crazy that backed me up to the point that I couldn't do anything.

He grabbed my elbows. I didn't want to drop it. Did he want me to drop it? The sharp little feet were scrabbling at my palm and he was shaking me. Jesus. He was, like, huge. I screamed at him, 'Get the fuck away from me! Get the fuck away!'

'Please,' he said. 'Please.' He wanted this one bird. He wanted it. But he had my elbows. I didn't know what he was going to do. He was crazy

322

about this bird, like my holding it was worse than what had already happened to it.

I charged forward with my shoulder. I pushed him hard. There was this kind of *oof*, but I kept pushing. My legs churned, sliding on spilt lettuce leaves. He went down the ladder steps.

I put the bird down, finally. Without him looming over me, I was able to pop it into a cage. It was going to die anyway. It wasn't sitting right; it was broken.

I looked down. Harry had fallen onto the back of his neck. His legs were diagonal up the steps; his head was flat on the carpet. His body looked short and strange to me from up here. It reminded me of Mantegna's laid-out *Dead Christ*, which everyone studies. The way he used foreshortening of the legs to position the viewer, anyone looking at the painting is right there, at dead Jesus's feet, near and kneeling. It's like I was right there with Harry. It's like this was real.

I had to walk sideways to get down past him. The phone rang. Four rings, the long beep again, 'Gretchen, Paul, and Harry...' Ha. Ha. Ha.

It was Gretchen. I listened. It's human nature to listen.

She was sorry, she said. It was she who had done it to the birds. She forgave, I don't know what. She needed to be picked up. Her mother was ... something. And the money.

She was suddenly bent on moving the money.

Charity. Immediately. I could hear the disgust in her voice. She was shoving the money away from her, like a plate of bad food. I needed until

Tuesday. I needed.

I deleted the message. I took the keys out of Harry's pocket.

I picked birdseed out from the tread of my shoes before I went downstairs.

The orange Sainsbury's bags sagged by the front door. I put the milk away, and the hot cross buns, and the coffee beans. It seemed important. My fingerprints wouldn't matter. They were already all over the place, they were supposed to be. It just seemed important that this not look sudden, not look caught-in-the-act. I pushed the empty bags in with the recycling under the sink. A small, white feather, which must have come off of me, was caught between them.

I picked it out very carefully. It was very important that nothing confuse the simplest explanation of what had happened, an explanation that didn't include me.

I cupped my hands around the feather, so it wouldn't waft away, and carried it up the stairs. At the end of the hall I stepped around the mess at the bottom of the ladder and inched my way up. At the top, the little bird, whose heart had beat so fast in my hand, was lying on its side but still visibly breathing.

I laid the feather on it. The little poof of white rode up and down, up and down.

I've driven their car before, once to get Gretchen to a lecture when her taxi didn't arrive, and another time to pick up a package. I'd volunteered as an acolyte and friend. It seemed like a long time ago. I shifted the seat for my shorter legs. I always put it back when I returned, to be ready for Harry.

I turned left onto Barton and stopped at the light at the bottom of Grange Road. Six other cars idled with me. A dozen pedestrians flowed past on both sides of the street.

A pair of women walked up Barton together, from out of Wolfson College. They were dressed up. One wore gold, the other white. Knee-length dresses and feminine coats. Gloves. The one in white had a veil on her head, a short one, grazing her shoulders. Her hair was down. They both carried flowers. They were arm in arm, like European girls. Like Therese and Annick. They were heading toward the river.

It was Alice. Today was Dr Keene's wedding. I'd forgotten.

They crossed the road in front of me. The light turned green. I went. What else could I do? There were cars behind me. There was nothing for it but to go forward.

Alice was so beautiful that I cried.

CHAPTER TWELVE

I woke up. It was dark and the clock said four. In winter, a dark four could be a.m. or p.m. and I didn't know.

I still had all my clothes on under the covers. My jeans felt stiff, like casts on my legs, and pinched my stomach. I tried to swing my legs over the side, but there was friction against the bedclothes.

I was still wearing shoes.

'What the fuck?' I said out loud. I kicked, hard, until the covers ended up on the floor. They sucked one of my shoes with them, and I had to crawl around down there and stick my arm into the tangle of blanket and sheet to get it back out. It was an awful lot of fucking work just to get out of bed.

I got dressed and went outside. The long line of twinkle lights across the shops were on. People bustled. So, four p.m. December shoppers from the villages were wide from the bags they carried. There wasn't room on the sidewalk for all of us; I got bumped on both sides. I put my hand on my cheek and shivered. How long had I slept?

My jacket wasn't warm enough. I didn't need one in California. I shouldn't need one here either; it's not like it ever snows. The only snow I got I'd had to make myself, little scraps of paper. The white Christmas reputation that England has is Victorian. You'd know that if you think about it. Those British-people-skating scenes on cards always have long dresses and muffs and sleighs. You don't get snow here now, except maybe one day a year. It snowed once last year, and it didn't stick or even slush. It hit the street and melted immediately. You could watch it happen but it didn't stay and pile up. Which makes it not really snow, not the snow that I dreamt about when I was a kid. Snow is only snow when it's accumulated. Snow is what happens after it's hit the ground. The falling is just the way that it gets there.

It's like a guy who touches you at a party isn't really a boyfriend. It's not like you can tell people the next day, *He's my boyfriend*. Because he's not, not until you see what sticks.

Nick looked upset. Not in my head; Nick wasn't in my head. He was in a car at the intersection.

I was stopped at the corner with the flower shop. I was flanked by a window of bright living things, and the doorway was like this halo over me. Flat brass flowers were embedded in the sidewalk all up and down this road, scattered like they'd grown up through the concrete by accident. Someone had designed them and cast them and pressed them in at random, all the way from here to beyond the river. God, it was beautiful.

I think he saw me. He looked right in my direction, but he didn't act like he saw me. There were other people around, so maybe he didn't. He wasn't driving. Someone else was driving. It was a woman. She drove the car through the intersection and on down Chesterton Road.

I leant back against the shop door. Nick. He wasn't gone. None of it had happened.

How much the fuck did I drink last night that I dreamt all that? Right?

I only needed to figure out how far back it all went.

I almost ran. I was so sure of what I'd find, I wanted to run. But I didn't, because of the narrow sidewalks and all those fancy shopping bags hanging from everyone's hands. So I kind of skipped and half jumped around, jogging but not really jogging, you know? I almost tripped over a busker's bucket of coins.

The gates were closed. Of course they would be – Monday. Museums close on Mondays because they're open on weekends. I didn't rattle the gates; I didn't need to. The window I was looking for was farther down the building. There – between the main stairs and the handicapped entrance. Over the giant Henry Moore. There. That window there.

Three Chinese vases, each as big as a toddler. I wrapped my fingers around the iron bars of the fence to hold myself up. None of it had happened. None.

It was Christmas. It was presents and snowflakes and cards with prints of Victorian skaters. I hadn't fucked it up with Nick; he wasn't gone. Maybe I hadn't even met him yet. If the vases hadn't been shattered, I hadn't even met Polly yet. I was still nineteen. I was young. I was happy. I was still a kid.

What a fucked-up dream. What the fuck did I eat last night? I had curry or something or a street vendor sausage with hot sauce. Right? What a fucked-up...

I'd wait till they opened. I had to go in. Maybe I could put my hands on the vases, just like a stroke or a pet, and no one would notice. They wouldn't have motion detectors, right? It's not like paintings, right? Because there isn't a guard on those stairs. And the vases aren't that old. They're not even that valuable. Just to me. I just wanted to touch them, like, to say 'thank you'. I wanted to draw them. I didn't have my sketchbook, but the front desk gives out these packets to kids who ask for them. They have paper and coloured pencils and even a little sharpener. I needed to draw those vases.

I've been waiting, like, my whole teenaged life for this. For something to draw. For something that's mine. For something that means something to me so much that when I draw it it's more than a stupid still-life or landscape or portrait that everyone says is amazing just because it's recognisable. Everything I've done up to now has been praised for looking like real life, but what good is it to just draw what everyone can see anyway? The whole point of art is that it shows the looker something that they wouldn't have seen otherwise. But you can't make that happen. You can't make yourself have something to say.

There are pictures that I drew when I was little, in the margins of books. It took forever for the library to get complaints about them, because they looked really good. They looked like stuff that was supposed to be there. Finally the librarian turned into fucking Nancy Drew and figured out that it was me. She just looked at who had checked out all those books. And she arranged a conference with my parents and told them that I'm an artist. I'm a fucking artist. Because my faces look like faces. It's such a fucking low standard. Are they good faces? Are they interesting faces? Do they tell you anything or make you feel something? Do they do something?

This librarian told my parents that I'm an artist because why? Because I draw hands with five fingers each, and I know the difference between an eye in front view and an eye in profile? Big fucking deal. An artist draws a face that stops you. Fuck, an artist doesn't even need a face. There's a Degas in the Fitz that's just a hand, a sculpture of a hand.

How would you feel if you held your hand like that, cocked back with crooked fingers? If you put your hand like that, everything else follows: You're angry. All he needed was a hand to fully depict anger. That's what an artist does. He takes something completely inadequate – like a single body part if you're Degas. And you make – what? You make something that stops people. Something that has more in it than can fit. Art is a fucking clown car. Right? It's something with more in it than anyone else would be able to fit.

So this librarian called me an artist. And people shouldn't be allowed to throw words like that around. Because she didn't know. She didn't know what that was supposed to mean. She just meant that I don't suck, that I'd drawn physically recognisable humans. She didn't have any standard higher than that. People like that shouldn't be teachers. Because people like me get told things and get the really wrong idea.

Up until this moment, I didn't really know if I was an artist. I had all these skills, but no vision. And now, right in front of me through that window, I had vision. It was this physical scene, just a stupid still life, right? But it was relief. It was profound fucking relief. And youth. And future. And Christmas. It's fucking Christmas on that shelf. Shit, I had tears on my face. They landed on the front of my jacket, and melted away in an instant like snow in England. Snow in beautiful fucking England. I was really here, and nothing bad had happened yet.

I didn't know if I could wait. If I'd had chalk I would have happily drawn on the sidewalk.

When I looked up again, there she was: Polly. What was she doing here? She doesn't start until next fall. She must be looking at the colleges.

She passed me by, without acknowledgement. I let out my breath. See? She didn't know me. She didn't know me yet.

I turned and watched her keep going, toward St Peter's Terrace. She must be checking out Peterhouse accommodation. That would make sense for a prospective student. It all made sense.

A poster farther down the fence reared up into view. It was hanging there, but not just hanging: It intruded and don't ask me how that works. I'm just telling you what was in front of me. It was a kind of panel where they announce new exhibits. I thought, *Someone beat me to it. Someone else is excited about these vases besides me, because there they are.*

It wasn't a drawing. It was a photograph. The Fitz was advertising the vases' restoration.

The image was a close-up, bigger than life-sized. I put my hand on it. I looked as close as I could, and I found them: the cracks. The picture was so real you could even find the cracks. I think I stood there forever. I don't think my blood even moved around my body. Everything just stopped. Even Polly must have stopped because when I looked away like a million hours later she was still just half a block from me. If the vases had been smashed and repaired, if I did know her, if everything had happened just like I'd dreamt it or nightmared it or just plain fucked it up, then who does she think she is that she can walk by me like we don't know each other? Who does she think she is?

I caught up with her in just a few stretched-out strides because I was mad. Anger makes people bigger, faster, longer-legged. My huge hand and long arm pulled her back by her collar. Her coat had a fur collar on it, fake and feathery. My hand plunged into the tickly mass to get hold of the wool neckline underneath. I pulled hard, to make her back up and choke. The coat was buttoned up around her neck and I pulled.

Then I let go so she could turn around. She looked indignant and I had on this innocent face. Her expression backed down, like she must have been mistaken. Like I hadn't choked her for a second. Ha ha. It's like – it's like, who wouldn't want to play with that? I wanted to smack her on the face and then say I hadn't, just to see if she'd take it. Maybe she'd even apologise for the mis-understanding.

'What the hell?' she demanded, rubbing her neck. 'What's wrong with you?'

'What's wrong with *you*, walking right past me? I'm here, you know? I'm right here!' I waved my hands in her face. 'I didn't think Gretchen's blindness was catching...'

The skin around her eyes was dark, like she'd slept in mascara. But she doesn't usually wear make-up. 'Liv, don't you know? Gretchen's dead. She's dead,' she said.

'I know,' I said. *I know. I know. I know. I know.* The vases are cracked, Polly is here, Gretchen is dead. But what about Nick? If everything's hap-pened, then why isn't Nick gone? Why did I see him in a car on Chesterton Road?

332

'I saw Nick,' I said.

And, just like that, there was this tapping sound behind me. It sounded like Gretchen's cane, tapping on the steps of the Fitzwilliam. I ignored it.

'Oh my God, what? Where?' Polly said. Her face didn't know how to look. It waited to hear whether I saw him dead on the road or on the news or buying a cup of coffee or in my own fucking head.

Then Harry brushed past me, his arm pushing mine as he went by. I know sidewalks can be skinny around here, but this one was plenty wide and there was no reason for it. It was like he just wanted to nudge me or something. I turned and watched him keep going. The clothes were different, and he had on this hat which wasn't like him, but it was obviously him. And I realised that all his niceness and can-I-make-you-tea is just as much bullshit as everyone else's because when you're really freaking out he'll just walk past you, right?

Polly grabbed my elbow. 'Did you really see Nick?'

I was, like, *What?* I made my face all innocent and said, 'What are you talking about?' Why didn't she ask about Harry? Had no word gotten around about Harry, only Gretchen? That isn't fair. But why would I expect anything to be any better for Harry than it is for me?

She looked hit. I said it again: 'What are you talking about?' and she actually started to cry. She looked like a well-trimmed poodle with that coat on. 'Nice coat.'

Her fists hammered me in the chest. I was up against the iron fence, and the hitting made my head bounce on the bars. It only lasted a few seconds. 'My mother bought me this coat!' she said. Then she let go of me, and I guess I slumped.

'Okay,' I said, 'I'll lay off the coat.'

'My mother bought me this coat,' she repeated. She crossed her arms as if I were going to try to take it.

'All yours,' I conceded.

We breathed at each other a little while.

'I just can't believe that Gretchen's dead,' she finally said. 'Old people die.' That tapping started again, behind me on the steps.

Polly opened her mouth like she wanted to argue about whether or not Gretchen was actually 'old' but instead she asked one more time, 'Did you really see Nick?' Like she really, really needed to know.

I thought it was sweet that she still thought he might be alive. Speaking of old, I was old now too. Because I'd been through something. I'd woken up thinking all kinds of people could be alive, and it turned out that none of them are.

I shook my head. Because I hadn't seen him, not the way Polly wanted me to have. I knew that now. I'd seen him the same way I see Harry and Gretchen, and would keep on seeing them, the rest of my life. Why Nick would bother haunting me is anyone's guess, because it's not like I had anything to do with whatever stabbed him or pushed him or held him underwater. Maybe he was just haunting Cambridge, and passing me was incidental. That would fit, wouldn't it? It's not like I mattered enough for him to even bother.

'Nick's dead too,' I said. What did she expect?

He's gone, he's dead. The police had dredged the Cam, because they thought so too. Did she ever really think he was coming back?

It was the smack I'd fantasised. The shock on her face was hilarious. She must have really thought he was coming back. Up until this moment, when I said what's been obvious for a long time. Of course he's dead. People like Nick don't just leave.

'You were going to take him back, weren't you?' I hurled at her. 'Never mind that he gets off with your best friend. You were going to take him back, and get on with being a tease and just holding hands.'

I stared hard, because this was fascinating. Look at her face: Things passed through it, things that could have become words but never got that far, never got that specific or that limited. That's what art is for, for catching these looks. I wanted to draw her so bad my fingers vibrated.

Then she spoke, and all the variety and vastness resolved and reduced into two bullet points: 'You're not my best friend. And I do wish Nick was back.'

There was a flapping sound behind me, like a dozen birds had suddenly taken off from the museum's roof. I didn't have to turn around. They would be Harry's canaries, round and fluffy and coloured like Easter candy. When the beating of their wings died down, I did turn around. Gretchen was gone.

When I turned back, so was Polly.

I checked an ATM. The transaction was going to take 'up to' two days, but that could mean today, so I checked. Everything was still the same. I was still in desperate need of money.

There are something like twenty banks in town and I passed, like, half of them. I checked my balance at each one. If I'd been on my bike I wouldn't have done that, but with everything in slow motion what else was I supposed to do? I was on foot because someone had taken it.

Bikes get stolen all the time in Cambridge, and it's not an idle thing. It's not like they get stolen by people who're going to use them. Then maybe someone who really needed a bike and had to get somewhere might be on mine. I could live with that. Maybe my bike would even be part of something important. But the bike stealing is more organised here. The person who took it is probably just selling it on, just doing business. Things like that make me sick.

I waited in a lot of lines. I pressed a lot of buttons.

Then, just like that: 10,003.45 pounds.

I looked over my shoulder. Did anyone see that?

I looked back. The number was still there. I jumped from foot to foot and shook my hands like they'd fallen asleep. Quick; end the transaction. No – celebrate! Withdraw cash. Buy something. Maybe one of those massively expensive coffees that's really some kind of mutant sundae with caffeine.

I pressed all the right buttons. But it spat out my card without any money. I tried again; the balance was there, but it wouldn't let me get at it. I grabbed the sides of the machine and tried to shake it, like when a bag of potato chips is hanging off the spiral in a vending machine. But this thing was, of course, embedded in the wall. There would be no shaking it.

The spiral with my money hanging off it wasn't in this machine anyway. It would be in a computer somewhere at the bank. The account or transaction might have been flagged, and put on hold. Perhaps they'd been notified of the death by someone incredibly thorough. Maybe everything to do with them was frozen already. Or, no, really, it could just be that things hadn't finished processing. Maybe there's this stage where the amount is acknowledged but not releasable yet. Maybe that's what they meant by two days and tomorrow everything would be fine. Right?

Just past Sainsbury's there was one more bank.

I waited in line behind a guy with a guitar on his back. He stuck in a card and punched a lot of buttons but nothing much happened, so he opened up his bag and rooted around in it. He got another card and held it in his teeth while he rebuckled the two straps on the front of his bag without taking off his bulky gloves. One side he got but the other one squirmed away from him over and over. He stood there, between me and the machine, wrestling with this stupid bag buckle while I rocked from side to side. The card stuck out of his mouth like a tongue. A mom with a stroller passed between us and rolled a dirty wheel over my shoe.

Finally he stuck the new card in the machine. A ten slid out. He got out of my way. I pushed my card in the slot and pressed the right buttons. The balance was there.

I tried withdrawal again. Ten had worked out pretty great for the guy in front of me, so I tried it too. Press, press, press, press, *whirr* ... money. Money.

Ten pounds.

I pinched it between my fingers and tugged. It didn't give right away so I pulled with both hands so hard that I rocked back into the person behind me. 'Sorry,' I said, but I didn't get out of the way. The machine asked if I wanted another transaction. Even with the money free I knew I couldn't get at the whole of it until tomorrow. A machine wouldn't be able to give that much; I'd have to wait in line and ask a teller nicely. It was already after five.

I just stared at the small piece of it that was in my hand. It was suddenly weird to me that it wasn't green. I'd been using this colourful money for over a year now but it was suddenly weird. It didn't look like money. It looked like a magazine ad. Like a travel agency poster. A poster for Tahiti, my own Tahiti, my own place to get away and grow into something that I knew I could be if people would just stop getting in the way.

I mashed the money into the front pocket of my jeans and whirled around. I thought I'd heard Gretchen's cane, but it was the person waiting behind me, tapping a pen against their card.

I rubbed my forehead. It was just a pen tapping a card. And the birds at the Fitzwilliam could have been any birds. There are lots of birds in Cambridge. Harry never wore a hat like that at all. I was just getting all 'Tell-Tale Heart' about things because of the waiting. Everything could be explained away, except Nick in that car. I'd seen Nick for sure.

Harry came out of the supermarket. I ducked into a doorway. He had those same two orange bags he'd left by the front door yesterday. He had that same hat on he'd had by the Fitzwilliam. No, Harry doesn't wear hats. What was going on? I had to look at his face.

I chased him toward Magdalene but there were crowds at the bus stops. By the time I got through he was gone.

I leant against the bridge to breathe. Of course it hadn't been Harry. He wouldn't carry groceries up Bridge Street; that's the opposite of the way to their house. A punt emerged underneath me. In the spring the river will be full of them, rubbing up against each other. But in today's cold and dark there was just this one. I squinted to see if it was Nick. But it wasn't. It really wasn't. He was too short. Of course it wasn't Nick. Why would Nick be punting?

I had to get it together.

If I'd seen a dead Nick, if I was seeing ghosts, then this money wouldn't get me anywhere. They wouldn't let me spend it on anything, not without sneaking up behind me or crossing in front of me or filling my ears with chirping and tapping and Gretchen's horrible thud against the front of Harry's car.

But if Nick had been real, if he was alive and back, then I'd know for sure that any tapping I heard was just someone busking on the drums, or bouncing a jackhammer into the street, anything, but not that cane.

If he was back, then I could get out of here tomorrow and get on with life. I could leave and not be followed.

He'd be with his family, wouldn't he? I had to know.

Madingley Road is a busy street and the cars whooshing by made a buzz in my head that blocked out other things. I felt like I was going to float up, which I think was from breathing in so much exhaust instead of oxygen.

Nick's family's house is on a corner. To get to the front door, you have to go around most of the place. The back of it is kind of right there, facing the crazy neighbour's fence.

This fluttering thing hit me in the face. Not a bird, not any kind of bird. It was a piece of ... it was a picture. It was a dozen little boys in black top hats. It was the King's College choristers. Nick was in the middle. That was him, when he was short and his voice was high. I recognised his face. I can always tell his face.

Another one landed on my foot. It was raining Nick. This one was of him as a blond teenager with a dark-haired little girl in front of some big European fountain.

I looked up. That dark-haired girl was grown up and throwing them out of the window. Wind blew them at me, instead of into the neighbour's yard she was aiming for.

'What are you doing?' I called out.

She flinched, and the top of her head banged into the window frame.

'Hey, are you okay?' I asked. I walked over to underneath her. The house didn't have high ceilings so upstairs wasn't that far up.

'If Mrs Cowley likes photos so much she can have them!' Alexandra kept trying to arc them over the fence, but the wind smeared them around the yard.

I picked up another at random. It was a blurry, blobby baby picture. My mom had pictures like that of me, from back in the day when you had to print a whole roll of film.

'Are you okay?' I repeated.

She looked at me with that kind of tilted head that people do when someone else is stupid.

'Hey!' I said. She retreated and shoved the window shut. I charged around to the front door. 'Hey!' I repeated, pushing it open.

This was Nick's house. There were full book-shelves everywhere. There was a cute bag on a chair, and a girly jacket on the floor. There was a table with two plates holding orange rinds and crumbs. There were two cups and two spoons, and a jagged-edged knife.

Alexandra cantered down the stairs on tottery high heels. She had on tights and a short skirt and a sweater. She hugged her arms around herself. 'You're Nick's friend, right? What do you want?'

'Where is he?' The house was mostly open-plan. It couldn't hide anything. Nick wasn't there, not on this floor anyway.

'I don't know.' Her mouth hung open in that last 'oh' sound. She rubbed her thin sleeves like she was cold.

I darted past her up the steps. She chased me. 'What are you doing?' One of the bedroom doors was sort of open. I pushed it the rest of the way.

341

The bookcase in here held old textbooks, framed certificates, and Nick's graduation photo: He looked like an Easter bunny in the University's traditional rabbit-fur cape and white bow around his neck. 'What do you want?' she persisted.

A drawer at the bottom of the computer desk had been pulled all the way out. It was full of pictures and negatives sorted into labelled envelopes. There was the window from which she'd dumped her and Nick's childhood.

The duvet on the single bed hung halfway off and the pillow was indented and askew. I gasped.

Alexandra hung back in the doorway. 'Mum must have slept in it,' she said. 'She does that sometimes. He's really not here. I, I really don't think he's coming back...'

The balance of the duvet must have reached some tipping point; it suddenly sagged and something round tumbled out. It came to rest at Alexandra's foot. It was a balled-up sock, a thick white one.

We both fell to hands and knees, like movie people ducking bullets. We stuck our faces under the bed.

There was a crumpled sweatshirt. And, where the duvet had slid off the mattress, a pair of jeans.

Alexandra squeezed the sweatshirt in her hands, but tempered her hope. 'Mum might have hugged his sweatshirt in bed...'

I pulled out the jeans to read the label. Inches, not a size. Guys' jeans. 'These are his,' I said. 'These are his clothes. Unless,' I added, 'you had a boyfriend over last night...'

'I wasn't even home last night!' she said, indignant, then ecstatic. Realisation bloomed. 'I wasn't even home...'

There's a famous sculpture of St Teresa in ecstasy. The expression Bernini put into her marble face would have been enough for anybody, but he positioned a hidden window to light it, and then threw in an extravagance of enormous gilt rods behind her, just in case the rays of the real sun didn't measure up. That's how Alexandra looked. She looked radiant. She looked lit.

'I saw him today,' I said, reflecting her happiness. 'On Chesterton Road. I really saw him!'

The money would come out of the bank tomorrow. I would leave a living Nick, and dead Harry and dead Gretchen, behind. I'd only been imagining things. They couldn't really follow me.

Tap, tap, tap...

All my muscles squeezed together hard.

I shook myself. That was just the noise of Alexandra's heels on the stairs. She was clattering down them because a car was pulling up.

I checked my hair in the dresser mirror. I wiped my mouth. I followed her down to see Nick one last time.

Tap, tap, tap.

Gretchen had no power over me any more. I knew the sound for what it was: knocking on a door.

Why would Nick knock on his own door?

The stairs decanted me back into the living space. It was a big room, for everything all at once: for sitting and eating and putting on coats. Only the kitchen had a full-height interior wall,

343

for more cabinet space, I guess. I ducked into that kitchen, behind that wall.

Alexandra opened the door to a man. She said, 'Morris!' and hugged him. Morris. That was the name of Polly's policeman.

'Alexandra,' he said. 'I need to see Nick. Is he here?'

'Is he alive? Is he really alive?' She jumped in place: bounce, bounce.

The policeman said yes. There were tears and squeals and stuff out of her, but he made her focus.

'Is Nick not here?'

'I think he and Mum are out looking for me.'

Her clothes were rumpled and stretched in a way that made things pretty obvious. 'Did you come home last night?'

'I was at a party. I slept at my friend Hannah's house. I didn't tell Mum.'

'Well, we need to call her now, all right? I need to speak to Nick.'

She came into the kitchen to use the phone on the counter, and Morris followed. I edged myself out the kitchen's other end, onto the living room side of the wall. I bumped into a suitcase. It cracked open and leaked a tie.

'They're on their way,' Alexandra told him, after talking to her mom. 'Dad flew home early, from New York overnight. He's upstairs asleep.'

'Really?' I blurted. That was a mistake. Before that the policeman hadn't realised I was there.

'This is Nick's friend,' Alexandra said, sweetly, gallantly. She was happy. She wanted us all to be best friends. She didn't even know my name.

But he did. 'Liv?' he asked, and it was totally not fair because he hadn't even bothered to meet me when Nick was gone. He'd fobbed me off on the assistant cop, the sergeant. 'No,' I said, denying it all. But he must have seen photos of all Nick's friends, or maybe spied on us, because he knew. He knew who I was.

'Why don't you go upstairs and wake your dad?' he suggested to Alexandra, but looking only at me.

I'd slipped the sandwich knife off the table, just in case. But it's not like I was going to use it.

I moved toward the door. The policeman put himself between me and it.

So it was his fault.

I got hold of Alexandra's arm. 'What are you doing?' she said. The knife jumped out of my pocket and pressed into her neck.

The policeman froze.

'It's all right, Liv,' he said evenly.

'I'm not doing anything.'

'Let her go.'

This is what makes me so angry: I wasn't even going to do anything.

He made this kind of leap at me, shoving his hand between my hand and Alexandra's neck. I moved as a reflex, not meaning to hurt him, but I sliced him across his knuckles.

I've spent a lot of time looking at hands; they're the hardest of all body parts to draw. This one was big and had blood on it, first just straight across, then also sliding down each finger, like clothes hanging from a laundry line.

He shoved Alexandra away with it, and she fell against the table. Orange peels popped up off plates; the two coffee cups toasted with a clink before wobbling over. There was blood on her shirt now, from him. I scrambled to the door but it opened in. I had to back up to open it all the way. I felt like I lost entire minutes, maybe hours, pulling that door back.

I plunged into the outside head first. He grabbed me around the middle with that one good arm. I elbowed him off me, but somehow I was back in the doorway, and he blocked my exit on the stoop.

I held my hands up. One of them still had the knife in it.

Out of nowhere, his good hand yanked me around, right around, like we were square dancing. This opened up his whole torso. His white shirt was this huge field.

It felt weird putting the knife in. His body was too soft and too hard at the same time. I didn't want it to be like this. It was like touching a guy you don't really like because you have to or else he'll yell at you or say things about you. I didn't push hard or move it around. I just rubbed it across, but the sharpness went in anyway. The knife did that. I was just pushing him away.

When our positions were fully reversed, I saw that Alexandra had a vase over her head, a huge urn from next to the fireplace. She looked like she was carrying water back from a well. She'd been about to smash my skull in, except that the policeman had heaved me away.

'What the hell did you do that for?' Alexandra shouted. She wasn't angry at me. She was angry at him, for pulling me out of her range and so

346

making himself vulnerable.

She couldn't balance the weight of it any longer. It shattered on the concrete stoop. We all jumped at the impact.

'What did you do that for?' I echoed, really curious. He sagged to one side, with the good hand kind of on his hip, I think holding him up. His shirt wasn't white any more. His cut hand hung down, limp at the end of his arm.

That good hand shot out and pulled my arm hard, twisting it behind me. We both went down, me front first. His weight on my back hurt. My cheek pressed into the concrete. I wiggled and whined. I thought it was a siren at first, but it was me.

His breathing was rough. He told me right in my ear that I didn't have to say anything, but that if I withheld something that would later be used in my defence, that would be a problem. He told Alexandra that there were handcuffs in his pocket and to get them on me, which she did, fumbling and I think freaking out. One of my hands was under me, and she had to dig it out. The other one was still held behind my back, under the policeman's chest, and held tight in his good fist. It was slippery from him bleeding on me. The cuffs were cold and she pinched my skin on purpose. 'Bitch,' I said.

'Keep still.' That was the cop.

'I didn't do anything,' I insisted. It was hard to breathe down there.

'We know about Gretchen, Liv. And Harry and the birds. It's over. Stop struggling.'

'I didn't–' But I didn't get the chance to say

that I hadn't hurt the birds. I'd only found them that way, but I didn't get to make that clear because a car turned the corner. Nick was home.

It was the car I'd seen on Chesterton Road, and the woman driving it must be his mother. He didn't see us yet. He was looking at her. He'd notice her change in expression any second, but for this moment he was only happy.

When we'd all first become friends together, me and him and Polly, we'd gone to the Fitz a lot. That was always my idea. Once we borrowed one of the kids' play kits they have: games and puzzles based on various galleries. Nick carried the plastic box, a clear tool-type box. Inside, the first game we picked up had been a kind of birdwatching in the ceramics gallery.

I'd never paid much attention to ceramics before. The whole point of these games is that they make kids pay attention to things they otherwise might not have. It works for adults too. There was a set of binoculars we shared between the three of us, and we prowled that gallery looking at every little piece to find representations of the half-dozen birds listed in the challenge. We horsed around, and made bird calls at each other, and tussled over the binoculars. That day, more than any other, is what I saw in his face in the car. Any moment he would look and see me and his face would get complicated. But for that moment in the car, and that whole afternoon in the Fitz, he'd been plain happy.

There are four Monets in the Fitzwilliam. I like the way the Impressionists would find one good moment and go after it. They wanted to show that for one moment the wind blew, or the sun reflected off the water this one way. They understood that life is mostly a mess and that good moments need capturing. Because light moves on. Wind dies. An expression changes.

Nick looked up. He saw me. His mother was already getting out of the car.

Alexandra called 999 on the policeman's cell phone. He was still breathing, but wasn't holding on to me any more. I could roll him off me. The cuffs had really calmed him down.

I thought: *This is my chance. Right?* In a moment, Nick would be out of the car, Alexandra would get through to the emergency line, Mrs Frey would stop freaking out and get it together. But this moment – just before all that would happen – was my chance.

I could run.

Into the jungle behind the house ... skirting the edge of the huge pond ... through back gardens and over a hedge ... between the medieval ridges and furrows of ancient fields ... sliding between tightly packed cars in the park-and-ride lot, cars that scream alarms when touched. This is where I went in my mind. This was my plan as my strength coiled.

My mind raced on, leading me. Onward up Madingley Road. Where was I taking me? There were two of me: myself, here, about to bolt, and myself, ahead, guiding me forward.

The solid me shoved off the policeman. I sprang forward and landed flat on my feet, knees bent, hands still cuffed behind me. I looked like a child bent to imitate a pecking chicken.

The soon-me, the just-ahead-me, kept running. I would make it. All I would have to do is follow.

The destination took me by surprise. Lawn, studded with thousands of short white crosses. The American Cemetery.

Both of us hesitated. Me, and me-about-to-be. How had it happened? How had we ended up there?

Britain had given the US the land for the cemetery in thanks after World War II. It's American. Even in my mind I'd run, somehow, home again. My fantasy had taken me roundabout, back to where I'd started.

I was still on the flagstones in front of Nick's house. Horror had frozen my escape. My imagination had betrayed me.

I was trapped. Not by the cuffs, though they hurt, or Nick tackling me to the ground, in a grotesque parody of what I'd once wanted from him, or by the distant sirens blaring toward us from the motorway. I was paused by those things, but I was trapped by realisation. I was trapped in my head.

Even in my fantasies I couldn't get away from home. Nothing would ever be new, ever. I knew that now. No place would ever be foreign enough that I wouldn't be me any more.

Nick was on top of me. 'Gross! Get off me!' I grunted, pushing. He was disgusting to me now. What had I ever been thinking? He was holding me down.

Alexandra kicked my midriff, just beneath where my shirt had gotten rolled up around my rib cage. She kicked my bare side, hard. I felt something crack. I think it was a rib. It got difficult to make my chest expand.

Her mother pulled to get Alexandra away from me. The girl resisted. 'You bitch!' she said, like I had to her, I think mistaking me for everything that had gone wrong. Mistaking me for why Nick had ever been gone. The toe of her shoe plunged in again.

The sirens got louder. Nick's dad stumbled out the front door, awake at last. He blinked, just coming to, as confused as a newborn. He almost tripped over the cop on his doorstep.

Alexandra abandoned attacking me, to fling herself at him. 'Daddy!' she cried out, melding herself to him. She was miniature against his adult height and barrel chest.

I squirmed. Nick must have felt my breathing shrink. He got off and rolled me over onto my back. That helped.

I really had seen him in the car this morning. A living Nick really was back. There had been no true ghosts, none of them. So I knew this was real too:

There! On that branch. The fluffy white canary I'd cupped in my hands. The last I'd seen, it was on its side, sucking and squeezing air in and out of its little orb of a body. I'd returned its feather. It had flown a long way to get to this tree, in this little wood at the edge of the city. I hadn't thought it would live at all, and look how far it had come.

'Hi,' I said. All around me people had other conversations. Bystanders urged paramedics. Bloody people explained where it hurt. The bird and I, we had our own thing going on. I'd tried to tell everyone that I hadn't hurt the birds. No one had listened, but we knew.

It wasn't afraid of me. It lit onto my stomach. This little poof of white rode up and down, up and down.

Thick hands brushed it away and scooped me up onto a padded mat thing. The bird hopped backward, away from the commotion. 'It's all right,' I croaked. I tried to make it shoo. There were too many feet, heavy and busy, crossing this way and that.

I couldn't turn my head on the stretcher bed, not far enough. I got slotted into the back of an ambulance. The last I saw for myself was a flash of white, maybe lifting up into the air. Or, that could have been the doors slamming. They shut with a bang and a click.

EPILOGUE

'I thought you were in jail.'

Nick flinched. He was in a hospital bed, one of four in the room, under a white sheet.

'That's why I didn't come sooner,' Polly explained from the doorway. 'I didn't realise you were here.'

Nick had to lean forward to see the whole of her, to see past the balloon bouquet tied to the metal arm of his bed, and through an absurdly coloured eruption of carnations.

'Some of us thought...' She took a breath, revised. 'Peter heard that you'd ... run over Gretchen, and that police had been called. And before that,' she said, squeezing her hands into a tight ball in front of her stomach, 'before that, we all thought you were dead.'

Behind a curtain, another patient coughed.

'I know,' Nick said. 'I'm sorry.'

The apology sucked Polly into the room. She got close, right next to the bed. Her fingertips grazed the sheet. 'I'm so glad you're–'

And, at the same moment, 'Your mum told me what your dad–' he said.

Polly covered her ears and stepped back. 'I know,' she said. 'I know.' Then, immediately, she replaced the subject: 'I know about you and Liv.'

He shook his head. He held up one finger, to ask her to stop. 'There was no "me and Liv". It ... I regret what happened with her,' he said. 'I regret – I shouldn't have pushed you like I did.'

'No, no, it was good. I shouldn't have stopped you. Us, I mean. Stopped us. It was dumb.'

'It wasn't stupid. We should have talked more before...'

'I wouldn't have told you,' she said. 'I didn't want to talk about it.'

She moved closer again. She pushed a balloon aside, and it bounced back against her head.

'Did you really slip on a plate?' she asked. 'In some old dowager's mansion?'

Nick's pause was filled with the creaking and heaving of someone else, someone very heavy, rolling over. The privacy curtain between him and Nick wafted.

'Yes,' Nick finally said. 'It was an old friend's

house. She wasn't in residence. I was stranded.'

'It must have been awful!'

He nodded, bouncing his chin against his neck.

'My mom's gone home,' Polly said. 'I asked her to. She hugged me goodbye this morning. She's divorcing my dad, did she tell you that too? Did she tell you that?'

'She only told me about what your father did.'

Polly looked up at the ceiling. A machine beeped.

'Well, it turns out that isn't everything. She came here to tell me something else, something added on. She kept trying to tell me, but I wouldn't let her get it out, until the day we went shopping for a coat. And then so much else happened ... I didn't think about it enough. I didn't think about it.

'The day that Dad did it, did the terrible thing, he was really stressed, because he'd confronted his boss about a safety problem at the mill. A forklift had run into a load-bearing column, and it wasn't being reported. They'd had an ugly argument and Dad thought he'd lose his job. I knew that already. He told the police, as if it mattered. As if it was some kind of reason. But Mom came here to tell me that it going public really shamed the company. They examined the column, and it turned out that a collapse was imminent. They kept it quiet that Dad was right, but they fixed it. Mom only found that out recently, from a friend of Dad's who still worked there. Five guys work in that area and they probably would have died. Because of Dad they didn't.'

'That's a good thing,' Nick said.

'I know. I know it's good. But it's not enough.

It's important to stay mad, you know? It's not like five guys make up for one guy. You can't average the people a person saves and the people a person hurts. They're *people*. You can't do that. Jeremy's dead. That's never going to be okay...'

'No,' he agreed.

'Liv's in jail now.' She rubbed her sleeve against her cheek. A nurse pushed a wheeled cart past the door, towards another room. It rattled like it contained small medical instruments, or food accessorised with metal utensils.

'Last night I had this dream,' Polly said, 'about Liv, that she was at Oxford instead of Cambridge. That she met different people, made different friends. That it was almost the same as here, but not quite, and so none of the horrible stuff happened.'

'Polly...'

'Do you think she had it just in her, the bad stuff, and that something awful would have come out of her no matter where she went? Or do you think it was just this one set of circumstances that worked together to push her in that direction? What do you think?'

'I think ... I don't know. I don't know.'

'Is it true that she hurt the policeman too? Were you there? People are saying that she stabbed him.'

'No, she cut him. She didn't stab him.' Nick mimed the difference. 'He's in intensive care.'

'No, he isn't. At least, not any more. He's here. On this ward.' Polly waved her hand towards the door. 'In the first room...'

Nick grunted, started to slide his legs off the

side of the bed.

'What are you doing?'

'I've got to talk to him.' Nick grabbed the crutches propped near his bed.

'Wait – why?'

'I need to thank him. For Alexandra. If he hadn't been there…'

'Is she all right?'

'She is. Because of him. She … she's upset, and angry, but she's all right.'

'Angry?' Polly's tone had changed. She wasn't curious; she was indignant. 'Why is she angry?'

Nick balanced on his crutches, stared at Polly. She squeezed her eyes shut. She accused him:

'She's like you with Cambridge architecture. You breeze past King's College Chapel. You trudge over Garret Hostel Bridge. Alexandra doesn't notice the safety of her life. She takes it for granted. I gawk and point at it. I'd put it on a mug. I'd wear it on a T-shirt if I could!'

'Polly, what are you talking about?'

'Alexandra doesn't know how lucky she is!' Polly hissed. 'The difference between someone you care about being gone and coming back, and someone you care about being dead, is a whole world.'

Nick needed both of his hands to hold tight for him to stay upright. But he nudged her arm gently with his elbow. Her breathing calmed.

'Do you know what I love about being here, in this country?' she said quietly. 'I love the sinks and their faucets for hot and cold. Not one tap, like I'm used to at home, where hot and cold mix together to make something nice to wash your

356

hands in. Here, most of the sinks have this one tap for cold and this one for hot. You can mix them in the sink if you want, but hot comes out hot and cold comes out cold. Side by side. There's something really true about that. Because I know I feel like that. I hate what Dad did to Jeremy, and I'm happy that those men at the factory didn't get hurt. I feel both of those things, not mixed into merely warm, but just as they are: something really terrible and something really good. It's like what I felt with you, in the Sedgwick, terrified and happy. I was terrified and I was happy. They didn't add up to indifferent. They were both just themselves.'

His shoulders were hunched up because of the crutches. She leant her head against one of them. He tilted his cheek against her hair.

Morris's abdominal injury was healing well, but his right hand was a wreck. He couldn't hold anything. He couldn't even hold a book.

'Are you bored? Is there anything I can do?' Nick asked.

Morris said no.

Nick hovered there. His left leg, still fragile, was bent at the knee and swinging just over the floor.

'I'm so grateful,' Nick finally said. 'We all are. I know what you did for Alexandra.'

Morris's voice was flat. 'Really? What did I do?'

Nick beamed. 'Alexandra had the fireplace urn. You pulled Liv around, away from her. That's how you got hurt. I'm so sorry you got hurt. But we're so grateful. Alexandra doesn't understand. She thought you did it to protect Liv. She's angry to have been stopped. She's just a kid. I had to explain it to her.'

'Why don't you explain it to me,' he said, all in one tone.

'You protected Alexandra, not just Liv. Killing someone, even in self-defence or defending someone else ... that's something a person has to carry around. It would have changed her. It would have ... it would have been a burden for all of her life. You protected her. Thank you. Thank you for that.'

Morris breathed deep through his nose. He didn't blink.

'Hi, Daddy!' A teenager bounded in, fresh from class. She was around the same age as Alexandra, but in the clothing of a different school. She dumped her backpack and kissed Morris's cheek, then promised to come right back. She headed for the toilets.

'You know what's the worst thing about being a dad?' Morris leant forward. He wrapped his good hand around Nick's crutch, and pulled himself up close to Nick's face. 'The kid is this thing you have to protect. She's so much more important than anything else. Even if you have to die, to keep her safe, you do it. You just do it, because if it comes down to you or her, it's her. That's it. It's just her. But here's the thing: Between me and the rest of the world, it's me. It's me, for her sake, because I'm her father. She needs me. She needs to not lose her dad to some nutter with a knife. What was I thinking? What the hell had I been thinking?'

He let go of the crutch. Nick rocked back.

Peter was sitting on Nick's hospital bed, arms crossed. 'I thought you couldn't walk,' he accused. 'I was told you'd never walk again and it would make you even more pathetic and everyone would point and laugh at you for as long as you lived.'

'I hobble,' Nick said. He forced a smile. Peter didn't. 'It's good to see you,' Nick said, trying to haul the conversation back to a proper start.

Peter resisted. 'Do the nurses usually let you wander? Is that wise?'

'I can balance all right,' Nick answered, as if the question had to do with his leg and not with his recent running away to Dovecote. 'I was visiting the Inspector. I had to talk to him. Did you know that he's Richard's brother? I could hardly believe it when my mother told me that. He's the one who caught Liv. He–'

'We all got to know him, Nick. We were all questioned by him. About you.'

'Yes, of course.' Nick still waited in the door-way, on one foot.

Peter stood up and to the side, to give him back his bed. Nick sat on it, legs over the side and back straight, rather than lying back down.

'Did you know that they dredged the Cam for you?' Peter demanded.

Nick nodded.

'That Richard considered postponing the wedding? Did you know that Polly's mother was arrested?'

'What?'

'Because of you.'

'I didn't know that.'

'A lot happened while you were off.'

'Is she all right?'

'She was only in a few days.'

'Days? My God. Polly didn't say.'

Peter lifted his head. 'She was here?'

'Half an hour ago.'

Peter sucked in a breath, then whooshed it out. 'I've got to ask you this. But ... you've got to tell me the truth.'

'About what?' There was so much he had to tell everyone, over and over again. Why he left, where he went, what he'd hoped to find and what he did find...

Peter leant in close and spoke barely above a whisper. 'Liv said you raped her.'

'What?' Nick gaped. 'What?'

'After they dredged the Cam she was upset. We all were. All day we'd prepared for the worst news. It didn't come, thank God it didn't, but all that coiled energy had nowhere to spring. Then she told me, and I was angry, and I didn't believe her. But it stuck in my head. It stuck there.'

'You didn't believe her,' Nick repeated, insistent.

'Not at first. No. Then maybe... The idea was absurd, but everything was already absurd. There was no reason for you to have run away, no reason for anyone to have hurt you. There was no ransom demand, no body... And I remembered the last time I saw you. You were upset about Liv and Polly. It came across like something on the scale of a pregnancy scare. But this was you, Nick, so at the time I thought you'd "led Liv on" as far as a kiss, or maybe not even that. Maybe

360

just words had been taken the wrong way. I hadn't thought anything significant of it.

'Then Liv told me you'd raped her. Having done that would make you run away. Or make Liv want to hurt you. It could even have made you hurt yourself. It was unthinkable that you would do it in the first place, but, if you had done it, that would make sense of everything else. Not just of you being gone, but now. What Liv did. Not why it was aimed at Gretchen and Harry, but why she felt she had to hit back at somebody...'

'No!'

'No what, Nick?'

'No to everything! No, I didn't rape her!'

'That's the truth?'

A leaf hanging from one of the carnation stems suddenly dropped. It sawed back and forth through the air on its slow fall, finally brushing gently against the cold floor. The slight sound of that soft friction magnified and elongated to fill the gap between asking the question and hearing the answer.

'I wouldn't do a thing like that,' Nick said.

Peter goggled.

'You wouldn't? Really? We all said that. "Nick wouldn't do that." Nick wouldn't just leave. That's what we told the police, over and over again. But that's exactly what you did do, so how the hell do I know what you would or wouldn't do any more?'

Peter avoided the bus. He wanted to keep moving. He believed Nick. He was relieved. But he was

361

still rattled by having had to ask him.

Nick was home, but home had changed while he was gone. Home had changed partly because he'd been gone. His absence had been a hole they all kept falling into. Now that he was back, he didn't quite fit that space any more. Now the people who cared for him most were poked by his sharp edges, and poked back with their own.

The south end of Cambridge, around the hospital, isn't the Cambridge that Polly and Liv swooned over. It's just ordinary brick houses, and then, after a good distance, Hills Road erupts with practical, undecorative shops and businesses. Only much farther beyond do the colleges and parks and expensive stores by which Americans mean 'Cambridge' cluster.

It used to be a fashionable prank for students to scale the University's towers. There's a famous leap from a student bedroom onto the Senate House roof, which has been forbidden for years. Peter had never been tempted. He'd never felt the urge to climb.

Until now.

He turned into Downing Street. He'd be caught, surely. But the question was, how far could he get before that happened?

Someone had had the bright idea to string the tower cranes building the Grand Arcade with Christmas lights; that's how much a fixture the cranes had become. They shone.

That's one of the last things Liv said to Peter: that she loved the cranes. That they were more beautiful, in their immensity, symmetry, and balance, than whatever they could build.

362

There's nothing so tall as they in Cambridge. Yes, there's the view from Great St Mary's bell tower, but it has a cage around the top to prevent jumping. You can press your face up against the cross-hatching to give your eye an unjailed look. You can see down onto the college lawns, and notice the plaids and stripes made by the mowers. But the cranes...

It was all too small, suddenly. Too tight. The history, the traditions, the glut of buildings.

Peter wanted height. He wanted to look at how big the world really is.

Cambridge is a transitional place. Some people stay. But most pass through on their way to somewhere else. They get their degrees. The cranes sum it up nicely – they'll come down when their job's done.

That's why it was urgent that Peter do this immediately.

The building site was fenced and locked. Peter knew there would be cameras. He tried to not look too interested. He wanted to shock whoever was watching. He wanted to give himself the most time he could.

Just scale the fence, jump down. The cranes were there. Just scramble up the base of one and grab on to the beginning of the latticed neck. He could manage that. Would alarms go off? How far could he get? Would whoever swooped in to get him down treat him like a criminal, or gently, like a potential suicide?

He just wanted to get up high. The air didn't feel breathable down among the buildings any more.

There's a famous Hubble image of deep space, full of distant galaxies and stars like a bag of sweets spilt across a blackboard. Hubble gets those kinds of pictures because it's above the atmosphere. It sees without fog.

That's what Peter wanted to do.

He wanted to try. He wanted to reach. He wanted to stand there just for a moment, and fling out his arms, and look down from a great height.

I'll come down without a fight, he promised himself. *I'll take what punishment comes. But I'll have that view in my head. That'll make it worthwhile.*

He grabbed the link fence and hauled himself up. He climbed, and rolled over the top, landing on his feet. The cranes were right there. He scrambled up a base, and gripped the bottom lattice in his hand.

The universe expands.

ACKNOWLEDGEMENTS

My heartfelt gratitude to all who contributed to *The Whole World*, especially:

My research sources, Keith Ferry, Dave and Gina Holland, Stephanie Hurd, Jon Coppelman, Dr Judy Weiss, Dr Sheila Picken, Jo Timson, Dr J. Alex Stark, Ruth and Elizabeth Doggett, Mingwei Tan of Peterhouse, and Detective Superintendent Mark Birch of the Cambridgeshire Major Investigations Team, for the generosity with which they shared their experiences and expertise. They know their stuff; all errors and liberties are my own.

My contacts at Magdalene College, especially Dr Glenton Jelbert, Dr Simon Stoddart, Assistant Bursar Peter Daybell, College Marshal Bob Smith, and Deputy College Marshal Michael Flanagan. I deeply appreciate the warmth and friendliness I've encountered whenever I've approached this college.

My early readers, Derek Black, Amy Mokady, Renee Cramer, Mary McDonald, Margaret Brentano Baker, and Eva Gallant, for encouragement and excellent advice.

Miss Snark, whose Crapometer set me on the right path at a critical moment.

Kristen King, for insisting on clarity.

Cameron McClure, for her artistic sensitivity and professional savvy.

Susie Dunlop and all the team at Allison & Busby: Lesley-Anne Crooks, Christina Griffiths, Sara Magness, Graham Montagu, Chiara Priorelli and Sophie Robinson. I'm honoured for my books to be on your shelves.

And, personally, gratitude to Dad, who loves me second to James Joyce; Mom, who embodies the compassion I attempt toward all my characters; and Gavin, the love of my life, who ensures that I have time to write.

Love to both Samuel, who brainstormed motives with me, and to Westcott. It's because of your pushchair that I learnt about that lovely old-fashioned lift in Earth Sciences.

The publishers hope that this book has given you enjoyable reading. Large Print Books are especially designed to be as easy to see and hold as possible. If you wish a complete list of our books please ask at your local library or write directly to:

Magna Large Print Books
Magna House, Long Preston,
Skipton, North Yorkshire.
BD23 4ND

This Large Print Book for the partially sighted, who cannot read normal print, is published under the auspices of

THE ULVERSCROFT FOUNDATION